PRAISE FOR

ROWING

"A textured portrait of one family's painful acclimation to changing sexual mores." —*Publishers Weekly*

"Evans has done a remarkable job in weaving a deeply colored and textured tapestry of images and emotions. Using news, music, and television programs of the late 1960s, she effectively re-creates a specific time and place. The vividness of the setting makes the human drama all the more poignant, as various relationships bloom briefly and die prematurely. Evans has written an anthem for failed romantics."

—*Booklist*

"*Rowing in Eden* is a dead-on portrait of the titillations and terrors of first love. Elizabeth Evan's Franny, like Fanny in Jane Austen's *Mansfield Park*, is not the most obvious choice for the belle of the ball. But that makes the thirteen-year-old's awakening to love even sweeter, and more surprising. Timeless as the feelings are, this novel also serves as a love letter to a very particular time and place: small-town Iowa in 1965, teetering, like Franny herself, on the crest of enormous changes."

—Lisa Zeidner

"A bittersweet story, lyrically evoking the awkwardness and excitement that thankfully come only once in a lifetime, to those in their early teens. . . . *Rowing in Eden* brings readers through a gamut of emotional experiences, and leaves them wiser at the close."

—*Denver Post*

ALSO BY ELIZABETH EVANS

Carter Clay

The Blue Hour

Locomotion

ROWING IN EDEN

A NOVEL

ELIZABETH EVANS

Perennial
An Imprint of HarperCollinsPublishers

A hardcover edition of this book was published in 2000 by HarperCollins Publishers.

First Perennial edition published 2001.

Designed by Jackie McKee

The Library of Congress has catalogued the hardcover edition as follows:

Evans, Elizabeth.

   Rowing in Eden : a novel/Elizabeth Evans—1st ed.
    p. cm.
   ISBN 0-06-019550-9
    1. Summer resorts—Fiction. 2. Teenage girls—Fiction. 3. Middle West—Fiction.
    4. Sisters—Fiction. I. Title.
   PS3555.V2152 R69 2000
   813'.54—dc21   00-025952

ISBN 0-06-095470-1(pbk.)

14 15 16 17 ❖/RRD 10 9 8 7 6 5 4 3 2

FOR H.P.

Acknowledgments

This project is supported in part by a grant from the National Endowment for the Arts.

Special thanks to my editor, Robert Jones, for his guidance; to my agent, Lisa Bankoff, for her championing of the work; and to my family, for the blessing of their love and support.

It was partly the unusual geography of the room that suggested to him the thing that he was about to do.

GEORGE ORWELL, *1984*

Part I

CHAPTER ONE

JULY. A QUEER, HAZY DAY. OVERHEAD, THE SUN MADE AN ODD white bulge in the pale, pale sky.

Like ice, thought Franny. Ice melting into a glass of milk. Or maybe a knee—eerie thought—maybe a knee or an elbow that poked out from a pool of concrete.

Franny Wahl.

Staring out through the plate glass window that belonged to the showroom of the Pynch Marina (many shiny boats hunkering quietly at her back). Frances Jean, she was. Thirteen years old. Face set in a look both obstinate and dreamy.

Frances Jean Wahl thought about the summer sky, yes. Made up her strings of words to describe the sun in that sky, but other words ran in her head as well.

We don't do that, Franny. Those were the words she meant to shut out by playing with words of her own.

We don't do that, Franny.

Outside the marina, Lakeside Drive ran bumper to bumper with irritable tourist traffic. This was Pynch Lake, a town of twenty thousand in the roughly rectangular state of Iowa. The noise from the traffic—coarse engine pops rising from a tangle of music and machinery on both the street and the lake—that noise poured through the marina's open door, and was overlaid by the sound of a radio playing in the back room.

"After late-breaking news, we'll return with Summer '65 Count-down," the announcer said in a voice that was as much a honk as the honks from the cars in the street, and, still, over all of this, Franny Wahl heard, *We don't do that, Franny.*

At the four-way stop, a pretty girl in a black swimsuit stood up from behind the wheel of her convertible and began to yell. The object of her fury: a man in a station wagon who had hoped to back his boat trailer into the lake via the ramp at the end of the parking lot that served both the marina and the Top Hat Club. Somehow, this man had gotten his trailer hung up on the curb in front of the Top Hat and now he blocked traffic for the entire intersection.

More horns.

The driver of the station wagon—mouth working in his red, red face—climbed from his car. *Something-something,* the mellifluous newscaster said of the closure of the investigation into the misconduct of Senate employee Bobby Baker. As Franny's father often became agitated by such reports, the newscaster's words gave the girl the same sort of passing qualm she might have experienced had the marina's fluorescent lights flickered. Still, she did not actually listen to the report. She did not much care about news of the nation.

She did, however, pity the driver of the station wagon. A big man. A good six foot five, two hundred and fifty pounds. His shirt had come untucked in back as, vainly, he tried to lift the boat and its trailer over the curb and into the street.

Franny let her forehead tip against the cool glass of the show-room window. She closed her eyes. Because she felt sorry for the driver. And appalled by him. And even a little humiliated by his plight. Because he reminded her too much of her father. Still, the driver did not entirely distract her from the words:

We don't do that, Franny.

She could not seem to stop herself from holding the words up for inspection, pouring them back and forth like a string of beads, a handful of pebbles. She—tasted them. Something a little chemical? Like copper? Like a penny held on her tongue?

KNOCK. KNOCK.

The sound made her start. There, on the other side of the plate glass window, stood a family of tourists, laughing, looking in at

Franny as one member of their group—a boy of six or seven, hair in duck feathers from a swim at the beach—lowered his fist from the glass. He scowled at Franny. "Wake up!" he shouted, the words damped but still definite through the heavy glass. Then his laughing father and mother set their hands on the boy's skinny shoulders and they moved him along toward the busy intersection.

We don't do that, Franny.

The honking in the street subsided. The man in the station wagon had finally driven his trailer off the curb. Traffic began to move again and, from the marina sales counter, Franny could hear the laughter of her big sister Rosamund as Rosamund spoke to the marina clerk about buying life-jackets for the family speedboat.

At the Wahl house, earlier that morning, there had been talk of the life-jackets. "You kids and your guests think you're indestructible." So Franny's mother had said to Rosamund, and the sharpness in Peg Wahl's voice had let Franny know that the conversation involved more than life-jackets. Though no one had pointed out the change, that summer Franny saw that the river of parties and guests that had formerly carried her father and mother atop its dashing blue now had tossed the pair aside. And who did the lively current carry these days? Franny's big sisters, Rosamund and Martie, home from their universities until September.

As she talked to Rosamund, Peg Wahl had been at work on that evening's dinner. With her substantial, sun-tanned arms sunk to the elbows in chicken parts and barbecue sauce, and her hair not yet combed for the day, Peg looked very much the farmwife she might have become had she not met law student Brick some twenty years before. Franny knew, however, that her mother could still bring up a shine on her once much praised looks (even now, her high cheekbones, chocolate eyes, and white-toothed smile attracted comparisons to blond and bubbly Doris Day).

Peg kept her voice low as she spoke to Rosamund; a few of her daughters' houseguests still lingered in the dining room, helping themselves to scrambled eggs and sausages from the breakfront.

"It's your dad and me that'll get sued if one of your guests drowns!"

Your dad and *I*, Franny thought, then blushed inwardly—a tingle swept across her scalp—at her mother's error, her own mental correction of the error, and the fact that, really, she was doing little more than eavesdropping. The Wahl house had begun its life as a lodge for hunters more interested in pheasants than privacy, and Franny sat, unobserved, on a set of stairs that allowed descent into either the living room or the big kitchen.

Franny's rule since June: Whenever possible, jump the four steps from the landing in order to show that you, at least, are not growing old and stodgy. You, at least, are young and alive, and the moment she saw an opening in the conversation between mother and sister—*slam!*—she jumped from the landing into the kitchen.

"Franny! How many times have I told you not to do that?" Peg said, but Rosamund laughed and drew close to Franny and linked arms with the girl.

Odd to be bigger than Rosamund now. Curious for the youngest to stand taller than the oldest by several inches. To be the same height as the nineteen-year-old Martie.

"Come to the marina with me, Fran," Rosamund said. "We'll take the boat!" She made a show of licking her lips. "And, after, we can go across the street to the Dairy Queen!"

An old green and white dinghy had been in the family for as long as Franny could remember, and had fallen to Franny the summer before, but when Rosamund said "the boat," Franny knew that Rosamund meant "the big boat." The big boat was a grand, gleaming thing, all burgundy leather and mahogany, a full-size automobile engine growling in its middle. When Rosamund drove the big boat, she looked even smaller than usual. Roosting on the very rim of the back of the driver's seat, she leaned forward and *down* to the steering wheel like a jockey to his reins. *A gentleman's den on the lam.* That was what Franny shouted that morning when she and Rosamund reached the middle of the lake, and Rosamund pushed the boat's throttle as far as it would go. Rosamund had laughed at what Franny said. Which was nice. Nice to have your big sister think that you were funny. Even if she only pretended to think you were funny, that was something. That was making an effort to be your friend.

But then the sisters had docked at the marina and started up the twanging boards to the sales area. The trouble spot—Franny anticipated it—was the gas pumps, where the knot of dockhands stood smoking their cigarettes. More than likely, Franny knew, one of the hands would make a remark as the girls passed.

But there was another possibility. A heart-swelling, breeze-on-your-skin possibility: that from that menacing cluster of sun-browned limbs and white T-shirts and blue jeans a miraculous boy might step forward, and look into Franny's eyes, and say something so right that it would be precisely as if Sir Walter Raleigh draped his cloak across a puddle for the passage of the queen. Then Franny could let down her golden tresses that the prince might climb to her arms, and love would fill all the nasty hollows in her head, and she would be who she always had been meant to be: the beloved, in love.

Passing by the dockhands. Okay. Passing. No moment of romance, but no embarrassment, either. Rosamund—not Franny, Franny was too nervous—Rosamund nodded coolly when one of the hands said hello. Safe, Franny thought, but then a sucking noise started up behind the girls, something so foul that she glanced back. Just to frown, that was all, but as soon as she and Rosamund moved out of earshot of the hands, Rosamund said, *We don't do that, Franny.*

Not that Rosamund sounded truly angry. Not the way that Franny's parents, or even Martie, sounded when they disapproved of Franny. Still, Franny had felt ashamed.

Yet, now, Rosamund chatted gaily with the marina salesclerk—as if whatever irritation Franny had caused on the dock were forgotten. Rosamund laughed and whooped a charming, "Oh, no!"

The clerk—dark, oily bangs flopped down in his eyes, a little Band-Aid on his chin—was not much older than Franny herself.

Still, Rosamund stood only five feet tall, and the advantage of the clerk's size clearly gave him a thrill. He blushed and towered. He tossed his pencil high in the air, caught it behind his back.

Not a special boy, Franny thought, so maybe it was greedy to want him to find her as attractive as he found Rosamund.

"I didn't really mean life-*jackets*." Rosamund closed her big brown eyes. Raised her chin. Solemnly moved it back and forth, as if she viewed some vast future visible only to herself—soon, soon, she would tell the clerk his fortune—then, quick, she opened the eyes once more and laughed. "I meant *belts*."

What Rosamund wore over her shorts that day: a sweater forgotten by one of the summer's male houseguests. Very big. Brown. V-necked. It seemed to Franny particularly wonderful on Rosamund, and see how Rosamund adjusted the black sunglasses that perched in her fair fluff of hair. That was wonderful, too, and watch the way in which, without ever taking her eyes from the sales boy, she fished a tube of lipstick from her shoulder bag and, using just one hand, removed its cap, and wound up the stick, which was a color called Pure Pearl.

Rosamund had let Franny try the Pure Pearl once. On Franny—why?—the fashionable frosty white mutated into something therapeutic, a salve, but on Rosamund it had the same effect as the big sweater, the frazzled straw bag slung over her shoulder, the none too clean but extravagantly purple brush that Rosamund used to "tease" her hair to cotton-candy heights. The same effect as the box of grapefruit sent home to the family from a stand near Rosamund's dormitory at the University of Miami. The same effect as that bit of Eastern accent she had picked up from New York friends at school, and the effect was: perfectly right.

"People won't put on the jackets," Rosamund told the clerk. "We have gobs, and nobody will wear them 'cause they make you look fat!" She puffed out her cheeks and drew up her shoulders to show the boy the effect of the bulky life-jackets. In response, he laughed and flopped his arms up and down.

He can't control himself, Franny thought, and felt some sympathy for the boy, and despised him a little, too. Poor thing. Looking silly, meaning to look cool. She understood that.

"So, okay," he said. "Let me check in back."

We don't do that, Franny.

We. Don't. Do. That.

To apply the Pure Pearl, Rosamund inserted the entire lipstick between her lips, then rubbed the stick back and forth. This extravagant method soon wore all of her lipsticks to an hourglass shape that broke in half; still, Rosamund had read in a magazine column that someone famous—Brigitte Bardot?—applied her lipstick in this way, and Rosamund put great stock in the advice of such columns. Knox gelatin made a girl's nails "drop-dead glamorous." A capful of baby oil in the bath left you "silky smooth." Just the day before, Rosamund had said to Franny, "Here's something great I read in that dating column. You're out in a car with a boy, and he gets fresh, okay? So you just press your finger to his chin and you say—very sweet, no need to be nasty—'Shall I drive us home now, or will you?'"

Franny had been thrilled that Rosamund shared such wisdom with her, and so she did not point out that it belonged to a predictable world, not the surprising one in which, say, just the Saturday before, standing in her friend Christy Strawberry's dark garage, Franny had found herself perfectly willing to let a fifteen-year-old by the name of Bob Prohaski press his tongue into her mouth.

Really.

Also, Franny did not really want Rosamund to know that she and Franny did not live in precisely the same world. Maybe if Franny did not acknowledge the menacing oyster-colored clouds above her own head, she could edge into that kingdom where Rosamund held her face tilted up to always sunny skies.

"You like turquoise?" the marina clerk called from the back room. "They're either turquoise or orange."

"Oh, turquoise, please," Rosamund said.

The honking in front of the marina picked up again. A crowd of pedestrians (two women with strollers, a group of teenagers, little kids being shepherded by adults) had worked up the nerve to cross the intersection of the four-way.

In winter, on Sundays, there were times when the Wahls drove the five miles into town from their own house on the far side of the lake without encountering a single car, but, in July, any day of the week, a trip "in" turned up flocks of cars with out-of-town plates. Shopping at the supermarket could involve parking a block or more from the store, and if you drove through town in the evening, you were bound to see the moth-pale flicker of little kids in light pajamas at play on the cots that their parents had set out on the porches and side yards of crowded rental cottages.

One of that pack of people who now crossed the Lakeside intersection was a clowning, blond-haired boy. Shirtless, teenaged, bright orange flip-flops on his feet. Franny wanted to see his face—was he handsome?—but the boy held his bare arms high, as if to shield himself from the drivers' fury. Oh. It was only Tim Gleason, the local boy Rosamund had chosen to be her summer "buddy." Tim Gleason had graduated from the Catholic high school that spring, then met Rosamund at Lindt's, the gift shop where both held summer jobs.

An attractive boy, Franny supposed. Though Rosamund's buddies did not *have* to be particularly attractive, Tim Gleason had silky blond hair, lime green eyes. His skin, however, looked a little raw, didn't it? Puckered from some sort of face scrub he had used too zealously? Franny started to raise a hand to wave, then lowered it. Risky to let Tim Gleason think she dared presume that he was her friend as well as Rosamund's—

"There must be some mistake, though. I mean, the check must have gotten lost in the mail or something."

Franny glanced back at the counter. Rosamund no longer spoke to the clerk, but to an older man, his face drawn, apologetic.

"You tell your dad to come in, Miss Wahl. We'll be more than happy to let you charge again once he takes care of his end. Your granddad was one of my favorite people."

The man smoothed his hands across what was clearly some sort

of ledger. Thin hands with wiry black hairs on their backs and fingers. A class ring. If Franny's father had been there, he would have
made them laugh at that man, his flushed cheeks, the ring with the
big red stone. *An honest-to-god graduate of Rinky Dink High!* her
father would have said. Something like that.

Eyes wide with fury, Rosamund strode toward Franny. "What
an ass!" she whispered. "Dad's check must have gotten lost in the
mail or something, so that *ass* is saying the account's overdue and
we can't charge!"

Franny raised and lowered her chin—serenely, she thought—to
acknowledge that she heard what Rosamund said. Peg Wahl—Miss
Johnson County of 1940—had trained all three of her daughters, by
example and knuckles in the back, to maintain a ramrod-perfect
posture at all times, and Franny had found that, sometimes, in tan-
dem with the posture, she could execute an impeccable pivot away
from distress. She could look, oh, as if she had never even intended
to make the purchase when the lady in the hosiery department at
Drew's announced, *I'm sorry, miss, but that account is delinquent.* If
her father happened to drink too much over Sunday dinner at the
Top Hat Club, Franny could slowly rise from the table and walk to
the powder room and stay there until it was time to go home—

"Here comes Timmy." Rosamund pointed out the window. "He
called before we left. I'm taking him skiing later." She glanced
toward the register. The clerk now stood with back turned, straightening a row of oars. His stiff movements hinted that he felt embarrassed for Rosamund or himself or both.

"How humiliating!" Rosamund whispered, but Franny fixed
her own attention on Tim Gleason. Did he check his approaching
reflection in the big marina window? The self-conscious fillip of
arrangement he gave to his hair suggested he had yet to spot
Rosamund beyond the glass.

"Anyone can see Tim's crazy about you," Franny whispered.

"But it won't be fun if I see!" Rosamund gave Franny a hug and
smiled. "Tim's cute, but wait. If Turner Haskin comes to visit this
summer, every girl in Pynch will be in love with him." Rosamund

raised the back of her hand to her mouth as she laughed. She had once explained to Franny how she had lifted this gesture from a British movie star for both its look of elegance and the fact that it concealed a gray mark left on her right canine by orthodontia.

"And no doubt"—Rosamund fluffed her bright hair with her fingertips—"our crazy sister will be first in line to throw herself at Turner's feet!"

The idea of Martie falling for a college friend of Rosamund's did not strike Franny as particularly funny, but she still smarted from Rosamund's remark on the dock—*We don't do that*—and so she laughed along at the image of Martie, head over heels for someone named Turner Haskin.

Followed Rosamund out the marina door.

Looked at the lake while Rosamund and Tim Gleason talked.

"I want just one *bite* of Dairy Queen. One bite," Rosamund said. "So, if I get a cone, will you eat it?"

Tim Gleason shook a teasing finger at Rosamund. "Just one bite? I know you! I'll *hold* the cone, but you'll eat it!"

"Meany!" Rosamund said, but her laugh lightened the word, which rose like a bubble, a toy, and when she looked out over the top of her sunglasses—Franny recognized the deft parody of the starlet in the old poster for *Lolita*—Tim Gleason laughed at that, too.

Franny's own perverse set of scruples—or self-consciousness, vanity, whatever it was—prevented her from even buying sunglasses: horror at the possibility that someone might imagine that she, Franny Wahl, imagined herself resembling any sort of celebrity! So it was that she had to squint as she looked out at the glittering lake.

What kind of name was Turner Haskin, anyway?

Beyond a moored houseboat, a "C" sailed past. The crewman stood on the leeboards, and even Franny knew that this would not be necessary if the skipper would let out more sheet.

Turner Haskin. Pinot noir. Yesterday, Martie and Rosamund had argued over how to pronounce the *y* in "Bob Dylan." Rosamund insisted the *y* was long, while Martie said, no, no, he took the name from Dylan Thomas, and Rosamund said, *yes,* that's why it's long, and Franny did not know which sister was right.

It would *not* be good if Martie fell in love with Turner Haskin, but Rosamund was right about one thing: Martie did fall in love with some regularity. The last heartbreak had come via an ROTC member from Des Moines. Funny, handsome in his uniform, that boyfriend possessed a handful of tricks with which to entertain a little sister (he could blow smoke rings through smoke rings; open his Zippo lighter with a swipe down the leg of his pants, and then, on the up-swipe, strike the thing to flame). As good as a brother, Franny thought the ROTC member, until he wrote a lengthy letter to Brick and Peg Wahl to let them know that he would not be seeing Martie anymore. He was sorry to say so, but, since starting college that fall, Martie had begun to swear and smoke and drink and generally behave in an unladylike manner.

"Read this!" Franny's father had rattled the blue stationery in Franny's face. "Read this, and see what nice boys think of crude behavior!" Peg shook and cried over the letter, but it only made Franny hate the ROTC boy for betraying Martie, and after she had handed it back, Franny went to her own room and climbed into her closet to dim the voices of her parents as they berated Martie over the long-distance wires:

Remember who you are, where you are, what you are!

Pretty is as pretty does!

So.

Were those little kids sailing past on the sunfish going to tip over? They half-wanted to, you could tell, but, no, a frightened mother shrilled from the marina dock, "You kids keep that boat upright or else!"

It might be *interesting* if beautiful Turner Haskin came to visit Pynch Lake—Franny was interested in beauty, all right—but she did not want him to come if his visit broke Martie's heart.

What time would that evening's party begin? Tim Gleason asked Rosamund. *Would there be a keg, or should Tim bring beer? Could some of Tim's buddies come by, too?*

Franny pressed her bare toes into the fat slugs of tar that some-one had used to fill a seam where the sidewalk slumped away from the marina wall, and Tim Gleason teased Rosamund about one of his friends. "You remember Ryan. You said he was so good-looking." Then Tim launched into a story of how, the night before, this Ryan had been very drunk and playing leapfrog on the parking meters in front of Viccio's.

"Everybody in Viccio's had put down their cues and come out-side to watch, and Ryan figures he ought to do something for a finale, so he drops his pants, and before anybody can think—we're all laughing our heads off—he leaps the next meter and, man, his pants catch on the pole and he belly flops right on the sidewalk!" Timmy Gleason began to laugh. "Christ, he's flat on his face, trying to reach around to untie his shoes so he can get free, and he's, like, come help me, you guys, but we're laughing too hard, and up comes that young cop, Haggerty. Haggerty asks what's going on, and Ryan—with his pants around his ankles and his bare ass in the air—he looks up at Haggerty and he says, 'I'm sorry, Officer, but I can't seem to get my laces untied.'"

Tim Gleason told the story well—craning his neck around for the last line, as if he lay flat on the ground and spoke to someone above him—but Franny did not know if she were allowed to laugh along with Rosamund, or if Tim Gleason would give her a look that said, "That wasn't for you." This summer, Franny often did not know what to do, and she did not want to do what she had done in summers past. Did *not* want to fish for crappies and bullheads. To make loom pot holders or drive go-carts or play miniature golf or endless games of Michigan rummy and Monopoly. To crew on the sailboat of the girl from down the beach—

"Be right back, Roz." Quick, she stepped from the curb and between the front and rear ends of two cars moving up Lakeside. No time to quake at the honks and shouts of the drivers. Just—try to look cool. Stay alive.

From the other side of the street, she turned to wave to Rosamund, who shook her head, but grinned just as she had the night she found Christy Strawberry and Franny smoking on the window ledge of Franny's room. An admiring smile. Maybe Rosamund had heard that shout from a passing car: "Hey, buttercup!" Which might have been meant for Franny? Because of her yellow shorts and shirt? Peg had told Franny that she should change before going to town, but Rosamund said, "She's fine, Mom," and now Franny was glad, glad, so glad she had to hold her face down to conceal her smile as she joined the line in front of the Dairy Queen stand—

Oh, the song that poured from the Dairy Queen speakers. It took her by the shoulders. It shoved her and her broken heart out into a cold, dark night, both terrible and delicious.

Though who had broken her heart? Who?

Misty-eyed, she surveyed the DQ patrons, the poor acne-pitted girl clerk behind the service window. At the back of the stand, the chubby owner shuffled around with a bucket and mop, a cinnamon-colored dachshund underfoot. Sweet thing.

Could that "buttercup" really have been meant for her?

Sometimes, it seemed to Franny that she did look pretty, but the next moment she might pass by a mirror and out would leap a creature so queer she might have been one of the Picasso ladies from the books at the home of her piano teacher; not just limbs akimbo, but nose and eyes, too, her face a primitive mask from which speech would surely issue in foghorn blasts, bovine bellows. To make matters worse: Recently, after a quarrel among herself and Christy Strawberry and Joan Harvett, Christy had telephoned to tearfully admit that, while angry at Franny, she had told Joan Harvett—*not that I really believe it, Franny*—that Franny's nose was too big.

A too big nose was a personal defect that had never occurred to Franny, but as soon as Christy Strawberry said it, Franny realized it must be true.

"What can I get you?" asked the girl behind the DQ's tiny screen window.

"Three medium cones, please." Surely ordering Tim Gleason a cone was the polite thing to do. If he rejected his, fine, she'd pitch it in a trash can. *No big deal. No hurt feelings here, man.* An odd boy, Tim. Sometimes, he was like a fish in the shallows, holding so still you did not see him; then, as if he did not want to be completely forgotten, he would make a leap, show himself. Franny would have liked to ask her sister Martie what she thought of the boy and of Rosamund's friendship with him, but Martie could be a whirlpool that sucked your words into her spin until your words were no longer your own. They became just—fuel for some dark momentum that Martie seemed to require to know that she existed.

While the DQ girl made up the cones, Franny watched Mike Zanios, owner of the Top Hat Club, cross the drive between his club's brick building and the marina. Mike Zanios and Rosamund called to each other, and Franny knew, any moment now, Zanios would give Rosamund a hug that lifted her off the ground—

There.

The Wahls had eaten Sunday buffets (prime rib, moussaka, chicken) at the Top Hat for as long as Franny could remember. Her father left his law offices each noon for lunch at the place. Still, Franny could not help wondering how Tim Gleason felt about that hug. Mike Zanios might be a family friend, but Rosamund and Martie both spoke of how charming they found his blue eyes and the brows that met in an ashen smudge, the silver streaks in his dark blond curls, the way he dressed in sandals and boat-necked sweaters. In addition, lately, Mike Zanios often drove out to the Wahl house after dinner, and while Brick Wahl mixed him a drink, Zanios invariably would shout up the stairs, "Roz, come on down and tell us the news of the American youth!" Something like that. Then Rosamund would wind up perched on the arm of whatever chair he sat in, and though she did not drink alcohol, she sometimes drizzled a bit of the man's bourbon onto a scoop of ice cream, and, later, as if there were nothing extraordinary about it, he would take her to the Top Hat to listen to the combo that played there in the evenings.

Tim Gleason stared at the lake while Mike Zanios talked to Rosamund. Poor Tim worked hard to appear detached, cool, but even from across the street, Franny could see the way bright lines of tension tweaked the corners of his mouth, his jaw.

"I do worry, Roz, that people might misunderstand your friendship with Mike." So Peg Wahl had said over a recent dinner. Rosamund just laughed and squeezed her mother's hand. "You're so innocent, Mom! *Everybody* in Pynch knows Mike has a thing going on with that sleaze who sings with the combo! Believe me, whenever I go to the club, she comes by to paw at Mike—so people can see he's hers!" Peg had seemed surprised by this, and asked Franny's father, "Is that right?" and Brick looked up from picking at his dinner to say he guessed so, honey, he guessed Roz meant that brunette with the green goop on her eyes.

So Rosamund was not in love with Mike Zanios. But maybe she was a little in love with the Florida guy, Turner Haskin?

"Look who we found!" Rosamund called as Franny returned with her triangle of ice cream cones.

Should she have gotten a fourth cone, perhaps? One for Mike Zanios?

As if he were a grave courtier, Mike Zanios bowed toward Franny. She smiled, but felt grateful that the cones in her hands precluded the possibility of a hug. It seemed to Franny that, like herself, Mike Zanios now considered her too big for hugs; it was awkward, however, to stop doing something you had done for years, especially when he and Rosamund kept it up.

"Hey, Roz." Tim Gleason jerked his head toward the marina dock. "You want me to gas the boat?"

Rosamund grimaced, perhaps in memory of the conversation with the marina clerk. "We'll stop at Moore's later," she said; then—with a wink to Franny—she took two of the ice cream cones, and presented one to Mike Zanios. "Farewell gift?"

"Why, thank you, ma'am!" Mike Zanios gave the cone an amused inspection, then raised it high in the air, like a standard, and hummed a bit of vaguely martial music while Rosamund and Franny and Tim Gleason made their way to the now empty dock.

"And, Timmy, this other cone's for you," Rosamund said, just before the three of them reached the boat.

"Ha!" The boy leaned forward with a laugh to thumb a spot of ice cream off the tip of Rosamund's nose. "Caught you!"

"It was one *lick*!" Rosamund protested, but Tim continued to laugh, *hee, hee,* in what seemed to Franny clear relief at having taken Rosamund away from Mike Zanios.

Was it possible that Franny had seen Mike Zanios's singer/girlfriend at some time and not known it? A brunette, her father had said, and Rosamund called her a "sleaze," which probably meant that Mike Zanios had sex with the singer.

Maybe he had even told Rosamund so. This was not impossible. In June, while Rosamund set about unpacking her suitcases—such wonderful things inside (the Pure Pearl lipstick, bars of lilac-scented soap with sprigs of lilac embossed on the front, an actual *bullfrog,* stuffed and posed to stand on its own hind legs and hold a tiny guitar)—Rosamund had revealed startling news to Franny:

After Rosamund's dates from the university took her back to her dormitory, they regularly went out for sex with town girls.

"But if you like a boy, and he likes you, how can you stand the thought of him kissing somebody else?" Franny had asked.

"Oh, honey, that's the way it works, is all," Rosamund said. "It doesn't *mean* anything."

To Rosamund, it did not mean anything. To Franny, it *did*. Just like it meant something to her when the boys at the junior high asked the girls, "Are you a *good* girl or a *nice* girl?" One answer was right and one was wrong, and a large part of the point of the question seemed to be to make a girl indict herself by her answer. A girl was supposed to remember that the correct response was "I'm a nice girl," because "A 'nice girl' goes out, comes home, and goes to bed, while a 'good girl' goes out, goes to bed, and comes home." Or maybe it was the other way around; on principle, Franny refused to memorize the correct response. Nice. Good. It was all stupid. People wanted to say stupid, vile, mean things about girls. Just that winter, at one of the high school basketball games, a freckly boy Franny did not even know had sidled up to her as she made her way to the refreshment stand. "You're Martie Wahl's sister, aren't you?" he asked, and Franny had turned, smiling, before that boy went on to say, "My sister says your sister's a whore." He was smiling when Franny slapped his face—a mess of Cheese Curls mortared between his teeth—and he continued to smile as he said, "I was telling you so you wouldn't turn out like her, but I guess it's too late, huh?"

Franny had never told anyone that story. For one thing, she knew that plenty of people believed that if a person were *called* a name, the name was deserved. To complicate matters further, the only other person Franny had ever heard call Martie a whore was her father.

Why was "whore" the ultimate insult applied to girls who were clearly not whores? Surely her father knew that Martie was not a whore. Franny knew. Still, *had* Martie been a whore, and that boy from the basketball game called her so from spite, Franny would have slapped him just the same.

Cold and hard. She stuck her hand over the side of the big boat and the speed fanned the lake water, cold and hard, against her fingers.

Just the same.

There were plenty of people who would think Franny were a whore if they knew that she had allowed handsome Bob Prohaski to stick his tongue in her mouth. Which meant she could not ask anyone for advice on the kiss. Certainly not her mother, who had sent Bob home, immediately, the day she came into the yard while Franny pitched grapes across the picnic table and into the boy's mouth ("I don't know what you're up to, but it looks awful!").

Certainly not Joan Harvett and Christy Strawberry, who spoke of sexual matters as if on the verge of nausea. *So-and-so let so-and-so French her. Feel her on top. Down below.* And not her sisters; though, it was true, last summer Franny had once watched through the staircase spindles as curvaceous Martie and the ROTC member entered into a clothes-wrinkling struggle on the living room couch. All that slow and serious movement had seemed so utterly foreign to Franny—like the first time she had seen a newborn puppy nurse or a cecropia moth make its way from its cocoon—that she did not judge it by any parental injunction she might have overheard. Martie loved the ROTC boy, and he loved her, and Franny watched their activity on the couch not from mere curiosity but from envy and sympathy and worry, too. Heart aching, she sensed that the sum of all that writhing could not equal Brick and Peg's taking center stage at a party to touch-dance to "So Rare." And suppose that Martie and the ROTC boy's species of living room struggle were all that was left for the rest of them? This impoverished, privately formed notion contradicted all that Franny had been raised to believe lay in wait for her grown-up self, but there was a measure of comfort in the fact that Martie appeared to know, at that acute moment, exactly where she lay, and that someone cared—at least for a while—for her movements and her breath and her lips.

The taste of the kiss that Bob Prohaski had given Franny in the Strawberrys' dark garage: elemental, almost a little bloody, reminiscent of the way that the old-fashioned porch screens at her own house tasted when she pressed her tongue to their rusty weave.

CHAPTER TWO

*C*HUNK. THE DARK, COLD WAVES SPANKED THE BOAT'S WOODEN hull, *chunk,* and then *chunk* again, and Rosamund bounced up and down on the lip of the seat's back in a way that looked both exciting and dangerous.

"Better put on a life-jacket, Fran!" Rosamund shouted over her shoulder. "Mom might be watching when we come in!"

"What about you?" Franny shouted back.

Tim Gleason turned in his seat to wag a finger Franny's way.

"Oh, stop," she said. "Just—stop."

As they drew closer to the steep bank of the Wahl property, it was possible to make out a sliver of sandy beach beneath the green ruching of scrub willow and rogue mulberry that grew along the shore. The bank's unmown grass and poison ivy rose up behind the scrub plants, and still held a large, crookedy cross of whitewashed stones that was a remnant of the property's stint as a church camp. Next came the bank's crown, with its crew cut of lawn and stand of oak trees, and the stout, white, gambrel-roofed lodge built by the Pynch Lake Huntsmen at the end of the last century.

"If I can't get out of this podunk town, at least I can live in a place with character," Franny's father had said when he bought the property with life insurance money received at his own father's death. Franny's rather elegant grandmother, Charlotte Wahl, still shook her head each time she drove out for a visit, but Franny felt a shimmer of pride in the place. As her father said, it had a history, and Rosamund and Martie agreed, and liked to tell how they and a boy with a BB gun had once wandered through the derelict lodge, and shot out whatever windows remained unbroken.

And wasn't it *ironic,* they declared, that when their dad decided to renovate the place, "we were the ones who had to clean up all that mess?"

Franny had helped, too, of course. That had been the summer before last. 1963. In June and July, she prepped and varnished hundreds of pieces of wood. She had been varnishing strips of molding in the front yard when a group of men arrived with a crane and wrenched the camp's little church right off its slab—the church gave a kind of gasp, then flew up into the air, like Dorothy's house in *The Wizard of Oz*—and off it was hauled, teetering and tottering on a flatbed truck, to be tacked onto the Baptist church in town.

"Look, Timmy!" Rosamund backed the throttle down, the big engine quieting to a low chortle. She lifted her chin toward the set of concrete stairs that ran up from the shore to the top of the bank. At the top of the stairs a girl in pink kissed a boy in surfer trunks. "Lovebirds!" Rosamund said, then sucked in her cheeks—attractive derision—which made Tim Gleason smile. If Rosamund did not take him seriously, well, he was clearly glad that she did not take the wooing and winning of others seriously, either.

The boy in the surfer trunks was new to Franny, but there were always new people. Earlier in the day, a gaggle of them had arrived—friends of Martie's from the University of Iowa—with sleeping bags, cases of beer, a favorite slalom ski, vanity kits in olive green, powder pink, fake alligator. The girl guests were mostly blondes in coon-dark eye makeup, pretty, but often red and puffed from the sunburns they acquired while "lying out" on the Wahl docks and lawns. The male guests: psychology and business majors in madras shirts; beer drinkers who wore their hair shaved across the neck despite the changing times. *Deadly dull* was Rosamund's analysis, but this did not prevent Franny from appreciating certain thick necks and shoulders, the sandy stubble visible on a hard jaw as its owner devoured Peg's scrambled eggs.

Whooomph! In the distance, a small explosion sounded: an

empty aerosol, or maybe a discarded gas can in the garbage heap of the farmer who hauled trash for both summer residents and the handful of year-round people like the Wahls. The Wahl house sat far enough from town that what lay across Lakeside Drive, there, in the almost-country, was the farmer's scruffy gray barn, pasture, and bits of marsh where, now and then, the cattails rustled with nesting red-winged blackbirds.

Should Franny tell Rosamund to smooth her hair before they docked? A teased bundle—a tiny haystack—had lifted during the boat ride. Where the roots grew in, the hair appeared black, but that was only a matter of contrast. In its natural state, Rosamund's hair was a soft oak, the color that Franny supposed her own hair would darken to by the time she went to college.

"We'll see," Peg Wahl had said when Franny announced that she would never dye her hair. It seemed to Franny that her mother viewed the tiny flaxen braid in her handkerchief drawer as not just a memento of her own blond childhood but proof that she was entitled to stay a blonde. ("People who never were blondes," Peg had said the time that redhead Martie subjected her hair to a bottle of bleach, "those people have no business trying to be blondes.")

"Hey, Tim!" Smiling, Rosamund steered the boat in along the dock. "Maybe we should ask that cute Cheryl Stafford if she'd spot for you this afternoon. I bet you'd like that, right?"

The corners of Tim Gleason's mouth twitched at this suggestion, and, not for the first time, Franny wished that Rosamund would not pretend that she believed Tim a boy on the prowl; that she did not know he preferred to sit by her side like a faithful pooch. Rosamund thought she did the boy a favor, of course. Still, it was too preposterous.

But, then—Franny flushed inwardly—*I'm* the one who's really preposterous. I'm the one.

Along with Tim Gleason, she scrambled from the boat, began tying the ropes.

Pre-pos-ter-ous.

"You're only saying you love me 'cause I said I loved you." So

Bob Prohaski had mumbled into Franny's hair after that kiss in the Strawberry garage. Heartbreaking words. The two stood near a dim but potentially dangerous clot of power tools, the acrid odor of oily machinery mixing with the powder-soft sweetness of the boy's worn T-shirt.

"You can't like a guy like Prohaski!" That was what the girls in Franny's honors classes had said back in May, but Franny was different from them. She could not make herself like those seventh-grade boys who considered it clever to flip up a girl's skirt in the hall, or even the nice ones who often measured four inches shorter than herself. Tough Bob Prohaski had the face of a Mongolian warrior and stood five foot ten and weighed a muscular one hundred and sixty-five pounds.

It was true, however, that Franny had come to see that Bob Prohaski was kin to those creatures that lolled in squares of sunshine, or sprang. Bob Prohaski's ultimate dream, shared in the Strawberry garage: to one day own a Harley-Davidson motorcycle and a house with a sunken living room. Still, it was nice he'd shared his dream with her, wasn't it? And that he'd implied Franny was the one he wanted snuggled up beside him in that sunken living room? And that he had stopped certain annoying boys at school from calling her on the telephone? Really, she was obliged to him for all of that and, so, in the Strawberry garage, wrapped in his big arms, she had insisted, "I do, too, love you, Bob!"

Preposterous.

WHIRRWOO! WHIRRWOO!

The wailing from the top of the bank meant that someone blew the emergency siren that Franny's father had picked up while in Des Moines for a state bar association meeting. Brick had intended that the siren be used to call in his daughters from boating. Its wail— *WHIRRRWOOOoooo!*—had proved far too disturbing, however, and so that handsome, silver siren generally sat on Peg's cookbook shelf, silent unless—as now—some wag picked up the thing and decided to give everyone a jolt.

Was the wag her father? No, but Brick Wahl did stand at the top of the bank. A massive man. Florid, with cheeks that hung big and soft as the velvet ropes that cordoned patrons of theaters and museums into entrance and exit. Though his red hair had started to fade, Brick's general effect was Big Little Boy, and this effect was heightened today by the fact that he wore soft yellow golf pants with matching cardigan and shirt. He might have been a giant toddler, just installed in his pj's for a midday nap.

The boy to whom Brick now spoke—Franny did not recognize him, but she understood from the way her father raised his arm that he talked football to the boy. It had been high school football that transformed Harold Wahl into Brick. Also: In the hand *not* clutching the imaginary football, her father held a drink. Scotch was his drink of choice, but, at this hour of the day, not much past noon, with houseguests about, that thermal glass might still contain a Bloody Mary. The houseguests—several now visible on the screened porch—always praised Brick for the pitchers of wicked Bloody Marys he poured at the weekend brunches.

"Mr. Ed!" Franny called as a harlequin Great Dane raced past Brick and barreled down the long stairs to the dock. "Come here, Mr. Ed!"

At the base of the stairs, Mr. Ed paused. Franny hoped he would come to her. His coat was the finest velvet and she would give him nice pats and scratches. The Wahl dog, a faded cocker by the name of Suzie-Q, had been put down the fall before, and Franny missed curling herself up against the animal's warm back, or pressing her nose to Suzie-Q's nose or to her lovable, asphalt-textured paws with their odor of toasted corn chips.

To Franny's disappointment, however, after Mr. Ed lowered his soft gray mouth to the lake, he shot back up the bank, silky skin slipping and sliding over his fine ribs and spine.

There were certain to be more guests on the lawn than Franny could see as she followed Rosamund and Tim up the steps, and she felt shy of the guests—who were generally nice until they knew she was just the little sister. Actually, she felt shy of her father, too. Until—last summer?—he had seemed to like Franny, even if his attention lay elsewhere. Now, more and more, both he and her mother stared at her as if she were dry prairie about to burst into flames.

Something was making him laugh. Something he himself had said? Something said by the young man or by one of the two girls in coolie hats who had joined them? He laughed his soundless laugh—the infectious one that he produced with teeth clamped together. His big cheeks, so shiny and well-shaven and spanked with Aqua Velva, jiggled in pink delight.

Hard not to smile at such delight. Franny herself smiled.

"And then"—her father squeezed his eyes tight; tipped his head back as if he might sneeze—"this fellow says, 'Why, surely you're too young to be flying across the country alone, honey!' and it turns out he thinks Roz is all of *twelve* years old!"

"Daddy!" Rosamund stopped at the top of the steps. Tim Gleason stopped behind her. Franny stopped behind Tim. "You're not supposed to tell everybody that story!" Rosamund said, but you could tell she was not angry, and, with a laugh, Brick Wahl reached out to wrap a big arm around Rosamund's shoulder:

"Honey! It's just you're so darned tiny! I'm sure he thought you were cute as a bug!"

"Cute as a bug." Tim Gleason leaned forward to give Rosamund a soft thump on the head with his fist.

And there was Martie, swinging on the tire that Brick and one of the boy guests had recently tied to the big pin oak. Today, Martie wore her long, red hair in a braid that hung straight out behind her when the tire swing went up in the air and Martie leaned far, far back—

Who pushed Martie on the swing?

Not a houseguest. No. Al Castor. A local boy. White-blond hair grown to his chubby shoulders during his first year at Cornell. Owner of the Great Dane. Repository of firecrackers and obscene riddles and faultless impressions of cartoon guys (Daffy, Bugs) and bodily eructations. Al Castor had been Rosamund's buddy-of-choice last summer; then he made the mistake of declaring his true feelings and, as Rosamund had said, that was that.

How do you like to go up in a swing,

Up in the air so blue?

Oh, I do think it the pleasantest thing

Ever a child could do!

So Martie recited while Al Castor pushed the swing. Franny knew that poem from an old book she had found after the family moved out of their house on Ash Street: *A Child's Garden of Verses*. By Robert Louis Stevenson. Peg Wahl had stored all of Rosamund and Martie's children's books (*Winnie the Pooh, In My Mother's House,* and so on) in the Ash Street attic and, by the time Franny was born, forgotten the books' existence. During the move, however, Franny had found the books and saved them. Now she had her own favorites from *A Child's Garden of Verses,* but she would never have shared them with this crowd. Martie's noisy recitation struck Franny as hopelessly naive, precisely the opposite of that fake baby stuff cooked up by the occasional girl guest who, say, toted a teddy bear with her sleeping bag, or made a show of sucking a giant lollipop.

"Higher, Al!" Martie cheered. "Higher!"

"Good Christ!" Brick gave a pained grin to the group about him. "That girl does hurt my ears!"

Though the others in the circle laughed at this remark, Franny pretended not to hear it. Even to herself, she pretended, and she told herself, *Yes, it is a Bloody Mary, you can tell by the way, after each sip, he raises his lower lip over his upper to clear away the juice and Tabasco and salt.*

"So, kids," Brick said, "how was your trip into the big city?" and Rosamund related a story that Mike Zanios had apparently told her and Tim Gleason regarding the mess that had resulted when one of his dishwashers bungled an attempt to sneak a bottle of Kahlua out the back of the Top Hat Club.

"According to Mike, Pynch's butterflies have been involved in an unusual number of fender-benders this morning," Rosamund said.

Don't mind me. That was the air Franny meant to project as she started across the lawn. *I'm just heading for the porch, there, don't mind me.*

"But, say, Fran."

She sighed. Turned. Her father wet his lower lip with his tongue. Screwed up one eye, then crooked his index finger to show that she should draw near, he had something to say.

"What?"

The members of the group stood quiet and her father must have noticed, for he gave a stiff laugh before he murmured, "Well, dear, I was just going to say you should give some thought to the way you walk."

Franny grinned—a stupid, frozen grin. Then, ears ringing—how strange, the sound was that of the smallest possible silver bells, falling like snowflakes—she started off across the lawn once more.

"And, Fran!" Brick again. Again, she turned. "Did you know that Prohaski was here while you were gone?"

"No," she said, the word a stone on her tongue, her face so hot she supposed she must appear not just foolish but a liar as well.

"Was he the one in the tight pants?" tittered one of the girls in the coolie hats.

"Those god-awful pants!" Brick shivered his big shoulders up about his ears.

"Actually"—Franny's voice trembled now—"actually, Bob's family doesn't have much money. His parents both work at the creamery. Bob just has that one pair of pants." A slight exaggeration. "Well, he and his brother share another pair."

"Uh-oh!" the girl in the coolie hat grinned. "I think I offended somebody!"

"Yeah, you did," Franny said, but Brick said, now, now, and here came Martie, calling out *choo-choo* as she crossed the lawn, locomotive style, arms working at her sides:

"Hey, people! *Que pasa?* Why so glum, chums?"

"Sh! Martie!" Brick lifted his finger to his lips and his thermal cup toward the branches of the oaks overhead. "Sh. You're disturbing all the little birdies up in the trees."

Automatically, the members of the circle raised their eyes to the branches at which Brick pointed; then they began to laugh as Brick went on in a soft, soft voice, "Now, I don't know about the rest of you, but, at a time like this, when all the little birdies need their naps, it seems to me the thing to do—the really responsible thing to do—is to head on back to the kitchen and make sure that whatever got left in the pitcher there doesn't go to waste."

CHAPTER THREE

THE FOLLOWING MONDAY MORNING, WHEN FRANNY WOKE IN her bunk bed, she felt slightly blank. Because the guests were gone? She supposed they did add dimension to her life. Borders. And—camouflage, yes, because a person could often hide out in the weekends' circus atmosphere.

With a sigh, she flipped her pillow. Flipped herself. Remembered: a Snow White nightmare. She never slept well after dreaming those goofy but horrible things (the evil queen forces Franny/Snow to wear a birdcage over her head, and that birdcage contains a woodpecker and the woodpecker will not stop pecking at Franny/Snow's head).

Outside the bedroom's old double-hung windows, the leaves of the big oaks rustled. Waves slapped the shore. A gang of jays let loose their raucous cries and flashed past like rocks shot from a sling. That *crack* would have come from the rowboat, tied up at the dock, swinging out to full length on its painter. *Eden,* Franny had painted on the rear of the boat after the Des Moines girl from down the beach had loaned her an anthology containing Dickinson's lines:

Rowing in Eden—
Ah, the Sea!
> *Might I but moor—Tonight*
> *In Thee!*

Franny's mother had never read that poem, but she objected to Franny's naming the boat *Eden*. Someone might think Franny meant to be suggestive, she said. Franny had painted over the letters, then, and painted in the number affixed to the poem: *#58*. Because she wanted to have that banner out there in the world. Because she had feelings like the poet in the poem even if she did not yet possess the person to whom she could attach such feelings.

If that made sense.

The Des Moines girl, Susan Thomas, seemed to think it made sense.

More morning noises: the thuds and howls from the antiquated pipes and taps. The mild thunder that meant Ginny Weston now dragged the vacuum cleaner out from the hall closet and across the floorboards. Which was a gift. Ginny Weston had cleaned for the Wahls since Franny was a baby, and the house always felt more peaceful to Franny with Ginny about, waxing floors, ironing, preventing any major outbreaks of domestic discord.

To rest her chin on her windowsill and stare outside made Franny feel as if she were a dog. A friendly dog. When she had her own house, someday, she would have not just one dog, but three or four. At the dock's end, the rowboat—white and green—appeared both mysterious and welcoming, like the boats in the van Gogh book at the home of her piano teacher. Boats with a thin stripe of red or some astonishing blue. *Red boats. Blue boats. Old boats. New boats.* (Was that a line from one of the old children's books? *The Friendly Book*?) Van Gogh's paintings of boats were somehow more like boats than any other paintings of boats that Franny knew. That is, the painting itself was somehow so clearly an object to be reckoned with, you felt as if you were in the presence of something magical.

Franny flopped back on the bunk. Pressed her toes hard against the wires supporting the mattress overhead, a fifties' thing whose cloth cover bore a design of bitter-yellow satellites and mottled-white planets on a sky of gray. When she pushed against the wires, their resistance traveled down her calves and thighs and made her feel pleasantly exhausted.

Tiny blond hairs had sprouted on her lower legs since the last time she shaved. Nasty-looking, but they felt nice, ticklish when brushed lightly with the tips of her fingers. "A girl should shave her legs every day during the summer," Martie had warned Franny, and Rosamund agreed but added that, on her spring break, friends had taken her to visit a farm outside New York City where there were girls who did not shave or wear makeup or even bras.

Fascinating. Repulsive. The idea that a girl could choose not to shave. A girl could choose to become practically invisible. Franny knew this was possible because there had been a girl in her seventh-grade gym class whom Franny recognized as potentially beautiful, yet no one at the junior high ever said a word about that girl. Sometimes Franny had wanted to tell her, "Look, you don't seem to understand, you could be beautiful!" But, then, she could be of other minds—one of them jealous of the possibility of the girl's entering the fray, another protective of the safe and happy world in which she lived, ignorant of her moon-maid charms.

And suppose the girl had not been ignorant. Suppose she had *chosen* to stay just as she was.

It must have been about eleven when Franny heard Peg calling for her to come to the basement. Franny did not find Peg in the laundry area, and so she stepped behind the fold-out screen that concealed the spot where Peg kept her "things": A set of metal shelves held a greenware crèche in a cardboard box and interesting sponges and other tools for ceramics; and there were boxes of pastels and tubes of watercolors, brushes, fierce-looking scrapers with toothed edges.

Peg herself sat on a stool in front of those shelves, reading the instruction booklet for the enameling kiln Brick had given her for their anniversary. She looked up, frowning. "They're supposed to send me something else—this isn't complete." She waved the booklet in her hand. "Could you run down to the mailbox and see if it came?"

Franny was relieved to be excused from helping with the house-work—Peg had assigned the girls to the bathrooms that day—and she smiled as she made her way down the hill and across the scruffy remains of the church camp's baseball diamond. What grass grew underfoot there was dry nubs, no more than weeds mowed to within an inch of their life; still, Franny's soles were tough from a barefoot summer, and she took pride in the way she could run on the stuff, run on rocks, on hot asphalt or burning cement.

A meadowlark sang on top of the sign at the edge of the property: DODGE BAPTIST CAMP. She hardly knew that she knew the local birdsongs but they ran in her head—they were part of her days—and she smiled as the lark swooped away and across Lakeside Drive and soared over that dream sweep of green and brown—swaying cattails and meadow and distant, thumbnail-size steers—that rolled up to meet a sky that seemed a pearly excrescence of the land itself.

A good day. Maybe she could slip away for just a quick walk through the Nearys' swamp where the high grass looked continuous but, in fact, grew in little hummocks a person had to jump from, one to the other, or get her feet soaked. Or maybe she could take a walk along Lakeside. Walk to the west until Lakeside ran out and there was farmland on both sides of the road and the lake was no longer visible. Or to the east, past the ramshackle neighborhoods of tiny cottages—

The big upside down U of the neighborhood's shared mailbox wheezed when she tugged on the door. Aluminum against aluminum. It made her shudder. And she felt suddenly guilty at the realization that she toyed with the idea that a boy other than Bob Prohaski might glimpse her by the mailbox, and like her. Yes. Just now, though she appeared only to sort her family's mail from the mail of the neighbors, she stood at the well, waiting for her prince to come, insert his reflection alongside that reflection of herself already held by the dark water.

Not much mail. An issue of *Life* magazine, a letter for her mother, a flyer from the Hobby Shack with a penned note on the front:

Peg—Remind me to show you the reds I got in my last firing—xo—Cele

Most of the bills and things went to Brick's box in town, or to the law office.

Did someone stare at Franny? If someone stared at her, she could almost always tell, and someone stared. She felt the eyes at her back, though she had heard no footsteps.

We don't do that, Franny, Rosamund had said at the marina, but you had to turn to know if you were in danger, didn't you? Or if your prince had come?

The Nearys' bull. That was all. An enormous black creature—Aberdeen Angus, according to her farm-girl mother—the bull stood stolidly at the edge of its private enclosure. "Hi, bull," Franny called, and waved the *Life* magazine the animal's way, but that was bravura. She did not feed handfuls of the taller grass from the ditches to the bull in the way she sometimes fed the old horses that pulled Mr. Neary's trash cart.

A bull that looks like a bull.

When the Wahls had first moved out of Pynch, they had gone to introduce themselves to the Nearys. The Nearys had merely stood silent in their yard and, finally, Peg pointed across the road at the bull and said, "My dad always told us, 'When you're in the market for a bull, make sure you get a bull that looks like a bull,'" and that line was now a family joke, something one of them could say when a conversation came to an awkward silence:

"When you're in the market for a bull, get a bull that looks like a bull."

Franny inspected the *Life* on her way back to the house. Some layout person had cut into the photo of the four U.S. soldiers on the magazine's cover in order to make one soldier's head lap the red block containing the bold white letters spelling out "LIFE." That soldier wore a silver ring on his finger that might have been a wedding band. He and another soldier were helping a third soldier—an injured man—cross a field while a fourth man, mouth screwed into an odd grimace, looked on.

The first page of the magazine showed a photo of a model in a kerchief. "Do you have to hide your hair to look prettier?" asked the advertisers at Clairol; and, next, there was the actor Louis Jordan, behind a pair of Foster Grant sunglasses. The magazine's many advertisements for liquor showed people having a wonderful time at elaborate parties. A model in a gold swimsuit and gold bathing cap and goggles promoted Revlon's new frosted lipstick and nail polish colors. Sugar and Ice was a faint, iridescent pink and Frosted Malt its beige twin, and Franny felt certain one of the colors would make a great deal of difference in how she looked, but *which* one?

From out of the pages of the magazine and onto the drive, something fell. A postcard. For Rosamund. Reading other people's mail was wrong. Of course. However, the handwriting on this postcard was so enormous, Franny could hardly have missed the explosive signature of Rosamund's friend Turner Haskin, and surely there was nothing wrong with looking at the picture on the front of the card. La Playa, Franny knew, was the name of the beachfront hotel belonging to Turner Haskin's father, and here was a photo of that hotel and its sandy beach, both of which looked as white and matte as confectioner's sugar. On the rooftop of the hotel, enormous burgundy letters stood up against the Florida sky to spell out the name: LA PLAYA.

"People like Frank Sinatra go there," Rosamund said when Franny brought the postcard inside, into the kitchen. Martie and Peg and Ginny Weston were in the kitchen, too. A rangy woman in beige glasses and beige slacks and a beige peasant blouse decorated with green rickrack, Ginny Weston sat at the breakfast table, testing the pin curls she would brush out before driving home to serve lunch to her farmer husband. Because of the growing midday heat, no one had bothered to turn on the overhead light, and it was dim in the old kitchen with its dark tongue-and-groove walls and ceiling, and Peg carried Turner Haskin's postcard to the little fluorescent over the sink in order to take a better look.

"Turner says they'll have Mafia bosses sitting next to movie stars. People who need privacy and expect the best." With a butter knife, Rosamund edged a pan of brownies left from the weekend, and ate the fragile slivers, one by one. "Turner says when a celebrity goes by, you pretend you don't notice."

Martie looked up from the eggs she was whipping. "Well, of course. You wouldn't make an ass of yourself by *gawking*."

"Martie!" Peg said in response to "ass," and Rosamund, with an amused twist of her lips, added, "It's not like you get a chance to see Frank Sinatra every day, Martie."

Ginny Weston gave a laugh as she wound a still-damp coil of hair back into place, and reinserted its bobby pins. "I couldn't go there, Roz! I'd probably scream if I saw Old Blue Eyes!"

"Oh, no doubt you and I would botch it completely, Ginny! A couple hayseeds like us!" Peg looked up from the can of tuna fish she was opening and she grinned at Ginny Weston. Sometimes it seemed to Franny that Ginny Weston was her mother's best friend, though Peg never had told Ginny to stop referring to her as Mrs. Wahl. *Mrs. Wahl.* Still, Franny had never seen Peg cry in front of her regular friends, but she had overheard numerous teary sessions between Ginny and her mother.

Which struck Franny as sad.

Also sad: the way that Peg forgot she was no longer the maker of lunches, and, so, regularly fixed large bowls of food—tuna salad, just now—that later she would have to throw out.

"Fran." Peg wagged a celery stalk Franny's way. "Stand up straight!" she said; and, then, "Not *that* straight!"

Rosamund, passing out of the kitchen, gave Franny a sympathetic wink. It was nice having the big girls home. The family seemed more like a family again. During the past school year, Brick often had said he had eaten a big lunch at the Top Hat and thought he would skip dinner. Peg came home from the Hobby Shack later and later; she had started working on enamels that fall, making everybody cuff links for Christmas, and more and more often Franny had ended up eating TV-dinners, alone.

The record that Rosamund now started on the turntable of the living room stereo: "You Were Only Fooling (While I Was Falling in Love)." Some old, old thing by an old, old group called the Ink

Spots. Antiquated falsettos and twinkly guitar strained into the kitchen. Martie sang along as she tended to her omelet on the stove.

"Ginny, did you see the picture where this Turner is the model?" From its spot behind a magnet on the refrigerator, Peg Wahl removed a newspaper advertisement (handsome, tuxedoed male assists his female equivalent in exiting a Lincoln Continental offered for sale by a Miami car dealer).

"Isn't he handsome?" Peg said.

Ginny Weston winked at Rosamund as the girl returned to the kitchen. "Be still, my heart!"

"But what's the deal, Roz?" Martie set her elbows on the countertop of the kitchen's island, then walked her feet up the cupboards across the way until she had made a kind of arch with her torso. "If his dad's place is so great, why hasn't he invited you there?"

"*Martie!*" Peg said, but Rosamund just laughed—a tinkling laugh that demonstrated how far above being insulted by Martie she was.

"I'm sure Martie didn't mean that the way it sounded," Franny said.

Martie looked injured. "Did I say something wrong?"

Rosamund smiled at Peg and Franny while the diplomatic Ginny gathered coffee cup and saucer and exited the scene. "Martie probably doesn't know I met Turner just before school let out," Rosamund said. "It's not like I'd rush off for a weekend with him whether it was at his father's hotel or—wherever."

"Of course not!" Peg said.

Steam from Martie's omelet pan rose with a hiss as Martie dashed the pan into the sink and protested, "I suppose you're implying *I* would?"

"Flower lady's on her way to the door," Ginny Weston called from the back hall. Peg shook her head at Martie, then grabbed the old Hopalong Cassidy mug in which she kept change.

"Flower lady, here!" a tiny, ancient voice cried. "Flowers!"

Franny was more than willing to follow Peg to the front hall, to shift moods. Though the flower lady drove a light green Pontiac on her trips around Pynch Lake, her stooped arrival at the door with her flower basket on her arm always made Franny feel as if she lived in some far-off, gentler days of tinkers and peddlers.

Peg picked out four of the old woman's tiny bundles—bachelor buttons, pinks, coreopsis, black-eyed Susans. "That'll be forty cents, right?"

The flower lady nodded as she moved her tiny bird-bone fingers in among her wares, setting things to rights. "You might like to see the tiger lilies I got in my car."

"Oh, I love tiger lilies," Franny said.

"Expensive," Peg murmured.

The old woman smiled. "Mrs. Wagner bought three dozen for her lunch ladies. She said they were a good price."

"That's nice for you, isn't it?" Peg fingered four dimes up the side of the sugar bowl while giving Franny a sideways smile that Franny hoped the older lady did not see.

"Trug" was the precise name for the basket in which the woman carried her flowers to and from her car. When Franny first had come across the word, she had known immediately that it described the basket carried by the flower lady. A perfect word: trug. So humble. Like potato. Like—hummock.

"Honestly!" Peg said as the woman returned to her car. Something in the set of Peg's chin let Franny know Peg's feelings were hurt, and, sure enough, as they hurried the little bundles of dripping flowers to the kitchen, Peg said, "Who all could Kay be having for a luncheon? And did you see how that woman was trying to shame me into buying her lilies?"

With the word "trug" now slipped over her own arm—its size necessitated holding the arm away from her side—Franny smiled at Peg and said, "Well, I didn't, Mom, but, then, actually, I was thinking about having some of your tuna salad."

Just to be nice. She knew the salad would make her breath stink at that afternoon's piano lesson.

*   *   *

A plump little quail of a woman, the piano teacher. A chain-smoker worn by recent widowhood. She gazed rather mournfully out a window obscured by ivy while she asked, "So, tell me, truthfully, did you practice at all this week?"

Franny mumbled frightened inanities about the difficulties of practicing with guests in the house, and how she would do better next week. She tried not to think about the hairy mole on the teacher's neck. A pathetic thing. Revolting. Like some furry pet cockroach that peeked out over the teacher's lacy collar.

With a rap, the teacher brought Franny's pile of books together on the corner of the piano. A Steinway. Once, Franny's father had come to fetch her at lessons and had stepped inside and admired the Steinway and played a version of "Mack the Knife" that the teacher seemed to find charming.

"Frances"—the teacher held the books out to the girl—"you need to consider whether you want to continue lessons."

Then it was over, and the next student could be heard, opening the screen door to the porch, coming inside. That girl was gawky, with hair the sickly yellow of the unguent Franny's family used for burns, but she had talent, and dedication, too. Usually, while waiting to be picked up at the lesson—why did her mother always have to be late?—Franny sat in a corner and looked at the teacher's art books while the talented student played. Today, however, mortification drove Franny onto the screened porch. It had rained while she was inside, and the raindrops had beaded on the porch's painted concrete floor. She extended the toe of her shoe to push one of the beads, see if it would roll, but it only smeared.

Her parents would kill her if she quit piano, she thought, and a queer pressure moved down her body, head to toe, as if she were being swallowed.

What was that?

Last winter, once, after a basketball game, she had waited for her mother in the foyer of the junior high school while the snow got deeper and deeper and the evening grew darker. All of the other students had been picked up and the janitors finally shut her into the foyer with the metal accordion doors that made a second defense against intruders. Friendly, good-hearted men, they did not realize it frightened Franny to be left alone in the dark building. The old one said to the young one, laughing, "I guess we can trust Franny not to let anybody into the foyer, huh?" and the young one said, "I suppose, but, hey, Franny, don't step outside till you're sure you're ready to go, 'cause otherwise you'll be locked out." Then each man left the doors he had locked, one man heading up the stairs to the second floor, the other disappearing down the hall. She watched the snowflakes sweep across the parking lot. A little while later, the janitors, both of them hunched against the wind, appeared in the lot and climbed into their cars and drove away and left the lot empty. Franny had told herself: She'll come now. Now. Now. The next second. In five seconds. When her mother did finally arrive—the car sour with the smell of those fired enamel plates Peg was bringing home from the Hobby Shack kiln—Franny had burst into tears. Her mother said she was silly, overly dramatic, and maybe she was. How could you tell?

The tall trees in the piano teacher's neighborhood cast such dense shade on the street in front of the teacher's house that the light there appeared green, and just suppose that this time Franny's mother really did *not* come. Not because she was hurt and unable to come, no, but because she simply did not want to come anymore.

"Frances?"

She jumped. The teacher stood in the open porch door though the talented girl continued to play her piece (something sprightly and slightly maniacal). "Do you want to try to call your mother? See what's holding her up?"

The teacher's telephone hung in the kitchen. It was easy enough to pretend to call. If she were actually to call, and Peg were still at home, she would be angry. *If I could be there, I'd be there.* How embarrassing, then, when Franny finished her fake conversation— did the teacher and the talented girl overhear?—to step onto the porch again and discover that the white Wildcat convertible, top down, now sat, idling, at the curb.

*   *   *

"So?" Peg glanced at Franny as she steered the car out of the piano teacher's neighborhood and back toward Lakeside Drive.

"So—what?"

"So how was your lesson?"

"She said"—Franny felt as if she swallowed a burr—"I should think about whether I want to keep coming."

"Oh, Fran! That means you're doing poorly! And when I think of all the children who would be thrilled to have a chance at a piano lesson!"

Franny ignored the tears escaping the corners of her eyes. She pointed up the street to her grandmother's driveway, the maroon Chrysler now waiting for a chance to back out onto Lakeside.

"There's Grandma," she said.

Peg honked. A hand emerged from the Chrysler. Waved.

"Well, at least she acknowledged me," Peg muttered.

Franny ignored that, too. From past experience, she knew that if she were to say anything negative about her father's mother, her mother would correct her. And if she said something positive, her mother would say, "Oh, well," implying Franny did not know the whole story.

Since there was nothing to say, Franny made a game of keeping hold of a glimpse of the lake as the road dipped close to the water, then away, then back again. Sometimes, she lost the lake completely as they started up a hill but then she found it again in the branches of trees. An entire field of it shimmered and shook silver when the car came level with the shore and passed Moore's Marina and Johnny's Casino—

"It'll kill your father if you quit, Fran."

"I'll try harder."

Peg gave her head a little shake. Before driving Franny to the lesson, Peg had complained of her own appearance in one of the hall mirrors—"I look like a cow!"—but now, chin lifted, short golden hair brushed back in Greek-goddess wings, she appeared impenetrable. Even the gold bangles that had slipped down her wrist and rested on her forearms as she drove contributed to this picture of competence, strength.

Tanglefoot was the name of Bob Prohaski's neighborhood, a dank, mosquito-infested place. The road to Tanglefoot lay just on their right, and if her mother were to turn, they would soon pass by the Prohaski house. Peg did not turn, of course—Tanglefoot would have been out of their way. On this stretch, for a time, the lake disappeared completely from view. On the right sat the pink motel that served as the dormitory of tiny Stanford Fanning Fellow College. Franny wished her father were in the car, then, because he would have made some tension-releasing joke about the school, which had been founded by an enormously successful and unscrupulous land developer after his son flunked out of several mediocre colleges. These days, well-heeled academic flops from around the region came to Pynch for easy credits and—if they were males—a way to avoid the draft. "Pompon majors," Brick called the girl students. "Stanford," he called SFF, and "School for Fools." Though not around Franny's mother, who had not gone to college, and was touchy on the subject.

Franny and Peg did not speak at all as they passed Stanford Fanning Fellow or Water Tower #2 or Woolf Beach or even the trailer court where a manic Irish setter—a beautiful creature with a glossy red coat but only three legs—made its usual barking charge at the car. In silence, they passed Mother Goose Miniature Golf. Crossed the causeway that spanned a short stretch of marsh dotted with those muskrat dens that Franny always hoped would one day turn out to be beaver lodges, a beaver being infinitely more appealing than a muskrat.

On the left: the chimney-shaped brick building that housed tiny Karlins' Grocery. During the spring, when her school bus had let out the kids who lived in the shabby homes huddled around Karlins', Franny sometimes got off with them and bought a pack of cigarettes or a Milky Way before walking the last mile home. A comforting old grocery, Karlins', with its scuffed wood floors and poor lighting and candy behind the counter. Franny felt loyal to the place, and to the house next to the grocery as well. A girl from her Sunday school, Kimmy Estep, had lived in that house, and, once, when Franny visited the girl—they must have been five or six at the time—Mrs. Estep gave them each two cents and they took the money to Karlins' to buy Sputnik gum balls. That had been long ago. The Esteps had kept the house nice and neat, but now the insulating bales of hay set against the foundation the winter before lay scattered about the yard, and the paint job had gone chalky. Whenever Franny's father glimpsed the place, he became infuriated, as if someone had given him a personal insult. *A pigsty. Somebody ought to get in there with a bulldozer. A couple of carefully placed sticks of dynamite could go a long way toward improving that spot.*

"What on earth?" Peg said, and pointed.

High on a ladder that leaned up against the old church camp sign at the edge of the Wahl property, there stood Martie, removing the letters that spelled out DODGE BAPTIST CAMP and handing them down to Rosamund.

"What are you two doing?" Peg called as the Wildcat drew up alongside the girls. "And in your swimsuits, no less."

Rosamund smiled and called back, "We're going to repaint the letters! Spruce things up!"

Martie climbed down from the ladder and she high-stepped through the tall grasses that grew in the little ditch that separated the property from the road. "We got this great idea!" She leaned an arm on the roof of the Wildcat. "We'll take a picture of the sign and the house, see, and paste it to a postcard, and then, Roz can send it to Turner Haskin. As kind of a spoof on his sending her that postcard of his dad's hotel."

In the end, Rosamund and Martie decided to scramble the freshly painted letters of the sign. "Poddigbattes Camp" was the result. Awful, Franny's mother said, and wanted the girls to put things right before their father got home, but then Brick did get home, and he thought the name so funny that he grabbed a camera and hurried the girls and the ladder back to the refurbished sign; and, there, he captured a shot of Rosamund pretending to be in the process of hanging the last of the letters, while Martie, below, supported the ladder with one hand and, with the other, slapped at a bug on her thigh.

CHAPTER FOUR

A GREAT HIT, THAT PODDIGBATTES CAMP PHOTO. THE SUM-
mer guests laughed at how the bull in the pasture across the road
seemed to lower in disapproval—or lust—toward pretty Martie
and Rosamund in their swimsuits. They loved to say the silly name:
Poddigbattes Camp. By the very next weekend, the photo had a
spot in the upstairs hall, along with a mishmash of other photos
that Martie rounded up after declaring the family needed to show
some pride, for Pete's sake (young Rosamund and Martie sailing
and taking swim classes and riding the horses they had kept as
kids; Peg as Miss Iowa Dairy in a photo taken not long before
Brick showed up at her parents' farmhouse to ask if someone with
a tractor might help him get his car out of a ditch). When Franny
had complained that no photo of her hung in the display, Peg
tapped on a picture of herself and Brick and the older girls, vaca-
tioning in Muir Woods. "You're in this one here," she said with a
wink that Franny did not care to consider. And there were Brick
and his father and Ralph Trelore in front of the offices of Trelore,
Wahl, and Wahl—Brick apparently unable to erase the look on his
face that said "Could somebody get me out of here?" Brick playing the piano. A much younger Brick polishing his yellow Mercedes, an open bottle of beer sticking out of his back pants pocket.

Franny considered this hallway display while, beneath her feet,
another party swelled and the Rolling Stones played on the
stereo—though not too loudly, as Brick and Peg were downstairs,

too. "Play With Fire": an insinuating, queerly seductive song. Franny could not help liking it, but the singer was cruel to the girl he addressed, and it seemed he was cruel because—because her mother was an heiress in St. John's Wood and neglected the girl? All of this hurt Franny's feelings somehow, yet also made her feel both a little dangerous and a little endangered—not entirely unpleasant sensations. And, really, she could not deny that Bob Prohaski's bending her arm behind her back—"Say uncle, Franny!"—was closer to the sentiments of "Play With Fire" than to those of the forty-five rpm that Franny herself had bought in May: "Hold Me, Thrill Me, Kiss Me" by Mel Carter.

A lull in the party below. Franny could hear the voices of Rosamund and Martie raised in debate.

"But absinthe is illegal," said Rosamund—using a touch of her New York accent for leverage—and Martie, "No, no, only absinthe made with *wormwood* is illegal."

Absinthe?

Across the bottom of the next photo in the hall display, someone had written by hand—with white ink—"Pynch Lake Huntsmen, 1897." Such dark, unsmiling men, the Pynch Lake Huntsmen, they might have been members of a vigilante group. Guns propped on their shoulders or stuck in the ground. Wool jackets as heavy as slabs of clay. In front of the men there sat a small hill that seemed, at first, incongruous, an awkward pile of dirt. Only slowly—and only to the patient viewer—did the hill finally resolve itself into a pile of hundreds of dead birds: pheasant and dove, quail of a sort no longer found in that part of the country.

Not for the first time, Franny felt an almost embarrassing advantage at having been born so much later than the huntsmen—as if she were sighted, and they the defenseless blind. Impossible the world had ever been so old and gray and humorless. At the same time, what a wonder that the lake rocks in the corner of the big fireplace behind the huntsmen were clearly the very same rocks that could be seen in that corner of the fireplace if she were to trot outside, now, sixty-eight years later!

This thought elated Franny so, she slipped the photo from its hook on the wall and started with it toward the stairs. She would show it to Rosamund. It was not so much Rosamund as her parents and Martie who objected to her being at the parties. Before this summer, Franny had always been allowed to wander through the noisy affairs her sisters threw when Brick and Peg went out of town, so why couldn't Franny just call Rosamund aside and ask if Rosamund felt as Franny did about the photograph?

"You two need to dance!" That was Martie's voice, down below. "Come on," Martie said, "I'll put on the Duke, and you can show us how it's done!" Which meant Martie spoke to Peg and Brick.

You sure you want a couple of old geezers out on the floor?

Well, just one song.

"Take the A-Train," Martie put on the stereo, and Franny peered down through the banisters to watch her parents dance in the middle of that politely smiling crew in the living room. They were good—especially Peg, moving on her toes as if she wore high heels instead of bare feet. Cheek to cheek they danced, Brick rumbling his shoulders around now and then, laughing, grinning as he spun Peg across the floor. Afterward, the guests applauded, and Brick said, "Now, that's what I call music!" A girl guest said that Brick ought to play them a tune on the piano, but Peg said, *Not tonight, kids,* she and Brick were going out for a walk, he'd promised.

Which Franny understood to mean that Brick was drinking too much. "Too hard," Peg would say, as if the drinking involved work, strain. There was a reason Brick sometimes drank "too hard." Peg had explained this to Franny after Brick had crashed into the what-not shelf at the home of Peg's mother and broken all of Delpha Ackerman's beloved Hummel figurines, and Delpha had called him a disgrace. Back at home again—Franny had been a sixth-grader at the time—while Peg and Franny tested the strands of colored lights for the Christmas tree, Peg had told Franny that her dad sometimes drank too hard because—here Peg took one of those breaths that Franny knew hurt when it expanded in your chest—*because* during his first year in law school, he and a girl had been in a car accident. "That girl died, Franny, and your dad claimed he was driving, but— he wasn't."

Why'd he do that? Franny had protested. Solemnly, Peg had picked up, then set down, a novelty bulb that remained in its box each year, as none of the Wahls' strands had a receptacle for the thing. Voice choked with tenderness, Peg said, "To protect her honor. Because she'd been drinking. Anyway, the point is, it's that memory—and having people think he was responsible—that's what makes him drink so hard. Now. Sometimes."

Franny had not known how to respond to this sad and terrible story, but she knew she must respond, her mother was waiting, giving a brisk shake to the felt skirt that would go around the base of the Christmas tree—such a pretty thing, with its red felt reindeers with the sequin bridles that Peg had stitched on, one by one—

"Well!" Peg cast a sidelong glance Franny's way. "I thought you were mature enough to understand, but I guess I was mistaken."

"No!" Franny threw her arms around her mother's waist, and insisted she did understand, she did. Which meant she had not been able to ask why her father had to protect the honor of a dead girl, or why their family had to suffer so for some stranger's reputation.

Up went the volume on the stereo below, suggesting that Brick and Peg were now out on their walk.

Franny returned the huntsmen's photograph to its hook on the wall. Of course she could not take it down to the party to show it to Rosamund. That would be preposterous. Pre-pos-ter-ous.

In her parents' bedroom, on the upstairs extension, she dialed the telephone number of Christy Strawberry.

"Hey, Chris, knock, knock!"

Christy Strawberry groaned. "Who's there, Franny?"

"Sacramento!"

"Sacramento who?"

"Sacramento objects belong in a church!"

"Well, Franny, I guess I'll just have to take your word on that one."

"Come on! Sacramento? Like sacramental? I'm making up city knock-knocks! Give me a city! How about—Detroit? Just—Detroit. *Troit.* Okay. Okay. It'll be—something with a troika. You know? Those Russian sleighs? This'll be good. Because it'll be something, like, I'm talking with a New York accent, see, and when I do the response, I'll say 'Detroit' so it sounds like I'm saying, 'De troika.' 'De troika's here to take you to the Russian Tea Room!'"

"What's the Russian Tea Room?" Christy Strawberry asked.

"It's in books, you know? People in New York City go there on special occasions, and they eat stuff, like, blini."

After Franny finished explaining to Christy Strawberry what she believed a blini to be, Christy told Franny how she and Joan Harvett had talked to a boy named Kirk Toomy at City Park's bandshell that afternoon. Franny did not know the boy—someone from one of the Catholic grade schools—but apparently he had swiped Christy Strawberry's madras scarf and she had chased him around and around the bandshell stage in an effort to get back the scarf, and *it was so funny, Franny*—

A small lamp sat on her mother's bedside table and Franny turned it off while Christy Strawberry talked, trying to make herself focus on the girl's words. At the start of junior high, when Christy Strawberry and Joan Harvett had asked her to go to the football games and things with them, she had been pleased. The girls in honors struck her as boring and frumpy. Christy and Joan were not hoods, but they liked boys and cigarettes and swearing out loud—*damn, shit, damn all this shit to hell*—and they pursued Franny's friendship in a way that no one else ever had. Especially Christy. Franny had spent most of the Friday nights of seventh grade sleeping at the Strawberrys' and even taking Christy along to her confirmation classes at the Episcopal church on Saturday mornings. Franny was the one in whom Christy confided when her father left her mother. Lately, however—especially when the two were together—Joan and Christy embarrassed Franny. Downtown, they shouted and hit each other over the head with shopping bags and insisted on practicing cheerleading moves. At the movies, they threw things at people and the screen. At City Park, they walked up almost on the heels of unknown but attractive older boys, then burst into fits of laughter and ran when the boys turned; and, sometimes, when Christy Strawberry talked to boys—or even talked about boys, like now, talking about Kirk Toomey—she began to speak like a little girl. *Fwanny*, she said. Which wasn't entirely her fault, Franny knew. Tiny Christy with her naturally curly brown hair and rosy cheeks and adorable bow lips had been groomed by her parents to be the next Shirley Temple, with tap lessons and ballet and all. Still, by the time the downstairs telephone clicked, and Rosamund came on the line—"Someone needs to use the phone down here"—Franny felt quite willing to say goodbye.

"Fwanny." Franny said this aloud as she lay back on the bed. In the dark, the ceiling sparkled with color, but that was just something your eyes did—and not even to please you, just from some sort of confusion of your eyes and mind.

Maybe she could walk down the beach to the cottage of Susan Thomas.

Knock, knock.

Who's there?

Des Moines.

Des Moines who?

Des Moines just ain't the same since the milkman stopped making deliveries.

It had been Susan Thomas who told Franny that Des Moines should, by rights, be pronounced *day-mua*. Susan Thomas went to a private school in Des Moines, The Bell Academy for Girls. Susan Thomas studied sculpture and oil painting at the Des Moines Art Museum. Maybe she would appreciate a joke built on the now standard mispronunciation of Des Moines.

However, if Franny visited Susan Thomas, Susan would almost certainly ask Franny to crew for her in Sunday's sailboat race, and Franny neither wanted to race nor to say no to the request.

So: Off the bed she rolled. Made her way down the hall to her own bedroom where, beneath the mattress of her lower bunk, lay a slim book of poems. Scarcely larger than a fancy invitation to a wedding, that book. *Poems for Lovers.*

She had kept a diary under her mattress until her mother found it, and let Franny know that the entries regarding Franny's undying love for the Beatles and the kiss she exchanged with a boy from her class were just the sort of thing that could land Franny in the girls' reformatory, and result in the loss of the Wahl family home, and Brick's being barred from the law. By the time Peg had finished, Franny felt grateful to be allowed to carry the diary to the ash can and burn it, and several months passed before she was able to look back on the day and realize her mother had been temporarily insane, and, worse, that Franny herself had been infected by the insanity.

"The sphere of our sorrow." That was one of Franny's favorite images in the book *Poems for Lovers.* It came from a poem by Shelley, which she read, now, by the light coming into her bedroom from the fixture in the hall:

> *I can give not what men call love,*
>
> *But wilt thou accept not*
>
> *The worship the heart lifts above*
>
> *And the Heavens reject not,—*
>
> *The desire of the moth for the star,*
>
> *Of the night for the morrow,*
>
> *The devotion to something afar*
>
> *From the sphere of our sorrow?*

The day that Franny had carried the poem down the shore to show it to Susan Thomas, Susan had said that if a poem made you feel as if the top of your head came off, that meant the poem was good. According to Emily Dickinson. And then Susan's father—who was a professor during the school year but tromped about in summer with his broad, nut-brown chest absolutely bare—Susan's father stopped in his thunderous passage across the Thomas cottage's echoey floor to add, one finger raised in the air, "'A period in just the right place is an ice pick through the heart.' Something like that." His quote came from Isaac Babel, he said, but Susan's mother corrected him. "No, no"—a kindly, abstracted lady who wore her gray hair in a pudding-bowl cut and walked the Pynch pastures, bent over, hunting for fungi—Mrs. Thomas said, "no, *Kafka,* dear," and Franny had made a mental note to look for something by Kafka the next time she went to the library—

A problem particular to the summer: all those unshod feet that did not provide the click of warning that meant someone headed your way. More than one someone, Franny decided as she wedged the poetry book back under her mattress.

"I get the skinny mirror!" crowed a female guest, and another said, "Well, hey, I like the fat mirror. It keeps you on your toes," and a third, "*I'll* take a realistic assessment."

Franny did not recognize the voices, but the girls had clearly been at the house before as they knew the trio of mirrors that Brick had hammered into place in the upstairs hall; and then Franny did recognize the voice of a certain newly engaged girl:

"*Anyway,* I sort of forgot about the fact that I'd helped out old Bruce with his hard-on and, my mom's, like, 'Elaine, what on earth did you get on your jeans, dear?'"

While the others erupted in laughter, Franny silently lowered herself into the dark recesses of her bunk. Let the engaged girl speak gaily and without constraint to her friends; Franny knew *she* was not meant to have overheard.

"'Elaine,'" one of the girls repeated in a high, mocking voice, "'what on earth did you get on your jeans, dear?'"

More laughter.

What the engaged girl had said—Franny made her breathing so quiet her chest ached—what the girl had said did not quite jibe with certain bits of information that Franny had received on the trail to and from the dining hall at Camp Winnebago. Those bits of information were now fixed in an odd amber of sunshine and shade that also contained the taste of unripened raspberries, the buzz of mosquitoes, the changes undergone by a certain small heap of scat—raccoon? fox?—that during last summer's four-week stay started out tawny and slick as a squirt from the craft hall's tube of ocher, but grew darker and darker until a colorless, long-haired mold overtook the shape, and, eventually, broke down its edges altogether.

Still: "Hard-on" must have to do with what the engaged girl's mother found on her jeans. Which went along, Franny supposed, with a recent afternoon in which she had tickled Bob Prohaski on the glider in the side yard. Without warning, Bob Prohaski had grown quiet. "Look, here," he whispered, and pulled at the waist of his pants to reveal a rim of moisture shimmering on his belly.

"Oh. Well, that's all right," Franny had said, and then she gave that big boy a sympathetic smile to ease what shame she assumed he felt at having wet his pants. But Bob Prohaski had put his arm around her and pulled her close and smiled at her as if he were not at all ashamed. And there was a reason, she realized now. Because the shimmer on his belly—she had not liked seeing his belly, the damp, dark curls flattened to the white skin—the shimmer there must have been made of the same stuff as the stuff on the engaged girl's jeans. Which also had something to do with certain cartoons Franny had seen in the books crammed flat against the piano teacher's bookshelves, behind *Masterpieces of the Louvre* and *Van Gogh in Arles*. It must have been the teacher's dead husband who had hidden those books behind the art books; the teacher probably did not know the books were there. And who would ever tell her? No one. No one could. It would be too embarrassing. And better not to think at all of that embarrassing night in May when Franny crawled into her parents' bed after a particularly bad version of the Snow White dream, only to reawake as something—neither elbow nor knee, something more like the rude nose of a dog—began to bump up against her from behind. "Wha'?" her father had mumbled when she sprang from the bed. Then he came wider awake and there was alarm in his voice as he called, "Who's there?" By then, however, Franny had made her way out the bedroom door and could pretend she had not heard.

Someone—the engaged girl or one of her friends—switched off the hall light before returning to the party below, and Franny's room went dark. Outside her windows, however, the ragged bits of sky not blotted out by the oaks still held their starchy blue, and in the bower of the bunk bed, she tucked her knees up to her chin, and felt pleasantly small, albeit in a theatrical sort of way. She thought of *A Child's Garden of Verses'* "Bed in Summer"—

> *In winter I get up at night*
> *And dress by yellow candle-light.*
>
> *In summer, quite the other way,*
> *I have to go to bed by day.*

—and how the summer light filtering into her room was very much like that in the book's illustration, magical stuff that revealed the checked counterpane on the boy's bed, and the bird that sang on a branch outside—

But, again, the light in the hall went on, and now Martie came down the hall, then turned into her bedroom.

Was she crying?

Oh, Franny did *not* want to go to Martie. Did not want to leave her cozy bower. Did not want to breathe in Martie's failure or despair or whatever it was—that exhausted air, that old-balloon air. Twice, Franny's feet drew back from the wooden floor before she made herself move into the hall, and even when she reached the small alcove that led into the bedroom proper, she hesitated before saying, "Martie?"

In front of her dresser mirror—a thing half-obscured by its wreath of souvenir tickets, matchbooks, faded corsages—Martie beat at her long red hair, which crackled and ripped beneath the brush. She looked curvy and grownup in her ivory shell and matching shorts, in lipstick and eyeliner and all, but her tears spilled over her full lips in precisely the same way that they had when she was a flat-chested schoolgirl in a merciless Dutch-boy haircut and horn-rimmed glasses.

"Hey, Martie." Franny put an arm around Martie, patted her on the back. "What's the matter, honey?"

"Oh, nothing! Except, just as Mom and Dad came in from taking a walk, your charming, teetotaling sister made a point of telling me I was acting drunk!"

Franny looked away, fixing her gaze on a chain of green gum wrappers—Doublemint—that Martie had made in the days when the gum-chewing ROTC member was her boyfriend.

"Well, that's great, Franny." Martie stepped away from the girl and resumed her hair brushing. "So I take it you think I act drunk, too? I love it! Everybody always takes Roz's side."

"That's not true."

"It is!"

"No!" Tears started to Franny's own eyes now. "This year, at a game, a boy called you a whore, and I slapped his face."

Martie set down the hairbrush. "A whore?" She took a seat on the edge of her bed. "Who was it?"

"Well, just some little jerk obviously." Sniffling, Franny sat down beside Martie on the bed. The combined weight of the pair on the old mattress made them tip, one into the other, and they exchanged teary half-smiles before straightening.

"I only told you to show I stand up for you," Franny said.

Martie patted Franny on the knee. "Well, thanks, Fran. I appreciate that." She stood and scowled at herself in the mirror. "And I am not drunk," she said before leaving the room.

Franny fished around inside the purse Martie had left on the bed. A cigarette smoked in the bathroom—that sounded like something to do. But Franny found no cigarettes. Just a comb. A package of tissues. A lipstick called Mighty Like a Rose. She wound up the lipstick—a clear, bright pink—then wound it down again.

The weekend before, after the Sunday brunch and numerous Bloody Marys, Al Castor—weaving a little, holding his hands over his white-blond hair, which, for some reason, he had now chopped ridiculously short—Al Castor had said to Franny, "Of you three girls, Roz is coolest, and you're second." Though she secretly had appreciated the fact that she had not ranked last on Al Castor's list, Franny was offended on Martie's behalf, and told Al Castor so. Who was Al Castor to make such a list, anyway?

But, it was true, she thought as she returned the lipstick to Martie's purse: She had never wished to wear the color of lipstick that Martie wore. And when people spoke of family resemblances, she always hoped the pronounced epicanthic fold of her own eyes (and the Ackerman dimple in her chin) would make it impossible for anyone to say, "You remind me of Martie."

Sometimes, when especially angry at Franny, Peg said, "You're acting like Martie!" and, then, Franny felt hurt, and then, guilty for feeling hurt. What made it so terrible to be like Martie, really? In fourth-grade Sunday school, Mrs. Dahlberg—plump, frisky, wedges of dark curl pressing against her very pink cheeks—Mrs. Dahlberg had explained that the love of parents was not a pie that had to be divided among the children, no, it was an ever expanding balloon that got bigger and bigger so there always would be enough love for each child. As if it were an indisputable fact—that was how Mrs. Dahlberg said what she had to say about the love of parents for their children, and Franny had cherished it.

There. Martie's cigarettes sat on the dresser. Winstons. In the dresser mirror, Franny considered herself with a Winston stuck between her lips. A pair of castanets sat in a dusty yellow bowl on the dresser and, to add a little flare to her reflection, she tried to slip her fingers into the soft brown and orange strings, elicit a clap of wood against wood. Hopeless. The things confounded her. She dropped them back in the bowl. Which also contained a yo-yo. And a brightly painted Mexican street toy that involved spearing a heavy block of wood on a peg. Martie had always been good at mastering physical skills—the castanets, the pogo stick—that required practice and patience, and that drew bursts of admiration that Franny herself found too short-lived to envy.

All that dust. She drew her index finger along the surface of Martie's dresser and brought up a good quarter inch of gray fur. Ginny Weston and Peg had agreed that Ginny would not clean

Martie's room as long as Martie kept the place a kind of shrine to her past.

What did the girl guests think when they dumped their sleeping bags and purses in here? Franny hoped—hard, almost like a prayer—that the girls did not think poorly of Martie. Martie certainly did like *them*. Almost all of the guests were people Martie invited. Rosamund might tell Tim Gleason to stop by with his friends—his "little friends," she always called the boys from St. Joe's, as if to emphasize the fact that she took none of them seriously—and, now and then, Rosamund might dance with a boy guest, but that was it. She had made it clear at the beginning of the summer that she did not mean to house girl guests in her extra twin bed, nor did she want people stashing their purses and things in her room.

Just in case her mother or father should be in the hall, Franny slipped the stolen cigarette down the front of her bra before stepping out of Martie's room. In passing, she glanced into Rosamund's room. Clean, spare. A single bottle of perfume sat on the dressing table and Franny knew its scent: Esoterique. The only item on the bureau was Rosamund's stuffed frog, its green throat raised in song above its tiny guitar. How kind and intelligent that brown-eyed frog seemed. Like someone with whom you could have a decent conversation.

A single travel poster adorned Rosamund's walls: Blazing-white buildings climbed rugged hillsides above the teal sea. MALLORCA, read the big black letters.

"Oh," Rosamund had said when Franny asked her about Mallorca, "it's a place in Spain that I'll probably visit someday."

CHAPTER FIVE

T HE RULES GOVERNING FRANNY AND HER ROWBOAT:

No boys on board.

No going beyond the Point.

No swimming off the sides.

Still, Franny liked the rowing, the way each stroke began in adversity and ended in progress; and that very tall girl now stepping into the rowboat, Susan Thomas—head a jumble of the juice cans upon which she wrapped her hair in an effort to make it fashionably straight—Susan Thomas appeared perfectly willing to let Franny do the work.

"*Merde!*" Susan Thomas settled herself in the bobbling prow, and stretched out her well-oiled legs as Franny began to row away from shore. "Just let me recuperate a minute," Susan Thomas said, setting the fat book in her hand over her face to block the sun.

Minutes before, the girl had telephoned Franny to announce that her father had measured her height, and now that she knew that she stood five foot nine, she intended to swallow the contents of a fifty-pill bottle of aspirin.

Franny had doubted that Susan Thomas was in real danger—the girl's mother stood close enough to the phone that Franny could hear her croon, *You're a lovely, statuesque girl*—but Franny had rowed down the beach anyway.

"Five-nine," Susan Thomas grumbled as she tried to position her head and its burden of juice cans on the prow's gunwale.

"Fashion models are tall," Franny said. "Maybe you'll be a fashion model." Susan was pretty enough to be a model, as far as Franny was concerned; but Susan glowered at Franny.

"Are you patronizing me, St. Frances?"

"No."

"All right." She lowered her book into place.

Anna Karenina was the name of the book, a selection from the Bell Academy's summer reading list that Susan Thomas had found at the Pynch Lake Public Library. Franny had accompanied her there, eager to breathe in the familiar smell of the old building and its books, and to see the creamy merging galaxies that the floor polishers buffed onto the black linoleum. She and Susan Thomas had gone into the woods behind the library, and Franny had shown Susan the area recently outfitted with permanent paths and the brass sign that read:

Francis Wahl Nature Walk

A gift from Charlotte Wahl to the city
in memory of her beloved husband,
Francis (1890–1963)

"Franny?" Susan Thomas again raised the book from her face. "You understand that's one whole inch since school let out?"

"I understand."

It would have been nice if she could have rowed the boat into the next cove over, even if the next cove contained only more of the same of what they saw in their own cove (trees and small summer cottages interspersed with the occasional campground or big year-round place). Martie always said that Franny had missed out on one of the best parts of living in Pynch by being born too late for the amusement park that had sat in the next cove; Franny knew perfectly well that a series of pastel ranch-styles recently had been built on the grounds of the old Funland site, but she still had a habit of watching for the hills of the roller coaster to rise again above the trees.

"Idiots," Susan Thomas groused as an inboard passed too close to the rowboat and the skier behind the inboard sent up a spray of lake water that looked pure white, like tossed pearls—though, closer to hand, over the side of the boat, sunlit, the water appeared a broth of lemon green.

"It's not *dirty*," Franny's mother always said when guests commented on the fact that they could not see to the bottom of Pynch Lake. "It's just bits of algae and reeds." Was that true? Franny's mother also had told Franny that the brown spots on lettuce were full of iron, and extra good for you, but when Franny shared this information in home ec class, the teacher laughed. "Where'd you get that idea?" she asked, and Franny felt stunned by her own foolishness. Of *course*. You could see that the brown spots signalled damage.

Still: Had her mother believed in the truth of what she said? You could hardly ask, *Did you believe that what you told me was true?*

"Actually, Susan," Franny said—though there was nothing she "actually" contradicted, or clarified, so maybe the word sounded foolish, but here it came again, along with a little throat-clearing— "actually, I thought of killing myself last fall." She watched to see if *Anna Karenina* would rise, and when it did, and there were Susan's long green eyes, she continued. "I had this crazy idea I was, like, spinning a cocoon—and when I got through, I wouldn't be dead, just different."

Susan Thomas nodded. "I'm not really going to kill myself," she said, then sat up and wiped the underside of her neck with her towel. "So, you feel like singing the Secret Seven?"

Franny smiled. "'Chances Are'?"

Susan Thomas gave an amiable grunt, and the pair proceeded to hum their way toward a mutually satisfactory key. After "Chances Are" came "Young and Foolish," and then "I'll Never Smile Again"—old love songs they had learned from a handful of record albums left behind by the last owners of the Thomas cottage. Slightly corny songs, the girls knew, but the lyrics' reverence for the beloved moved the girls, and as they sang they smiled at one another, and nodded, and sometimes clutched their hands in front of themselves in an attitude of fervent prayer.

"I'm going to start drinking coffee, like you," Susan Thomas said when they finished "I'll Never Smile Again." "Do you think that'll help?"

"It might." Franny tilted her own face up to the sky. Was there any color in the world quite so rose as the rose with which the summer sun limned the closed lids of her eyes? Bain de Soleil was the brand of tanning oil that now cooked on Susan Thomas's skin. Expensive stuff. Franny recognized the scent: rich, musky, the way she imagined biblical oils of anointment must have smelled. Her own mother bought Rexall's house brand and said not to waste it.

"If I were a guy, I would definitely give flowers to my girlfriend, wouldn't you?" Susan Thomas said.

"Of course." The ROTC boy had sent Martie roses. And both Rosamund and Martie had received mums for homecoming dances and orchids for spring formal. But nobody had written them poems, as far as she knew. "I'd write her poems, too," Franny said.

"Boys," Susan Thomas groaned, and Franny smiled and groaned "Boys," too.

On the shore near the Camp Winnebago docks a dog began to bark—a chubby beagle, tail stiff with guard-dog fury—but Franny knew the animal to be a lovable old thing whose hindquarters performed a hula dance at the prospect of a pat on the head, and she called out, "Hey, Cocoa, it's Franny!"

On the dock below the beagle lay a woman: facedown, heavy limbs tanned to the dusty hue of a pecan shell. That would be Mrs. Siebold. The Siebolds—jolly summer people from Waterloo—had been friends with Franny's parents last summer, and the summer before that, too, but, these days, the couples only exchanged waves at the Top Hat when they happened to eat there at the same time. Which Franny suspected had something to do with a trip her parents and the Siebolds had made to a University of Iowa football game the fall before. "Three hours is not a few minutes!" So Franny had overheard Peg say as she and Brick arrived home from that trip. At the time, Franny and her sitter, a high-minded lady in orthopedic shoes, sat watching the TV in the long, sunstruck chamber that had served as the trophy room for the Pynch Lake Huntsmen and the dining hall for the church camp. "The den," the Wahls called the area, but that was only because they had had a den in the Ash Street house. Both Franny and the sitter kept their eyes on the *Amateur Hour* contestant—a man who played "I Left My Heart in San Francisco" on a saw—until Brick, laughing and red-cheeked, had bounced into the room and declared, *Say, we had a ball! The game was a dandy!*

"Franny!" Susan Thomas cried.

In fright, Franny jumped up in the rowboat. Like some giant, mindless wave, a large red and white inboard now bore down upon the rowboat—so fast, and with prow so high in the air, that Franny could not see the driver at all.

"Hey!" She waved her arms high. "Stop!"

The inboard's prow dropped lower into the water as the engine's roar became a low gurgle, but the boat still came on.

Three boys. Two grinning. One looking harsh, almost reproachful.

"Who are they, Franny?" Susan Thomas cried as the inboard pulled up alongside the rowboat. Franny flushed; maybe it was an outcome of attending girls' school, but Susan Thomas sometimes behaved as if a boy could not even hear a girl talk.

"Hi, girls!" called one of the grinners.

Franny looked down at the copy of Emily Dickinson she had brought onboard. Still, out of the corner of her eye, she could see the boy. Cute. In the surfer mode. Hawaiian print swim trunks. Shock of blond hair.

"What'cha reading?" he said.

"Franny," Susan Thomas cried, "do something!"

The surfer's stern-looking friend—a handsome boy, with the surprise of a silver tooth—put his foot on the rowboat's oarlock, and said a squeaky, "Franny!"

Franny cast a low glance back toward the bank—home—to see if anyone were in view. But, please, not her parents because her mother would be sure to say, "What were you doing to attract them in the first place?" and if her father heard her mother, he might go along with her mother's suspicions, or he might decide to chase down the boys, give them a scare.

Someone did stand at the top of the Wahl bank. A sturdy male. He waved both arms over his head. Franny waved back even before she understood that she waved at Bob Prohaski, who now started down to the dock, taking two concrete steps at a time.

Another push on the oarlock by the boy with the silver tooth. Susan Thomas lay her head upon her knees and wailed.

"So what're you doing this afternoon, *Franny*?" the boy asked. "You and your friend bringing in radio transmissions on her orange juice cans?"

Haw, haw, haw.

"You think if your boat goes down you can use her head for a pontoon?"

Haw, haw, haw.

"Bob!" Franny stood up to shout and wave. "Bob!"

He was too far away to hear, she knew, but the boys in the inboard did look toward the shore. Even at that distance, Bob Prohaski's arms and legs appeared slightly bowed by muscle.

"That's my big brother, there! And that's our speedboat in the lift! He'll come out here! You better watch it!"

"Like we're really scared," said the boys, and then, "bitches" and "sluts" and "sloppy" something—a word Franny did not know—and with whoops and hollers, they sped away.

Though the rowboat rocked wildly in the boys' wake, Susan Thomas managed to whimper, "Thank God they're gone."

"No kidding." The boys' words rang in Franny's head as she set the oars back into the water. "Bob doesn't even know how to swim, let alone drive a boat."

Susan Thomas peered toward the shore and Bob Prohaski, now waiting at the end of the Wahl dock. "So that's him, huh? Why'd you say he was your brother and not your boyfriend?"

Franny flushed. "Just—to make him sound older." She began to row in, then, quickly, with a sense that, really, she ought to rescue Bob Prohaski. Though the boy never said so, Franny understood that not knowing how to swim made him nervous around water. On an early visit to the Wahl house, he and Franny had dangled their bare feet from the dock, and one of his shoes had fallen into the lake. The fear that rumpled his cheeks before Franny jumped in to retrieve the thing—a cheap, canvas slip-on—had made clear to Franny what it would have cost for Bob Prohaski to jump in the water, or to have to go home with one foot bare.

"He's good-looking, all right," Susan Thomas murmured as Franny rowed closer to shore. When she grinned at Franny and wiggled her eyebrows, Franny could not help grinning back. Bob Prohaski *was* handsome. Still, Franny sincerely hoped that in Susan Thomas's company he would *not* talk about, say, his big brothers' grinding some guy's teeth into a curb outside the Knights of Columbus Hall, or a bowling alley, or another spot equally foreign to Franny's experience.

Bob Prohaski stood at the end of the dock, unsmiling, appraising Franny. He liked to look at her. Liked her to know he looked. Creepy, Franny thought, but flattering, too.

"Howdy!" she called. Not a greeting that belonged to her. A greeting that belonged to some other cheerful girl in some other circumstance. A Martie-sort-of-greeting that made Franny look down into the unbailed water in the bottom of the boat.

"What was going on out there?" The boy's voice floated toward them, low and flat. No hello. No acknowledgment of Susan Thomas at all. From the start, Bob Prohaski had made it clear to Franny that as long as he had her and his big brothers, he did not need anyone else.

"They were just some jerks, Bob." She brought the dinghy up against one of the old tires that hung from the dock posts. The jarring roused a muskrat that snoozed in the sun-warmed water that had gathered in the tires. With a sickening *plop,* the creature dropped into the lake, and Franny gave a screech that sounded, she knew, girlishly guilty. Which made her irritated with herself, and then with Bob Prohaski *and* Susan Thomas, both of whom looked at her as if she had lost her mind.

"There was a *muskrat*." She pointed to the triangular ripple of water now heading away from the dock.

"So, were those guys trying to pick you up, Fran?"

She did not answer as she set the oars into the boat. Bob Prohaski's anger still took her by surprise; the way he wrapped himself up in it as if it were a luxury item. Sometimes, she could not help liking the anger. It bestowed upon her a new power: She could put an *end* to that anger by wrapping her arms around Bob Prohaski's neck, saying something sweet or funny.

"Were they anybody you know?"

"Oh, Bob." She laughed. As if she were just a little weary of male attention, so used to it that she no longer gave it a second's thought; she was, in fact, almost Rosamund herself. "They were probably from out of town. We didn't exactly *chat* with them, you know."

The boy folded his big arms across his chest, a gesture that enhanced his look of junior-hit-man/thug-in-training, which Franny sometimes found appealing; sometimes, appalling. "Anybody bugs you," he said, "I'll kick his teeth in."

For Susan Thomas's benefit, Franny crossed her eyes. Then did her best to conceal the fact that she glanced up the bank toward the house. Just as she suspected, there stood her mother, a watchful shimmer behind the screened front porch. *Tom Pocaski.* So Peg referred to Bob Prohaski. *John Polaski.* Always the wrong name. And always with a face, as if the name were a piece of hair she hurried to remove from her tongue. Because he looked older? Because she knew he came from battered Tanglefoot, where the dirt roads left the houses looking as if big animals came in the night to rub their backs against the siding? The one time that Franny had seen the Prohaski house, a big piece of plywood filled the picture-window frame and gave the place a forlorn and dangerous air, almost as if it was a clubhouse for criminals.

"Wait," Franny murmured as she stepped from the boat and Bob Prohaski reached out to embrace her, "my mom's up there."

"Oh, yeah?" The boy turned toward the house and bowed.

"Don't do that! Please. I've got enough trouble."

"Sheesh!" On hands and knees, Susan Thomas clambered onto the dock. "Why are your parents so paranoid, Wahl?"

A word Franny had learned from Susan: paranoid. Used by Susan the time she overheard Brick and Peg berate Martie for including on her school insurance form the fact that Brick's father had died of complications from diabetes.

Did Bob Prohaski know what "paranoid" meant when he brought his broad-boned face close to Franny's own, and said, "Yeah, Franny, why are your parents so paranoid?"

"Bob"—she stared at a gash that ran through one of the boy's dark eyebrows, the blood still bright beneath a slick of salve— "what happened there?"

"Oh." He grinned and tapped a finger against the cut, apparently to prove the thing did not hurt; then he winced at his own touch. "It's no big deal. My old man took a swing at me. He'd had too much to drink, is all."

Susan Thomas gasped. "Your *dad* hit you?"

Bob Prohaski laughed. Tweaked Franny's chin. "You ain't going to cry about it, are you, Franny? Remember when we seen that dog—"

"I am *not* going to cry." Franny bent to tie the painter to the dock. Still, for the boy's dad to hit him hard enough to break the skin—it did make her feel like crying. And it frightened her, too, that Bob Prohaski had told them about the blow. And that his dad had had too much to drink. There was no denying that, sometimes, her own home trembled and shook with slaps and screams and terrible threats. Once, just after they had moved from town to the old lodge, she had crawled out of her bunk and into the narrow space between the mattress and the cold wooden floor because a madman chased Martie through the house. *Whore*, the madman called Martie, and *filthy bitch,* and Franny could hear that he hit Martie with something that snapped against her skin and made her cry out, and Franny wet her pants, certain the madman already had killed Rosamund and her mother and father, and would find her next. Of course, the madman turned out to *be* her father, and no Wahl ever mentioned the incident again. Such incidents did not happen. Or they happened in every house? Now and then, some parent hit some kid with a belt or a brush, a shoe, but—that was not who they were, not the Wahls, and Franny wished Susan Thomas would be quiet, and not embarrass Bob Prohaski by going on and on about how it wasn't right—

"Hey." As if he did not hear Susan Thomas at all, Bob Prohaski moved in close to Franny, and began to tickle her, hard.

"Stop it!" She wriggled away from him; then—just in case she had sounded too grouchy and hurt his feelings—she drummed up a smile. "Goofy," she murmured.

"Do your sisters have company up there?" Susan glanced toward the top of the bank. "I hate walking by their company."

Bob Prohaski hawked and spit in the lake. "They don't bother me. I could whip any of those guys."

"Oh, *well*." Franny started up the stairs at a brisk pace. "Just—ignore them, both of you."

A cluster of out-of-town guests sat on the far picnic table, another had gathered around the glider. Two boys, faces red and contorted, did pull-ups on opposing limbs of a small hackberry.

"Here come Franny and her little friends!" one of the girl guests said. Nothing too dreadful, and Franny smiled the girl's way. But, then, Susan Thomas made a mistake. She scratched at her ear and, immediately, a boy on the glider gave a high-pitched moan, "Oh, daddy!" and let his tongue loll while he twirled his fingers about in his ears—apparently to suggest that he mirrored some lust-crazed look on the girl's face.

"I have a mosquito bite!" Susan Thomas protested.

"Come on!" Franny shepherded the pair onto the screened porch where, Rosamund and Tim Gleason sat, side by side, on a wrought-iron loveseat recently cast off by Brick's mother. Had Franny and her friends disturbed an intimate moment between Tim and Rosamund? No. Rosamund was showing the boy her photo albums of university life.

Those albums. Franny knew their photographs by heart: Excitingly messy dorm rooms in which pretty girls stuck their tongues out at the camera and hoisted glasses filled with the gold of beer. Peach and blue sunset beaches where big boys stood with their arms wrapped around the bare shoulders of Rosamund. There—Franny could recognize the photo even upside down—a black-and-white Rosamund wore a banner of paper towels upon which someone had scribbled GIRL WITH SMALLEST SHOE. And, there, Rosamund in cameo pink stood on a stage at a formal dance. Beside her was a boy known campus-wide as a "stud"—so Rosamund had explained the first time that Franny inspected the photos—and the "stud" grasped the microphone upon which he was making a drunken announcement to the entire assembly:

He didn't want anyone to have the wrong idea about his dating Rosamund Wahl. "This," the stud announced via the microphone, "is a girl as pure as the driven snow."

As pure as the driven snow.

Tim Gleason gave Bob Prohaski a sardonic up and down. "Hey, Franny," he said, "your mom's been looking for you."

"I was in the bay the whole time," she protested.

"Sh. I want to hear." Rosamund turned, smiling, toward the set of French doors that stood open to the living room. Something went on, there—Peg Wahl's voice rose above a ripple of low titters and hoots:

"Now, *Ron,* dear!"

On the living room's shantung couch, just beyond Peg, Franny could see the boy guest named Ron. Prone. A plastic bag of ice cubes clutched to his forehead.

"No, Peg, please," said the boy with a weak laugh.

"Now, Ron!" Peg rose up on her bare toes. Showed her big white smile. In her hands were two pot lids, and she lifted the lids high in the air, as if she were about to crash them together. "Is it really true, Ron, that you wanted me to come out here to practice my cymbals?"

The boy waved a feeble hand her way while the others in the living room laughed all the harder, and called, "Come on, Ron, you know it'd do you good." A girl at the opposite end of the shantung couch was applying polish to her toenails, and did not look up from her task, but her shoulders trembled with laughter.

"So, Franny"—Franny and Susan Thomas and Bob Prohaski turned back from Franny's mother to Rosamund—"I'm going to take Timmy skiing this afternoon. You guys want to be spotters?"

"Oh," Franny said, but before she could ask Susan Thomas and Bob Prohaski what they thought, Peg stepped onto the porch, pot lids lowered to her sides.

"Frances Jean," she said.

"I never went beyond the Point, Mom."

"*And* I told you not to wear that T-shirt anymore."

"I forgot." A lie. But there was nothing wrong with the T-shirt. It was just a big T-shirt from the men's department of Drew's. Crew neck. Short sleeves. Red and white stripes.

"Come to the kitchen after you see your friends to the door," Peg said.

"But they just got here!"

"Did you clear it with me? Have you done your piano?"

No.

"All right, then."

When Franny entered the kitchen, she found Peg yanking open and slamming shut the cabinets' old wooden drawers and doors—a number of which did not want to open or close at all because of the summer's humidity. "Twenty-three sixty-seven," Peg muttered with a glance Franny's way.

"What?"

Peg raised a finger—*shh*—and made what Franny thought of as her "devil face": one brow cocked high, eyes open demoniacally wide, a look that would have been funny had Franny not known better. Always, in the past, there had been both the mother and father whom she loved, and who loved her back, and the monster mother and father—who maybe wanted to kill her for not doing or being what they wanted. The monsters had been almost transparent, hard to see, a little like ghosts. Now, however, they were increasingly opaque if not yet entirely familiar, and they fitted themselves over the mother and father in such a way that, sometimes, for days on end, Franny could not make out even an edge of a loving parent.

"Twenty-three sixty-seven." Peg began to rifle through the contents of the purse on the counter.

"Mom"—Tim Gleason in tow, Rosamund entered from the dining room—"do you know where this morning's paper is? Timmy and I want to see what's at the movies this week."

Peg pointed to one of the ladder-back chairs at the breakfast table. "There," she muttered, and "twenty-three sixty-seven," and then, "oh!" She gave a derisive snort. "Guess who I saw at Hayes's, Roz? Cynthia Sandvig! With that *thing* she married!"

Rosamund laughed. "So what was 'the thing' like?"

"A goop! He sat there the whole time we drank coffee and he had this goopy smile on his face"—Peg produced an imitation of the "goop's" buck-toothed, simpleton smile—"and he never said 'boo' or, 'Gee, Mrs. Wahl, I've heard such nice things about you!' or anything else for that matter."

"'Goop,'" said Tim Gleason. "That's a new one to me, Mrs. Wahl."

"Twenty-three sixty-seven." Again, Peg opened the purse on the counter. "Franny, you haven't done something with my checkbook, have you?"

"Of course not. And how am I supposed to practice piano with all those people in the living room?"

Peg waved the question aside, then turned with a smile to Tim Gleason. "You don't know the Goops, Tim? The girls *loved* the Goops. 'The Goops they lick their fingers, the Goops they lick their knives'"—

While Rosamund and her mother recited the "Goops" poem for smiling Tim, Franny edged into the back hall. It was darker in the back hall, and even a little cooler. That flicker of noise from a few feet off meant that her hamster, Snoopy, was shifting positions as he slept away the day. She drew closer to the cage, its toasty perfume of animal heat and cedar bedding. "Hey, Snoopy," she whispered. She pressed a finger against the tiny metal bars of the cage, and stroked the bit of soft, soft fur that poked through. The weekend before, a party guest had put beer in the water bottle that hung on the side of Snoopy's cage, and, this afternoon, sometime, Franny meant to sneak the cage up to her bedroom for safekeeping.

"Here's one that's supposed to be good, Tim," Rosamund said. "*The Pawnbroker*."

Tim Gleason groaned. "It's depressing, right? Why's your daughter have to go for all these gloomy movies, Mrs. Wahl?"

Peg laughed, and told Tim Gleason if he wanted to see something cute he should see *Do Not Disturb* at the Lake—Franny noted the way in which Peg paused before she pronounced "theater," no doubt wondering if the pronunciation that sounded best to her mental ear were correct. Long *a*. The way her farming parents had said it. Franny hoped Tim Gleason did not hold such things against Peg.

On the blackboard that hung between the kitchen and the back hall, Franny drew a small asterisk. "Creamettes," Peg had written on the board. "Peas." Did an asterisk have a connection with asters, those flowers the flower lady brought around in autumn, tiny bundles of sky blue that went straight to your heart? Franny studied the tips of her fingers, now dusted in yellow chalk. *Whorls*. Even when she merely mouthed the word, she felt as if a marble pressed down on the middle of her tongue.

"Don't mess up my shopping list, there, Fran!"

Franny edged away from the blackboard to lean on the sill of a window so old its rusty screen gave the countryside below a sepia tone that made the view appear antique—until a shiny white convertible came over the rise past the Nearys' barn: Peg's Wildcat, top down, Martie behind the wheel.

"You don't suppose one of your friends picked up my checkbook, do you, Fran?"

"*Mother*," Rosamund chided while Franny turned from the window to ask, "You mean, stole it? My friends wouldn't steal your checkbook!"

In the driveway, Martie gave the horn the toot that she and her high school friends had shared: a set of three longs, followed by two sets of two shorts. Then the front door of the house opened, and Martie leapt into the kitchen, one sandalled foot and tanned calf preceding the rest of her. "We're ho-me!" Martie sang, and did a spin that twirled the ends of the bandanna print blouse tied up in rabbit ears above her belly.

Tim and Rosamund did not look up from the movie ads they studied, but Franny said hello to Martie and the girl behind her, a high school pal named Deedee Pierce. Peg waved at the girls. "Twenty-three sixty-seven," she repeated, then, again, turned to dig about in the purse on the counter.

"Uh, Roz? Tim?" Martie cocked her head to one side. "Hellooooo, you guys!"

Deedee Pierce—a large girl given to leaning against walls and talking out of the side of her mouth like a cowpoke—Deedee Pierce said with a drawl, "They're probably hiding their happiness at seeing you, Martie. They're probably the bashful type."

Rosamund gave Deedee Pierce a glance that Franny thought was too cool. Rosamund could not abide Deedee ("She's a vulgar cow! Of course she can't get a date!") but, really, Deedee sometimes could be nice, and funny, too—

"Well!" Sandals snapping, Martie did a bit of a tap dance across the kitchen floor. Swung her arms this way and that. Stopped with a flourish, hands high. "Bashful or not, here we are! *And* we picked up a birthday cake for Roz!"

Franny sneaked a peek at Rosamund, who had made it clear that, this year, she had decided to stop celebrating her birthdays, and would appreciate it if everyone else would comply.

"Rozzie?" Martie cupped a hand to her ear. "Do I hear a thank-you?"

Rosamund stood up from the kitchen table and raised her hands before her face, palms outward, suggesting Martie was a gale that blew twigs and trash into Rosamund's eyes and nose. "Thank you, Martie," she said—her voice now slightly choked by all that debris—"but I think I made it clear a birthday celebration wasn't necessary this year."

The crestfallen Martie asked, "So you don't *want* a cake?"

"You may have your cake, Martie." Rosamund smoothed her hands across the pages of the *Gazette*. "Let's just not make a big deal of it, okay?"

"Will you look at this?" Peg lifted the missing checkbook from her purse. Gave Franny a look that suggested she believed the girl had just planted it there.

"So." Martie leaned her forehead into Deedee Pierce's broad upper arm. "I don't suppose anybody bothered to take messages for me while I was gone?"

"That Ed from Lake Okoboji called," Peg said. "He'll call back. And, oh, Roz, I forgot: Mike Zanios called while you and Tim walked down to the mailbox. He wanted to know if you'd like to hear some visiting piano player on Monday night."

"Jeez"—Martie grinned and set her hands on her hips, some imitation of comic exasperation—"why's Mike never asked any of the *rest* of us to come listen?" Then, without waiting for an answer, she hurried on, "By the way, Frances Jean, I saw that Prohaski out on the road, hitchhiking. Was he here again?"

Tim Gleason began to whistle the refrain from an old Sonny James song called "Young Love." Rosamund slapped his wrist— playfully—and Deedee Pierce laughed. "You don't know the half of it, Tim," Deedee said, and launched into a story of how, as a small girl, Franny had sat in front of the Ash Street house and pretended to baby-sit an even smaller girl. "She was trying to make the big guys driving by in their cars fall in love with her, weren't you, Fran?"

Franny rolled her eyes, though the story was true. She felt thankful that she could change the subject by announcing, "Someone's coming up the drive."

"Eduardo?" Martie said with a smile for Deedee Pierce. Deedee smiled back, but when Martie ran for the front hall, it was all that Franny could do to keep from calling, "*Martie*, beware!

Remember Roger! Remember Steve and Mark and Daryl!"

"*Eduardo?*" Tim Gleason raised an eyebrow as he pronounced the name. He lifted one of Peg's copper aspic molds—a leaping fish—off its peg on the kitchen wall, and cradled it in his arms. "Eduardo?" he crooned to the fish.

Rosamund sputtered a laugh at this, but Deedee Pierce growled a low, "Shut up, you two."

"Now, now," said Peg, but she grinned at Tim Gleason and Rosamund, and what did that mean? Franny felt right in *not* laughing—really, she did not see what was funny about Tim and the fish, and she appreciated Deedee Pierce's defending Martie—yet *not* laughing made Franny feel somewhat superior, and surely that contaminated whatever was right about not laughing.

"Here's Eduardo, everybody!" Martie called as she pulled into the kitchen a handsome, fair-haired boy who grinned rather shyly, perhaps because his nose was painted with a slick, white coat of zinc oxide.

"Eduardo!" Peg cried, and Rosamund, too, "Hey, Eduardo!"

Eduardo! Eduardo! As if they'd been missing him! Eduardo was no object of ridicule! Eduardo was their pal! Embarrassed, confused, Franny edged into the back hall. Who was this Eduardo from Lake Okoboji, and would they all hate him tomorrow, and did they even like him today?

Farther down the hall, Franny peered in at the hamster. Still asleep. "Snoopy," she whispered. She wished he were awake. But this was not his time to be awake. She listened to the laughing and talking of the others in the kitchen; then, as quietly as possible, she picked up the cage and made her way out through the garage and around the house to the screened porch. There were guests out there, but they ignored her and, after a little grappling with the door, she managed to carry the cage back into the house, and up the stairs to her bedroom, and there she set it on the floor of her closet for concealment and safekeeping.

CHAPTER SIX

ANOTHER WEEKEND. ANOTHER PARTY ABOUT TO BEGIN. THE song Franny's father played for the young guests who stood in a circle around his baby grand: "Satin Doll." "Satin Doll" was one of Franny's favorites of the songs Brick played, and she sat on the stairs and she listened through the banisters.

Apparently, none of that evening's guests knew the lyrics to the song, but each time that Brick reached the refrain, the group blurted a raucous "My Satin Doll!" and howled with laughter. Which would have irritated Brick under certain circumstances, Franny knew—she had learned, long ago, that Brick did not like people to sing along with him—but this evening he smiled. At the engaged girl. At Al Castor, who was using a barefoot toe to slide back and forth on the floor the shot glass that Brick had brought out with his bottle of scotch. A strawberry blonde stood by the piano, too (swaying, eyes closed, slender arms hugged to her sides). That morning, in the kitchen, the strawberry blonde had declared, "Man, it's hard to get Brick off the ivories once he gets started," after which a second guest cut her eyes in the direction of Franny, just then putting bread into the toaster. "I mean," the blonde continued in a rush, "because he loves to play so much! He's so good!" At the time, Franny had felt too hurt on her father's behalf, and too embarrassed, yes, to speak up in his defense, and so pretended to have heard neither the insult nor its retraction.

But look at Brick, now, tossing his big head back and holding it there, mouth open wide while his long, chubby fingers leapt so nimbly across the keys. And look at the smiling guests. They did like to hear him play. At least, sometimes. But, sometimes, it was true, he did play beyond his welcome, or when he was in no shape to play more than two or three measures in a row without an error—

"What's going on down there?" Peg stepped out of her bedroom and into the upstairs hall, then hiked up her skirt and began to pull her blouse straight beneath the skirt's waistband.

How did she dare do that? What if someone saw? Franny did not mean to see—pretended not to see—those little pillows of flesh that pooched out between the tops of Peg's nylons and the binding rubber of her girdle. "Better hurry, Mom," she said, but, by then, Peg had lowered the skirt, and stood pouting at her backside from over one shoulder.

"Martie told me my stomach sticks out, Mom," Franny said.

"Oh, you girls are ridiculous."

"But do you think I should do sit-ups or something?"

"*I* think I should have had sons! Now, remember, if anybody comes upstairs after your dad and I leave, you tell them they are not allowed up here. And *you*—are not allowed down there."

"That's right!"

Both Peg and Franny started at the voice from the landing below: Martie, peering through a plume of cigarette smoke shot baby blue by the rays of the falling sun that now reached deep into the house. Pretty rose-pink shorts. Matching tank top. Curtain of marmalade hair concealing one eye; a corny provocation in Franny's book, but apparently not in the mind of "Eduardo," who meant to drive all the way from Lake Okoboji for that evening's party.

"And no *bugging* the guests, either," Martie said.

"Bugging the guests? I'm glad to be *away* from your guests."

"Mother—"

"Hush, both of you," Peg said.

With a wave of her arm, Martie heralded Peg's descent to the group below. "And *heeeere* she comes, folks!"

Brick just had begun his intro to "I've Got a Crush on You" but he abandoned it now in order to take up the "Miss America" theme.

"'Scuse me!" Rosamund rushed past Franny and down the stairs, and, a few minutes later, along with the other guests, she called "Bye-bye" to Peg and Brick, and "Have a good time" and "You kids be in by one!" As if Brick and Peg headed to a party as lively as their own, and not to dinner at the Top Hat Club.

From Peg and Brick's own bedroom window, Franny watched her parents go. In the dusky light, convertible top lowered, the white Wildcat and its white leather interior made a kind of gorgeous cloud in which Peg and Brick floated down the long driveway toward Lakeside, and, for a moment, it was almost possible to believe that the world continued to belong to them. They were Peg and Brick, and she was pretty and fun, and he was big and popular, and their living in Pynch Lake was just a temporary affair, soon they'd be on to bigger and better things.

There was no denying, however, that at the end of the long driveway another car sat, idling. That second car was also a white convertible, but full of young partygoers who politely waited for the parental car to clear the drive before making their own approach.

Honk, honk, honk! *Hey, how you doing?*

The passengers of both cars waved and called to one another, and beeped their horns as the Wildcat pulled onto Lakeside Drive. So pretty, the taillights of the Wildcat advancing up Lakeside. Twin rubies. Still, Franny felt queer as the lights disappeared at the crest above the Nearys' farm. Disassembled. As if someone could pass a hand between her torso and her limbs or push her head right off to either side of her neck. For a moment, she wished she were accompanying Christy Strawberry and Joan Harvett to City Park's bandshell—but, no, she could not have borne the company of the noisy juvenile delinquents her friends had set their hearts upon.

Also, the last time Joan Harvett had stayed at the house, Franny's mother had sworn to Franny that she had heard the girl talking about Franny on the telephone. "You'd gone into the bathroom," Peg said with what seemed to Franny grim satisfaction, "and I surprised her!" Franny was not sure she wanted to know what Peg had heard, but Peg had continued, "Mostly, it was ha-ha-ha stuff, but she acted plenty nervous when I walked in."

"Here you go, dog!" In the yard below her parents' window, one of the male guests threw a ball or something out into the yard for Al Castor's Great Dane, Mr. Ed. In the dusk, Franny could not make out the face that belonged to the voice—it was a dark cloud, a stone, but the boy's bleached T-shirt glowed like coals gone to white ash, a thing so simple yet so beautiful it took Franny's breath away, and when the extension on her mother's bedside table began to ring, she jumped.

"It's me." Bob Prohaski. But Martie was on the kitchen telephone, and Martie said, "You can't talk now, Frances! Eduardo may be calling me! He may have had car trouble!"

"Well, give me at least a minute, Martie."

"*One* minute. And that's it!"

"So, you're staying upstairs, right?" Bob Prohaski said after the kitchen's receiver clicked in its cradle.

Franny lay back on the bed, and explained how Peg had assigned her both to stay upstairs and to keep the guests downstairs. "It's like being a vestal virgin," she said, then gave an awkward laugh because maybe she should not have said "virgin" in front of a boy—the word was so loaded—and, indeed, Bob Prohaski responded with a gruff, "You better be a virgin—"

"*Jesus Christ,* Frances!"

Franny winced and raised her head from her mother's pillow as Martie zoomed into the room and around the bed.

"Have a little consideration!" Martie grabbed the receiver from Franny's hand, and barked into the mouthpiece—"She can't talk now!"—and hung up the telephone.

"Damn it, Martie!"

Imaginary skirt held out to the sides, Martie dropped a curtsy. "Watch your mouth, dear!" she said, then bounded out the door and down the stairs.

Under the circumstances, Franny supposed it would not be so

dreadful to call Bob Prohaski back in order to say, "Sorry about my sister." But she had never called a boy on the telephone and, just now, did not care so much about the lost call as Martie's meanness.

"Stay there, Dick!" Another voice from the yard below. This time a girl. When Franny stepped to the window, she could see a boy in the driveway. Dick, she supposed. And the girl must be the glimmer now hurrying toward the ghostly slab of concrete that had once formed the foundation for the church of the Baptist campers.

The rough noise of vomiting reached Franny, then, and she felt a little queasy, and she worried for the girl, too, but, almost immediately, the girl (white shirt, white pants) came back through the tall grasses around the slab and toward the lawn.

The boyfriend rubbed the girl's neck as they passed beneath the lavender light from the lamp above the drive. Neither of them seemed to notice the old car lumbering up the drive. No—now the car stopped. Began to back *down* the drive, apparently having determined it was at the wrong address, or that other guests already had filled every possible patch of drive or lawn closer to the house.

Let the car belong to Eduardo. Though she was angry with Martie, Franny thought, Let it be him, and let him tell Martie he loves her and make him really mean it, and then Martie can do the same, and be safe, comforted, quieted.

She pressed her nose to the window screen while the driver backed into a spot near the road. The first door of the car to open was the passenger-side door. A slender boy climbed out and plucked at his pants legs, stomped his feet. Dark pants, light short-sleeved shirt. It was not until he stepped from the shadows of the trees that lined the drive that Franny recognized him as Artie Stokes, who, along with handsome Darren Rutiger, had been one of Rosamund's "buddies" in high school.

How vulnerable former bad-boy Artie Stokes looked now! As if he were on his humble way to some humble church to seek absolution for past sins—cherry bombs in the rest room toilets, drag racing—that no one cared about anymore. Poor Artie. Even his blond hoodlum's pompadour now signalled obsolescence.

Franny had heard that Artie Stokes had tried to enlist in the army but been found to be too skinny. At any rate, whatever he had done in the two years since he and Rosamund finished school, it had not made him appear as confident as the boys in madras button-downs who strutted and yowled at the party below.

"Oh, Artie," Franny whispered. She would not have been surprised to find out the boy had a tie stashed in the glove compartment. Just in case. And Darren Rutiger, now emerging from the driver's side of the car—despite the fact that Darren Rutiger had a good fifty pounds on Artie, Darren looked pretty defenseless, too. But maybe Franny imagined that. They were having fun, weren't they? Exchanging a flicker of fake punches as they made their way up the drive and into the yard light?

She opened her mouth to call down a greeting, then balked. It had been almost a year since she had last seen the pair, and that had been at Karlins' Grocery, when Peg stopped to pick up a gallon of milk. "Is this necessary?" Peg murmured when Franny gave the boys a hug. Franny had blushed, but the answer was *yes*. Artie and Darren had been kind to Franny. In the old days, they had not objected to her coming along when they took Roz for a drive. When Peg and Brick were out of town and the big girls had parties, Darren and Artie had given Franny cigarettes and sips of beer, and Artie used to sing "Nature Boy" for Franny, and then listened, without laughing, when she sang, "Where Is Your Heart?"

Of course, she understood that the boys' kindness was largely the product of the fact that both were half in love with Rosamund. Still, they were kind, and, once, when Darren Rutiger felt dejected, and talked to Rosamund about a quarrel with his dad, he had held Franny in his lap, and stroked the back of her head for a good fifteen minutes.

Impossible not to smile at the way that Artie Stokes now leaned his raised forearm against the front door as he waited for someone to answer the bell. So familiar, that posture! It suggested a casual, rakish attitude toward life, yes? That hot-rod, James Dean attitude so popular with boys in the fifties?

But how long could you keep your arm up like that—sustain

that attitude—if no one came to see who waited at the door? To spare the boy the answer, Franny called down a croaking, "Hey, Darren! Artie!"

Both rolled their heads back on their necks. "Franny?"

"How're you guys doing?"

Darren Rutiger laughed. "Well, pretty good, but nobody's answering the door!"

Franny smiled. She felt happy—happy and excited and useful. "Just wait. I'll tell Roz you're here."

"Attagirl." Darren's voice was smoky, languorous, just as Franny remembered it. "A movie-star voice," Martie always said. Neither she nor Franny had understood why Rosamund was not crazy about the boy.

"Oh, Franny!" With a jerk of her chin, Rosamund indicated that Franny should follow her out of the noisy, party-crowded kitchen and into the dark and empty dining room.

"So—where are they, Franny?"

Franny pointed toward the front door. "Out there."

"I was *hoping* they'd leave if we didn't answer." Rosamund sighed. "Okay. You—stay here," she said, then edged around a couple cuddling in the kitchen doorway.

The young men who followed Rosamund into the dining room a minute later were a pair Franny thought of as The Golfers (large specimens, very tanned, always wearing the sort of coordinated country club clothes that Franny's father wore on his days off).

"Franny, I'd like to introduce you to my new boyfriend," Rosamund said, with a wink at the taller of the two young men.

Franny flushed. "You're not even going to let Darren and Artie come in?"

"Franny." Rosamund rested her head on Franny's shoulder. "If they come in, they might start a fight with somebody, and who knows what all?"

"But—"

"*Franny*." Rosamund took a step back and fixed a stern gaze on the girl. "They're the ones who broke in the house when we went to Florida the first time, remember?"

At this bit of information, the golfers pushed back the sleeves of their cardigans; and Franny, astonished at her own daring, blurted, "But we always knew they were the ones who broke in, Roz. You were still friends with them, after that. You told me they just took stuff from the liquor cabinet."

Rosamund eyes flashed wide: *That's enough*. Then she turned and, reasserting the Peg Wahl posture—"Remember, the top of your skull is connected by string to a star directly overhead"—she began to move toward the door, with the golfers close behind.

"Roz—" Franny hoped Rosamund would turn back; instead, someone else seized Franny's elbow from behind. Martie. Redolent of cigarettes and beer, and asking, "What the hell are you doing, twitching your ass around down here?"

"Back off, Martie," Rosamund called over a shoulder. "She came to tell me Darren and Artie are here."

Martie released Franny and broke into a broad smile. "Darren and Artie!" She pushed ahead of the others, and by the time they arrived in the hall, Martie was outside, giving hugs to Darren Rutiger and Artie Stokes and yelping *How the hell are you?*

"Hey, Martie," the boys said, but even Franny—standing at the back of the hall with the golfers—could see that Darren Rutiger and Artie Stokes' eyes remained fixed on the screen door, behind which stood Rosamund.

Darren Rutiger offered Rosamund one of the sleepy smiles that Franny had always found so endearing. *Bedroom eyes*. Rosamund had once told Franny that was what you called heavy-lidded eyes like Darren's.

"Hey, Roz, I'm going in the service," Darren said. "Thought maybe you'd invite us in for a farewell drink."

"Not tonight, guys." Rosamund sounded regretful, but also firm. Skinny Artie Stokes blinked hard before he looked down at the ground, but Darren laughed and asked:

"Not even for one drink?"

Rosamund stared out the door and into the dark beyond the light from the mercury lamp. "You don't need a drink."

"Rosamund Wahl!" Martie gave a hiccuping laugh. "Would you get real? These are old friends!"

"Yeah, Rosamund." Darren Rutiger wrapped an arm around Martie's waist. "You're not going to let your big sister be a bad hostess, are you, Martie?"

Martie handed him the can of beer in her hand. He took a long drink, then passed the can on to Artie Stokes. "I don't see why they can't come in for a drink, Roz," Martie said.

"Roz?" In one move—Tweedle Dee and Tweedle Dum, thought Franny—the golfers stepped up from the back of the hall to the door. "Is there a problem here?"

Martie glared at Rosamund. "I don't believe this! Did you ask them to do this?"

Rosamund lowered her head, but held it aimed at Martie as she said a clipped, "Would you, please, *please,* go inside?"

Martie turned to Artie and Darren, but this time it apparently did not escape her attention that the boys watched only Rosamund. "*I* give up!" she said, and threw open the front door and stormed inside, past Rosamund and the golfers and Franny.

"Okay," said the taller of the golfers, "I think you fellows can see that Roz would like you to leave."

Darren Rutiger exchanged a little boy's grin with Artie Stokes, then rubbed his hand across his mouth as if to contain a laugh. "And who would you be, bud? Dean Martin?"

"That's right." The first golfer nodded, then pointed to his companion. "And this is Sammy Davis. We got to go do our act now, fellas, so, good night."

After the golfer had shut not just the screen door, but the inner door, too—an awful moment, to Franny's mind—Rosamund let loose a deep breath. "Promise me you won't do that ever again," she said to Franny. Then she and the golfers headed across the dark dining room toward the distant gold of the den, where Martie and Al Castor could now be seen dancing with the wild-eyed Mr. Ed.

It seemed to Franny that the front door made a great deal of noise when she went to open it again, but no one came running to check on her and, after a moment's hesitation, she called down the drive, "Artie! Darren! Wait!"

"Franny? Is that you?"

"Just—wait."

In the crowded kitchen—a nervous beat ticking away in her right eyelid—Franny excused herself to a girl who blocked the cupboard where Brick and Peg stored their liquor.

"Hey, there." Someone crouched down beside Franny as she knelt to study the bottles: scotch, bourbon, vodka. Richie Craft, she realized. Boyfriend to the beautiful girl who stood in the window of Stacey's Sweets and stirred the big copper kettle of caramel corn with a wooden paddle. Sometimes, when Franny and her friends went to Stacey's, they saw Richie Craft standing outside the shop window, trying to make the girlfriend laugh. He seemed nice. He had a band called The Craft and they had cut a record that received plenty of play on the local station. With his chin as big as a heel, his shiny brown hair soft around his long face, Richie Craft always made Franny think of the photo of Oscar Wilde that appeared in the copy of *The Importance of Being Earnest/Lady Windermere's Fan* that she had found at the library's book sale.

"I've seen you at Stacey's, right?" Richie Craft asked. "So, is the liquor cabinet open for business?"

She shook her head. Behind a bottle of peppermint schnapps were bottles of—brandy, Kahlua. Carefully, she set the schnapps back into place.

"What's she doing?" someone else asked, and Richie Craft stood, and said he didn't know, and then Franny stood with the bottle of bourbon. Pulled two glasses from the cupboard over the sink. Filled the glasses. Set the bottle back in its cupboard.

"Have fun!" Richie Craft murmured as she left the room, and she murmured back, "It's not for me."

The bourbon sloshed onto her hands as she walked, its chill a surprise. Where were the boys?

Sitting a ways off, on the old church slab. "Is that really you, Franny?" Darren Rutiger called. "When'd you start looking like that?"

Artie Stokes laughed. "Hey, Franny goes steady with Bobby Prohaski now—Larry's little brother, man. I told you that."

Whap. Darren Rutiger slapped the side of his head. She had forgotten he did that. "Well, hey, why don't you go with us? Forget that Prohaski kid!"

"Here." She offered them the glasses of bourbon. "These are for you guys. It's bourbon."

Darren Rutiger glanced toward the house as he took a glass. "They're drinking *bourbon* in there?"

"No. I took this for you guys. It's my folks' stuff."

Artie Stokes leaned low to the glass. "There must be eight ounces in each of these! You trying to get us drunk, girl?"

"So what if she is?" Darren Rutiger laughed. "Hey, Fran, did Martie tell you to bring us this?"

She shook her head. "Martie's a jerk."

"Uh-oh. Trouble in Petticoat Junction!" Darren Rutiger gave Franny a hug. "Well, thank you kindly, ma'am. But, then, we've always been pals, haven't we, Fran?"

She smiled. "Sure."

"Hey, I bet Brick and Peg try to keep you under lock and key now, huh?"

She knew enough to respond with a wry pucker of the lips that might mean any sort of reply—amusement, girlish or tomboyish disgust, even agreement—before she stared off through the backdrop of the old baseball diamond to the road beyond.

"Hey, Artie"—Darren Rutiger raised his foot to give a nudge in the knee to Artie Stokes, who was now trying to separate the pages of a bloated *National Geographic* that someone had left on the slab—"Artie, remember the night we got wasted and sneaked into Camp Winnebago to visit Franny?"

Artie did not look up from his work on the magazine, but he nodded. "Roz didn't want to see us *that* night either."

Darren Rutiger ignored this. "Man, we thought maybe we'd spy some cute counselor taking a shower or something, and instead we ended up with that big old mama chasing us around."

"Yup, we're going, 'Franny, Franny,' and old Franny's just sawing logs." Artie Stokes looked up at Franny then, smiling, and she smiled, too. Though she had slept through their visit, she had been proud the next morning when the counselors called her to view the bouquet the boys had left outside her tent and the torn-up flower bed around the Camp Winnebago flagpole.

"Whew!" Darren Rutiger's eyebrows rose as he lifted his lips from his glass. "Good stuff!"

"Like we'd really know," murmured Artie.

How long would it take for the boys to finish those drinks? Too long, it appeared, and Franny extended a hand toward Artie Stokes' glass—his seemed to hold more than Darren's—and she asked, "Can I taste it?"

"Oooh, Franny!" Darren laughed. "Watch out, babe!"

He was right to warn her. The sips of beer she had taken in the past tasted nothing like that foul swig she now swallowed. "Oh!" she cried. "Oh!" Her shoulders shook and she panted for air, and the boys moaned in delighted sympathy.

"Poor Franny!" Darren Rutiger patted her on the back. "You never tried hard stuff before, huh?"

Eyes tearing, she shook her head; then, quick, took a second swig, this time from Darren Rutiger's glass. While she shook anew, Artie Stokes asked, "But, hey, Fran, who the heck were the clowns in the golf clothes?"

"Just—college boys. Nobody special."

"Ah. College boys."

It was not a nice thing to do, she knew, but to assure Artie Stokes and Darren Rutiger that college boys were not so marvelous, she proceeded to act out the way in which the taller of the golfers had tried to air the bathroom that morning: jerking the door back and forth, lighting matches, spraying window cleaner in the air. She was not nearly so funny as the boys' laughter suggested.

She knew that. No doubt, the alcohol in their blood made up a large part of her wit. She herself felt suspiciously good, and had to resist the urge to stretch her mouth into queer, experimental shapes.

"So, Franny." Darren Rutiger made an amused, luxurious noise, and stretched his arms high over his head. "Rozzie's getting too big for her britches these days, huh?"

Back at work on the stiffened pages of the magazine, Artie said, "Darren"—a brief warning—and Franny said, "Believe me, Darren, Martie's worse. When I went downstairs to tell Roz you guys were at the door, Martie was, like, 'What're you doing down here?' and—" Franny broke off. Even with the bourbon in her veins, she could not repeat what Martie had said.

Twitching your ass.

"Maybe Martie's starting to worry about the competition, Fran! If you were just a little older—but, hey, I bet you've already got quite an education, being around the big sisters, huh? You must have seen plenty."

"Oh, pf!" said Franny. *Pf!* Which sounded like one of the old-fashioned expressions people used in Nancy Drew mysteries, and made her snicker.

"Well?" Darren nudged her shoulder. "Am I right?"

"I don't know!" She started to laugh—then the oddest thing, her gums went bone-dry, and caught her upper lip in a horsey snag—so silly it made her laugh even harder, and she bent over at the waist so no one would see.

Darren Rutiger laughed his low, buzzing laugh. "What is it?" he said, and laughed some more. "What, Fran?"

"Well." She straightened. Stifled a laugh that came out through her nose. "Once, I did see Martie—on the couch."

"Is that right?" Darren Rutiger raised a silencing finger toward Artie Stokes. "Who with?"

"Oh." She blinked away the memory of the ROTC boy, fast. Somehow, she knew, it would not do to say the name. And why had she said anything at all? "I don't—it was a while back."

"But you'd remember something like that, Franny!" Darren

Rutiger chucked a finger under her chin. "Or maybe there've been a bunch of guys, and that's why you can't say?"

She shook her head, hard. "Just the one. Just once."

"Okay, okay." He settled an arm around her shoulder, then looked off with her across the road toward the swamp. Which was nice. There were stars. The dark swamp jingled and whirred with baby frogs and crickets. She was consoled, then, and—

"I bet it was Roger Dale, wasn't it? Clothes off or on?"

"On!" She pulled away from Darren. "And it wasn't Roger, and they were—kissing is all."

"Yeah, but, like, *grinding* away at each other, right?"

"Hey, Darren." Artie Stokes stood. "Maybe we should get going, man. You don't want old Franny getting in trouble with her sisters after she was nice enough to bring us these drinks."

Franny stared at the magazine now spread open on the slab beside Artie Stokes. Even in the night, she recognized that two-page photograph of windmills in Spain, the golden sails like scalded cream.

Darren Rutiger raised his hand to his mouth and made a noise, a kind of "Sssss" which sounded like an air brake on a semi-trailer. Uncanny. He took a seat on the church slab. Sipped from his glass of bourbon as if he hardly knew that Franny existed. Looked over Artie Stokes' shoulder at the photo of the windmills. All of this was intended to make her feel alone, she understood, but when he spoke again, asking, "So were they grinding away, Franny?" she could not seem to stop herself from answering:

"Well, they were *close.*"

"How close?"

She hesitated. "Like—cement."

"You mean, like a cement *mixer*?" Darren asked, a puff of laughter pushing out the last syllable.

She shook her head. She had not given much thought to the description. She meant only to offer an idea of the kind of completeness she had sensed in that moment between the ROTC boy and Martie.

"Man, Artie!" Darren Rutiger rocked back onto his elbows and raised his face to the trees and the sky overhead. "Here we sit with our old friend Franny, and she's giving us the lowdown on her big sister's sex life, and we're drinking her dad's primo bourbon! Who says we didn't go to the damn party?"

How jubilant he was! While Franny was miserable. Not only had she betrayed Martie, the boys—at least Darren—seemed to think she had offered them the bourbon as a blow against Brick. *I only brought it because I felt sorry for you.* That was what she wanted to say, but that wasn't the whole truth, either. She wanted them to like her, too. She was preposterous. She was—

Darren Rutiger threw a twig at her shoulder. "So, Franny, that booze got you feeling tight, babe?"

"Tight" was not the right word. She did not mean to give him the right word—which was more like "loose," and so she said, making her voice as casual and steady as possible, "No, but I've got to go now. You guys can—just take those glasses with you. My mom'll think they got broken, or something."

"Aw." Darren made a little boy's pout that he was handsome enough to get away with. "So *you* want us to leave, too?" He stood, then, and pulled her into his chest, which did feel nice, so big and solid and warm, the soft scuff of his cotton shirt against her cheek—

"Say good night, Darren," said Artie Stokes.

"All right, all right." Darren raised his hands in the air, like a man being held up, and Franny began to back away through the foxtail toward the clipped lawn and the drive.

"Good to see you guys," she said.

"Right." Darren Rutiger picked up his glass from the slab, raised it her way. "We'll never forget you for this, babe!"

Artie Stokes lifted his glass, too. "To old pals."

"But, hey, hey, hey"—Darren Rutiger began to laugh—"look who's coming now!"

Martie: hoisting a six-pack of beer over her head, and calling, "It's me!"

To the boys, Franny hissed, "Don't tell about the bourbon."

Quick, grinning, they set their glasses on the slab behind them; then Darren hurried on ahead of Franny to give Martie a hug considerably more intimate than the one he had given her back at the front door—now, a nuzzle to the neck, the cheek.

"So tell me, Martie," Darren said, "am I wrong, or is Rozzie getting too big for her britches?"

Martie threw her head back and gave a yip of delight-filled ire. "Wasn't she a perfect bitch? But, Frances Jean, what are *you* doing out here?"

Darren Rutiger winked at Franny as he took Martie's hand and spun her out to arm's length.

"No" was the word Franny mouthed at the boy, and he must have understood what she meant because he stopped looking Franny's way as he gave Martie a second spin.

"You're sure looking good, Martie! Must be that college life. The rest of us gotta slug away at the old job, lug that barge, tote that bale, while you're out breaking the boys' hearts between classes." He turned to Artie Stokes. "Is that fair, man? We come home and rub Ben-Gay on our sore backs, and Martie, here, is out living the high life?"

Artie laughed and Darren went on, "Hey, Martie, remember the good old days when you'd sit behind me and rub my shoulders while Señor Siquieros told us about his family in old Mejico?"

"Frances Jean, get inside," Martie said. "Pronto."

"But, Martie—"

"You want me to tell that you were out here with Darren and Artie after Mother specifically told you to stay upstairs?"

"But—"

"You're not wanted." Martie pointed toward the house. "*Go.*"

"Hey, you," a voice called as Franny made her way up the stairs, but another voice—the voice of Richie Craft, she thought—said, "No, man, that's the little sister."

In her parents' dark bedroom, the only things perfectly visible were the long sleeves of a white shirt on the ironing board—white, dangling, one on each side of the board: the arms of a man who finally died on that piece of the wreck he had hoped might keep him alive long enough for rescue.

Outside, things were clearer. From the bedroom window, Franny watched Darren Rutiger and Martie make their way down the drive. Artie Stokes stayed behind on the church slab, smoking. Maybe Artie still hoped Rosamund might come out to him. Maybe he saw himself as a kind of watchdog for Darren Rutiger. Or for Martie.

After a while, Artie stood. Worked a beer from the six-pack Martie had brought outside. Punched holes in the top.

Into the closed space she made by cupping her hands over her mouth and nose, Franny breathed her bourbon breath. "I'm a bum," she whispered. "Dear God, please help me not to be such a bum."

She still stood watching out the window an hour later when a white station wagon hesitated at the end of the long drive, then turned and parked along the edge of the moon-blond plot that held the single apple tree that remained of the Nearys' old orchard.

The car's driver began to walk toward the Wahl house. A male. Artie Stokes looked up as the newcomer passed but Artie did not call out an hello, and the newcomer did not seem to see Artie. A light-haired boy in a white shirt, khaki Bermudas, loafers. For a dazzling moment, Franny thought: Martie's old ROTC boyfriend, come to make amends!

But, of course, the boy was actually "Eduardo" from Lake Okoboji, and now Eduardo's loafers scuffed the front steps. He rang the doorbell. Folded his hands behind his back. Waited.

Maybe no one would come to the door, the way no one had come to the door for Darren Rutiger and Artie Stokes. Maybe the boy just would—go away.

But maybe not.

Down the stairs Franny pounced. Through the noisy living room and out through the screened porch. She knew the yard, even in the dark, and made her way along the rim of the bank without trouble, then cut back across the far side of the property and came up from behind the church slab.

"It's just Franny," she whispered as Artie Stokes flinched. "Sh."

The scene now unfolding on the front steps included Rosamund, Tim Gleason, and Eduardo (head tilted to one side, hands in his pockets in what Franny suspected he meant to serve as a jaunty pose).

She dug her fingertips into Artie's arm. "What have they been saying?"

He shook his head—"Can't hear"—then Rosamund disappeared inside the house, leaving Tim Gleason and Eduardo on the steps.

"But who's that with Roz?" Artie asked.

"I need to find Martie," Franny said.

WHIR-OOOOO! Rosamund stepped out from the front door, the silver emergency siren raised to her lips—*WHIR-OOOOO!*—while Franny made her way across the rough ground to the faded car in which Darren and Artie had arrived.

She knocked on the side of the car. No answer. "Martie?" she whispered. Half-sick, she rose up just high enough to look inside: empty.

WHIR-OOOOO! WHIROOOOooooo!

"Whir-oo!" called a mocking voice out of the dark beyond the end of the drive, and a couple began to take shape there. The girl's head lay on the boy's shoulder. The two appeared wonderfully anonymous. Content. In love. Unfortunately, as they drew closer, they became Darren Rutiger and Martie, using each other for support as they made their drunken way up the drive.

"Martie!" Rosamund called. Her voice scratched a warning into the night sky that was sharp and bright as lightning. "You've got company!"

Martie stopped and woozily disengaged herself from Darren Rutiger. "Eduardo"—*Martie's* voice: It was the bleat of the lamb that quails at the lightning—"is that you?"

Edwardo did not reply.

Moving a little faster now, though her legs seemed hardly sturdy enough to carry her; raking her fingers through her mussed hair, Martie called, "When d'you get here? I about gave up—"

"I guess so," the boy murmured.

Darren Rutiger, now several paces behind Martie, raised his face to the moon and delivered a wolf howl.

"Darren Rutiger!" Rosamund hurried down the drive, her hands raised in the air. "Get off our property or I'm calling the police!"

"Hey, Roz." Darren Rutiger reared back a little, but his voice was as smooth as ever. "Get off your high horse. I was with Martie, not you. Hey, Martie—" He broke off as Martie put her hand on the arm of Eduardo, and Eduardo turned aside.

"I mean it, Darren," Rosamund said.

"I know you do." Darren considered Martie and Eduardo for another moment, then called, "Hey! What's-your-name! Eduardo!"

"Shut up, Darren," Artie Stokes murmured, his voice just loud enough that Franny could hear, and when Eduardo did not answer, Darren continued, "Well, whatever your name is, man: Too bad you got here so late."

It did not occur to Franny that she had covered her eyes until she heard the slap that made her uncover them, and there was Rosamund, shoving at Darren Rutiger, who now held a hand to his cheek. "Get out!" Rosamund shouted. "You are a—nasty person! Nasty! Just—get!"

Which might have been the end of things had Darren Rutiger not begun to laugh at Rosamund. When Darren Rutiger laughed at her, Rosamund kicked him in the shins.

"Hey!" he protested, and then Martie sat down on the front steps and started to cry, and Eduardo, making a sound Franny would have preferred never to have heard, smashed his fist into the lap siding of the old lodge. The cry of pain that followed the blow made something inside her convulse, and, for a second, she thought that Artie Stokes might step into the drive and hit someone or something himself—there was a shifting in the air alongside her—but, no, after a brief salute to Franny, Artie Stokes headed toward the gray car at the end of the drive, and, then, Darren Rutiger headed that way, too.

Only Franny watched Artie and Darren's departure because Rosamund now was enlisting Tim Gleason and his friend in the white T-shirt to drive Eduardo to the emergency room, quick, someone had to cut off the boy's class ring, the finger was swelling, *Go on, before my parents get home.*

Spooky: the number of party guests who now stood just beyond the light from the mercury lamp, looking back and forth between Rosamund in the driveway and Martie on the front steps. Martie, still crying, pushed Mr. Ed away as he tried to lick her salty cheeks.

"Franny," Rosamund called as Franny made her way down to the drive, "what are you doing out here?"

"I—wanted to help."

"Good luck." Rosamund shook her head. "Really, the best thing for you to do would be to get inside in case Mother and Daddy come home." Rosamund turned to watch the car carrying Eduardo move off down Lakeside. "Go on. Really. I'll try to help Martie settle down in just a minute."

CHAPTER SEVEN

T HOUGH THE WAHLS' CHURCH ATTENDANCE HAD FALLEN OFF sharply since their move to the far side of the lake, the next morning, when Franny woke, she instantly felt "Sunday." Sunshine and moisture had already made the morning as glossy as a photograph, and she found herself thinking of the repentant Baptist campers of the nineteen-fifties, how they would have filed out of the lodge and into the day, made their way across the drive to the little church. Skinny-necked boys in outsize white shirts and ties. Girls in full skirts and straw hats and white gloves. Franny would have appreciated an opportunity to join those girls that morning. To look down at her gloved hands, just as they had, and say the requisite prayers.

On this Sunday morning, the Wahls' out-of-town guests fled the house eagerly and early, rolling up sleeping bags and packing cars before Peg even had a chance to start the brunch.

"What on earth?" Peg said when she came down to the quiet kitchen and found Franny, there, alone with the newspaper. "Did something happen here last night?"

Franny's eyeballs felt parched when she raised them to her mother's face. *Look blasé. Blink, but do not blink too much. Look dumb, but not too dumb. Not infuriatingly dumb.* Her mother knew about the scene with Eduardo? Did not know? This was a test to determine if Franny would tell the truth, the whole truth, and nothing but the truth?

"I was upstairs. If anything happened, how would I know?"

Sickeningly brave, Franny felt. Perhaps witnesses would now

pop out from the broom closet and drag her to a confession.

"You girls"—Peg's smile bristled with bitterness—"you girls are thicker than thieves."

Keeping the dumb look on her face, Franny moved off to the den where she lay down upon the floor and watched *This Is the Life*. Her sisters made fun of the show's religious slant, but its stories of troubled families seemed more realistic to Franny than most of the stories on television.

Out in the kitchen, Rosamund asked Peg what time they were meeting Brick's mother for lunch at the country club, and Peg complained about Martie being impossible to wake up, and then Martie's voice sounded in the kitchen, too:

"How're my beautiful mother and my beautiful sister on this beautiful Sunday morning?"

Trying to sound chipper, Franny supposed. And to show gratitude to Rosamund for last night's display of loyalty.

Her father, on the other hand, came directly into the den from the stairs, and moaned, "It's hell to grow old, Fran."

From her spot on the floor, Franny turned to smile at him over her shoulder. He smiled back as he lowered himself onto the creaky leather couch, but he looked terrible—jittery, puffy, pink-eyed. Some mornings, he was sick to his stomach, but no one acknowledged the fact: The faucets ran loud, the toilet flushed, and that was that.

"Hey, girls," he hollered toward the kitchen, "any coffee out there?"

"Coming right up, sir!" Martie called back.

Martie herself looked a little pasty above the collar of her pink bathrobe, yes, but she had washed her hair and piled it on top of her head in a pink towel. She was making an effort. "Frances Jean," she said as she carried a clattering cup and saucer toward their father, "I can't believe you watch that garbage."

Franny pretended not to hear, made no move from her spot on the rug, a hard sisal thing that left a giant paisley pattern on her skin if she lay on the floor for any time at all.

"Awful quiet around here this morning," Brick said. "Where'd everybody go?"

Martie laughed. "Just sit tight! I'm going to make us a killer pitcher of Bloody Marys! I figure I ought to know how, right, since I learned at the feet of the master?"

On *This Is the Life,* a family with a shoplifting son received sufficient counsel from their pastor that things were looking up by the time the theme song began. The song, and the candle that flickered on the screen while it played, always made Franny's heart hurt in just the way it hurt at certain love songs. Could the singer be Bing Crosby? Franny would have asked Brick what he thought, but Brick despised Bing Crosby, and here came Martie, again, this time pressing the television's off button with a flick of her hip as she carried Brick his Bloody Mary.

"Martie!" Franny protested.

"Sh." Martie dropped down beside Brick on the couch. "You know what I'd *love,* Dad? To hear you play 'Satin Doll.'"

"Aw, honey. Not just now."

"Come on!" Martie hopped to her feet and held out her hands. "Franny, wouldn't you love to hear Dad's 'Satin Doll'?"

"Sure," Franny said. Even though she could see her father did not want to play. Because if she did not say, *Sure,* even if he did not want to play, he would feel hurt.

Come on, Martie mouthed at Franny, and now Martie's eyes jiggled with tears. What did the tears mean? Were they leftovers from the night before? *Cheer him up,* Martie mouthed.

Franny forced herself to her feet and went to join Martie in holding out a hand to Brick, to help him stand.

"For God's sake, girls"—he shook his head—"you think I can't get up by myself?" He stood then, with a grunt, and he called out to Rosamund, just entering the den, "Your sisters, here, seem to have decided I'm some kind of cripple!"

This made Rosamund laugh. "Oh, Daddy," she said, and she shook her head at her sisters' folly.

*   *   *

That afternoon—why did it always happen that way?—by the time the Wahls arrived at the Pynch Country Club for lunch with Brick's mother, they were twenty-five minutes late.

"And I'm the one she'll blame," Peg said as the family hurried up the walk.

"Don't be ridiculous." Brick ran his finger around the collar of his sport shirt. "*I'm* the officially errant son."

The country club manager—in short-sleeves and tie and fat wristwatch—pointed the family toward the large table where Charlotte Wahl sat waiting on the old dining porch. Stately, dignified, her seamed forehead and nape surrounded by an ever present gray doughnut of hair, Charlotte widened her dark eyes at her son and his family as they wound their way through the linen-covered tables, most of them now empty of the lunch crowd.

"I thought you'd gotten lost," Charlotte murmured, then offered her cheek to each in turn.

"That's a beautiful suit, Grandma," Rosamund said, and Brick said, "Yes, indeed! You're looking well, Mother-o-mine!" and he threw a long leg over the back of a Windsor chair—not an entirely graceful move, but he got himself seated, and proceeded to make a show of tucking his napkin into the collar of his shirt. For his mother's benefit. As soon as she sighed in mild dismay, he gaily tossed the napkin onto the table. "Of course, you always do look well, don't you, Ma? Mom? Mother?" He glanced toward the bar. "Where's our boy Jimmy this afternoon?"

"He'll be by," Charlotte said. "Don't get frantic, dear."

Brick leaned over the table to screw up one of his bloodshot eyes at his mother. "Do I look frantic, dear?"

Charlotte did not respond to her son's question, but said, "The Brinkleys stopped at the table while I was waiting. They'd had the chicken, and advised against it."

"Well, well!" With a laugh, Brick pushed back his chair and stood and saluted. "If the Brinkleys advise against the chicken, by God, I shall stand against the chicken!" He winked at Franny. She smiled, then wished she had not when he started off toward the bar.

Charlotte Wahl watched the departure, but did not return the helpless shrug of alliance offered her by Peg.

"Do you think Dad'll get us something, too?" Martie asked. "I'm sure nobody would object if we all had a little wine with our meal—"

"*I'd* object," Charlotte and Peg said in one breath, and Rosamund whispered, "You already had a Bloody Mary, Martie."

Martie fanned herself with the big menu. "I don't see why you guys eat here, anyway. You always say the food stinks."

"Martie!" said Rosamund, and Peg did her best to smile at the approaching waiter as she added in an undertone, "We have to use our minimum, Martie."

"I'd forfeit it," said Martie.

"Good afternoon, ladies." The waiter was a tiny boy with pointed ears whom Franny recognized from the newspaper as a high school wrestler.

"So, tell us," Martie said to the boy, "what does your chef cook *well*?"

A bracing moment, for which Peg apologized to the young man; then, while everyone placed their orders, Brick—scotch in hand— resumed his seat and Charlotte began to explain why Franny really ought to wear her hair tucked behind her ears.

"You don't want to look like an Afghan hound, now do you?" Charlotte said with a chuckle.

"Ruff, ruff!" Franny replied, which made the departing waiter smile, but did not put an end to the matter, no, because Brick agreed with his mother. *She looks like she just crawled out of the sack, doesn't she? Somebody loan that girl a comb!* and this inspired Martie to reach around behind Franny and pull the hair away from Franny's face.

"Better, right?" Martie said. "Right?"

"Stop!" Franny shook her head out of Martie's reach, and though Rosamund gave her a smile of sympathy, Charlotte said, "We're right, though, Fran. For a moment, there, you looked lovely." She pointed her chin Brick's way. "Have you noticed how much she looks like your cousin Grace, Brick?"

"*Grace?*" Franny tried to think who Grace might be.

"A second cousin," Charlotte said. "You wouldn't have met her, I suppose. She lives off in Texas."

Nh. A little noise escaped Brick Wahl's nose. *Nh.* He raised himself up by the arms of his chair and peered down upon the men gathered on the putting green that fanned out below the raised porch.

"Brick?" Peg said. "Your mother asked you a question."

"Grace." He shook his head as he resumed his seat. "Christ, she was a character! Remember how she'd complain her breasts were too big? Oh, they made her hot! Oh, she couldn't find clothes that fit right!"

"Harold!" Charlotte Wahl lowered her eyes. "Really—"

"Well, she did!" Brick glanced at the females gathered around the table as if their presence made him itch. "If you ask me, her breasts were the best thing that ever happened to her."

At this last, Martie gave a gulping laugh and blushed, earning a stare from Peg, who then said "Isn't it"—but switched to a half-hearted, "Here's your soup, Brick."

"French onion." With a flourish, the waiter lowered a bowl into place before Brick, then handed salads around to the others.

"I always find that pepper mill business embarrassing," Franny whispered to Rosamund as the waiter began to make his way around the table. Rosamund nodded, but whispered back, "It's supposed to be part of the charm of service."

"Say, young man."

The girls joined the others in turning toward Brick, who was making a horrible face toward the bowl of soup in front of him. "Could somebody in the kitchen actually think I'm fool enough to eat this swill?"

The waiter's smile revealed nubs of teeth, as pitted and gray as rock salt. "If there's something you'd rather do with it, sir," the waiter said, "please, be my guest."

"Young man"—Brick raised his reddened eyelids at the boy—"don't tempt me."

Charlotte, Peg, Rosamund, and Franny looked down at their

plates, but Martie darted a hand across the table. "Let me taste it, Dad," she said. "I'm a connoisseur of onion soup."

"*What?*" Brick laid his hands over the top of the soup bowl. "For God's sake, I said it was awful!"

"Mr. Wahl?" The manager appeared from behind the waiter. "Is there a problem?"

"Would you say it's a problem if your soup tastes like piss, and your waiter's a smart-ass?"

At a distance, the manager conferred with the waiter, then returned to substitute a salad for the offending soup and to introduce a new server.

It was Rosamund who broke the silence that followed by announcing that she knew a game they could play. "Wait." She rooted around in her bag for a pen and a cocktail napkin she said she had brought home from Mike Zanios's Top Hat Club.

"Here it is!" She held up a napkin containing a sketch: pouty lips, pouf of blond hair falling into big, doe eyes.

"What's that?" Peg asked.

"It's Roz!" Franny said. "Can't you tell? A caricature. Did Mike Zanios draw it?"

Rosamund nodded. "But it's the back I want you to see. We were playing this game called 'word golf.' See how it works? In this one, we performed a miracle! One letter at a time, we changed 'blood' to 'wine'! Well, '*wines*.' Mike thought of that."

"You guys have so much fun together!" Martie said. "Let's you and I go to the Top Hat, Roz! Sometime this week!"

Rosamund smiled off out the window. "You wouldn't think Mike was in his forties," she said. "I mean, he's read Hemingway. And Camus."

Charlotte Wahl gave a dry laugh. "Dear, I'm practically an antique, and I've read Hemingway and Camus. Your grandfather read Hemingway, and no doubt your father did, too." She cocked an eye at Brick—just then chewing hard on a bite of dinner roll and looking around the dining porch like a bored boy.

"Isn't he the one who blew his brains out?" Peg asked.

Rosamund nodded. "He'd developed a tragic view of life."

"Puh!" Brick stood up from the table. "He couldn't write anymore. That's what I heard." Brick picked up his drink and moved off to the upright piano at the rear of the porch.

Everyone at the table watched. Pretended not to watch. Charlotte and Peg sat straighter in their chairs and took delicate bites of their salads. The girls followed suit, and then Charlotte, who was the bankroller of her granddaughters' college educations, began to ask questions about what Martie and Rosamund would study in the fall. Franny, however, could not help noticing that a woman in a red sundress approached the piano. The woman leaned forward and said something in Brick's ear that made him nod and smile. Which, unfortunately, made Franny think of a cartoon from the hidden books at the piano teacher's house: A woman stands behind a smiling, seated male, her very large breasts covering the male's eyes as she asks, "Guess who?"

To Franny's relief, Brick did return to the table when their entrees arrived.

"Actually," Charlotte said—she smiled up at Brick as he resumed his seat—"I don't like my beef rare, but Brick's daddy trained me to eat it this way. He was a tyrant on beef."

Brick laughed. "But remember how he loved those greasy old pork ribs at Arnie's? Remember that, girls?"

Rosamund smiled. "And he'd always make sure Arnie brought the favor basket around for us."

"'Get the big picture,'" Martie sang out. "Remember how he'd tell us, 'Girls,'"—she tucked her chin to her chest, made her voice deep and commanding—"'make sure you get the big picture.'"

"The favor basket," Charlotte said. "You girls loved the favor basket."

Martie threw her hands down on the edge of the table. "Remember the black and white Scotties with the magnet bases?"

Remember the parrots at Drake's?

And the wishing well at Halford's?

The time Roz got sick on cherries jubilee?

Oh, yes, said Peg and Brick and Martie and Rosamund, and sometimes Charlotte, too. Now and again, one of them gave Franny a look, *Join in,* though, in fact, Franny had not even been alive in the days they discussed, or if she were, she had been too small to remember. This was a common enough pattern (sometimes it was "Remember how Kendrick at the stables used to flirt with your mother?" or "Remember how Daddy used to come in at night to say prayers and teach us 'I Have a Little Shadow'?"). Really, she would not have minded the reminiscing so much had the others not acted as if she were a killjoy for refusing to pretend to have shared those same pleasures. However, it was a fact that the only time she remembered her father ever coming to her room to say good night was after he threw her notebook at her when she did not understand his way of explaining a math problem. Neither her father nor her mother had taught her how to sail or drive a motorboat or ride a bike, let alone a horse. Unlike the big girls, she had not owned a horse. In fact, the only times she had gone to the stables were when her mother picked up the big girls after their rides.

Which was not to say she did not have childhood memories.

She remembered her parents' parties at the Ash Street house (downstairs in winter, on the patio in summer). The tree house. Playing king and slave with the neighborhood girls. The thrill of "scooping the loop"—up Clay and down Main, past City Park, and on Lakeside to Clay again—when Rosamund first got her driver's license. Rosamund dressing Franny as a mascot for her junior high school's basketball games and taking her out to buy noisemakers and candy the time that Brick and Peg went to Minneapolis for New Year's Eve. Rosamund inviting her along to the drive-in for hamburgers with Artie and Darren—

"Hey, Zanios!" Martie cried, and, sure enough, Mike Zanios—dark blond curls still wet from the clubhouse shower, gym bag slung over one shoulder—now cut across the dining porch to the Wahl table.

"Don't get up!" he called.

Brick did rise, of course, to take Mike Zanios's hand, but the ladies stayed seated; the last time they had come to the club together, Charlotte Wahl had told Franny that she was now of an age when she should stay seated.

"How'd your game go, Zanios?" Brick asked.

With a bow toward Charlotte and Peg, Mike Zanios said, "Brick likes golf, but I only play because it makes me feel virtuous; like I just ate a helping of liver or cooked carrots." He laughed then, and set his hands down on Rosamund's shoulders, who tipped her head back and smiled up at him.

"Rosamund," Mike Zanios looked down at the girl and murmured, "you smell—delicious."

An awkward moment, Franny thought. Rosamund colored, and then Peg tapped her nails on the table—Peg appeared surprisingly frosty—and she asked, "Well, Roz? Aren't you going to tell him you swiped some of your old mom's perfume?"

Dully, Rosamund said, "It's Mom's perfume."

"Ah." Mike Zanios apparently recognized that his compliment had gone sour, and he winked at Peg, and said a lively, "No wonder you smell so nice!" and, then, Brick asked if he had ever told Mike the story of how the man on the Miami airplane mistook Rosamund for a twelve-year-old—

"Excuse me." Franny stood and started toward the rest rooms. She had not gotten far when Martie called from behind her, "Wait!" and so she waited, staring at the ceiling tiles pocked from an era when games of darts were allowed near the bar.

"Was it that idiotic story about the man on the plane that drove you away?" Martie whispered. "I mean, are we supposed to believe a grown man mistook a platinum blonde in a push-up bra and eyeliner for a twelve-year-old?"

Franny blurted a laugh, though she could not tell if Martie meant to imply that Rosamund had invented the airplane story, or that the man on the airplane had, indeed, said those things to Rosamund but not meant them. If she could have thought how to do it, Franny would have asked Martie to clarify the matter. She also would have asked what had happened between Martie and Darren Rutiger the night before. Also, did Martie know: Were she and Franny the Cinderellas? Or were they the evil stepsisters? Were they bound to find handsome princes, in the end? Or would they be forced to dance on burning coals, and have their eyes pecked out by a flock of crows?

While Franny went into the toilet stall, Martie whispered outside the door, "Anybody with half a brain can see why Dad trotted out that story, right? I mean, Zanios is drooling over Roz, so Dad's trying to tell himself that Roz *is* twelve. Maybe he's even trying to tell Zanios that Roz is twelve."

This made a certain amount of sense to Franny but it also depressed her. She hurried to wash her hands and leave the bathroom, and was somewhat cheered, upon returning to the table, to find Mike Zanios gone and the others now standing beside their chairs. Soon, they would be home and Franny could go to her room, and be by herself, and read poetry and write in the journal she had bought when she last went shopping with Christy Strawberry.

The waiter/wrestler stood leaning up against the bar as the family moved toward the door. He nodded. Maybe he did not mean to look ironic—maybe that was just his face. Franny glanced away from the ironic look. Her father, however, stopped right next to the boy, and the words he said to the boy made Charlotte Wahl gasp "Harold!" and the bartender, Jimmy—a slender mustachioed man who had always been friendly to Brick—step out from behind the bar.

"That's enough, Mr. Wahl," Jimmy said.

"You damn betcha that's enough!" Brick's upper lip quivered in agitation. "You get rid of this pipsqueak or forget about my business!"

His voice low, the bartender said, "I wouldn't threaten to take my business from a place I owed nine hundred dollars. Sir."

"Jimmy!" The little manager bustled toward them, all the while nodding apologetically to Charlotte. "Folks, please—"

Peg put her hand on Brick's arm—"Honey"—but he shook her off, and banged open the door on his way outside.

Charlotte Wahl was not an easily ruffled woman. On that day, however, as her daughter-in-law and granddaughters walked her to her car—Brick already sat scowling behind the wheel of the Wildcat—Charlotte declared, "Well, that's one more place I'll never be able to show my face again because of Harold."

"Oh, men!" Peg—looking wan—did her best to smile at her daughters as if they all had just shared a bit of fun.

Charlotte climbed into her Chrysler. Shut the door. Turned on the motor. "Are we dismissed, then?" Peg muttered.

No. With a hum, the Chrysler's electric window descended into its velvet slot. "I'm sending him a check," Charlotte said to Peg. "See he uses it to pay off that bar tab. I don't ever want to hear about that again."

"Hey, you guys: Knock, knock."

In the front seat, neither Peg nor Brick gave any sign of hearing Franny—neither had said a word since the country club—and in the back, Martie and Rosamund looked Franny's way with some irritation.

"Come on! Somebody ask 'Who's there?'"

"Who's there?" said Rosamund.

"Honolulu!"

"Honolulu who?"

"Now listen carefully, okay? Just—say 'Honolulu who?' again."

Rosamund sighed. "Honolulu who?"

Franny grinned as, carefully and slowly, she enunciated, "*Hon! Oh, it's Lulu, who you've been waiting for! I can see her coming up the sidewalk!* Hon-o-lu-lu. You get it?"

Rosamund groaned, but Franny laughed and, meaning to fill the car with the sound of merriment, she added, "No, it's extra good because I used the 'who.' *And* the person who answers *isn't* Lulu, see? It's somebody else, so you get the answer once removed, and I don't know if I've ever heard anybody do that before."

Rosamund smiled a little, then pointed out the window. "There's your favorite cottage."

Franny felt grateful to Rosamund for remembering the favorite cottage, a tiny place shingled in chocolate brown and sitting in a hollow below the road. Enormous basswoods surrounded the cottage, and the green moss on the roof was simultaneously sharp and soothing. Something else, however, had made the place magical to Franny:

One night, long before they had moved out to this side of the lake, the family had driven by the spot and Franny had seen a group of anonymous, enchanted kids through a window that let into the cottage's pitched upstairs. A golden window. The children conducted a parade with batons and paper hats, and Franny had thought, *I want to be one of them.*

Though, of course, she could not be one of those children if she lived in the cottage now. Now, she would have to be something else. Someone's beloved, maybe? A wife?

Back at the house, all three daughters filed upstairs, as if they had agreed to leave the first floor to Brick and Peg. Franny followed Rosamund into her room, and sat on the edge of one of the twin beds while Rosamund stood at her dressing table, and—with an occasional sigh—shifted into different patterns the photos she meant for the pages of her new album.

Rosamund—Franny wanted to ask Rosamund something. In her head, she kept forming the name *Rosamund,* preparing to ask her question, which was: Had Peg ever said to Rosamund, "Don't look too nice because then Dad will spend all dinner looking at you?" Sometimes, Peg said this to Franny and Franny wondered how to respond. Of course Brick had never spent a meal looking at Franny. He hardly spoke to her, if he could help it.

At any rate, Franny felt relieved that she had not asked Rosamund the question because here came Peg, smiling rather timidly, knocking on Rosamund's door frame.

"So what are you girls up to?" she asked.

"Nothing much," Rosamund said with a glance toward Franny.

Would they talk about the scene at the country club, Franny wondered? Would they like her to leave?

Peg stepped to Rosamund's side. "That's a handsome young man, isn't it?" She pointed to the album on the dresser, and Franny stood so she might look, too.

"James." Rosamund shook her head. "He's the one who got my friend Pam in trouble." Rosamund pointed at another picture, this one of a tanned girl in bra and underwear—perfect figure, perfect underwear—who stuck out her tongue at the photographer.

"So"—Peg glanced over at Franny, hesitated, then asked—"what happened?"

Rosamund smiled the nonchalant smile she used for stories with a bit of shock to them. "Pam was lucky. Her rich daddy came to school and flew her down to Mexico and that was that."

Franny tipped her head to one side—an attitude she hoped might suggest that she did not quite understand the story. In fact, she had heard it before, and knew that Rosamund meant the girl had had an abortion. Which, Rosamund said, was no big deal except in the United States, where it was illegal, so girls tried to do it to themselves with hangers and things, and ended up dead.

It startled Franny that Rosamund could speak of such things to their mother—the closest Peg had ever come to speaking of anything sexual to Franny was to tell her that if a boy ever tried to touch her, she should lift her knee between his legs as hard as she could. Still, from certain remarks that Peg had made over the summer, Franny gathered that Rosamund had told not just Franny, but Peg, too, that she was friends with a Miami heroin addict and a rich boy who stole cars for kicks. That she knew people from New York who sometimes went to Greenwich Village and smoked marijuana while they listened to jazz, and that her friend David, as Rosamund put it, liked boys better than girls.

Peg picked up the photograph of Pam. "After you were born"—she raised her eyes to meet Rosamund's eyes in the dressing table mirror—"people told me I couldn't get pregnant while nursing. Well, at first, I thought I just hadn't got my period back, but, pretty soon, uh-oh, I started getting sick in the mornings."

Rosamund gave her head a sympathetic shake. "Poor Mom."

"I tried everything!" Peg continued. "Bethie and I drove across every railroad track we could find. I took hot and cold baths and drank a whole cup of gin"—Peg made a face of revulsion, then laughed—"your dad and I rode horseback for hours—"

Franny had heard this story before, too. She knew that Rosamund had heard it, as well, for Franny had been in Rosamund's company at least once when Peg told it. Still, Rosamund behaved as if the story were perennially fresh and important. She managed to look both grave and amused, the perfect combination.

"Oh." Peg raised a finger to her lips as Martie's bedroom door opened: Sh.

"Hey, am I invited, too, guys?" Martie called, and stuck her head into Rosamund's room.

"Actually"—again, Peg winked into the mirror at Rosamund— "I'm just leaving, Martie."

Mother and daughter turned sideways to pass each other in the doorway, then, with a yawn, Martie flopped down on the nearest twin bed. "Guess I drove her away, huh? Could you believe Dad at the club, though?"

"It wasn't that big of deal, Martie." Rosamund waved a hand in the air. "Just—forget it."

"Sure." Martie raised herself on one elbow in order to peer around Franny to Rosamund. "We're supposed to be as pure as the Lennon Sisters, but Dad can be Mr. Toilet Mouth any old time."

Rosamund licked a photo corner. Pressed it to the album page with the ham of her hand. "He was just—he shouldn't have had a second drink before we went to the club, is all."

"Or a third, for that matter." Martie slid off the bed and moved to Rosamund's side, where she reached out a finger to set a photo square on the page.

"Martie"—Rosamund warned—"this is *my* album."

"Sorry, Your Highness! Hey"—Martie smiled at Franny—"you know what Dad'd really like about us being the Lennon Sisters? He could shut off the TV whenever he got bored!" She made the classic "pig face"—nose pulled high by a finger of the left hand; lower eyelids dragged down by the fingers of the right—"Remember who you are, where you are, and what you are, but never mind if your father tells a waiter to fuck off!"

"Will you shut up, Martie?"

To Franny's surprise, Rosamund's eyes were pink with misery, and filling with tears.

"I would think after *your* behavior last night"—

Martie folded her arms across her chest, stood taller, straighter. "What about my behavior, Rosamund?"

Rosamund did not answer, but Franny said, "Come on, you guys. I'll tell you another knock-knock joke if you're good."

"What *about* my behavior?"

"Well—you'd been drinking too hard." Rosamund slowly closed the photo album. Sniffled. "And you *know* why Dad drinks too hard sometimes. So you shouldn't criticize him."

Franny watched Martie's face to see if this change in the subject would satisfy her, and when Martie did not object, Franny added, "Because of that car accident, right?"

"Of course," Rosamund said, and Martie burst in, "You know I think what Dad did was beautiful, Roz!"

"I hate that girl, though," Franny said.

Martie and Rosamund looked at one another, then at Franny. "What girl?" Rosamund asked.

"The girl who *died*."

"But, Franny," Martie said, "she's dead."

"I don't care. You can hate dead people. She messed things up for our whole family, and I hate her."

"Well, all right," Rosamund said. Her lips started to twitch with suppressed laughter, and then Martie laughed out loud, and Franny bolted from the room and down the stairs and out the front door, running until she was a ways down Lakeside Drive.

A cool blonde, that was how Franny imagined the dead girl. Carefree, laughing, wearing some strapless thing that pressed tight around her breasts and under her arms. If that girl had somehow miraculously been able to arrive at the Wahl house, Franny would have barred the door against her without compunction. Pushed her away. Beat and scratched and kicked—

The sky over Lakeside Drive was a thin shell of glass, the inner curve of a lightbulb that now softened the asphalt road and baked the sandy shoulders and made the swamp exhale the vegetative breath of old men. In certain of the cottage yards she passed, grownups were at work: a man started charcoal in a grill, a couple spread a sail out to dry on a lawn. They were a distraction and plucked at her taut thoughts so that something like an off-key note rang through her, and she fixed her eyes on the patch of brown that was the Thomas cottage. The paint was the color of cattails and there was shade around the Thomas cottage—a homely shade made up of pine boughs that drooped like the wet swimsuits and towels on the Thomas clothesline—and it comforted her.

Turandot was the opera playing inside the Thomas cottage. The windows were open and the music came through the screens. Franny and Susan Thomas had listened to *Turandot* several times, and, once, "Nessun Dorma" made Franny cry, but, just now, the music left her ashamed. A few nights ago, over dinner, she had mentioned that the Thomases often played opera music, and Brick laughed and said, "Ah, yes, academics and their fraus tend to be a pretentious bunch," which was not what Franny had meant to say. Franny had meant to say how interesting it was that you did not need to know Italian to know that you listened to something beautiful. Yet she had laughed along with the rest of the family when Brick boomed a bit of fake opera in a fake language.

So what else was new? She set her knuckles to the Thomas door and knocked and Susan Thomas came, smiling, to let her in.

CHAPTER EIGHT

Because Ginny Weston had removed the vinyl cloth from the breakfast table that morning, after Franny jumped from the landing into the kitchen, and took a seat at the table, she spied the familiar but usually hidden spot where, years ago, a dreamy, love-struck Martie had written into the tabletop with a ballpoint pen:

ROGER
+
Martie
LOVE

You could feel the incised letters if you ran a finger across the wood. You could see the old oily black ink at the base of the tiny grooves.

"Look at this!" Brick had shouted when he saw Martie's declaration of love. "Our beautiful table defaced by just one more example of your asinine behavior!"

"But I love Roger!" Martie had said, which made Brick, and then Peg, even wilder, less rhetorical.

Roger Dale had calluses so thick from work on his family farm that he once entertained Franny and Martie by paring his palms with a steak knife. Right at this table. And hadn't Franny been sitting at this table—eating breakfast, just like now—when Peg screamed at Martie because Martie had come in from a date with Roger Dale bearing a hickey on her neck? "If ever I catch you in a horizontal position with a boy, you won't leave this house again till you graduate from high school!" Peg had said.

"Don't answer that phone!" So Franny wanted to shout up the stairs to Ginny Weston or Rosamund—everyone else had left for the day. The caller would almost certainly be Susan Thomas on the line, confirming that Franny meant to crew for her.

"Telephone, Franny!" Ginny Weston called down the stairs.

Susan Thomas.

While Franny told Susan Thomas, no, she was sorry but she could not crew today, she stared at a brass pitcher of daisies that sat on a shelf above the telephone. The rime of corrosion—white, black, turquoise—that bit into the pitcher's rim increased her squeamish feelings about the conversation, and she found she lacked the strength to offer the excuses she had considered earlier (I have chores, I'm grounded, I have to practice for my piano lesson at three).

Susan Thomas sat quietly for a time, but then, voice scratchy with both irritation and hurt feelings, she said, "It's because my parents tag along to the races, right?"

"No!" Actually, Franny was touched by the way that the Thomases followed Susan's tacking from their speedboat. Really, Franny did not know what it was that made her need to stay home. "I'm sorry," she murmured.

In a rush, Susan Thomas said, "My dad told me if you said no today, I can't ask you anymore. Since you're—unreliable. So, 'bye."

"Unreliable." The word buzzed in Franny's veins. Unreliable. He loves me, he loves me not. She reached out to pluck a daisy from the pitcher—for Bob Prohaski?—but the rough and leafy stem of the flower was entwined with other stems, and when she pulled, up came the whole bouquet, a putrid mess, the stems all gone to rot, and, quick, she hurried the pitcher out to the garage, set it on top of the freezer.

So. She started up the stairs. She would ask Rosamund, *Do you think I'm unreliable?* and Rosamund would say, *Of course not.*

At the top of the stairs, a chiffon scarf covering today's pin curls,

Ginny Weston stood polishing the newel post.

"Ginny"—Franny stopped with a yelp—"that's my shirt you're using for a rag!"

Ginny Weston inspected the striped T-shirt, now splotched with the orange of O'Cedar polish. "Your mom give it to me before she left, hon. Said it was rags. Sorry."

Franny found Rosamund in her bedroom, retroussé nose almost touching her dressing table mirror, mouth open in concentration as she applied mascara to her lashes. Franny took a seat on one of the twin beds. Smoothed her fingers back and forth on the corduroy bedspread. Darker in one direction, lighter in the other. Calming. Like fields of oats moving in the wind.

"Mom gave Ginny my T-shirt for a rag."

Rosamund turned to offer a pout of sympathy and a grin. "Probably 'cause you're getting to be such a hot tomato. And I've wondered, lately, if Mom's going through the change."

The change?

"When a woman stops having her period." Rosamund turned back to the mirror and began to groom the mascaraed lashes with a tiny comb. "It drives some of them crazy. Turner Haskin's dad has this mistress who's going through it, and lately she's been trying to seduce Turner!"

"His dad has a *mistress*?"

Rosamund laughed at Franny's surprise. "Oh, Fran," she said, "last night, I wish you could have seen it! A guy at the Top Hat sat in with the trio, and Annette, Mike's whatever you call her—*the singer*—she started flirting with the guy, so Mike and I pretended *we* were flirting. But wait—" She reached to her bedside table to raise the volume on the little radio there. A grown-up sort of song strained through the tiny speaker. Violins, a crooner. *You're out of reach-something-something*—

"Pretty," Franny said, albeit warily because suppose Rosamund said, *No, no, it's ghastly*.

"It is, isn't it?" Rosamund smiled. "A boy who wanted me to date him—he used to play that whenever I came into a party."

"And—did you ever go out with him?"

"No, but people got so they'd wait for me to show up—just to see if he'd still play the song."

Franny traced her initials on the corduroy. "Listen, though, Roz," she said, "what do you think I should do about Bob Prohaski?"

"Come on." Rosamund hopped up from her chair and signalled for Franny to follow her into the hall. "Timmy's taking me to work in just a minute." In front of the mirror at the top of the stairs, she stopped to tease her hair a bit higher. "So, why do you need to do anything about that Bob, anyway?" she asked.

The ringing bells of some TV game show indicated that Ginny Weston now had taken up ironing in Brick and Peg's room; still Franny answered in a low voice, "I don't—he's not that smart."

Rosamund laughed. "At your age, they don't need to be smart! And maybe they never need to be smart as long as there's lots of money and lots of honey!"

Lots of money and lots of honey. Franny could not believe that Rosamund meant that. That was some jingle that she had picked up from her Miami pals, or, maybe, some old movie. *How to Marry a Millionaire,* maybe—one of those movies designed to make you think that all a woman wanted was to be coddled and cosseted, that the only passion a woman really felt was for fur coats and diamond rings.

"Anyway, you can always tell him you can't see him. Tell him your mother disapproves. Which isn't even a lie."

True that her mother disapproved, Franny thought, but a lie that Franny would stop seeing him for that reason. If she loved him. If she loved him, she would never stop seeing him for any reason.

Rosamund shook her head at the mirror. "I know I don't actually look this good," she said, and Franny, now idly considering herself in the nearby "fat mirror," tugged Rosamund down the hall, toward the mirror closest to her own bedroom. "This one's best," she said. "I mean, most accurate."

"For bodies"—Roz nodded—"but it's got some kind of warp toward the top that stretches faces long."

Franny moved closer to the mirror, up next to Rosamund. Compared to Rosamund, Franny looked half-baked, didn't she? Maybe when she started to wear makeup—but, no, her face would still be long, shadowy, droopy-eyed.

"But, Roz," she said, "why doesn't Mom come out and say she disapproves of Bob?"

"She does!" Rosamund tilted her head onto Franny's shoulder. Smiled into the mirror. "Over and over again, hon!"

Franny smiled at Rosamund's reflection, then flushed and looked away—just as she would have had she come between a flirtatious glance and its target—when she understood that Rosamund's smile was only practice.

After Ginny Weston left for home that morning, Franny carried the library's Emily Dickinson book, along with her new notebook and a pen, to the screened porch. She closed the French doors separating the porch from the living room, then curled into one corner of the love seat.

In fear of her mother's ever again discovering a diary of her thoughts, Franny had written on the front of her new notebook, *Franny Wahl's Selected Poems of Emily Dickinson,* and, these days, instead of making personal entries, she copied into the notebook whatever Dickinson poem seemed closest to her own heart and mind. Today:

> *The Soul selects her own society—*
> *Then—shuts the Door—*

Unreliable. Susan Thomas's father had called her that? Well, maybe someone had once called Emily Dickinson unreliable, too. Emily Dickinson did not much like to go out in public.

> *I've known her—from an ample nation—*
> *Choose one—*

At the creak of the French doors' opening, Franny leapt from the love seat, crushing both journal and poetry book to her chest.

Brick. Looking abashed. "Sorry if I frightened you, dear," he said. "I just came to pick up some papers."

"Oh." She raised her hand to her neck and laughed at her heart-thumping panic. "I'm—okay."

"Well, good. That's good." He ran his hand over the top of his crew cut. Back and forth. "I forgot your mom wasn't going to be here this noon. I thought I'd have lunch with her."

Franny nodded. Maybe he was feeling worried over something, and needed Peg to tell him it was all right. Sometimes Peg could do that for him, Franny knew—they all laughed about it, and called it "fluffing up Brick."

But suppose Franny made him lunch. Suppose it cheered him, and he said, "This is real tasty, honey. You're growing up to be a fine young lady." It was not impossible. Susan Thomas's parents said such things to Susan, and, just a few days ago, at the China Castle, Franny and Christy Strawberry and Joan Harvett had seen an entire family whose contented members bent so close over their little table that their heads almost touched. *Check out the cornballs,* Franny had whispered to Joan Harvett and Christy Strawberry, though her longing to leap into that cozy circle actually made her dizzy. Her thoughts skipped—little blanks—as if she were a scratched record, and to save herself, she began to sing a very loud rendition of *"Cuando caliente el sol,"* which forced not just that charmed family to look up, but other patrons as well. Christy and Joan had found this hysterically funny, but Franny had known her behavior was hideous. Even then, she knew.

"Dad?" She stepped out into the kitchen where Brick now shook aspirin from the bottle they kept by the sink. "If you haven't eaten, I can make you lunch."

"Oh?" he said. He would have preferred to stop at Mike's Top Hat on his way back to the office. She could see that as soon as she spoke. Eat a steak sandwich. Have a drink. Still, he nodded. He meant to be nice. "I guess that'd be okay."

*   *   *

Supposedly, when Rosamund and Martie had been small, Brick always came home to the house on Ash Street for lunch. Maybe if he had come home when Franny were growing up, she would have known him better. This beefy man with fine red hairs on the backs of his big fingers, now lifting to his mouth a spoonful of soup: What did a person say to him?

"So, how's your soup, Dad?"

He gave her a winking grimace. "Awful salty!" he said, but in a voice so enthusiastic, so peppy, she wondered if she had heard him right.

"I made it like they said on the can."

He smiled and nodded. "Awful salty!" He pushed back his chair from the table, and picked up his sandwich from his plate. "Think I'll be okay, though, once I scrape some of the glurp off this sandwich!" As if he were some comic sneak, Brick raised his shoulders and tiptoed to the bread board and, there, snatched up a knife and scraped off the mustard and mayonnaise Franny had put on the bread.

"Ta-da!" He smiled at her, and winked, as if they now had triumphed over the small disaster that was her making of the lunch. But then something made him frown. Something outside. "Ahem." He jerked his head toward the window that opened on the sideyard. Took a long, whistling in-breath. "Looks like somebody's on his way up to the house from the road."

Bob Prohaski. And not alone. She could hear the sound of two boys laughing as they made their way around the garage to the front door. Brick widened his eyes—very wide, an awkward-looking stretch that actually made it possible to see the bulge of the cornea—but did that mean she should go outside or not? She took a bite of her own sandwich. Chewed.

"Aren't you going to go say hello, Fran?"

Without answering, she stood and carried her plate to the sink. She could tell he watched as she walked to the back hall, and this made her movement awkward, stilted.

*   *   *

"Franny!" Bob Prohaski grasped her hand and pulled her down the front steps to the mulberry tree, beneath which sat a smiling, berry-eating boy whom Franny did not recognize: Legs akimbo on the lawn. Big, bare belly. Blond baby face.

"Roy Hobart," said the boy, and waved a purple palm.

"He went to Holy Family," Bob Prohaski said. "He's starting at St. Joe's in the fall."

Roy Hobart shook his head. "Bob and I were having a blast at Shelly McDonald's but there wasn't a thing would do for Bob but we come see you!" Roy Hobart gave the house an admiring look. "I heard this can be a rocking place."

Bob Prohaski grinned and grabbed Franny to his chest. He smelled of sweat and dust from having hitchhiked to the house. A person was not supposed to like those smells, and the fact that Franny did made her wonder if perhaps there were something wrong with her. Maybe she was too much of a sensualist. Sensuous? Sensual? One of them was okay, and one was not, and Franny suspected she was the wrong one.

"I missed you," Bob Prohaski murmured, then grinned at Roy Hobart in a way that made Franny feel uncomfortably on display.

Roy Hobart snorted. "Take a look at his right hand if you don't believe it."

Franny backed out of the boy's embrace and took hold of the hand. A series of scrapes marked the knuckles, and the skin around the scrapes blushed with infection. "What happened?"

He squeezed her to him again, so tight it hurt. "Hit a wall," he said with a surprised laugh.

"He hit a fucking wall!" Roy Hobart dropped onto his belly and began to softly pound the ground with his fists.

Franny tried to break free of Bob Prohaski's grip, asking in pained breathlessness, "But why would you hit a wall?"

"'Cause I missed you!" Bob Prohaski crowed.

Franny struggling to free herself, Bob holding her tight, the pair moved about the yard in a kind of bumbling dance. Behind the mulberry tree, they went. Past the pump house, up onto the front steps and down again. A dance of resistance and restraint.

"Stop!" Franny pleaded. "My dad may be watching!"

A guffaw rose from deep in Bob Prohaski's chest.

"You might mention you were drunk when you hit that wall, Prohaski!" Roy Hobart called.

"I'm *stopping*, Bob," Franny said, "*really*." She leaned deep into his steamy embrace. "Stop!"

Panting happily, he stopped. Placed a damp kiss on her ear. From the house came the sound of piano music. "Cantabiles." The piece that Franny should have been practicing for this afternoon's lesson.

"Who's in there?" Bob Prohaski asked.

"My *dad*."

"Christ"—the boy gave a panting laugh—"that sucker does hate my guts!"

Franny shook her head. "Please, don't call him that."

"What do you want him to call him? 'Papa'?" Roy Hobart gave Franny a look of shrewd appraisal. Clearly, she disappointed him. She was not the girl he had expected. Bob Prohaski, on the other hand, looked at Franny with new interest, as if she were, perhaps, a pet that had just locked him out of the house; despite the inconvenience, the new trick tickled him, and he smiled, and wrapped her hair around his fist, and pulled her head back so that she had no choice but to look up into his eyes.

"That hurts, Bob!"

"You," he murmured in her ear. "You—"

"More likely her papa hates your dick than your guts!" said Roy Hobart, and trumpeted on a blade of grass: *Plh! Plh! Plh!*

For one moment, Bob Prohaski grinned at Roy Hobart, but then his face grew dour. "Watch your mouth!" He let go of Franny's hair and smoothed his hand down her neck. "Have a little respect, man. This is my girl, and I've been missing her."

Plh! Plh! Roy Hobart lowered his blade of grass. "That's why you got drunk, right?"

Franny turned from the boys. The wrong thing to do, she understood immediately. Bob Prohaski would take her turning away as the kind of concerned disapproval that boys expected girls to demonstrate over their antics; really, she just wanted to turn away, get her bearings.

"You mad, Franny?" Bob Prohaski whispered in her ear. From behind, he placed his hands on her waist. She felt like a pioneer woman when he did that. Strong and loving. As if he were the one for whom she waited. But she knew that if she turned around, looked at him, all of that would fade.

"Listen," he whispered, "I'm going to get you a present. And you know what it is?"

It was good he could not see her face; that she could say, without looking at him, "You don't need to get me anything, Bob. Really. I don't want you spending money on me."

"Money? No, this is great. I went into Hanson's with my brother to make a payment on his class ring, and they got these watches on chains." He reached over her shoulder, made claws of his fingertips. "Right near the door, if you know what I mean."

"No stealing! If you get caught, you'll end up in Eldora!"

"Rod got his girl one." Bob Prohaski pulled Franny's arm behind her and twisted the wrist. "I'm going to get you one, too."

Though she did not want to embarrass Bob Prohaski in front of his friend, it occurred to her that, if she had to, she could kick him in just the way he had told her you could kick a man when you needed to "massacre" him, fast, in a fight—which was perhaps the same way her mother meant you could kick a man if he put his hand in some private place.

"You're hurting me again!" she whispered. "Stop it!"

He did not stop, however, but went on in a rush, "What this watch does—it's a little acorn, see, and you can open up the top and tell what time it is."

It hurt to break loose from him—the skin on her wrists burned—but then she was running, bounding barefoot across the lawn and around the house and down the concrete stairs to the dock, where the boards bounced and sang beneath her feet.

The icy temperature of that spring-fed lake momentarily took away her breath, but the water quickly became skin, and her shorts and shirt became the wafting fins of a sea creature, and she swam away from shore.

"Franny!" Bob Prohaski called from the top of the stairs. "Get back here!"

Could she elude nonswimming Bob through the use of pools and lakes and rivers and ponds? She gave a panicky laugh, then choked on a bit of water, which brought her up short, and she turned to look back.

On the dock, Roy Hobart now bent over at the waist, unlacing his shoes.

"No!" she shouted. "I'm coming! Stay there!"

The thought of being in the same body of water as Roy Hobart alarmed her, and she thrashed her arms and legs in a mad effort to return to the shore as quickly as possible.

Bob Prohaski seated himself on the dock as she drew near, and she called to him, hoping to sound gay, "Fancy meeting you here, mister!"

"Jesus." He pulled off his shoes. "You're a funny girl, Franny!"

She smiled, but did not feel funny or nice or even safe. Since the boys' arrival, the sky had gone beige and granular, like lard. Maybe it was going to rain. She treaded water there at the end of the dock. Parsnips, or some other vegetable grown underground, that was what Bob Prohaski's wan town boy's feet resembled as he dangled them over the edge of the dock. They made Franny pity the boy, and she tugged on his toes to make him laugh again before she hoisted herself from the water.

"Whoa, Franny!" said Roy Hobart.

"Franny." Bob Prohaski grinned. Tried not to grin, dividing his glances between her and the now leering Roy Hobart. "Here—" He snagged a towel from the seat of the rowboat, and threw it her way. "Put that around you!" he barked, and though she did as he said, she felt mortified and furious and started up the dock in silence.

They came after her, Bob Prohaski hissing at Roy Hobart to be quiet, just shut up, man, be cool.

Her father was loading a case of empty deposit bottles into the old Mercedes when Franny and the boys came around the side of the house to the driveway, and when he saw the girl, he let the case drop into the trunk with a thump.

"For God's sake! You're making a display of yourself!" he declared.

She flushed, then waved a vague hand toward the boys. "They're just leaving. I'm going in to do my practice."

Brick slapped his hands together. Something about that slapping—the slow motion of it, and the way he, then, drew a finger up to the edge of his lip and pulled—let her know that he had been drinking while she was outside with the boys. She hoped the boys did not know. It had occurred to her recently that if people knew your father drank too much, you might be less safe in the world.

"Guess he ain't going to offer us a ride to town," Roy Hobart murmured as Brick disappeared into the garage.

The boys began to work their way across the old baseball diamond, down into the ditch, and, then, up and out to the road. The size of the Nearys' bull, penned in its private triangle of pasture, must have intimidated them for they bent down and took up rocks from the shoulder of Lakeside Drive before sticking out their hitch-hiking thumbs.

A green car whizzed past as they started to work their way, backward, down the road. Next: a gray station wagon, empty but for its male driver. Out this far, there were not so many opportunities for rides, and Franny shouted from the drive, "Put down those rocks! You guys look scary!"

Bob Prohaski cupped a hand by his ear.

"The rocks look scary!"

He shook his head—apparently he could not hear what she was saying, and he started toward her.

No! She pantomimed holding something in her hand, crouching, setting the thing down. At her back, Brick's shoes scuffed the drive. "What do they have the rocks for?" he asked.

She hesitated. Bob Prohaski stood in the ditch, holding up his rock-filled hands as if to say, *Now what?* To please her father, it seemed to Franny that all she needed to do was to laugh; to act as if the boys were silly, dismissible, hardly even real. And so she did, saying, "They're scared of the bull."

Brick shook his head and he laughed, too, but then he did something that left Franny feeling both thankful and betrayed:

He raised a hitchhiker's thumb high in the air for Bob Prohaski to see. He mimicked holding on to a steering wheel, then pointed to himself and, then, to the spot just beyond the Poddigbattes Camp sign, where, sure enough, a minute later, he stopped the old Mercedes in order to give the boys a ride to town.

CHAPTER NINE

A CCORDING TO MARTIE, FRANNY WAS IN FOR A TREAT. MARTIE meant to take Franny somewhere special before driving her to piano lessons—*Hurry it up, I left the car running, we're wasting gas*.

Franny sighed on her way to the piano to fetch her books. The truth of the matter: Special trips with Martie often ended in disaster, or at least unpleasantness. There had been numerous occasions in which, supposedly on an outing to the Dairy Queen, Franny found herself endlessly "scooping the loop" or, say, languishing on a pile of automobile tires while Martie visited a certain on-duty gas station attendant. "You should feel privileged Deedee and I let you in on this!" Martie said the time that Franny protested a series of trips back and forth past a rival's house in order to watch the comings and goings of a cinnamon-haired "Donny"—trips that finally did stop when the girl's furious father darted out from behind a tree and snapped off the Mercedes' radio antenna.

"So"—Franny settled herself in the convertible's front seat, piano books on her knees—"where we going?"

"It's a *surprise*." Martie lowered her sunglasses into place, released a drag of smoke.

"Can I have a cigarette, too, please?"

"*May* I." Martie handed the girl the pack from her purse. "And as you can see, it's my last one."

"*May* I. If you stop at Karlins', I'll buy you more."

"I don't approve. Nor do I approve of you wearing T-shirts anymore. You don't see me wearing T-shirts, do you?"

Franny looked down at the dry clothes into which she had just changed. "I'm not *wearing* a T-shirt."

Martie frowned. "What?"

"I'm not *wearing* a T-shirt!" Franny hated conversations in the car with the top down, having to raise her voice so everything felt like an argument. "Did *you* tell Mom to get rid of my T-shirts?"

"We discussed it."

"Sometimes, Martie, you're nuts. I swear to God."

Martie smiled at the road ahead. "And you, my dear, are rude, crude—and *skewed*." She leaned forward to turn up the radio. KIOA. From Des Moines. The crackle and hiss were hardly bearable. It had been the ROTC member who had assured Martie—and Franny, too—that KIOA was far superior to the Pynch station, and, even now, Franny felt a little disloyal when, lying in bed at night, she tipped her clock radio this way and that in an attempt to bring in the more famous stations in Chicago, Oklahoma City, Little Rock.

"Horses." Martie pointed her cigarette toward a pair of bays that stood in the dense shade of an old oak that grew close by the road.

"Pretty," Franny said.

Martie gave her cigarette a practiced flick out the window. "You've never been around first-rate horses, have you? There's a girl at school—her father's Scotsman Potato Chips—and he bought her a prize Arabian. He sends a trailer back and forth whenever she likes—the way you do if you're a serious horse owner. *I'm* the sort of person who should have a horse like that. I mean, that girl's won awards, but I'm sure I could have, too. If I'd had her horse, and a chance to compete and all. I mean, I love horses more than anybody loves horses, right?"

Franny scrutinized the passing fences, the trees. She refused to do it, to declare, *Yes, Martie, you love horses more than anybody*.

"When Dad got rid of my horse—not that it was a great horse—he said I didn't ride enough!" Martie laughed harshly. "How was I supposed to ride if nobody drove me to the stables?"

On their left, a large basswood had been split in two by a recent storm and, for just a moment, Franny thought of reminding Martie of the time, years ago, that a tree in the vacant lot near their house on Ash Street had been hit in that same way. A group of neighborhood kids—big and small—had spent an entire gray-green misty Saturday puttering around that tree, popping up out of its still leafy branches, sucking on green wood. It had been Martie who introduced Franny and the others to the delicate sweetness to be found in the green wood beneath the bark.

From past experience, however, Franny knew that if she were to mention that day, now, it was unlikely that Martie would remember Franny's presence at the scene at all; instead, Martie would remember only that a boy named Eddie Graham had happened by, and invited Martie on a hayride.

An invitation which, of course, Franny remembered, too.

As if she did not live just her own life, no, she lived her sisters' lives as well.

With a swing of the wheel, Martie turned the Wildcat into the tiny lot in front of Karlins' Grocery, pulled past the pair of antiquated gas pumps, and parked.

"*I'll* go in," Martie said. "You're underage."

Franny settled back in the convertible. Stared out at the dusty lilac bushes that grew between Karlins' and the now dilapidated former home of her old Sunday school friend Kimmy Estep. Franny had slept in that house once, her first overnight ever, an occasion fraught with strangeness. Mr. Estep had joined the girls at Crazy Eights while Mrs. Estep settled herself on the couch with the baby. The Esteps seemed entertained, but Franny found herself overwhelmed by the idea of a father playing a child's card game with his daughter and his daughter's friend. She felt nervous. Mr. Estep sat in an easy chair while the girls sat on the floor, and each time that he leaned forward to pick up cards from the hassock they used for a card table, the floor lamp turned his bald head into a glowing bulb that looked as if it might melt or explode with its own heat. Franny had never before given a thought to Mr. Estep's appearance, but that night she grasped at straws. She decided Mr. Estep's baldness—or some other terrible vulnerabil-

ity, some form of retardation—had made him and his wife out-
casts who had nothing to do on a weekend night but stay home
with their children—

"'How's Roz?'" Martie said as she got back into the car, slamming the door shut.

"What?"

"'*How's Roz?*' I see Al Castor in there, and that's about the
first thing he says to me! Anyway"—looking quite keen now, Martie pulled out of the lot and back onto Lakeside—"you want to
know where we're going? To a rehearsal of The Craft."

In order to conceal her interest in what Martie had said, Franny
busied herself with lining up the books in her lap (the roughly covered Schaum from which it seemed she would never graduate; the
slick *More Etudes*). She stared straight ahead at the causeway. A
rehearsal of The Craft. Martie should have warned her. At least
Franny could have combed her hair, then.

"You can't tell anyone because it's at a *house*. Which is why I'm
taking you. It wouldn't look good if I went alone."

Franny squinted past the silver sheets of swamp water, as if it
were important to hold on to a view of Mother Goose Miniature
Golf's plywood Miss Muffett and her dangling spider—both of
them now disappearing into the cloud of pesticides with which a
masked figure fogged the course's perimeter.

"Well?" Martie cast a sharp glance Franny's way. "What do you
say? It's a privilege, you know."

It would have been nice to be able to show Martie pleasure, but
Martie might well decide Franny was too enthusiastic, and then
blow up at Franny, and not let her go to the rehearsal at all, and so
Franny said only a quiet "Thanks."

"'*Thanks*'? Jeez, they're only being courted by Columbia
Records, Franny!"

Franny nodded. Would Richie Craft mention Franny's taking
the bourbon from the liquor cabinet? "Martie." Franny pointed
ahead to the three-legged setter, now dashing out from the trailer
court and toward the road. "There's that dog."

"Any-*way*," Martie said, when they were safely past the setter, and it headed toward what Franny assumed was its home, a pink trailer whose artificial geraniums were forever toppling out of their pink window boxes.

Woolf Beach. Then the water tower. As they passed the chain-link fence surrounding the swimming pool of Stanford Fanning Fellow College, Martie stubbed out her cigarette and said, with a shake of her head, "Did you hear Mom and Dad actually suggested I take a summer school course at SFF? In typing, no less!"

"Weird," Franny said. "Well, you know they're weird."

In town, the trees grew thicker, and arched over the street, and Franny tilted her head back to stare up at that shuffle of milky sky and green, green, green, but the canopy thinned when Martie turned onto Lincoln Way. The sky opened and Franny straightened in her seat, and looked about herself. She had a vague memory of this area as cornfields, then a clearer memory of days when the gallows of framing stood up against the cerulean sky of a long gone autumn.

The house before which Martie brought the Wildcat to a stop was a ranch-style. White shutters with a purely decorative function. The overgrown yard in front and around the sides of the place was a wild patch amidst the neighborhood's trim green lawns. According to Martie—now putting her sunglasses in their case, and the case in her purse; making an effort to appear very businesslike and grown up, Franny thought—according to Martie, Richie Craft's parents had moved to Arizona the summer before, but had kept the Pynch Lake house so that Richie could finish his last year of high school with his band. "Isn't that cool?" she asked Franny. "That kind of support for your kid?"

"Turn On Your Love Light" was the song the band played. The bass thumped in Franny's chest as she and Martie approached the home's ivied entry. Franny could not help grinning—just the way she grinned when the drums in a parade passed by—but when Martie saw that grin, she flared her nostrils at the girl.

"You sure you can behave yourself?"

Franny resisted the urge to scoff. She stared at a tendril of ivy that had worked its way under the brass street numbers—630—affixed to the entry wall.

"Remember who you are, where you are, what you are," Martie murmured. "We sit quiet. We listen to the music. If anything seems inappropriate—if anybody offers us a drink or anything—we get up and go. Immediately."

Franny pointed to a tiny plastic box lit up by a tiny lightbulb: the doorbell button. Martie shook her head. "He said just to come in."

The front hall of The Craft house was dark but it was possible to see the grimy path that cut through the celery green carpet and the gouges in the wallpaper.

Wide-eyed, Martie brought her mouth close to Franny's ear to say, "Would Mom and Dad kill us if we did something like this to a house of theirs, or what?"

It was not far from the front door to the wide portal that opened on what had clearly been the family's living room. Now the room contained nothing but the band members and their musical instruments and beat-up boxes and trunks and cords and electric fans that stirred the heavy white drapes that hung, closed, at the windows. On the carpet, her back against the living room wall, sat Richie Craft's beautiful girlfriend, the caramel-corn girl from Stacey's Sweets. In her lap lay a yellow cat. A perfect picture, but the girl quickly disturbed it by jumping to her feet and striding past Franny and Martie in a huff.

Franny tried not to gawk, but weren't those baby-doll pajamas she wore? In the middle of the afternoon?

Also: Did a person look at the hands of band members while they played their instruments? Did she portion out her glances: a glance at the drummer, then the boy guitarist, the piano player, the trumpeter, then Richie?

At the break, Richie Craft mumbled an apology for the behavior of his girlfriend. He tucked a slice of his dark and shiny hair behind his ear, then pulled it out again. "She's just in one of her moods."

Martie nodded agreeably. "That's okay. Oh, and this is my little sister, Richie."

"I remember," Richie said with a smile, "sure." Then, so he and Martie would not find her in the way, Franny knelt to pet the fat gold cat now rubbing up against her legs.

The Craft's possible contract with Columbia was the topic of Martie and Richie's discussion. And The Craft's manager, Tony Zanios, brother to Mike Zanios. Was Tony any good, and how was Richie supposed to know? Maybe he stunk. What'd Martie think of the horns they'd added? Were horns good?

Martie began to talk about the days when Richie Craft had played with a group called The Countrymen. "'Scotch and Soda,'" Martie said. "I loved that!"

"And 'Green Fields,'" said Franny. "You guys came to a chili supper at my grade school and you played 'Green Fields.'"

"Hey, Phil," Richie Craft called to a prematurely balding young man just then fiddling with a portable organ in the corner, "this one liked our 'Green Fields.'"

Phil smiled at Franny and nodded, then asked Martie if there might be a party out at the house that weekend, he'd heard there had been some good parties. Martie said, yeah, there had been, but they were taking a little break from parties just now, and then Richie turned to talk to a boy at work on an amplifier, and Franny slipped off to find a bathroom, and maybe a comb—

How odd that house felt! Every curtain had been drawn against the day, and the strained light that came through the white cloth reminded Franny of the nursing homes to which she and her seventh-grade Y-Teens group had gone caroling at the holidays. Two thin slabs of the kitchen counters' olive Formica were missing, which gave the counters the look of an incomplete puzzle. The oven door lay on the table in the breakfast nook. Still, the sink was not piled with dirty dishes. Trash did not spill out of bags. It could have been worse.

She supposed the door to her left might lead to a powder room, but, no, that was the broom closet, and she blushed as if caught snooping. The next door—its handle sticky with honey or jam—led to a set of basement stairs; but then came a hall in which she could see, through a far door, the ticking of a bare mattress, a tumble of sheets and blankets on the floor—

Someone was crying. A girl, of course. It seemed Franny could hardly go anywhere lately without finding a girl, crying.

"Hello?" She stepped into the hall, then walked a bit farther until, on her left, a door opened onto the bathroom that seemed to hold the crying girl.

"You okay in there?" Franny called.

"Who's that?"

Franny stepped through the doorway. On the wall were a pair of the plaster mermaids Franny remembered people hanging in bathrooms back in the fifties—though someone had modified these two: added four red paint nipples, one of which had dripped all the way to the tip of the mermaid's tail.

"Over here."

In the room's pink tub, behind a pink shower curtain, lay Richie Craft's girlfriend, stretched out, toes pressed against the spigot end of the tub. "I've seen you before," the girlfriend said—*growled*. Suddenly self-possessed, the girl sat up and wiped away her tears. "What are you doing here?"

Back in the living room, the band began to play "Green Fields" and, hoping to appear nonchalant, Franny waved a hand toward the music. "We just came to hear the practice. Are you okay?"

"'Are you okay?'" The girl gave Franny a murderous look. She held up an aspirin bottle. Empty. White with dust. "Take this to Richie," she said. "Tell him I took every last pill in here, and the bottle was full when I started."

At Franny's interruption of "Green Fields," Martie's face went red in anger and shame. The band members looked peeved, too, but when they understood what Franny said, they rushed to the bathroom.

Because Franny led the way, and Martie followed, by the time the others pressed into the room, the two sisters found themselves awkwardly boxed into the far corner, one of them on either side of the pink toilet. *How many aspirin were in the bottle*, Richie Craft pleaded with the girl, and Martie called toward the door, "Get an ambulance!"

"What is that bitch doing here?" the caramel-corn girl demanded. "Tell her to get out of here!"

"She's just trying to help, Patty. Now stop it," said Richie Craft, and then he and the pompadoured drummer climbed into the pink tub and lifted the girl out.

"Put her in my car!" Martie said. "I'll take her!"

"I'm not going anywhere with you!" The girl stuck out her tongue at Martie, and then at Franny, too. "You bitches stay away from Richie or I'll scratch your faces off!"

Sorry, Richie mouthed to Martie as he and the drummer backed out of the bathroom with the girl, who alternately struggled and hung like dead weight.

From the bathroom window, Franny and Martie watched the group pile into the car. When Martie sighed, Franny thought she understood: It was difficult not to feel left behind. After the car disappeared up the road, the house sat solidly silent. There was no sound but the twitter of birds outside the bathroom window, the whir of water leaking from the toilet tank.

Franny reached down and jiggled the handle on the tank. It was an automatic gesture, like turning off the lights when you left the room. You never let a toilet run or Peg would yell, "Somebody jiggle that handle!"

"Hey, look." Martie pointed at the toilet: A small heap of white stuff—cottage cheese?—rested in the base of the bowl. When Franny recoiled, Martie said, "It's *aspirin*. That girl dumped the aspirin in there but the toilet didn't flush them all."

It was irrational, she knew, but Franny felt cheated, almost disappointed by the news. "So, she was just *faking*?"

Martie leaned over the sink to the medicine cabinet mirror and wiped at the makeup smeared beneath her eyes. She had been crying a little, Franny realized.

"Well," Martie said, "it's for sure she wasn't faking being pregnant."

"Pregnant? How do you know she's pregnant?"

"What do you think she was wearing, Fran?"

"Shorty pajamas?"

"*Maternity* clothes." Martie glanced at the toilet, then pressed down on the handle until all signs of the aspirin were gone.

CHAPTER TEN

Rosamund Wahl never did say just when Turner Haskin would arrive in Pynch Lake. "He'll come when he comes, if he comes at all," she said lightly, and, using that same light voice, on the last day of July, she strolled into the den and jingled her key ring, and asked Franny and Joan Harvett—the girls were watching *P.M. Matinee*—if they would like to ride out to the airport to pick up Turner Haskin.

Very cool. As if the arrival of Turner Haskin were a trip to the Dairy Queen. In the car, however—driving at speeds that thrilled the girls—Rosamund did speak of Turner Haskin with some ardor:

In acting class, he had learned to speak to a camera as if it were flesh and blood. Rosamund once saw a clip of him and was truly impressed. "He's not sure acting is his path, but I know he could have a career like some of those serious but terribly good-looking stars. Like, Laurence Harvey or Montgomery Clift."

In addition, Rosamund informed the girls, Turner Haskin could tell if you were a virgin just by watching the way you walked. "We'd all be at the beach or a club and a girl would go by, and he'd say, 'That one, yes, that one, no.'"

"That's so cool!" Joan Harvett squealed, and abandoned her attempts to curl her eyelashes in the sunshade mirror, and fell back against the car seat. Franny doubted anyone possessed Turner Haskin's supposed skill, but she wanted to participate in Joan's wonderment, and so she added, "His dad has a mistress and she's been trying to seduce Turner."

"*Franny*," Rosamund demurred.

"You said it was no big deal."

"Still."

In the airport parking lot, Rosamund offered around her tube of Pure Pearl lipstick and Joan gave it a try. "Do I look awful?" she whispered to Franny as they climbed from the car.

"You look fine."

Joan moaned. Tugged at her short-shorts. She was a sturdy, excitable girl, a compulsive hair-comber and executor of sit-ups for her board-hard little belly. The only thing that looked a bit off about Joan was the four pink patches left on her cheeks by the Scotch tape she used to "set" her cheek curls each night.

"I bet he thinks I'm a turd, Franny."

"Hsss!" Franny raised her hands in cat's claws at the girl, then whispered, "He's coming to see *Roz*, Joan."

The Pynch Airport was a simple, concrete-block structure, just large enough to support a coffee shop frequented not so much by travelers as by the farmers and businessmen who stopped in for the cinnamon rolls. Franny had rarely visited the place, and with the big fans blowing her shirt against her skin, and the polished concrete under her bare feet, she felt foreign, there, uprooted.

"Oh, my god," Joan Harvett yowled when Turner Haskin (tall and dark and handsome, yes, and perfectly stylish in baby blue pants and cordovan loafers) ducked out from one of the small planes that served the airport.

"What'd I tell you?" Rosamund said, then stepped away from the girls and up to the gate.

"Let's give them privacy," Franny said. She led Joan Harvett back to the terminal's front doors. A long panel of lawn and pink and yellow snapdragons had been planted between the two roads that led up to and away from the building. On the outer edges of the roads, broad swaths of mowed grass ran for a hundred yards or so, up to fenced fields of corn, the stalks tall now, their long leaves stirring, a little eerie in the sunlight.

Isn't it green here? Those were the first words she heard Turner

Haskin say as he and Rosamund came up toward the doors. *Isn't it green?*

Over a candlelit dinner that night, Turner Haskin told the Wahls all about his opera-singer mother. "She could have had a brilliant career but some fascinating man always wanted her to fly some-where with him. How could she stay home to practice *Un Ballo in Maschera* when Mr. Mankowitz needed her opinion on where to build a villa on the Côte d'Azur?" Turner Haskin threw his hands in the air in imitation of his mother's pleasant dismay. The evening air was soft and warm on the skin, and everyone laughed. Brick and Peg smiled and nodded. Rosamund looked proud. Martie, who had been disgruntled about giving Turner Haskin the use of her room, now stretched her arms so far across the dining room table that she gripped the other side.

"The family of a friend of mine has a place on the Riviera! Such lovely people!" Martie tossed back a gulp of the Beaujolais Brick was pouring as he made his way around the table. "They know how to live!" She paused to shake her head and grin at Brick and Peg in some sort of loving reproof. "They have a maid, and the maid wears a uniform, and—it's cool, it's professional."

Brick paused at Turner Haskin's elbow to say, "You should understand, Turner, this comes from a girl who, a few months back, didn't think we should have cleaning help at all. At Christmas, we were capitalist pigs, right, Martie?"

Martie smiled at Brick and raised her glass in a solitary toast. "Oink, oink," she said gaily, then confided to Turner Haskin, "My father likes to tease me about the period when I dated a member of SDS. Milton Altman. Have you ever heard of him? Apparently, his family was of B. Altman fame, but Milton ends up helping write the Port Huron Statement—"

"Oh, Martie, Martie," Peg Wahl said quite merrily, "if I were you, I'd take some of those stories from school with a grain of salt." Peg had exceeded her usual single glass of wine that evening, and she now began to relate a story in which she happened to make a surprise visit to a girlfriend at Iowa State. "In all innocence, with her roommates right there, I said, 'Celia, why have you got a picture of the library on your dresser?'—not knowing Celia had been passing it off as a photo of her family home!"

While everyone laughed at Peg's story, Brick, poised behind Franny's chair, set his bottle of wine over Franny's empty glass of milk, then said, "What the hell?" and filled it.

Everyone laughed at that, too, and they laughed again when Franny said, imitating Brick's basso voice, "What the hell?" and took a swig of the slightly gray concoction.

"Brick!" Peg cried. "She'll make herself sick! Franny!"

Franny grinned at Brick, and finished off the glass, and that made everyone laugh, too.

Turner Haskin had lived in Milan and New York City as well as several Florida resort areas. Turner Haskin made being the child of divorced parents sound like a treat. Of course, he had received the best of care. Been spoiled by doting relatives and the staff at his father's hotel. If his mother did go on tour, his Italian grandmother stuffed him with candy apples and cannelloni—

"Candy apples," Brick broke in. "Boy, that brings back memories! When I was in college, working in the kitchen of this little breakfast joint—Barney's—my sis stopped by one day." Brick took a sip from his wine. "My parents thought a boy should put himself through school, but sis had everything nice, and she lived in the sorority house and all. So this one day she shows up at Barney's with a big box of gorgeous candy apples! 'Gosh, sis,' I said—I was mopping the floor at the time—'I'd sure love to have one of those,' and she looks straight at me"—Brick reared back and made his voice high with girlish indignation—"'But, Harold, I have just enough for the sisters!'" Brick laughed wryly. "As if I weren't her actual brother, you see?"

Peg leaned forward to tap Turner Haskin on the arm. "She was spoiled rotten. Got everything while Brick had to scramble."

Turner Haskin smiled at Brick. "Well, someone should have told you, Brick, that the best way to avoid trouble with brothers and sisters is to be an only child."

"Ah hah"—Peg threw herself back in her chair so hard it gave an ominous rock, but that did not stop her from continuing—"accidents do happen, though!"

"Ahem, dear," said Brick, and looked down at the table.

"Oh, no, Dad!" Martie grinned. She fanned a hand in front of her face—like a person who smelled a bad odor—then went teary-eyed. "Let Mom tell how she rode back and forth over the railroad tracks, trying to miscarry me—"

"That's enough," Brick murmured, and turned what Franny thought of as his mad bulldog stare on Martie. As for pale-faced Peg—the rest of the Wahls held their breaths while Turner Haskin turned toward Peg and began to explain how, because of her beauty, for a time his mother had been pursued by RCA as a possible torch singer, "Someone like Helen Merrill—"

The name Helen Merrill meant nothing to Franny, but in an effort to wipe out these last moments, she jumped in, too. "If I was a singer"—

"For Christsake," interrupted Brick, "don't they teach you kids the subjunctive anymore?"

Franny supposed her teeth might look a little inky, but she smiled as she climbed onto the arm of her chair and warbled to the tune of "Begin the Beguine":

"When they subjunct the subjunctive—"

"What the hell does she think she's doing?" Brick asked Peg.

An old trick of his: to suggest that what she was about to do would bring her shame, and she could avoid that shame if she behaved as Brick wanted. In self-defense, Franny plunged right into a throaty version of "I Can't Get Started."

"For Christsake," Brick muttered, but she did not stop, she did not dare stop. Rosamund—looking both amused and skeptical—smiled and sat back in her chair to listen. Peg—still waxy from Martie's words—began to clear the table, and Brick looked down into his lap the way he did when he considered the sermons of the minister at St. Mark's too solemn. It was Martie who seemed most inclined to knock Franny off her perch, clamp a hand over Franny's mouth. Martie's eyes had gone perfectly round with dislike.

Terrible to keep singing, impossible to stop—the top of Franny's head ached—but at least now it did not matter so much that Martie had brought up Peg's attempts at miscarriage because now Franny was the monster, just hatched, and Franny wanted to be the monster because—because the monster was the only thing to be. Be the monster or be nothing.

"That was good!" Rosamund said when Franny finished, and Turner Haskin smiled, though Brick and Martie shook their heads, and, from the door to the kitchen, Peg said only, "So where does your mother live these days, Turner?"

Peg and Brick were charmed by their guest. In the kitchen, later, Franny overheard Peg whisper to Rosamund, "He knows how to ignore a clod like Martie, doesn't he?" and while the girls finished cleaning-up, Peg showed Turner Haskin where she kept the extra keys for her Wildcat, and Brick explained that Turner could charge gas to the family's account at the Sinclair station on the way into town.

"Believe me," Brick said, "if you're around for any length of time, you'll need to get away from this brood!"

In an effort to demonstrate that she had her own life, Franny decided that she would go upstairs with the hamster and the copy of George Orwell's *1984* she had found in the boxes of books the big girls had brought home from school; however, while she was on her way to fetch Snoopy, Tim Gleason—fresh from a shower and clearly unaware of the arrival of Turner Haskin—showed up at the front door. Franny had to let Tim in, and then Deedee Pierce, who was wearing a violently pink turban. "I got a hideous haircut," Deedee Pierce whispered to Franny, "but Martie said I had to come by, immediately, to see this Turner."

Since the bad party, it seemed that Martie spent most of her time with Deedee Pierce, and Franny felt grateful that Martie had a friend in Deedee, and she joined the pair, now, in peeking across the landing and into the living room:

Turner Haskin sat next to Rosamund on the shantung couch

and looked at the liner notes of a record album he had brought from Florida. Poor Tim Gleason slouched in the wing-back chair, apparently studying the patterns his knuckles made where they pressed out against the pockets of his jeans.

"You hear that?" Martie said to Deedee Pierce. "When *I* tried to get Roz to listen to Mose Allison, she dismissed me entirely!"

Deedee Pierce drew her head back into the kitchen once more. In addition to the turban, she wore an elaborate, rattling seashell necklace that she twiddled with her fingers. "What do you say, Franny? That's some serious hunkiness, there, right?"

Franny's shrug made Martie and Deedee laugh, but it was true, she did feel vaguely disappointed by Turner Haskin. He was good-looking and his voice was low and well-modulated and he moved smoothly and said amusing things. She was *impressed* by the value that Rosamund ascribed to him in much the same way she would have been impressed by a painting if someone had told her it was worth a million dollars. Even if she had not cared for the painting, she would have found it hard not to think: a million dollars! Still.

"He's handsome and all," she whispered, "but he reminds me too much of those guys who model underwear in catalogues."

"Some complaint," said Deedee Pierce.

Franny turned to Martie for support. "You know what I mean. He's not as *sexy* as, like"—she hesitated—"Darren. I don't think. Do you?"

As if uncertain how to answer, Martie looked toward Deedee Pierce, who began to laugh uproariously. "Oh, Franny," Deedee Pierce said, "you're so naive!"

Franny shrugged, then proceeded with her plan to go upstairs with Snoopy and the copy of *1984*.

The very next night, she finished the book. She looked forward to talking to someone about it in the morning. Unfortunately, she discovered that no one wanted to talk about anything but Turner Haskin.

From the screened porch, her mother and her mother's friend Bethie Coontz spied on Turner and Rosamund as they returned from a trip to town in the boat. Bethie thought he looked like Rudolph Valentino. No, Rock Hudson, or maybe a dark Alan Ladd.

Franny joined the women on the porch just as Turner Haskin bent to give Rosamund a kiss. The women poked each other in the sides and laughed. "Woo-woo!"

That very afternoon, girls who somehow had heard of Turner Haskin's presence at the Wahl home—girls known and unknown—began to appear at the Wahls' front door. Hair and makeup perfect. Excuses ridiculously transparent. *Yes, they wondered if they could borrow a slalom ski? Make a call on the telephone?* Even Christy Strawberry, arriving for the afternoon, immediately asked, "So where's Adonis?"

"Skiing." Franny pulled Christy Strawberry out to the screened porch where she had left her copy of *1984*. She would have liked to ask Susan Thomas what she thought of *1984*, but she had not spoken to Susan Thomas since that "unreliable" business.

"You've got to read this." Franny pressed the book into Christy Strawberry's hands. "Just—try the first page."

She smiled in anticipation of Christy's looking up from the book as soon as she read that the clock had struck thirteen. When Christy did not look up, Franny thought how, once the girl finished the first chapter, Franny might share with her the fact that yesterday, in imitation of the book's hero, she had found an old fountain pen of her father's and used it to copy one of the Dickinson poems into her journal.

"But, Franny"—tiny rosebud mouth half open, Christy looked up from the book—"you know he's already famous, right?"

"Sure. People study his books at college and stuff."

A look of confusion passed over Christy's face. "Turner Haskin writes books?" she asked, before Franny erupted in laughter.

"So, Turner," Franny said over dinner that evening, "did you ever read *1984*?"

He nodded, then, to her confusion, said, "I don't believe so, Franny."

Rosamund smiled. "You'll never find anyone who writes as well as Hemingway."

"But Orwell wrote *1984,*" said Martie.

Rosamund nodded. "But *I* like Hemingway."

"Did you ever read it, Dad?" Martie asked.

"Hemingway?"

"*1984,*" Martie said.

"I bet you did." Rosamund turned toward Turner Haskin to say, "Daddy's a great reader."

Brick laughed. "I don't know about that, dear."

"You almost became a writer though, right?" Rosamund said.

Brick waved a hand in the air. "Oh, well." His voice was gruff. "I got drafted. By the time I got out, I had two kids to support. That'll make you give up on being a writer."

Turner Haskin nodded sagely. "So, you decided on the law after you came home from the war?"

"I can't say I ever decided on the law," Brick murmured, then raised his voice to add, "and I made *damn* sure I didn't go to war. They trained me as a pilot, and I wasn't too shabby, but I didn't see any point in getting shot up when they'd pretty much finished things over there." He grinned at Turner Haskin. "I flunked my tests three times, if you get my drift."

Peg and Rosamund and Martie all smiled reminiscent smiles that suggested they knew this story. Franny did not recall having heard it before, and she felt relieved that Christy Strawberry had been unable to stay for supper. Christy's father had been a prisoner of war in Japan.

"Anyway, about *1984,*" Franny said, and launched into details of Big Brother and O'Brien and Thoughtcrime.

"That's so silly, though!" Carefully, Peg picked open the hot foil wrapper in which she had baked a loaf of garlic-buttered Italian bread. Now and again, the steam inside the foil made her pull back her fingers and wait. "Anybody ever tried to torture me, I'd just tell them what they wanted to hear, right off, and then go about my business."

Brick nodded. "Sure. In your heart, you'd know what you believed."

"That's what the main character of *1984* thought," Franny said, "but it wasn't as easy as that. They could get you confused." She tried to explain how Big Brother's government had begun to ruin the language; then she found herself rushing on to describe the way in which they finally broke down the hero, Winston Smith: "With rats. Remember, Martie?"

As if cold, Martie rubbed at her arms. Nodded. "They put a cage on his head. They put rats in a chute that opened into the cage. That was what made him betray the girl he loved."

Brick leaned toward Rosamund. Whispered something in her ear that made her smile. Rude, Franny thought, and when the others smiled and turned toward Brick and Rosamund—what was their secret?—Franny hurried to add, "I could see how that drove Winston nuts because I've had nightmares where I'm Snow White and the wicked stepmother puts a birdcage over my head and there's a woodpecker in it, pecking at me—"

"Honey"—Peg patted the back of Franny's hand where it lay on the table—"that's enough, now," and Brick said, yes, he thought Roz ought to tell Turner the story of that gentleman on the airplane who thought she was just twelve years old—

"You think that's bad?" Martie shook her head at Franny, but smiled before continuing. "At our last party, a guy from Iowa State asked me to introduce him to Fran!"

Peg frowned. "Wasn't Franny upstairs during the party?"

"I probably went down for a glass of water or something," Franny mumbled, and then Turner Haskin—quite diplomatically, Franny thought—broke into high praise of Peg's lamb chops:

There was a bit of rosemary in the glaze, yes? Rosemary and red wine?

Peg served lamb chops that evening and not the spaghetti with meat sauce she had meant to serve because, before leaving for Lindt's that morning, Rosamund had explained to Peg—delicately, and with a hug—that Turner had "a hard time" with ground meat. Because he was used to fine dining. Because of having grown up eating food prepared by world-class chefs at his father's resort.

After that conversation, Turner had driven Rosamund to work. Certain rituals had been established in the first days of his visit. At noon, if Peg did not need the car, Turner drove to town again, and he and Rosamund ate lunch at the Top Hat Club, often with Brick, who declared Turner "good company." In the evenings, after dinner, Turner and Rosamund usually went back to the Top Hat to listen to music. Turner liked world-weary jazz, and so the Wahl house was now filled with "Your Mind Is on Vacation" and "Meet Me at No Special Place," and Brick did not object too much because Turner also professed to enjoy Duke Ellington and Art Tatum.

Turner took to calling Franny "Little Sister," and for some reason—because they wanted to be like him?—other people began calling her this, too. Even Brick and Peg and Martie did it now and then—and Martie had even agreed to Rosamund's request that, in deference to Turner's visit, they continue to hold off on having parties for a while.

Turner showered twice a day and used a fresh towel and washcloth every time, and Peg seemed delighted to keep up his supplies, though the Wahl girls continued to receive their weekly allotments of single bath towel and washcloth ("Rosamund," "Martie," "Franny" read Peg's felt-tip markings above the assigned towel bars). Each morning, Turner drank a pitcher of orange juice for breakfast. His own pitcher. On the screened porch overlooking the lake. Alone. "I'm funny about it," he said, and Peg and Rosamund fussed over the cans of concentrate in the freezer as if they were hatchlings in an incubator. When Turner found Sunshine Brand "a little funky," Peg said, "Next time, we'll buy Minute Maid."

And Rosamund, sounding proud, "It's because he's actually from Florida. He's used to just stepping outside and plucking oranges from a tree. He's a connoisseur."

At the time, Franny had stood in the back hall, adding feed to Snoopy's cage, and thinking that Rosamund was not nearly as inter-

esting with Turner Haskin in town; and then Rosamund had lowered her voice and, with a knowing laugh, said, "Of course, Mom,
he's a connoisseur of many things, as you might guess."

Peg laughed. "Oh, I suppose so!"

Franny had stopped her chores, then, and stood stock-still—*not*
because she wanted to hear more of that conversation in the
kitchen. No. She was silent because if she had to overhear, she at
least did not want her mother or Rosamund to know she overheard.
Because she understood that they meant sex. They were laughing
about the fact that Turner had had sex with many women—maybe
he was one of those dates who went out for sex after he took
Rosamund home?

In the kitchen, Rosamund had then explained to Peg how Mike
Zanios's singer/girlfriend always sang a certain song to Turner
when he and Rosamund visited the Top Hat—"You Better Love
Me While You May"—and how Turner could tell the singer was no
virgin.

"I swear, Mom! He knows, just by the way a girl walks!"

"Well." Peg sounded dubious, if amused, but then she added,
"If it's true, I wish you'd ask him about Martie!"

"Oh, *Mom*!" Rosamund loosed a peal of giddy laughter. "You
are terrible!"

But, of course, Rosamund meant "terrible" as a kind of compliment. You could feel that way if someone's dark side amused you, or
flattered you, somehow. Franny knew that. Indeed, a few days later,
when she and Joan Harvett and Christy Strawberry went shopping,
she found herself behaving as if nothing could have been more pleasant than to have Turner Haskin for a houseguest. As she and the girls
made their way down Lakeside, she explained about the Top Hat
singer's crush on Turner, and how, yesterday, Rosamund had gotten
hold of an old recording of "You Better Love Me While You May"
and played it on the stereo in order to tease Turner.

How outrageous that song was! A woman coming right out and
proclaiming both her desires and her desirability! Really, it made
Franny laugh in delight, but she did not know how to tell Christy

and Joan this, and then Joan changed the subject, asking, *Hey, isn't anybody else worried Allen's won't get our outfits in before the first football game?*

Cheerleading. It seemed impossible to Franny, now, that she ever could have cared about cheerleading. Still, it was necessary for her to act as if she cared, and she said, "Sure," and here came her mother's Wildcat up the street—unmistakable, the way the right headlight drooped like a weak eyelid ever since a mishap for which no one had taken the blame. At sight of the car, Franny felt a moment's panic, as if she were doing something wrong, but it was Turner Haskin who sat behind the wheel.

Now slowing. For a moment, Franny thought he meant to stop and say hello, and she felt a flutter of pride, but, no, he only waved and drove by.

"He is so cool!" said Joan and Christy.

Franny nodded, though lately, more and more, "cool" struck her as conjured, a thing that hurt the soul of both its practitioners and admirers. Franny wanted passion. Passion could hurt you, too, of course, but passion was not fake. Passion *arose*. Was not arrived at. Was not achieved. But she could not discuss that with Joan and Christy. With Susan Thomas, yes, she could have discussed it with Susan Thomas, she thought regretfully.

"But, really," she said as the Wildcat disappeared from view, "I don't know that I trust Turner."

Christy Strawberry laughed. "You don't trust anybody!"

The words gave Franny a shock, but maybe the girl was right. And look at Franny herself. The day before, out in her rowboat, she had pretended not to hear Bob Prohaski call to her from the shore. Seated on a cushion in the hull, reading, she had scooched farther down, let the unbailed water in the bottom of the boat soak her shorts and the back of her T-shirt.

"Go away," she had whispered, "please." A rusty Folger's coffee can bobbed in the unbailed water beside her head. Thumped against the hull.

"Hey, Franny!" Bob Prohaski called.

The ribs of the hull had bit into her spine. Penance, she had thought. To pass the time, she played word golf. "Love" to "hate." She felt pretty sure that "lave" was a real word that meant something like "wash." "Lave" to "late" to "hate." Three moves. That was too easy. How about "yellow" to "orange"? Too hard? You could go to "fellow" and then "fallow," or "mellow" and "mallow" but without paper and a pencil—

The sun left blue-green dots on her eyes. Was Bob Prohaski still on the dock? Suppose her boat drifted to shore?

Wait. The hull of the rowboat hummed with the approach of a trolling motor. Closer, closer now—

She scrambled up onto her knees in order not to be caught in the bottom of the boat, and there sat Bob Prohaski, grinning, while a little man in a striped engineer's cap—a farmer fishing the shallows in an outboard—drove up alongside the dinghy.

"How you doing, hon?" The fisherman flashed the mouthful of false teeth that perched in his skull-thin face. "You ain't hiding from this fellow, here, are you?"

The rowboat tilted dangerously as Bob Prohaski—arms held out like wings—stepped from the outboard and onto the middle seat of her rowboat. For a moment, he had swayed there, then crashed into Franny, and struck his knee, hard, against the hull.

The fisherman guffawed as he pushed off from the rowboat, "Attaboy! Cop a quick feel!"

Bob Prohaski moaned and rubbed at the knee while edging back onto the rowboat's middle seat. Bright pink gum had shown as his mouth contorted in pain.

"You okay, Bob?" she asked.

WHIRWOOooooo! WHIRWOOooooo!

"Jesus." He shook his head and kept one eye closed while continuing to rub his leg. "Is that your old lady?"

On the top of the bank. Silver siren raised to her lips. *WHIR-Woooo! WHIRWOOOOOoooo!*

"How come she didn't use that thing when she knew I was calling you?" Bob Prohaski had asked.

"Were you calling me?" Franny said in a small voice just as Peg shouted from the bank, "NO BOYS ON BOARD!"

"I can hear her, Franny. How come you couldn't hear *me*?"

Franny flushed. "What'd she say?"

He gave a dark laugh. "Are you deaf? 'No boys on board!' Jesus, your family lives in the dark ages, don't it?"

She nodded. "Move to the back, and I'll row us in."

When he stood, the boat began to rock and, quick, he crouched, seized hold of the seat. "I can row us," he said uncertainly.

"No." Franny had given her head a shake. "I better be the one, Bob." To placate her mother, she knew, it was best to behave as if there had been no boy in the boat at all.

The house sat empty when Joan Harvett's mother dropped off Franny after that afternoon shopping trip with Joan and Christy. On impulse—feeling a little nervous—Franny hurried down to Lakeside Drive and made her way to the cottage of Susan Thomas. What she would do, she thought, was present her visit as a literary call. She would ask if Susan Thomas had read *1984,* and see where things went from there.

"Come in, Franny," Mrs. Thomas said when she arrived at the door. "No need to knock."

Didn't the cottage smell odd, though? Like permanent-curl solution?

Mrs. Thomas waved at the TV set now on in the cottage's main room. "I was getting some news about Johnson's latest escapades."

Politely, Franny looked at the program: Some government official behind a microphone spoke of the president's decision to double the numbers of draftees from seventeen thousand a month to thirty-five thousand a month.

Mrs. Thomas plunked herself down in a wheezing rattan chair to stare at the TV. She wore one of her funny hats, something that looked as if it might have come from an army surplus store. A pith helmet? Was that what it was called? It seemed Mrs. Thomas had forgotten Franny, and the girl wondered if she were meant to search out Susan on her own; but then Mrs. Thomas stood up with a groan. "I don't want to say he's as bad as Goldwater would have been, but who knows what he'll do next?"

Franny had assumed that, like her own parents, the Thomases had voted for Goldwater, and she did not know what to say. In silence, she followed Mrs. Thomas in the direction of Susan's room.

"If you think it stinks out here, wait till you get to Sue's room. She is—*depilating*." Mrs. Thomas gestured toward the bedroom off the kitchen, where, on the floor—eyes closed, legs covered with hair remover, kitchen timer ticking beside her head—lay Susan Thomas.

"Mom!" the girl protested when she opened her eyes and saw Franny in the doorway. "How embarrassing!"

"I thought it was important you two talked," Mrs. Thomas said, "and I'm sure Franny's seen things just as silly."

"I wanted to come before," Franny said after Mrs. Thomas left the room. "I'm sorry about being unreliable and all."

"Oh, well." The girl sat up. She scraped a set of fingernail initials through the cream on her leg. S.T. read the suntanned skin beneath. "I got a kid down the beach crewing—he's fine."

It was good to be with Susan Thomas. She had not read *1984*, but she, too, had been reading more Dickinson, and the two discussed favorite poems; and then Franny explained how she used the Dickinson poems to record her own thoughts. "And, lately," she added after a moment's hesitation, "sometimes I put my own poems in the journal, too, since my mom never reads poetry."

Susan Thomas seemed confused by this last, and as Franny did not want to tell Susan about her mother's reading the old journal or about its demise in the ash can, she hurriedly recited one of her poems.

"I wish you went to Bell," Susan said when Franny finished. "Half of the girls are boarders, you know? They live in dorms. When I start ninth, I'll be in Mrs. Rogers' English, and we'll get to do a whole anthology of student work. Your poem would definitely get in."

Earlier in the summer, Susan had shown Franny last year's Bell

Academy "annual," a book full of photographs of the ivy-covered buildings, and of girls in dark blazers and plaid skirts doing things like debate; and girls in white choir robes holding candles and singing madrigals for a special ceremony at Christmas. There was something wonderful and yet strange about the place—maybe because there were no boys?

Franny could not imagine herself there, and she certainly knew her parents could not afford to send her, and so she just smiled whenever Susan Thomas mentioned the school, and said, "It sounds great."

CHAPTER ELEVEN

THE FIRST WEEKEND IN AUGUST A COLD SNAP ARRIVED THAT made the summer days strangely thrilling. To shiver and pull on heavy clothes and dense stockings—Franny's scalp constricted with the pleasure of it. Snoopy cradled against her cheek, she stared out the back hall window, and across the road to the gray fog that hung above the meadow and the swamp, which seemed a new world. Even the voices of the guests moving about behind her vibrated and echoed in some novel way.

Because of the turn in the weather, and the exhausting of possible places to take Turner Haskin, Rosamund had agreed it might be good to throw a party that weekend, and, now, in the downstairs bathroom, girls who initially had refused Peg's offers of old jackets and sweaters got into the spirit of things and donned ill-fitting items and laughed over their appearances. In the den, as if fall had arrived, a couple of boys made a lot of noise talking about football. One boy sat at the kitchen table, reading an Ian Fleming novel of Brick's, while others—sometimes including Peg—played cards on the porch, or in the dining room. One group had spread out a game of Monopoly on the living room floor. A girl seated beside Brick on the piano bench tried to sing along with his "Time After Time," but Brick kept breaking into improvisations that shut her out, and finally she went to play cards.

That was Friday. Saturday night, the night of the party, girl guests rushed in and out of the upstairs bathrooms to consult the hall mirrors.

"Little Sister!" one of them called as Franny started down the stairs from her bedroom. "What're you reading?"

"Emily Dickinson." Franny held up the book.

The girl smiled. "Hey," she said, "'I'm nobody. Who are you? Are you nobody, too?'" and Franny smiled back before she reached the landing and made her four-step jump into the kitchen.

At the sound of her landing, Brick looked up from mixing drinks for Mike Zanios and Turner. He frowned at Franny, then turned to Peg to say, "Somebody's got to talk to her about that."

"Yup," Zanios muttered as he used the tip of his index finger to wiggle back and forth the tiny rudder of a complicated model ship that belonged on the mantel in the den but now—inexplicably—perched on top of the kitchen stove.

Franny pretended not to have heard what her father and Mike Zanios had said. She made her gaze vacant—she was hardly there, no need to say hello to her—and as if she had come to the kitchen for just this reason, she picked up the telephone and dialed Susan Thomas.

While she listened to the ringing, she watched Mike Zanios out of the corner of her eye. He seemed to be in a foul mood. He ignored the conversation between Brick and Peg and Turner—something about the model boat and the man who had given it to Brick. Maybe Mike Zanios felt awkward because he could see that Peg and Brick were dressed to go out, and that the big girls meant to have their own party at the house? And, no doubt, he missed his evenings with Roz, too.

Ten rings. Eleven. Her mother now said something teasing to Turner Haskin, then smiled at Mike Zanios. She looked pretty and cheerful, though a few weeks before, she had worried that she and Brick would not be invited to the Henleys' annual party; then, when they had received the invitation, for a time, she had worried they might have been on a second list, one made up of people who would be asked only after regrets came from those on the first list—

"Hey, Frances," Mike Zanios called, "how long you going to let that ring?"

She shrugged and hung up.

"That's a girl," he said. "Now go on and tell your sister I'm here to take your parents to the Henleys' and she ought to come say hello before we leave."

Franny nodded, okay, and turned to fetch Rosamund, but before she could, the introduction to the song that Zanios's girl-friend always sang to Turner Haskin—"You Better Love Me While You May"—began to play on the living room stereo, and Rosamund appeared on the landing, grinning, casting her arms open wide as if she were about to sing.

"Oh." The moment she saw Mike Zanios, Rosamund's cheeks went red. "Mike, I—"

As brightly as possible, trying to help, Peg said, "Roz, Mike stopped by to take us to Henleys'!"

"Just"—Rosamund lifted her chin—"excuse me."

Before anyone else in the kitchen had a chance to speak, Mike Zanios—his own face now a little gray—turned to Turner Haskin and, peering over the rim of his drink, said something about making a pousse-café next time Turner and Roz came into the club. Did Turner know how to make a pousse-café?

Out in the living room, Rosamund's recording of "You Better Love Me While You May" came to a scratchy stop. Then, from the back hall—a welcome interruption—Martie called an halloo and toted in a case of beer that she set on the kitchen floor so she could wrap an arm around Zanios's neck, and give him a kiss on the cheek.

Though Zanios continued to look grim, Brick and Peg and Turner Haskin and Franny all said hello to Martie, and their hellos stuffed a little distance between this moment and the embarrassing moment with Rosamund's record. Martie, of course, was overjoyed at the welcome she received, and Franny was pleased on her behalf; earlier in the day, Franny knew, Martie had been upset and crying over not receiving a response from a boy named Terry regarding tonight's party. Now, however, Martie clapped her hands together, and threw open the refrigerator door.

"Anybody need a brewsky?" she said, and popped the lid from a bottle and held it up for takers.

"Hey, Martie"—Mike Zanios smiled but something in his narrowed eyes gave Franny a chill—"maybe you should lay off the beer. You're getting a little broad in the beam, aren't you?"

Could he really have said that? The words hung in Franny's chest like something dead, birds with broken necks, but her parents' faces maintained fixed smiles. Martie herself smiled. Turner Haskin blew a puff of air at the sail of the sailboat on the stove, and the sail swung out an inch or two. Well. Franny shook her head. "That"—her voice tottered—"that was rude."

"Oh, settle down," Brick murmured darkly. And Martie mouthed a beseeching *shhh*.

Franny locked eyes with Zanios, a move she found uncomfortable but not impossible. "And it's not true," she said.

"Franny. Enough." Peg set her hands on the girl's shoulders and turned her toward the stairs.

She was glad to leave, and hurried up to the landing and then down into the living room where Rosamund now slid a Ray Charles album out of its case.

"How mortifying!" Rosamund whispered when Franny drew near.

"Don't worry about hurting *his* feelings. The jerk." She explained what Zanios had said to Martie, then added, "It wouldn't be nice in any case, but it's not even true!"

"Franny." From the landing, now clipping on a pair of earrings, Peg called, "We're taking off, so you need to—" She pointed toward the second floor.

Franny rubbed the bridge of her nose with two fingers. A scholarly gesture, she thought; one that suggested that *had* she been invited to the big girls' party, why, she could scarcely have torn herself away from her book of Emily Dickinson.

"Remember, Frances"—Martie stepped up from the kitchen to join Peg on the landing—"if anybody at the party tries to go upstairs, you tell them 'down.'"

Rosamund rapped the edge of the album cover on the top of Franny's head. "Franny Wahl," she said—still sounding a little gloomy, though she smiled—"we dub thee Keeper of the Stairs."

Keeper of the Stairs. After Peg and Brick and Mike Zanios left for the evening, and the girl guests had all descended to the first floor for the party, Franny set her book on the top step, and went to the mirror closest to the top of the stairs. Folded her arms across her chest. Sneered, "Get thee back to the first floor."

Did she look tough? She twisted her lips. Put a little poison in her gaze.

A couple appeared on the landing, and they paused there, looking up, heads tipped together in conference. If they started to climb the stairs, then she would have to say, "You can't come up here, guys," but the couple moved away without a word.

So her power was *not* imaginary—though, of course, it was really the power of Brick and Peg, a sovereignty sufficiently substantial that it could be vested in her thirteen-year-old self.

She was reading, again, when a scowling Martie began to climb the stairs. Was she already a little drunk? Franny wondered as Martie called a loud, "Frances Jean, did you let someone up there?"

"No."

Martie grabbed the newel post at the top of the stairs and pulled herself up the last step with both hands, apparently unaware of the oddness of this movement.

"You okay?" Franny asked.

"No, I'm not!" In the mirror at the top of the stairs—one eye squeezed shut—Martie watched herself take a swallow from the can of beer in her hand. "I wanted Terry to come tonight!" She sniffled noisily, then examined the book in Franny's hand. "Emily Dickinson. Emily Dickinson was, like, a spinster. What would she know about love or anything else for that matter?"

When Franny did not bother arguing with her, Martie handed back the book and headed downstairs once more.

It was almost nine-thirty—the party in full swing—when

Franny decided it would be stupid for her to go all night without a snack because of some stupid rule. As she made her own way down the stairs, she did her best to ignore that atmosphere of gelid confidence that immediately rose to her knees, a flash flood that swirled about her waist, climbed to her neck—

"We making too much noise for you, Fran?" called one of Martie's college friends, Nancy-something-or-other, a nice girl.

"I was just thirsty."

The girl and her boyfriend smiled encouragement. "Big book!" said the boyfriend, nodding at the volume now closed on Franny's finger. A lucky boy, Franny thought. Just saying "big book" seemed to make him happy. A boy whose old battle with acne had left him with skin that was a sheet of pie dough rolled out over gravel—still, he was happy. Nancy-whatever-her-name-was was happy. And there was Rosamund, dancing with Turner Haskin—a cool and restrained sort of dancing, Franny thought, but they looked happy, too, and Franny, feeling diminished, did not jump the four steps into the crowded kitchen but descended slowly, with eyes lowered.

Sweater cuffs and the hands that extended from them comprised her view. The hems of pants. Belts. Loafers. "Excuse me," she said. As bland as a server as a wedding reception. "Excuse me, please."

"Hey, Franny." A very sunburned and drunk Al Castor pulled her toward the back hall. "We gotta talk."

"Uh-oh!" said a voice across the room. "Jailbait, Al!"

"Shut up, asshole," Al Castor growled.

It was painful to look at Al Castor that evening. Even his lips were sunburned, crisp and brown as a piece of fried chicken. His eyebrows were now bleached as white as his hair. But Franny smiled at Al. She suspected she knew what poor Al wanted to say to her, and she was right:

Had Rosamund ever talked to Franny about him? About what happened before they all went back to school last fall? He knew he'd come on too strong, and he thought if they could just talk—

Franny nodded. She patted the boy on the shoulder. "I'm sure Roz still thinks you're a great guy."

"Ha." Al Castor listed this way and that. Thrummed his fingers across the wires of the hamster cage as if the cage were a harp—just once, but poor Snoopy dashed to the far corner and cowered there.

"Anyway, I'm not supposed to be down here, Al," Franny said, "I just came to get some pop," and she backed out of the hall, passing Tim Gleason, who sat in a ladder-back chair beneath a planter of half-dead ivy. Tim Gleason looked a little drunk, and very forlorn, the soles of his tennis shoes turned in toward one another. No doubt, he waited for Rosamund to remember his existence. The tendril of ivy that lay on his shoulder made him appear especially baleful.

"You've got some ivy on you, there," Franny could have said, "Or, here, Tim, let me move that thing." But she suspected Tim Gleason would prefer to remain ignorant of a minor debasement rather than have it pointed out by a thirteen-year-old.

Orange soda. The first bottle of pop to hand. Awful stuff that tasted like dust, mildew.

"Hey, you."

Somehow she knew that voice that rose above the buzz of the party crowd called to her. "Hey. Wait."

She did not allow herself to look up, but quickly hurried back across the kitchen. Sandals, loafers, tennis shoes. The first step of the staircase appeared and she was moving up. One, two, three and she was on the landing.

She cried out, then, in fright as something clutched her ankle. Just in time, she turned to see a young man fall up the stairs after her.

"Wait!" he said. A silver-haired young man with eyes not merely blue but somehow light in the dark, like one of those creatures that lived miles and miles down in the sea—

The truth: She put her hand to her heart. For one perfect moment, she believed in everything. She was the fairy-tale princess who looks at her reflection in the well and finds the reflection of the prince who stands behind her.

When this prince smiled, however, the reflection in the well stirred. This prince lived *inside* the well and was about to pull her in.

Franny took a frightened, stumbling step up the stairs. "Nobody can come up here!" she cried when he began to follow her once more.

"But you'll let me come up, won't you?" he said, and walked his chest into the hand she held out to stop him. "Why are you up here?" He looked about in the dark at the top of the stairs. "What's your name?"

"You have to go *down*."

When she pushed on his chest, he rocked back precariously. "Whoa!" he said, and while he grasped the banister to keep from falling, she hurried down the hall to her room. She closed the door behind herself and leaned against it.

"Hey," he called. "Where'd you go?"

Several moments passed before she heard his footsteps descend the stairs. There. Gone. She did not move away from the door. The room before her had turned queer: poisoned and brilliant. The wooden walls and floors were odd and grainy in the light from the ceiling fixture. Each dark knothole in the wood formed the spinning center of a galaxy, a beautiful and active part of some vastness that signalled either great meaning or meaninglessness. And if it were meaning-lessness—well, it became meaningful from sheer grandeur.

She jumped at a knock on the door at her back.

"Who is it?"

"Me." Rosamund. "One of Timmy's little friends wants to dance with you."

Franny opened the door. "Who?"

"That doll who was just up here?" Rosamund laughed. "I doubt you missed him!"

Franny flipped through pages of the poetry book in her hand. Oh, yes, she was just casually looking through a book of poems. That was how fast her heart had gone undercover. Because she knew that if Rosamund sensed the way it had instantly rebuilt itself from go-cart to dragster, she would put a stop to it, quick.

Rosamund—Franny could imagine how Rosamund saw things: Rosamund was taking Franny to her junior high's basketball game as a kind of mascot. Or Rosamund saw the moment as a little like the time that she and Martie had made up Franny's face and teased and sprayed her hair into a French twist and brought her downstairs to show off their handiwork to Roger Dale.

"So, can I tell him you're coming?"

"I'd have to—comb my hair." Franny hesitated. "And what about Martie?"

"Don't worry about her." Rosamund smiled. "I'm supposed to tell you he'll be waiting at the bottom of the stairs."

If he were not at the bottom of the stairs as soon as she arrived . . .

She arranged her face in what she thought of as her toughest "drop-dead" look, but knew, already, this moment was nothing for which she could prepare herself beyond the sort of steadying a person might do in anticipation of the doctor's inserting a needle.

He was waiting. He looked up at her as he took a sip from the can of beer in his hand. In the brighter light that shone into the living room from the den, his beard announced itself a granite that did not belong on boys even close to her own age. Worse, what she felt when he took her hand already seemed historical, like some substance that had sat too long unused and turned corrosive.

"I'm thirteen," she said.

He bent nearer than necessary, breath canny with booze and cigarettes and coffee. "What's that?"

"I'm thirteen."

"*Thirteen?*" He threw back his head and gave a raucous laugh. So the whole thing was a joke? Maybe something cooked up by Tim Gleason? Sickened, she turned to go.

"No! No!" With a fervor she had never heard from a real-life male, ever—except behind anger—he said, "Don't go! Please."

She did not want to be aware of Al Castor and the others watching from the big green couch. Dancing Nancy-something-or-other and her boyfriend: watching. Franny was Cinderella at the ball, but undisguised. Cinderella still wearing her cinder rags, her bare feet.

"Thanks for coming down," he whispered. He wore a V-necked sweater but no shirt and the skin along his collarbone bloomed pink and tan, absolutely tantalizing. His hair was longer than the hair of the boys she knew, thick, brushing his collar. He took a long drink from his beer and there was his man's neck . . .

"You're quiet," he said. "So. Thirteen. I don't remember, do thirteen-year-olds know how to dance?"

"I know how to dance."

The song was a fast one, but he kept his fingers on her shoulder, a profound and confusing intimacy. Really, the only dancing she had ever done, she had done in front of the hall mirrors or with Christy Strawberry and Joan Harvett. The only male she had ever danced with in her entire life was Al Castor; at the Fourth of July picnic, Al had asked her to dance because he loved the song "Peppermint Man" and the big girls were taken.

"Hey, Frances Jean"—Deedee Pierce called from the dining room—"isn't it time for you to go to bed?"

"With *whom*?" another guest cackled, and then Al Castor yowled, "Don't put any ideas in Marvell's head, man!"

Franny pretended not to hear the remarks, and this made— Marvell?—laugh. He brought his face close. "Too tough to care?" he murmured.

She supposed he imagined her merely embarrassed; in fact, to Franny, many things simply appeared extraneous: her parents, the friends of Martie and Rosamund, Martie and Rosamund themselves. They existed like the blinking yard lights of homes across the lake: small, colorless, too far away to be of consequence. She could not think about them. She had to dance. She had to consider this moment to which she was pinned like a warrior by an arrow to a tree, at the same time that she had to consider very small rules, like the fact that she could not even ask, "What's your name?"

To ask "What's your name?" might be to ask too much.

And, of course, when the song ended, she would have to walk away immediately—in case he meant only *one* dance. And then the song did end, which broke her heart; the magician pulled back his cape and not just the rabbit but the magician and the entire stage disappeared, too.

"Thanks," she said, and started toward the stairs.

"Don't go!" He clasped her hand in his. No one had ever looked in her eyes that way. He was a little drunk, of course. She knew that. Still, his gaze was steady and full. Unfortunately, she could not return it—not without acting, at any rate. Not without the most terrible strain. And what did that mean? That she was not meant to be a lover? She *felt* like a lover, but maybe being a lover meant a willingness to act in a way that was not natural to you?

They began to move to the music again, his hand, once more, miraculously, on her shoulder, but surely everything would stop any moment now. She would turn back into a pumpkin, bombs would fall, the filmstrip inside her head would break—

"Don't you even want to know my name?"

What difference did it make if she knew his name? She felt sick with happiness and confusion. The living room where they danced was her family's living room but now it was something else, too, something charged with significance.

"I'm Ryan Marvell. Like in the comic books? You want some of this?" He offered his can of beer to her. When she took a sip, he laughed. "Don't get drunk now!" he said.

It disappointed her that he could disappoint her—this offering her something, then warning her against it—but she accepted the disappointment, and said, "I've tasted beer before."

"Yeah?" He pulled his face long, as if to hold back a laugh. "Your dad give you a sip? Uh-oh!" He squeezed her hand. "Somebody over there looks like she'd like to bite my head off!"

In the dining room, Martie now stood in glowering conversation with Deedee Pierce.

"That's my sister," Franny said—just as Rosamund looked toward Franny and waved with a flourish that reminded Franny of the waves that parents gave their children while the children rode the merry-go-round.

"I've met Roz," Ryan Marvell whispered, "but the other one's making me nervous."

Still, he did not leave. He put his hands on her shoulders and guided her toward the screened porch—dark that night, closed off because of the weather.

"Franny," he said. "I like that." He squinted into the darkened porch. "Where do you sit here, Franny? I can't see."

The table lamp she flicked on was too much, he said, and she flicked it off and, eyes flashing with adjustment—heart juddering with joy—she led him by the hand to the wrought-iron loveseat. "Here," she said.

With a laugh, he pulled her down beside him. "You know, I think my parents met your parents at some parties before," he said. "Your dad's the lawyer, right?"

She nodded.

"Thirteen." In the half-light, with one eyebrow raised, he seemed skeptical, almost amused, but then he rubbed his chest with the flat of his hand as if it ached, and she could almost believe that he felt as baffled and heartsick as she did.

She folded her hands in her lap and entwined the fingers. This is the church. This is the steeple. He began to tell her a story of how, the day before, he and Tim Gleason and their buddy Warren had been at City Beach, and met a group of silly girls from Waterloo, and convinced the girls that he was the drummer for the Beach Boys.

"They wanted my autograph!" Ryan Marvell laughed with a boy's delight. "I gave them my autograph! Me, *Denny Wilson*!"

Franny laughed, partly in thanks that she was not one of the tricked girls, but instead the girl who learned of the trick. Being the girl who learned of the trick made her feel a little like Rosamund. Ryan Marvell's story was the sort of story that Rosamund often told, a story in which she was immune.

Franny was not immune, and knew that Ryan Marvell knew that she was not immune. It was acting on his part that he pretended to believe she were immune, and she almost wished that she were a girl who did not have to think: This is something he can do, and do well—watch out.

He was it, after all. The one.

She could not help feeling joy at meeting the one, though surely it was all too good to be true. He seemed as joyous as she was. He wrote her name in the air with the coal of his lighted cigarette. Before too long, he would put his arm around her. She would like that, but regretted that it would happen so soon because, now, side by side on the loveseat—a loveseat in her very own house, rendered permanently, irrevocably magical—they smiled at each other, smiles so broad they could have been a couple of five-year-olds, just tucked in for their first sleepover.

There. He came close, his chin grazing her cheek. A nervous laugh jarred loose from her, and he murmured, "I like the way your breasts move when you laugh."

Oh. She looked away, her teeth beginning to chatter. She would have preferred to leave her breasts out of it, but he went on, in a whisper, "It's a compliment, honey."

Honey. As if to keep her company, he drew up his shoulders and made his own teeth chatter. "Okay," he said through chattering teeth, "look. I work at the miniature golf course. Tomorrow, you could come there, couldn't you? There's no problem with that, is there? And—Roz takes Tim skiing. We could get her to take us along, right? That'd be one way we could see each other."

Franny did not say that Tim and Rosamund saw her as a kid, not someone to include in what would amount to a double date. She looked out the porch screens. There: the familiar dark and bouncing limbs of shaggy oaks, the night sky strangely white with the cold. Like your breath in the cold. The earth's warm breath, and when he leaned in to kiss her, she did not shut her eyes. She did not want to lose a minute of his face, any sensory information she could get while this lasted—

"FRANCES JEAN WAHL!"

Bits of light shot through the flower pattern of the table lamp's cut-paper shade: slice of leaf and petal, dots of stigma. A startling portion of Martie's face loomed above the shade.

"Remember who you are, where you are, what you are!"

Franny managed a shaky laugh. "Jeez, we're not Hanovers, Martie," she said, delighted to finally use a line she had invented for imaginary repartee with her parents.

"We are Wahls!" Martie glared at Ryan Marvell. "And you leave that light on, Frances! If Mother and Father were to come home and catch you—" She exited with a fling of her hair.

Ryan Marvell laughed. "Do you guys really call your dad 'Father'?" He pretended to nibble on fingernails he plainly did gnaw at other times: down to the quick, a devastation Franny took as a sign of a sensitive nature. A good sign.

"*I* call him 'Dad,'" Franny said. "I don't know where Martie got that 'Father' stuff. Some old movie, maybe. You know, like, the hoity-toity family's eating breakfast and—yeah, the maid's pouring the daughter her cup of coffee—and the daughter goes, 'Father, dear, could I take the car to the city today?'"

Ryan Marvell threw his head back and laughed and kissed her hand. "Do you know what a terrific girl you are?"

"We better go back in the other room, " she said, and stood up, fast. She wanted to shed his words, hold on to them for dear life, not believe them at all.

He held out his hands to her and she pulled him to his feet. The expression on his face was a tender one. If it were an act, so be it. He ran the play she wanted to be in, again and again. "Thirteen," he said. "That isn't good for us."

At "for us" she tried to laugh. She did not want to hear another one of his wonderful words, and she kissed him, just to stop his mouth—

"Hey, Franny!" Laughing, peering around one of the porch's French doors, Deedee Pierce called, "What would your boyfriend with the tight pants think about all this?"

Ryan Marvell smoothed his hand down Franny's back. "Let's go outside," he whispered, and she nodded, okay.

*   *   *

Later, she would not understand how it was that she let him lie down on top of her on the bank. "Let me keep you warm," he said, but, of course, they would have been warmer in the house. His beard scratched her chin. That was new. His kisses assumed open mouths and tongues and when he pressed against her she understood that he meant for her to feel the ridge of his penis. Which was all right, now that she knew this was a natural thing. She tried, however, to detach that moment with Ryan Marvell from the word the engaged girl had used: hard-on. She wanted her experience entirely uncolored by the rest of them.

"I love you," he crooned. He sounded desperate but blissful. "I love you, Franny." He raised his head and smiled, sweet as a dog paddling in open water. It was shameful that he said he loved her. That he thought her foolish enough to believe him. Still, she wanted him to say it. He had to—or she would sink into the earth. Because she loved him, too, and wished she could be with him without having to watch for someone to come their way. The house, big and white, lit by the mercury lamp to a lavender pallor—it shone in the windy distance: a ship, a dream, breathing. Twigs from the oak trees bit into her scalp. Her parents would tear her limb from limb if they found her in these arms.

How long did she lie there with Ryan Marvell murmuring her name? He was on top of her, he was under her, they rocked in the cool night air. In his thrall, she tried to weigh how awful that hand under her shirt, on the bare skin of her back, might be in the eyes of the world; and, more important, in the eyes of Ryan Marvell himself. Surely he understood that she had never done such a thing before. Still, he complained when she stopped his hand's movement toward her breasts.

He lifted his face and looked down into her eyes. "You love me, too, don't you?"

"Yes," she said miserably. It was not a glory. It was an admission. What good could come of it, barring a miracle? "I've got to go in, though. My parents will be home soon."

He protested briefly before standing to help her brush the

grass and twigs from her hair and the back of her shirt.

"Marvell!" From across the lawn, Tim Gleason now wobbled their way, his arms wrapped tight about his body. Teeth rattling with the cold, he cried, "Jesus, you guys! Are you guys nuts?"

Ryan Marvell lay a kiss on top of Franny's head. "Tim," he said, very grave, "you know Franny."

When Tim Gleason groaned, Ryan Marvell guided him off across the yard, saying to Franny, "I'll be right back, okay, honey? Stay there, okay?"

She looked out at the choppy lake. A single boat sat in the bay. The lamp at its prow threw a circle of yellow on the dark water. The boat and the lamp suggested some sort of menace, though Franny knew the boat belonged to Mr. Judd. Mr. Judd would be putting down his nightly trail of corn and cat food for the enormous carp that he lured to his dock, caught, and buried because no one could abide all of those bones.

"Old Jughead, now, he likes a struggle," Brick would say of Mr. Judd, laughing, able, as most men, to find amusement in the wrong-headedness of others so long as it did not intrude on his own turf.

A third person joined Ryan Marvell and Tim Gleason. A boy in a white St. Joseph's letter jacket. Franny recognized him as the person who had helped Tim Gleason drive "Eduardo" to the hospital at the last party. He, too, was shaking his head, telling Ryan Marvell he was nuts, what was he thinking of, *Come on, man!* Franny smiled as if she heard nothing. As if she were quite comfortable standing on the top of the bank, looking out at the dark water and the lights across the lake. Her heart beat wildly, but she stood straight and tall and, just as her mother had taught her, she pictured that star connected to the top of her skull, and hoped this made her appear wise beyond her years, and even lovable.

Part II

Part II

CHAPTER TWELVE

THE NEXT MORNING, WHEN SHE WOKE, THE LIGHT IN HER
bedroom was the color of the clay that she knew how to find, here
and there, by digging in pockets along the shores of Pynch Lake. In
that cool, clay light, she pressed her fingers and strands of her hair
to her nose, and she held them there, sniffing for traces of Ryan
Marvell. Who had kissed her. And danced with her. And told her
he loved her. All of which felt much grander than anything she had
ever expected, and came as more of a shock because it had happened in the world as she knew it, in her own home, where, after sitting with Ryan Marvell on the landing, she could feel the familiar
pattern left on the back of her thighs by the sharp metal treads of
the steps.

But, then, where else could a miracle occur? A thing happening
in real time in a real place: that was what made a miracle a miracle.

Beneath sheet and spread, she knotted her hands together, and
squeezed them tight. Tighter. They sang with the fact of flesh and
blood compressed against bone. It was necessary to do this, though
she did not know why. She would be—please, let her—like Super-
man, who once saved the day by squeezing a lump of coal so hard
that it became the perfect replacement for the diamond eye stolen
from the natives' idol.

But what was it that a human being could become under pressure? How did you get to be the princess so beloved by the prince
that you could never, ever again be returned to life among the cin-
ders? The stories suggested that the answer to the latter was a foot

small enough to fit into a tiny glass slipper or a backside sensitive to the pressure from a pea, but what about love?

No need to ask, "Am I in love?" or even to think, "Now I am in love." Love was an eagle, dangling her high in the sky. Look around. The thin air and the beauty of the clouds robbed her of breath. Look down at her life, her house, her town, suddenly so small, the lake's blue fingers calmly invading the land, the land invading the water.

However, when she finally did descend the stairs and stop on the landing, she found—and this was no surprise—the now sunny world continued on as if nothing had occurred. At the stove, Peg was explaining to several girl guests the proportion of Lea & Perrins she used in her scrambled eggs. In the far corner of the kitchen, Rosamund ran the blender that whirred the orange juice for which—pitcher in hand—Turner Haskin stood waiting. Thinking it camouflage, a kind of veiling of herself in the daily, Franny jumped from the landing—slam!—before she hurried to the sink to draw a drink of water from the tap.

"Hey, Franny"—one of the girl guests stepped away from Peg's circle to whisper—"that guy you were with last night was some babe, but how *old* is he?"

Franny shrugged to suggest the girl's question was irrelevant, the guy was irrelevant—

"Franny!" A furious Martie motioned from the dining room— *Come here!*

Better not to ask what Martie wanted while within Peg's earshot. Still, Franny hated taking those steps into the dining room, asking, "What is it?"

Martie tugged Franny toward the front door where bars of morning sunshine now crashed into the house like demolition dust. "Tell me what happened last night," Martie commanded.

"Martie"—Rosamund stepped around the corner of the breakfront—"are you torturing Franny?"

"I want her to tell me what went on with that guy or I'm giving Mom and Dad a full report!"

"Of what?" Rosamund asked. "That she danced a couple of times with some cute guy? Don't be a jerk."

Franny caught the spirit of Rosamund's defense, and added, "He was nice. He said maybe we could all go skiing sometime."

Like a cartoon housewife, Martie crossed her arms and tapped her foot against the floor. "And how old is he?"

Franny shrugged. "I don't know. And I've got to go. I'm crewing for Susan."

A lie, but she did not feel guilty at telling it. She was willing to tell as many lies as necessary to protect the possibility of seeing Ryan Marvell again. She was willing to make the lies true.

"Susan," she called ahead of herself when she spied Susan Thomas gathering swimsuits and towels from the Thomas family's clothes line. "Hey!"

"Franny!" Grinning, Susan Thomas dropped her work and started across the scrappy yard. "I just heard!"

Franny raised a finger to her lips, and kept it there until she reached the girl. "What'd you hear?"

"Al Castor was out on the dock with Bryce Campbell, and they said you were at your sisters' party with some older guy!"

"Well, yeah"—sick and proud, she smiled, she shook her head—"it's a mess, though."

Susan Thomas grabbed Franny by the forearms, and jumped up and down, laughing. "Oh, my god, you're in love! I can tell! St. Frances! You're in love!"

"You feeling okay, sweetie?" Brick asked her over that evening's dinner.

She nodded. Ryan Marvell had said he would call at six-thirty. It was now six-thirty.

Brick turned to Peg. "Where's Martie?"

Peg raised her eyes and went on spooning green beans onto her plate. "Oh, she's off with Deedee, all upset about some boy not coming to the party last night."

"Someone she's interested in," Rosamund explained to Turner.

"She throws herself at them. That's her problem." Brick took hold of both sides of his end of the dining room table, and gave the table a shake that made the others reach out to steady their glasses. "Christ."

When Brick lifted his head again, his face was twisted. He's going to cry, Franny thought, and started from her chair to offer comfort—

"'But, Dad!'" Brick leaned his torso deep over the table, craned his neck toward each of them in turn as he shrilled, "'But, Dad, I *love* Billy Bob Joe!'"

Franny did her best not to run into the kitchen to answer the ringing telephone. Rosamund and Peg and Turner Haskin were all laughing at Brick's imitation of Martie—Rosamund so hard that tears stood in her eyes—and Brick, pleased, laughing a little himself, turned to Peg to say, "Did you know I was as funny as all that, toots?"

Rosamund gave a helpless sniffle. Peeped out from over the edge of her big cloth napkin. Burst anew into a series of breathless laughs as Franny exited to the kitchen.

Ryan Marvell seemed to have no idea that his actually calling her at the time that he had said he would call—his calling her at all—constituted one more miracle. He was at Viccio's Pool Hall, he said. Could Franny meet him at the Romero that night? Maybe get Rosamund to take her? The Craft was playing. Eight o'clock.

"Come on, Franny," he said, as if she were being difficult, or coquettish, but she had never been to the Romero in her life. No one her age went to the Romero. She tried to imagine a way to cover the five miles between her house and town. Running past Karlins' Grocery. Down the hill and over the causeway. Past the miniature golf course. Woolf Beach. Stanford Fanning Fellow.

Was it possible that she could row there and back without being missed? That Rosamund would drive her in, and bring her home again? That she could pretend to go to Christy Strawberry's for the evening?

The click and crack of pool balls—exotic to Franny's ears—sounded behind Ryan Marvell's words, and there was easy male laughter in the background, too, and then a deep voice moved in close to the telephone and began to sing the refrain from an old country hit called "They Say I'm Robbing the Cradle."

"Go away," Ryan Marvell told the intruder but he sounded elated, as if nothing in the world could make him gloomy. "Listen," he said, "let me talk to your folks, Franny! Good old Brick and—what's your mom's name?"

"Peg."

"Sure, Peggy and Brick. Let me tell them I love you."

"I love you, Franny," a strange voice trumpeted above the noise of the pool hall, and someone else, "Is he telling her he loves her, man? Marvell, has this girl got you whipped, or what?" and Ryan Marvell laughed and laughed, as if love's defeat filled him with joy.

A backward zoom out of the old garage and all the way up into the tall grass around the old church slab.

"Hey!" The milk in the bowl of cornflakes in Franny's lap sloshed over the bowl's edge and onto her thigh.

A forward zoom. Sharp left down the long drive. Franny pressed one bare foot against the Wildcat's glove compartment, and not just because she imagined this might save her if some slow-moving truck pulled out from one of the little side roads, but, also, to steady herself against whatever Martie meant to say.

It seemed Martie had worked to make herself look awful that morning: dowdy elastic-waist skirt, dark red lipstick, hair pulled back by one of the plastic headbands they all wore when washing their faces.

"So what's this all about, Martie?"

"It's about your friend Ryan Marvell." For emphasis, Martie slammed her palm against the steering wheel. "He's going to be a freshman in the fall."

"A freshman," Franny said. A soothing balm flooded her brain. "But that's great—"

"In *college*, Franny. A freshman at SFF."

Of course. College.

"So what do you have to say to that?" Martie demanded.

Franny had nothing to say. She carried the most delicate and precious and vulnerable of potions; the wrong words might jostle it, destroy its ineluctable qualities, or even cause an explosion.

Surely Martie understood that it was a wonder that Ryan Marvell existed and that he cared for Franny. Surely she understood love was not a part that could be turned down. In fact, maybe that was what love was—finding the one who released you into the role of lover.

Couldn't Martie and everyone else just turn away, and allow Ryan Marvell and Franny to pass, as quiet as Mary and Joseph in a Christmas pageant? Just for a while? Until the miracle was over?

"Listen up, toots!" Martie said. "Timmy told Roz this Ryan said he made out with you at the party."

Franny's disappointment was solid, a good-size pebble, but she found she could swallow it, make it a kind of meal. "So what if he did," she said. After all, she had told Susan Thomas about kissing Ryan Marvell—though not about the way he tried to put his hand up her shirt; not about the way he said he loved her. Like Franny herself, Susan Thomas would have considered both suspicious.

Past Karlins' Grocery the Wildcat darted; then it rushed out from the stretch of shady trees into the causeway's bright sunshine. Beyond the causeway and the swamp lay Mother Goose Miniature Golf, whose silly name did not detract from its new role as sometimes-center of the universe—that center making gorgeous if unnerving shifts that depended upon where Ryan Marvell could be found at any particular time—and even though she hated Martie, just then, Franny could not stop herself from crying out, *"Look,"* for a heron, bright as a bead of mercury, now stood atop the nest of a muskrat. Absurd bird. Snooty and lonely and ugly and gorgeous, and, to Franny, all of this was absolutely connected to Ryan Marvell, as were the last few soggy cornflakes in the bowl in her lap, the towel she had used to dry her face that morning, the way her signature had unfurled yesterday when she wrote her name on the birthday card to be sent to her Grandma Ackerman in southern Iowa.

Suppose Ryan Marvell were at Mother Goose right this moment?

"That's where he works, isn't it?" Martie said. "Deedee told me girls go there to flirt with him."

"Watch out." Franny pointed to the trailer court setter, now returning to his car-chasing after a dip in the lake. The driver of an oncoming station wagon honked at the dog, and the horn played the first phrase of "When You Wish upon a Star."

Standford Fanning Fellow appeared on the left. Ryan Marvell meant to go there? She could not think about what that meant except that he was impossibly old and, oh, she shivered as the Wildcat sped past the road that led to Tanglefoot and Bob Prohaski's house.

"I can't believe you!" Martie reached out her hand, and brought it down in an awkward slap that grazed, first, Franny's cheek, then her shoulder. "Can't you behave like a lady?"

"A 'lady'?" Franny tried to spit out the word but the slap had jarred her and a sob cracked the word into something unrecognizable. "Don't be—disgusting," she said.

With a lurch, Martie pulled the Wildcat into the drive of a pretty yellow Cape Cod. Ivy on the fireplace. Scotch pine towering above. The front door opened and out stepped Tim Gleason, carrying a large, red book.

For Franny, Tim Gleason's new role as friend of Ryan Marvell had made him gather substance and meaning, and she straightened in her seat as he bent down and peered into the car. "Where's Roz?" he asked.

"Rude," Martie muttered in Franny's direction, as if they were cohorts; then she informed Tim Gleason that Rosamund and Turner Haskin had driven Mike Zanios to Des Moines that morning so Mike wouldn't have to leave his car at the airport. "Is that the yearbook?"

Tim Gleason drummed his fingers on the car's convertible top.

"I thought Roz was coming," he said. Reluctantly, he handed the big book through the window to Martie, who handed it on to Franny.

St. Joseph Catholic High School. A black cross wrapped the front like a ribbon, dividing the cover into four equal parts. How dank and impoverished that linking of school and church had always seemed to Franny in the past—something smelly and moldy about it all—yet now the two aspects connected to Ryan Marvell, and the resulting triangle gave off a potent aura of mystery.

"Page fifty-two," Tim Gleason said. "Bottom of the page."

Franny opened the book: attractive young men and women in formal dress sat around a party table. Tim Gleason was one of them. And Ryan Marvell. Oh. With his arm around the bare shoulder of a very pretty girl. Who was not Franny. Which was wrong, of course, yet Franny still appreciated seeing the face of Ryan Marvell. Ryan Marvell before she had known him. The photo struck Franny as far more magical than the one that showed Peg pregnant with Franny—or any family photo that showed her infant self living a life she could not remember. Both Ryan Marvell and the girl grinned, as pleased as punch, supported all around by friends.

"Who's that with him?" Franny asked.

"His girl. Noreen Frye. A really *nice* girl."

Franny licked her lips. Tim Gleason's head remained in Martie's window, a dark blot she refused to turn toward. "What do you mean, 'his girl'?"

"Until you came along, he planned on giving her a *ring*."

"Here." Martie pulled the book from Franny's hands, and flipped to the section of senior photos. Noreen Frye. Blond hair, warm and lovely eyes, yes, but did he like her still? That was all Franny cared about.

"Do you know what it means that he was going to buy her a ring?" Tim Gleason asked.

Before she answered, Franny steadied herself against something that offered itself without explanation—some not entirely wholesome appendage she seemed to have sprouted in support of this love for Ryan Marvell. "I guess it must mean he likes me quite a bit," she said, then flipped through the senior photos pages. Ryan Marvell. His face. Look at that. Look at that chin. Those eyes like sparklers under the cliff of his brows. "Oh," she said aloud, without meaning to.

"Damn it, Franny!" said Martie.

As if she could do something about the way she felt! As if knowing Ryan Marvell had meant to marry a Noreen Frye once upon a time—even last week—might cauterize her soul, and she would simply say, "I hadn't realized!" and go away. She lowered her head into her hands. The photographs had sealed her fate more exactly by documenting that Ryan Marvell was, indeed, what she had imagined him to be: that is, made for her eyes. And her eyes made to behold him.

"Listen, Noreen's a really nice girl," Tim Gleason said. "She's broken up about this."

Franny glanced up at Tim Gleason, his face so earnest and agitated. She wanted to make an appeal to him: Would you stop liking Roz because somebody told you to? But no one ever spoke of Tim Gleason liking Roz, and so she said only—voice low, ashamed at having to defend herself—"Well, I'm a nice girl, too."

Tim Gleason made a face, as if she had said something loathsome. "You see *that* girl?" He reached into the car to tap a finger on a photo of an attractive girl in the row below Ryan Marvell. "Donna Nelson," read the type below the girl's picture. "Now, that girl's a mink, Franny. Does Franny know what a mink is, Martie?"

Martie groaned. "Just—drop it, Tim."

"A mink's something you don't want to get a reputation as, Franny. A mink's, like, a *whore*."

"Oh, really?" Franny found that, just then, she hated Tim Gleason for not being his own self—a boy in love with Rosamund—and, instead, being one of the creeps who despised girls for giving boys what the boys apparently wanted. "You mean, this Donna has sex for money?"

Tim Gleason smiled the thin smile once more. "As a matter of fact, Franny, she just gives it away."

"So—the boys who have sex with her are whores, too?"

Martie groaned. "Franny, just—shut up."

"You shut up! How does Tim even know about this girl?"

"Guys talk," Tim Gleason said.

"Okay." Martie handed the yearbook out the window. "That's enough, Tim."

"No, it's not." Tim Gleason bit down on his lip, but his chin still trembled. "If Roz were here—you want guys saying stuff about you, Franny?"

Without a thought, she flung herself between startled Martie and the steering wheel. She was a dog, then, barking at another dog, and it did not seem entirely impossible that she would bite. "*You're* the guy talking about that Donna!" she said. "I don't want anybody going around saying stuff like that about anybody!"

"*Franny.*" Martie tried to press Franny back into her seat, and in the scuffle and upset the girls missed the approach of a middle-aged woman with a potted palm in her arms.

"What's the problem here, Tim?" the woman called.

The girls settled back in their seats. Tim Gleason backed away from the car. "No problem, Mom," he said. "They're just leaving."

Whatever Martie had to say on the ride home—how their mother and father had hit her the time they found her "making out" with Roger Dale, how they had threatened her again and again with reform school—Franny did not want to hear it. She slumped against the car seat, and turned away, eyes closed. She made herself into the smallest possible wave, moving up to, and away from, a sandy shore. Up, back. From that day forward, she vowed, she would speak to Martie only when absolutely necessary—

"Reform school!" Martie murmured. "Is that insane, or what?"

Franny distracted herself by inventing ways by which she might obtain a photo of Ryan Marvell without actually asking him for a photo. To actually ask him for a photo—that would be to ask him to agree to the reality of their romance. Which might be to ask too much.

"Look, I know you're mad at me," Martie said, "but there's nothing you're going through that I haven't gone through worse."

Franny opened her eyes to slits. The Wildcat was passing the far end of the Nearys' farm. She could see the Poddigbattes Camp sign in the distance. If they had not been so close to home, she believed she would have jumped from the car, taken her chances on bones, skin.

"Looks like somebody's at the house," Martie said.

On the front steps stood a boy and girl of about Franny's own age. The grandchildren of Mrs. Conover from down the beach. "I don't want to see them right now," Franny said. "Just—drive by."

"Don't be silly!" Martie honked the horn, then pulled the convertible to a noisy stop by the front steps, and called, "Howdy, guys!" before whispering to Franny, "Get out and talk to your friends!"

"I could kill you," Franny hissed, but she did her best to smile as she walked over to the pair. The Biancos. They had had a nice time together, two summers ago, when Franny first had moved out from town, and they had come from New Jersey to visit their grandparents. Marie, with her almost lidless brown eyes, had become very pretty since then, and though her sweet brother had gone from soft to stout, Franny would have known him anywhere. Billy. With his big black glasses frames forever sliding down his nose.

It was decided that—for old times' sake—the three of them should test the apples on the Nearys' remaining tree and, while they walked down the drive toward the orchard, Marie leaned close to Franny to whisper, "Our grandma made sure to tell us you were 'busty.' Like we'd faint if we saw you without being warned!"

Franny blushed. "She probably meant Martie," she whispered back, and bent to pick a handful of the butter-and-eggs that grew along the road.

"Hey, Franny," Billy Bianco said, "remember how you got us to roast acorns? You'd read some book where the Indians ate acorns?" The boy wrinkled up his nose at the memory. Franny laughed. No more than a week before, she had eaten a few waxy bites off an acorn, just to recall its acrid taste, the curling of her tongue.

"And remember how Billy always *wanted* us to be Indians so he could kill us?" Marie asked.

Franny liked the Biancos for remembering things—so much so, in fact, that it seemed to her that if the Biancos would only stay the summer, she might be restored to her old life. She would not tell them about Ryan Marvell. Or even about Bob Prohaski—

With a shout of exuberance, she ran ahead and jumped for a branch of the old tree, and though the bark hurt her hands, she managed to swing back and forth several times.

Unfortunately, when the Biancos caught up with her, they explained that they were in Pynch Lake for only two days. Tomorrow night, they would take a plane to California to visit their father. Billy Bianco, halfway up the apple tree, struggling a little, explained that their parents had divorced since their last visit to Iowa:

"That's one reason we didn't come at all last summer. Vacations, now, we're usually at Dad's."

If the Nearys' apple tree had been healthier, then perhaps Bob Prohaski would not have spied Franny and the Biancos in the tree. As things stood, however, years of disease had left a great gap in the branches that faced the road, and no sooner had Bob Prohaski stepped from the Oldsmobile that had brought him from town than he began to move down into the ditch and toward the tree, the big muscles beneath his cut-offs and T-shirt pumping.

He heard about Ryan, Franny thought, and the thought must have shown on her face, for Billy Bianco asked in a breathless voice, "Do you know that guy, Franny?"

Before she could answer, Bob Prohaski began to shake the limb upon which she stood. "What's going on here?" he demanded over the swishing leaves, the clunky beats of Franny's heart.

Though too high up in the tree for a safe jump, Franny jumped. The jolt of the earth rose through her feet to her shoulders, and the very top of her head, but she was okay. "Bob, these guys are my neighbors' *grandkids*," she said. She tried to send a smile of reassurance up to the pair, though Billy Bianco's eyes had already acquired the milky look that Franny had noticed on other boys in the presence of Bob Prohaski. Playing dead, maybe?

"Get down here, man!" Bob Prohaski shouted. He grabbed the fat limb supporting Billy Bianco and began to shake it. "I'll kill you if you've been messing with Franny. How'd you like that?"

"There's Grandma!" Marie Bianco shrieked, and all eyes turned toward the Cadillac that now made its ponderous way down the main drive toward Lakeside. "Grandma!" The girl and her brother began to slip and scrape their way down the backside of the tree as the Cadillac came to a stop.

The grandmother—a fragile but erect woman—leaned out her window. "Is that Franny with you?" she called happily—one split second before Bob Prohaski grabbed her grandson by the scruff of his T-shirt. Immediately, the grandmother screeched in alarm, and tried to put the Cadillac into park. The car lurched forward and died as Franny grabbed a handful of Bob Prohaski's own T-shirt and whispered an ardent, "Bob, let go of him! You're all wrong! Let go!"

From a safer distance, Marie Bianco called, "Let him go, you creep! Let him go!"

Bob Prohaski turned toward Franny. For a moment, she thought he meant to spit at her, but then he released Billy Bianco, and the boy took off, running, for his grandmother's car.

"It was a misunderstanding!" Franny called after them. "Really."

Neither Mrs. Conover nor the Biancos looked her way as they drove off in the Cadillac, and Franny knew it was preposterous for her to wave as the car turned onto Lakeside, but she waved anyway, as if she and Bob Prohaski saw off guests after a weekend of fun and hospitality.

Their jagged breaths filled the silence that followed. The whistle of the air through her nostrils frightened Franny a little, but she rustled up a smile when Bob Prohaski gripped the back of her neck with his hand and started her up the drive. She kept her mouth shut.

Things were not so bad as she had thought: He did not know about Ryan Marvell.

"You hear the woodpecker?" she asked when they were in the shade of the oaks. He made no reply. "It's a red-headed wood-pecker," she said.

She was wondering if she should tell him about her Snow White dream—just to fill the silence—when he brought his knee up behind her knees and collapsed her onto the lawn. "Hey!" she cried.

With a grin, he flipped her onto her back, and straddled her belly. "See, I thought you were messing around on me. I didn't see the girl up there." He brought his face close. Something like cotton had gathered at the corners of his mouth—something like the foam that caught in the rocks along the shore. She had seen that same foam at the corners of her father's mouth when he was in a fury. "I guess you know now what I'd do if you messed around on me."

She glanced off to one side to conceal what was in her eyes: the thought that he was dull, but dull in the dangerous way of dull knives, which slip and cut because they lacked a good edge.

"FRANCES JEAN WAHL!"

Here came Martie, barreling across the lawn, and what did Martie begin to do but kick at Bob Prohaski? Who scuttled off of Franny, shouting, "What the hell?"

"Get up immediately, Frances Jean!" Martie shrieked.

"Like I *asked* him to sit on me!" Franny stood and brushed her-self off. "You are so nuts, Martie!"

"What the hell's going on?" Bob Prohaski repeated.

"Just get out of here, bud," Martie said. She began to push Franny toward the front door, saying as they went, "I'm nuts? What's that make you, Frances? Messing around with a Prohaski *and* that Mother Goose jerk!"

Impossible for Franny not to look back to see if Bob Prohaski had heard that last.

He had heard. His eyes narrowed, and not just in suspicion, but in pain, too. "What's she talking about, Franny?"

"Oh, Bob." She wanted to go to him, then, take it all back, offer comfort, but Martie continued to push her toward the house, and to shout, "You get off our land," and, really, Franny wanted that, too. She felt half grateful for Martie's shoves, and went along with it when, with a bang, Martie opened the front door and pushed Franny inside.

"Unless you want the police to come!" Martie called over her shoulder.

Bob Prohaski burst into furious huffs of laughter. "My uncle's with the police, bitch! You don't scare me."

"That's your mistake, then!" Martie shouted at the boy before she slammed the big door shut and locked it.

"Martie," Franny said. "I hope you understand he *tripped* me. I don't even like him anymore."

"Yeah. Now you're in love with some guy who's going to college in the fall." Martie held her head down as if she did not want Franny to see her smile, but she let Franny see her eyes. Because she could not help but find some happiness in Franny's being in love? Because it made them more alike?

"What on earth was all that?"

The girls turned. In the doorway to the back hall stood Peg. The mask of cosmetic clay that she sometimes put on her skin had dried and cracked around her mouth. To Franny, the clay always made Peg look a little frightening, but Martie laughed at the effect and went to Peg and put an arm around her.

"Good news, Mom," she said. "Franny doesn't like that Prohaski anymore," and, with a thumb, she directed Peg to the small rectangular window in the front door.

Peg peered out. "Well, say, he's halfway down the road already, girls. Would that be too soon to celebrate?"

CHAPTER THIRTEEN

IN HER BEDROOM, ON THE FAINTLY BLUE-LINED NOTEBOOK
paper she had recently purchased for fall, Franny drew a log cabin
with a stone path up to its door and *K*'s of curtain at the windows.
A home as rustically functional and removed from the real as the
Boxcar Children's boxcar, the Swiss Family Robinson's tree hut,
the Flintstones' pile of rocks. She set a little mailbox at the end of
the path, and wrote upon it RYAN MARVELL.

In the next room, Deedee Pierce and Martie applied Peg's clay
mask to each other's faces in preparation for that evening's dance
at the country club, and listened to the records that Martie always
played when feeling lovelorn—just then, Brenda Lee's "All Alone
Am I."

Did something inside the brain carry a code for that downward
spiral of violin notes—falling, falling, like leaves—that the brain
read as "sad"? Franny was thinking about how poems created such
effects when the telephone began to ring. She ran for the upstairs
extension, but it was only Rosamund, calling to say that she and
Turner Haskin were back from Des Moines with Mike Zanios's car,
and did Peg want anything at the store?

"Are you on the line, Franny?" Peg asked from the kitchen telephone. "Come downstairs and set the table. One extra place."

While she gathered silverware in the kitchen, Franny decided
the dinner guest must be the owner of that rectangle of flattop she
could make out over the back of an easy chair in the den.

Daiquiris. The smell of rum and limeade filled the kitchen and Franny could see her mother in the den, the empty blender pitcher in her hand. "Oh, Brick!" Peg sounded displeased with something Franny's father had said, and Franny edged toward the doorway to listen.

"Think about my cousin Grace," her father was saying, "but, hey, here's Fran now!"

She started. She had not realized she was in his line of sight.

"Come on in! I want you to meet an old friend of mine!"

Franny lay down the silverware and entered the den. She could see, now, that her father already had drunk quite a bit. Even if she had not heard the liquor in his voice, she would have known from the way he leaned back in his chair, hips toward the edge of the cushion, long legs shooting out into the room. Still, it was Franny to whom Peg gave a dirty look as she left the den with the empty pitcher. What was that about?

The guest turned out to be an old law school buddy by the name of Hank Ayles, a trim and friendly man with a disconcerting amount of gray fuzz on his arms and forming his owlish tufts of eyebrows. "Your father's feeding me daiquiris," Mr. Ayles said.

Brick nodded at Franny. "We were just discussing a phone call I received this afternoon." He winked at Mr. Ayles, and Ayles winked back. "This man from the miniature golf—Mother Goose?—he's got a problem. Johanson? You know that name?"

Skin prickling—could they see?—she shook her head.

"Well, he seemed like a nice fellow, but he's all upset. Apparently, he's twenty-eight years old with a wife and kids and, this afternoon, someone called him and threatened to beat him up. Under the impression you were his girlfriend!"

While regaining her breath, Franny did her best to arrange a reassuringly juvenile expression on her face (wide eyes, gaping mouth). The idea that someone could be beaten up because of her made her knees go wobbly with distress. Still, her voice sounded quite normal to her ears when she said, "I don't even *know* of anybody named Johanson, Dad."

Brick nodded. "That's about what I figured, honey, but I told him I'd ask you about it. He was pretty shook."

"I guess." She made an effort to meet her father's eyes. "What do you bet—what do you bet that Bob Prohaski got some crazy idea in his head?"

That Bob Prohaski. Thus evoked, it seemed to Franny that Bob Prohaski stood across a field, a banished figure that she and her father could contemplate together. The sight of Bob, there, left her a little lonely, a little frightened, but Brick was massaging the bridge of his nose, laughing. "This Prohaski's a bruiser," he told Mr. Ayles, then turned back to Franny. "Better call him off, dear. He's got Mr. Johanson quaking in his boots."

Franny was quaking, herself, but no one seemed to notice. Mr. Ayles sat forward in his chair and waited that perfect deferential second to see if Brick were done talking; then, tilting his head to one side, Mr. Ayles asked what Franny had done over the summer, and she told him the sort of things she could: a bus trip with the Y-Teens to Minneapolis to shop at Southdale and view *The Sound of Music*, sailing with Susan Thomas—

"Playing miniature golf," Peg muttered as she came into the room to refill the men's glasses.

"You know what's funny?" Franny said—though almost as she spoke she sensed the foolishness of flashing a minor truth around in an area where serious lies could be exposed—"I haven't even played miniature golf since early June."

"Best years of your life, right, Brick?" Mr. Ayles said.

Brick rumbled a laughing assent. "Hell to grow old," he said and briskly rubbed his hands over his face and neck as if trying to wash away the signs of his age.

As soon as possible, Franny headed up the stairs to her parents' bedroom, and located the Prohaski family's telephone number in the local directory.

"Oh," said Mrs. Prohaski, "he don't want to talk to *you*."

Three Hobarts lived in Pynch, but one of them was a doctor, and one showed a rural farm delivery address, and Franny felt certain Bob Prohaski's chubby pal Roy was the son of neither a doctor nor a farmer, and so she tried number three.

"You," Roy Hobart said. "What do you want besides a fat lip?"

"A Mr. Johanson called my dad and said somebody claiming to be my boyfriend threatened to beat him up. I don't even know this Mr. Johanson, Roy! Will you tell Bob that? And, please, not to hurt him?"

Roy Hobart laughed. "So who's the guy we should hurt?"

When she did not answer, Roy Hobart said a low "Fuck you" and hung up.

Dear God—knives and spoons on the right of the plate, fork on the left—*please let things work out all right. Please don't let Bob hurt Ryan or that other man.* So ran the prayer Franny was praying as Turner Haskin and Rosamund arrived at the house in Mike Zanios's car.

"Fran, we have to talk," Rosamund whispered the moment she and Turner Haskin entered the front hall.

Something else? "What is it, Roz?"

"I hope we're not mistaken," Martie called down the stairs. "We thought we heard the blender going. Could somebody be serving daiquiris?"

"What *is* it, Roz?" Franny whispered again.

"Follow me." Rosamund stepped into the living room and, apparently as some sort of cover, she and Turner Haskin began to rifle through the albums leaned up against the stereo cabinet. "We ran into Timmy downtown," she murmured. "He told us about that business with the yearbook. He felt bad, I guess—about you being upset—so he told Ryan and now Ryan's coming *here*. To meet Mom and Dad. So they'll let you go out with him! Timmy told him it was crazy—"

"He's coming here?" The information went down like a piece of candy, accidentally swallowed: an experience of sweetness, then that lurch of fear and loss of breath and the sweetness gone out of reach. Still, it seemed to Franny that the odds had changed. The odds that a person as wonderful as Ryan Marvell would want to be with her were surely more unlikely than the odds that her parents might decide to let her see such a person.

"Maybe it will work, Roz," she pleaded.

"Franny! It will *not* work, and Daddy and Mom will kill me!" Rosamund pulled the album in Turner Haskin's hands away from him, and plunked the record inside onto the stereo turntable. "We're going to treat this whole thing as—a funny misunderstanding. You talked to Ryan for a few minutes the other night, and he thought you were cute, and asked you to dance, but had no idea you were so young—"

"I have to see him, though, Roz!"

"Hey!" Brick shouted from the den. "Someone's knocking. Can't one of you get that?"

"I've got it!" Rosamund called, then hissed at Franny as they rushed toward the front door, "Let me handle this!"

No one stood at the front door, but *Ay-yay-yay* said Rosamund, and pointed toward a funny old brown and white car in the drive. "That's his car." She stuck her head out the door and looked around. "Where is he?"

"I hear knocking," Franny murmured.

"Hey!" Brick again. "Who's getting that door?"

"Where is he?" Rosamund started toward the back hall, Franny following close behind, but then they heard Peg, using her voice for guests:

"Just a minute. Hold on, there. It's stuck."

In the back hall, left over from the days of the camp or, perhaps, even the hunting lodge, there stood a door that no one ever used, but that Ryan Marvell had apparently taken for the entrance allotted friends who came to call. Franny and Rosamund and, then, Martie, too, arrived at this door just in time to hear Ryan Marvell introduce himself to Peg.

"Actually, you've met my folks at the Paulsons', Mrs. Wahl. My dad's Ben Marvell."

Peg nodded pleasantly. "Oh, yes, he owns the theaters."

Something in Ryan Marvell's smile let Franny know that he had seen her though he did not look her way. "I was wondering if Franny was home, Mrs. Wahl. If I might speak to her."

Peg started at the cluster of daughters she found behind her when she turned, but she smiled. "You have a visitor," she said to Franny.

Maybe Peg saw in Ryan Marvell a polite improvement over Bob Prohaski, and missed his age. Maybe—Franny's thoughts swam, dipped—maybe by some miracle, he had actually become younger. Maybe people had been mistaken about his age—

"I don't believe this," Martie muttered, then marched after the departing Peg and Rosamund for a moment, leaving Franny and Ryan Marvell alone in the dim hall. She did not hesitate to step into his open arms. They were blessed. They were the candle that flickered at the end of *This Is the Life*. They were the couple in "So Much in Love." But then came the sound of hard soles on wood and Franny and Ryan Marvell drew away from each other just as Brick and Martie and Deedee Pierce poured into the narrow back hall. Brick was swearing and Martie was saying "statutory rape" and Deedee Pierce was laughing, *Oh, boy, old Franny's got herself a mess now*.

"Scum," Brick called Ryan Marvell. Mr. Ayles and Turner Haskin and Peg and Rosamund had moved into the kitchen by then, too. *Dog. Slime. Yellow-bellied sapsucker*, Brick said. Colorful, childish insults that steered so close to obscenity they would have been funny if Brick had not bawled them out like a power saw, his eyes red and bulging with the effort and emotion.

"Dad," Franny protested, "stop!"

But he went on. He was a fire, a spectacle.

Had anybody ever spoken to Ryan Marvell the way Brick spoke now? When Brick finally paused for breath, Ryan Marvell leaned forward a bit—"Well, you see, sir," he began, but Brick did not mean to listen to a word. He yelled, he grew redder in the face, and finally Rosamund said what Franny could not bring herself to say:

"You better go, Ryan."

Ryan Marvell pushed his fists deep into the pockets of his pressed chinos. "Well, I don't know," he said, and looked out the back door toward the swamp, the meadows.

"What does he mean, he doesn't know?" Brick demanded.

Ryan Marvell turned toward Franny. "We'll talk later?"

"The hell you will!" Brick shouted, and it became necessary for Mr. Ayles and Turner Haskin to restrain Brick then, Mr. Ayles taking hold of Brick's belt from behind and Turner Haskin pressing against him from in front while Ryan Marvell exited through that never used door.

"You stop your crying this instant," Brick shouted at Franny. "I'll be damned if I'll have shenanigans like this under my roof!"

"And don't you give me a dirty look, Roz," Martie said. The scene had left her looking hot and sweaty in her party clothes. She might as well have already been to the party and come home after a long night of being sick in the ladies' room. "And Franny"—Martie tried to wrap her arms around Franny, but Franny wanted nothing to do with Martie, and she moved across the room to stand beside Rosamund.

"Martie." Rosamund pursed her lips. "I don't know what you think you accomplished here, but I'm sure we could have found a more graceful means of handling a boy's coming by to say hello."

"Huh!" Martie thrust out her chin at Rosamund. "You might think so. After all, you're the one who introduced them."

"No," Franny said, "it wasn't Roz," but Brick burst in, "At that party? Is that right, Roz?" Turner Haskin and Mr. Ayles had let him go now, but he looked as if he wanted to run in circles, the way Suzie-Q had used to do when people set off fireworks on the Fourth of July.

"It was all quite harmless, Daddy," Rosamund said, and rubbed her hand up and down Franny's back. "I don't know why Martie caused all this trouble."

"*I'm* the one who told them how old he was, Roz," Deedee Pierce said.

Rosamund nodded. "I could have expected that. Ryan's handsome and cool"—she shrugged—"no doubt you envied Franny."

Deedee Pierce laughed. "Don't get snotty, Roz. You know the other night wasn't so innocent as you make it out to be."

"That's right!" Martie said.

"What in heaven's name?" Brick looked about to cry. "Shall we drag out our dirty laundry for all the world to see?"

"Peg." Turner Haskin smiled gently at Peg, then pointed to the mushrooms now blackening on the stove.

"Oh!" Peg pulled the pan from the fire. "Our dinner!"

"Don't worry about dinner." Mr. Ayles gave Peg a wink of sympathy, then grabbed the bottle of rum from the counter and nudged it into Brick's back. "Brick and I will just head back in the other room to talk over old times, right, Brick?"

"And I don't want that Prohaski scum around here, either," Brick shouted as Mr. Ayles guided him back into the den. "There's going to be some changes around here."

Peg set her hands on top of her head. "What a mess! What a mess!"

"Now, Mom," Rosamund said, "calm down," and she linked her arm through Peg's arm as if the two of them were going for a stroll, and then she suggested Turner Haskin take the Wildcat into town and buy himself a hamburger while she and Franny and Peg had a talk upstairs.

"What about me?" Martie protested.

"I don't want to talk to you!" Franny cried.

"I was trying to help, brat!" Martie said, and kicked a foot in Franny's direction.

"Martie." Rosamund waved goodbye to Turner Haskin as he made his way to the garage; then, one arm still linked through Peg's arm, she settled the other around Martie's shoulders and said a soothing, "Let Mom and me talk to her now, Martie. You go to your dance, and we can talk later, when you don't have company."

Though Deedee Pierce responded to this with a snort that signalled both amusement and loathing, Martie wilted under Rosamund's arm.

She cocked her head toward the front door, signalling to Deedee that the two of them should, indeed, make an exit.

Dread filled Franny's heart as she began to climb the stairs with Rosamund and Peg, but, halfway up the stairs, Rosamund turned and pressed the back of her hand to her mouth as if suppressing a giggle. "How many pitchers of daiquiris have Dad and Mr. Ayles had, anyway?" she whispered, as if blame for everything—the appearance of Ryan Marvell at the door, the appalling quarrel—could be laid at the feet of too much rum and limeade.

And suppose Rosamund's intimation were right? Maybe Franny's father would feel differently about Ryan Marvell tomorrow?

Rosamund waved Peg and Franny into her bedroom, and Franny, heart full of hope, said, "Ryan really is nice, Mom."

"Oh, Franny," Peg said, "he's going to college, honey!"

"But we're all going to stay calm and cool, right?" Rosamund said, her voice light, almost teasing.

Peg smiled wearily as she took a seat at the dressing table. "I'm working on it," she said. "His mother—I seem to remember the mother was quite charming."

Franny stroked the wales of the bedspread back and forth. Charming. Of course she would be charming.

"He's a good friend of Timmy's," Rosamund said. "He was trying to do the right thing, coming here to meet you guys."

"Irregardless," said Peg.

Rosamund nodded, eyes closed. "I know. Of course."

They both looked at Franny then. "I didn't know he was so much older when I met him," she said. "I really like him, Mom."

"I didn't think—I mean, they could end up serious about each other," Rosamund said. "He was supposed to be getting engaged, and now apparently that's all off."

"Engaged?" Peg shook her head.

It seemed to Franny that Peg sounded almost impressed, and so Franny dared to plead, "Couldn't you just talk to Dad about it, Mom? Couldn't we just see if he'd calm down?"

"He's not going to calm down." Peg's voice was unusually shapeless, so unformed by any design that Franny knew she could believe her.

"You're a brilliant and lovely girl," Peg said, "and you probably are mature for your age, but—we wouldn't be good parents if we let you see someone so much older."

Brilliant and lovely? Franny wanted to press up against the words. That Rosamund and her mother believed Ryan Marvell actually cared for her was, in itself, a miracle; really, in its way, this moment with Rosamund and her mother was almost as dazzling as her evening with Ryan Marvell. Look at the three of them, sitting there in Rosamund's room, talking! What they had in that room—it possessed a glow that Franny could only have imagined being given off by some dream version of her family—

But, then, a bellow sounded from the den below, and Peg whispered, "I know your dad can be a trial. His drinking's alienating everyone from us—"

"Well, Mom," Rosamund said—almost brisk—"you could always divorce him."

The idea that such words could even be spoken knocked a wall right out of the bedroom, and let in with a crash the beautiful, spooky dusk and all of the universe beyond—glorious, perilous—and Peg did not even sound angry when she responded, "Oh, Roz, honey, you don't divorce somebody after twenty-five years."

"But why not?" Franny felt giddy. "Christy's parents are getting divorced. Turner's parents are divorced. Lots of people—"

"Franny." Peg shook her head slowly, thoughtfully. "Now, you know we're not getting divorced."

"But his drinking—you just said it's awful."

"But we know why he drinks, Franny," Rosamund said—almost impatiently, as if she had not been the one to bring up the idea of divorce in the first place.

Franny nodded, though she did not understand how it was that Rosamund and her mother—and Martie, too—could so easily hold on to the string that kept the bright balloon of that old story above their heads. She herself felt tugged about each time she touched the thing.

"Well"—Peg smiled wearily as she stood up from the dressing table—"I suppose I better go check on him."

Now? Franny did not understand. They could not stop talking now, surely.

"And I better get ready for Turner!" Again, Rosamund linked her arm through Peg's arm—imagine doing that!—and, with a little sidestep, the two of them headed out the bedroom door and into the hall.

Come back, Franny wanted to call to them, but she was a creature pulled out of the water and left gasping for air on the unfamiliar shore.

What about Ryan Marvell? Did they think she now would—could—just say, "Okay, if you don't think it's a good idea, I won't love him"? Who were they if they thought that was possible?

Limp, panting a little, she lay back on the bed.

The thing about Ryan Marvell—the special and amazing thing—was that he had chosen her, while the rest of them were only stuck with her: a member of the family. The rest of them did not care about the fact that he had chosen her, but, to Franny, it meant the world.

Quietly, she made her way down the stairs and through the living room while her father continued his rant in the den. She passed out through the screened porch to the grassy bank where she had kissed Ryan Marvell. She lay down. Smelled the grass. Felt the twigs beneath her head and back. No one could take from her the fact that she had lain here on the bank with him. Not that, or his smile, tonight, when she stepped into the back hall.

From his smile, she had seen that he was purely *happy* to see her—happy in that way that her father used to be happy to see her when she was small and ran out to the car to greet him. Even happier. Because it did not seem there was something else Ryan Marvell waited for: She was it.

At the thought of losing that smile, the pain of it, she grabbed the scruffy grass of the bank with both hands as if it might hold her to the earth.

"Franny?"

She recognized Turner Haskin without looking up; the light blue pants, the perfection of their creases. After giving a careful, but debonair hike to each knee of his pants—a Cary Grant kind of gesture, Franny supposed—Turner Haskin crouched beside her on the bank. He gazed off at the lake, his chin lifted just a touch.

"Roz sent me out here," he said.

Franny nodded. It would have been pleasant to give him a little shove. Not so he'd get hurt, really—just so he'd topple over, have a clumsy moment.

Eh-hem. He cleared his throat. Thinking? "Franny," he said. He pointed his index finger out over the lake, then cocked his thumb the way a boy would when pretending his hand was a gun. "A penis is like a loaded rifle, Franny: Safe till it shoots."

She stared at the lake while Turner Haskin blew imaginary smoke from the tip of his imaginary gun. "Get my drift?"

She hoped her silent nod would make him go away, and soon enough the radiant blue pants did move off toward the house, and, shortly thereafter, the headlights of the Wildcat swung across the old lap siding, and the lawn, and the oak trees, and her back, and Rosamund and Turner Haskin drove away for the evening.

Beyond the dark ruff formed by the trees on the other side of the lake, the sky pulsed with heat lightning. Eventually, Mr. Judd came out and began to fiddle with the fishing poles he had rigged up on his dock. A queer thing: her sense that she had to stay outside until someone called her in.

Stars fell. Great numbers of them. But, of course, they were not stars. Meteors. She could swear some of them made a little zipping sound as they moved, a sizzle like sparklers tossed into the lake on the Fourth of July.

At the beginning of the summer, had something gone wrong, Franny would have called Christy Strawberry or Joan Harvett. Now, she thought of calling Susan Thomas, but she hesitated because if

Peg knew that Franny called someone outside the family, Peg would almost certainly accuse Franny of judging the conversation in Rosamund's room as deficient, and that conversation needed to be shown respect, enthroned, built upon.

Well, then, the person she should talk to was Peg, wasn't it?

Though Mr. Ayles's car remained in the parking area, and Franny could hear his voice and the voice of her father in the den, the downstairs was perfectly dark. From upstairs, however, light from Peg and Brick's bedroom window shone on the lawn. Peg would be reading her craft magazines. In bed. A pillow behind her back. Franny could picture her exactly. Reading under the lamp with the ugly green shade that Peg wanted to replace but felt she must use until it wore out.

Franny did not dare turn on a light in the front hall for fear Brick would come to see who was there; and so, very slowly, she worked her way through the dark dining and living rooms to the staircase, and up the stairs.

The door to her parents' bedroom stood slightly ajar, and it opened the rest of the way when Franny began to knock. There stood Peg, in the center of the room, red-eyed, a fistful of her nightgown balled up in her hand.

"I hope you have some idea of what you've done!" Peg cried. "Your father may just pack up and leave us altogether!"

"Mom," Franny pleaded, but Peg backed away, shouting:

"Don't give me that wide-eyed look! I'm not dumb! There's only one reason a college boy would come to see you, which gives me a good idea of what you were up to the other night!"

"Mom, please." Franny did not understand what was happening until she heard her father's footsteps begin to pound their way up the stairs.

"What the hell is she doing now?" Brick bawled, while from below, Mr. Ayles called, "Come on back, Brick. Come on, pal."

Her father was a bear, coming at her. She tried to crouch in a ball in the corner, by the bedside table, but he yanked her to her feet. "Get up!" he shouted.

"Brick," Mr. Ayles called, his voice full of misery. "Come on back down here, buddy."

Brick did not respond to Mr. Ayles. Like an athlete too long confined by bad weather, he seemed delighted to use his muscles. His face contorted into something almost a grin, he picked Franny up by her hair and rushed her into a wall while Peg slapped at whatever bit of girl she could find. Arms, face, back, neck—

Both of them: close, personal, astonishing.

"I'll teach you." Her father's big head and lips snarled alongside her right eye. Revolting. Him. Not him. She felt his spit on her cheek. "I'll teach you to act like a whore."

CHAPTER FOURTEEN

THE CAB DRIVER WHO CAME TO TAKE TURNER HASKIN TO THE airport was a jolly guy with a gap between each of his pumpkin-colored teeth and a crescent of sunburned backside visible between his T-shirt and low-hanging pants. That noon, the winds were high enough to raise whitecaps on the lake, and at first Peg and Franny and Martie, waiting at a polite distance while Rosamund and Turner kissed goodbye, could not hear what the driver called to them above the wild swish of oak leaves, the buck and crack of the sheets on the Judd clothesline.

"I said, 'I never picked anybody up out this far before.'"

Though a little misty-eyed at the sight of Rosamund and Turner Haskin's farewell—and laughing at themselves for being misty-eyed—the trio nodded politely at the driver's words. Nodded when he admired the Wildcat and said he'd rather have gone to the airport in *that* than his old cab any day.

Franny was relieved when Turner Haskin threw open a door of the cab and climbed in (she had sensed that Peg was on the verge of explaining to the driver that, of course, her daughter would have given her boyfriend a ride to the airport had he not called a cab in order to spare her a depressing goodbye, and wasn't that a gentlemanly thing to do?).

"So"—as soon as the cab started up Lakeside, Peg turned to Rosamund with a giddy smile—"so," she asked, "is this serious?"

Martie sniffled and laughed. "Of course it's serious!"

Rosamund, however, lifted her shoulders. "Too soon to know."

"But your dad and I thought you really liked him!" Peg protested.

"I do really like him." Rosamund smiled at the now empty road. "He's as handsome as a movie star and he's smart and absolutely charming."

Martie made a sour face at this response, but Peg seemed to like it, and she smiled at Franny as if to say *See what nice things await you if you behave?* That smile of Peg's—it suggested that the scene of three nights before had never happened at all. Just this morning, however, Peg had come to Franny's bedroom door to plead, "You have to be nicer to your dad! Every night since that Marvell came here, your dad's left his shoes by the bed. In twenty-three years of marriage, he's never done that. I think he's planning to leave us!" The next thing Franny knew, Peg had flung her arms around her and begun to weep, and Franny—confused by the rare embrace— promised to be nicer, really, Mom, though she could not think that she had ever *not* been nice to her father; and remembering that moment, now, as Peg—half playful, half chiding—said to Rosamund, "If I were you, I sure wouldn't let Turner get away," Franny felt irritated, and obliged to object:

"Why don't you say *Turner* shouldn't let Rosamund get away? Did you tell Turner that?"

Peg laughed as if this were pure silliness, and Franny wanted to object to Peg's laughter as well, but the telephone had begun to ring inside the house and—quick, to conceal whatever might be on her face—she stooped to pick up one of the small green acorns that had fallen onto the drive. Chucked it at the garage door. See? She did not care about the telephone. Not a bit. Let Martie be the one to hurry ahead to answer.

"Rosamund"—Martie stuck her head out the door to call— "Mr. Z. calling."

Rosamund wrinkled up her nose as Martie disappeared into the house once more. "Did she mean Mike?" she asked Peg.

"Probably. He probably wants to thank you for driving him to Des Moines."

"Oh, dear." Rosamund stopped to hold open the front door for Peg and Franny. "I don't feel like talking just now. Could you tell him I ran Franny into town, Mom?" She glanced toward Franny. "You're ready to go, aren't you?"

Yes. To Christy Strawberry's and, later, from Christy Strawberry's to the carnival now making its annual visit to Pynch Lake. At the carnival, she would see Ryan Marvell.

Amazing that she had arranged to do such a thing. That, yesterday, she had arranged to be by the pay phone at Karlins' Grocery, waiting for his call. That she had picked up the ringing pay phone when it rang. "Is that wild or what?" Ryan Marvell had said after Franny told him of the call her father had received from the manager of Mother Goose Golf. "Johanson told me all about it, too, and I acted totally dumb, and, like, 'Hey, man, I'll help you out if anybody tries to hurt you!' and now Johanson thinks I'm a real pal!"

"I shouldn't have gone this way." Rosamund tapped her nails on the steering wheel as a group of pedestrians crossed in front of the Wildcat. "This is crazy."

In a ring around the grassy center of City Park, the machinery of the big carnival rides—the Ferris wheel, the Bullet—rose above the trees. The carnival's herd of semitrailers pulsed and whined in the streets surrounding the park. Still, it was possible to see the band shell, and, on stage, a bee of a girl in black and gold sequins, twirling a baton.

"Do we go right when we get to Payson, or left?"

"Left." Franny smiled at the full-size cutout of the winking Dutch boy that stood behind the plate-glass windows of Grant's Hardware. The day before, on the telephone, Ryan Marvell had mentioned that his father was making him paint the family garage, and now the world of ladders, brushes, and buckets of paint shimmered with significance, trailed banners of gold.

"So"—Rosamund cleared her throat—"I guess you're meeting Ryan at the carnival tonight?"

Franny glanced her way. Rosamund was smiling a profile smile, nothing collusive, but a smile nonetheless. "Just be careful," Rosamund said. "Don't get hurt," and Franny smiled back as if she were as lighthearted as Rosamund herself.

"And watch out for Martie," Rosamund added with a laugh, then murmured a more somber, "everybody watch out for Martie. This morning, I swear to God, she would have followed Turner into the shower if he hadn't barred the door. It's—weird. She's always wanted to date everybody I've ever dated."

"Poor Martie," Franny said; her love for Ryan Marvell made her generous. "Maybe she isn't sure if a guy's any good unless you've already gone out with him, Roz."

Rosamund shook her head. "That would be too pathetic."

But not necessarily untrue, Franny thought, and switched the topic by asking how Turner Haskin would spend the rest of summer.

Wasn't it curious, she thought—while Rosamund went on about Turner at some length—that in just one week, the formerly flavorless brick buildings of St. Joseph's had magically popped out from behind Mailer's Auto Body and the Red Owl. All over Pynch, sacred ground accumulated: the staircase where she and Ryan Marvell had met, the pay telephone at Karlins' Grocery where they had planned tonight's meeting, the loveseat where they first kissed, the street she now knew to be the street on which he lived; *and* there were the streets that led to his street, and, then, all streets. He was her Rome.

But what he gave, he could also take away. He had even changed the carnival. The rides rattling on their tracks, the booths for games of chance, the buttery lights against the red paint and gilded mirrors of the merry-go-round—if he did not come to meet her tonight, all of that would wait in darkness, as if only he controlled the switch that could make the pleasure begin.

It was Christy Strawberry's mother who drove the girls to the carnival. On the radio, the newscaster spoke over a background of sirens. He was in Los Angeles, where black people were rioting, burning things, sometimes the very buildings in which they lived. The governor had called out the National Guard.

"How depressing," Mrs. Strawberry said. "Maybe I ought to go to your carnival, too, take a ride on the merry-go-round."

In the backseat, Franny and Christy clutched each other's hands. Of course, if Mrs. Strawberry—so recently abandoned by Mr. Strawberry—wanted to accompany the girls to the carnival, they would have to let her. And Franny would be forced to smile a warning to Ryan Marvell: *Not tonight.* And maybe her life would be ruined.

"Don't have a heart attack!" Mrs. Strawberry said into the rearview mirror. "I wish you girls could see your faces!"

The girls found Joan Harvett leaning up against the front of the chamber of commerce building. She was not alone, but with a bone-thin, heavily made-up girl whom Joan introduced as Lola Damon. "She just moved here from Minneapolis! Isn't that cool?"

Franny sneaked peeks at the girl. In the queer light made up of the dusk and the carnival lights, Lola Damon's teased hair—surely dyed that flat black—and her pale, pale makeup gave her a spooky look.

"Nobody in the Cities can believe I'm living in *Iowa*," Lola Damon drawled.

"She'll go to Roosevelt with us in the fall," Joan Harvett said, and Christy and Franny smiled and said "Great."

The night was perfect. The globe lamps marking the park's old underground toilets lit up the iron guard rails so exquisitely that when Franny stepped through the ring of rides and into the grassy center of the park, for a moment she felt magically lost, she was in Paris or London at the turn of the century, and those stairs led to the trains—

"Look, Franny!" Joan Harvett pointed to the bandshell, and Franny's heart let loose a spangly cymbal crash as she momentarily mistook for Ryan Marvell the long-haired boy to whom Joan pointed: Richie, from Richie and The Craft.

"Franny's been to their practices," Joan told Lola Damon.

"Well, *one* practice," Franny said.

"Hey, there!" A cluster of big boys in matching gray sweatshirts now bore down upon the girls, like a truck out of control—

What're you doing? Joan and Christy and Lola protested as Franny turned and ran. Though complaining all the way, the three girls followed her down the stairs into the park's rest room:

God, Franny, some of those guys were really cute!

Franny laughed, but she felt buzzy and strange and a little embarrassed as she stepped up to one of the trio of smudgy mirrors over the rest room sinks and began to comb her hair.

Lola Damon joined her at the mirrors. "I should have stayed up there."

"So you wear mascara?" Christy Strawberry said as Lola Damon pulled a mascara wand from her jeans pocket. "At Roosevelt"— Christy broke off with a squeak. "What happened to your arm?"

Lola Damon looked down at the arm in question as if, for a minute, she did not know that Christy Strawberry referred to the row of rusty scabs that marked its surface like so many dried-up earthworms. "Oh. Chicken." Concentration on her application of the eye makeup constricted the girl's voice. "Won four, lost three."

Christy Strawberry drew closer to the scabs. "What's 'chicken'?"

"You know!" Joan bugged her eyes at Christy, as if to say, *At least pretend.* "It's when you put a cigarette between your arm and another person's arm—it's more fun if it's a guy, right, Lola?—and you try to not be first to pull away."

"So—you get burned?" Christy asked.

"Boys like it." Lola Damon began to work on her lower lashes. "It shows you can stand up to a hard time if you have to. Like, you could be good for a girlfriend."

"Oh, pff!" Franny said, but Christy continued to stare at the burn marks as if they contained a message she needed to decode.

"I'm going to see if I can go up against Bob Prohaski," Lola Damon said with a glance Franny's way. "Joan told me you dumped the doll! I live just a couple doors down." She stuck the mascara into her pants pocket. "I hear Bob and his big brothers are going to beat up your Ryan Marvell."

The moment slid out from under Franny's feet. Her ears filled with a kind of hiss. "What? And how do you know his name?"

"I guess you told me?" Lola Damon said to Joan Harvett.

"Joan!" Franny protested.

"Like anyone couldn't find out," Joan said. "Like everybody doesn't already know."

Quickly, Franny headed up the rest room stairs. She felt obliged to the many people—sweethearts, picnickers, families with toddlers—who had spread blankets and bedspreads out across the center of the park, and so made it necessary for a person to concentrate upon where she stepped next, not talk. "Testing, testing, one, two," Richie Craft called over the bandshell microphone. Franny recognized the trio of tough high school girls who stood next to him on the stage: hoody girls who got in fights and stole and stood in foyers on Main Street and called out things—almost like boys—when other girls walked past. Franny was surprised to see them with Richie Craft, but then the caramel-corn girl joined the group—she was much more visibly pregnant than when Franny had seen her at the Craft house—and she slung an arm around one of the tough girls while Richie continued testing the microphone.

"There's Greg and those guys." With a jerk of her head, Joan Harvett indicated a stretch of street given over to the pinball arcade; then she shouted—apparently for the benefit of the Roosevelt boys at play on the machines—"Let's go on the horses!"

Christy and Lola Damon and Joan ran toward the park's playground equipment. "I get dibs on the pink horse," Christy cried, "the pink one's mine!"

The three girls took seats upon small resin horses meant for toddlers. The horses bounced woozily upon their thick metal coils while the girls tossed their hair and limbs.

Franny was miles from them, miles, lonely, cold. She stroked the tops of her arms with her palms. If Ryan Marvell did not come. If he did not come . . .

She stared across the park at a battered booth of white ply-wood. Even from here, she knew the wobbly bits of bright yellow before the booth operator were toy ducks. Little ducks that bob-bled on a narrow tank of water, and after you paid your dime, you plucked a duck from the water, and the number on the bottom cor-responded to your prize.

"Come on, Franny!" Christy Strawberry called from her wob-bly perch.

"Franny's being a poo-oooop," Joan Harvett called in a singsong voice, but she was wrong. Franny knew it felt nice to play on equipment. If she could have gone on the horses without some-one assuming she did it in order to get attention, she would have.

BOOM. With whoops and hollers, Greg Hopper and his friends now jumped aboard the playground equipment's little push merry-go-round. *BOOM*. They jumped up and down on the metal plates.

"Franny"—Christy Strawberry abandoned her horse and rushed up to tug on Franny's arm—"come on! Help us talk to them!"

No. Those boys made her uneasy. In June, she had been at Joan Harvett's when Greg Hopper and another boy had come by and, in lieu of conversation, for what seemed like hours, the boys had thrown rocks—successively larger and larger ones—at a metal shed across the alley.

"Come on, Christy!" Joan Harvett and Lola Damon now grabbed Christy Strawberry's arm, and, walking backward, began to pull her toward the merry-go-round. "If Franny doesn't want to talk to them, that's her problem."

"But, Franny," Christy pleaded over one shoulder, "don't you at least think Greg's cute?"

"Sure," she said, but she knew she sounded like her Grand-father Ackerman the time the family had taken the train to the Grand Canyon. "Don't show me *that*," the old man said if anyone pointed out a pretty bird or a clump of mistletoe or some other item of interest. "I'm saving my eyes for the canyon."

"Whoa, Nelly!" Joan Harvett stopped in her tracks. Elbowed Lola Damon. "Look at what's coming our way!"

Franny knew it would be Ryan Marvell even before she turned, and so she murmured, "Please, be quiet! Please!"

"*That's* him?" Christy Strawberry yelped.

Biting his lip, pretending to be scared, yet all the while doing a kind of dance of awkwardness that required real grace as he skirted picnic blankets, and coolers, and a little kid who toddled forward onto her hands, diapered rump in the air.

"Do we have chaperones tonight, or what?" Ryan Marvell called ahead of himself.

"Oh, my god!" Joan Harvett covered her eyes with her hands. "He's beautiful!"

Under her breath, Franny begged, "Sh," while Ryan Marvell laughed and did a little trick with his cigarette; somehow he drew the thing inside his mouth, as smooth as a train into a tunnel, and then made it appear again, standing upright on his tongue, like a little man from a cuckoo clock. Disappear. Appear.

"How do you *do* that?" Lola Damon asked, and smiling Christy looked over her shoulder at the boys on the playground equipment—for a moment, Franny feared Christy might call the boys to come admire Ryan Marvell, too—

"Puh!" Ryan Marvell made a funny face as he tossed the spent cigarette onto the ground. "Believe me, you don't *want* to do that," he said, "but, hey"—he set his arm around Franny's shoulder—"what about Franny, here? Isn't she great?"

Sure, sure, the others said, at which Franny crossed her eyes; she knew the girls would be angry if she accepted the compliment, which, really, had nothing to do with her, everything to do with Ryan Marvell, who probably could have led those starry-eyed girls down to the shore, walked them right into the lake—

"RYAN MARVELL!"

The crowds on their blankets and everyone else in the grassy middle of the park looked in the direction of the bandshell.

"RYAN MARVELL," Richie Craft called into the mike, "WHAT ARE YOU DOING WITH THAT FEMME FATALE?"

Ryan Marvell laughed. "Is Richie right?" he asked Franny. "Is your old boyfriend still planning to beat up me, or my boss? Richie told me the guy's a Prohaski."

Lola Damon stepped up close to Ryan Marvell, almost as if—against her will—she wanted to sniff at his shoulder, lay a hand on his neck. "His name's Bob," she said. "He's pretty tough."

"The one named Larry"—Ryan Marvel grimaced—"I know he put out somebody's eye at the Romero."

Lola Damon nodded. "And Rod knocked out some teeth last week."

Ryan Marvell put his hand over his mouth and did a jig of imagined pain. "Are you going to get me killed, Franny?"

"I'm sorry," she said miserably.

"Oh, hey." He stroked her arm. "Don't get gloomy, now. But, remember, if you come see me at work, you have to use a different name." He snapped his fingers and smiled. "Something French, maybe?"

Franny turned to the girls to ask, "Why is it guys always think French girls are so wonderful?"

The girls grinned. Ryan Marvell grinned. "It's their mouths," he said, "the way their mouths go '*Je t'adore.*'"

Christy Strawberry's eyes widened. "You speak French?"

"No. But if Franny, here, would like me better if I did, I'd learn! I'd be a regular French-talking fool."

"Actually, I'm *part* French," Franny said.

Ryan Marvell nodded, then added with a sweet wink, "I could tell the first time we kissed!"

The other girls' laughter was so perfect—so absent of criticism—that Franny laughed, too. Everything was perfect, really, except for the scowling Roosevelt boys on the playground equipment, one of whom now stuck his fists up under his shirt and strutted across the merry-go-round as if he were a vain, big-breasted mama.

"Uh-oh," Lola Damon said. "See those big guys over by the Wild Mouse? Well, the one that looks like Bob—that's Larry Prohaski."

"Shit!" Joan Harvett said. "He's looking right at you, Franny!"

"He doesn't even know me!" All this agitation irritated her. Christy Strawberry jumping up and down like an excited puppy, whimpering, "Oh, Franny!"

"He is looking at you, though, Fran," Ryan Marvell murmured. "You and me."

"Come on!" Christy Strawberry pulled Franny toward an opening between a corn-dog booth and a kiddy ride (tiny boats going round and round on dark and noisy water). "You two gotta split up!"

One eye on Larry Prohaski, Ryan Marvell said, "Okay, okay, but look for me when the band takes a break, okay?"

"I don't think the Prohaskis would actually *kill* him, do you?"

"Joan!" Franny protested.

"Sorry. I was just saying what was on my mind."

The girls sat on the edge of the geranium-filled brick planter that made a border between the sidewalk and the little parking lot in front of the dark offices of Trelore, Wahl, and Wahl.

"They could make it so he got arrested," Lola Damon said. "For statutory rape. Because you're thirteen."

"I'm not having sex with him!" Franny protested.

"It doesn't really mean *rape*," Lola Damon said. "Anyway, I don't think they'd do that. They want their own revenge, you know?" She laughed. "Christ, in Minneapolis, guys kill each other all the time! There's even a gang, the Baldies—they're so bad, they put razors in the toes of their boots, and if they kick you in the shin"—Lola Damon snapped her foot forward—"the razor cuts something and you never walk again."

Wow, said Joan and Christy. Oh, my god.

Franny stuck her fingers into the deep grooves of the letters chiseled into the law office's wooden sign. Trelore, Wahl, and Wahl. A crisp white sign, the chiseled letters highlighted with gold. Rosamund had told Franny stories about a gang in Miami that were almost identical to Lola Damon's stories. Razor blades. Babies eaten. Piles of bones. Even the name of the gang was the same. And the rival gang of the Baldies was the Eagles. Wonderfully frightening, Franny had thought when Rosamund first told her the stories, but now she wondered if both girls' stories might be just stories. *Did you ever actually see a Baldie?* She could have asked Lola Damon that. As a means of dimming the admiration on Joan and Christy's faces. But, instead—using Rosamund's deadpan manner for telling such tales—she said, "Where my sister goes to school, in Miami, the gang guys are drug dealers, too, and when they need more customers, they'll just walk along the matinee lines and stick a needle full of heroin into little kids—ten-year-olds, whatever—and, bang, they're addicted for life."

Joan and Christy looked appropriately horrified; Lola Damon, chagrined. Franny's story had triumphed over Lola Damon's story. Because it was a better story. It was not just evil. It was evil injecting itself into innocence—

"Anyway!" Lola Damon jumped off of the brick planter. "I don't know about you guys, but I am bored out of my mind!"

Just five more minutes, Franny mouthed at Joan and Christy, and Joan said, hey, why didn't Lola show Christy and Franny her splits and handstands? "So they can see how good you'd be at cheerleading."

Lola Damon shrugged—"Oh, cheerleading," she said with a slight sneer—but threw her hands forward and her body followed as she executed a perfect handstand on the law office's sidewalk. She seemed about to perform another, then, hurriedly, she pulled at her disarranged shirt and called, "Hey, Larry!" and stepped straight into the path of that out-size young man she had earlier identified as Bob Prohaski's big brother.

"Lola!" the girls hissed, but Larry Prohaski stepped around Lola Damon without giving her a glance.

"Woo! Aren't you hot stuff?" Lola Damon laughed. "I'm new neighbors to you, but if you don't want to meet me, how'd you like to meet Franny Wahl, here?"

Immediately, Christy Strawberry and Joan Harvett took off,

running. "Come on, Franny!" they shouted, but Franny shook her head and the girls edged back, muttering, *Jesus, Lola, what are you thinking, Jesus.*

Larry Prohaski stepped closer to Franny. His appearance of strength was rendered more frightening—mindless—by the fact that he wore glasses so thick they gave his eyes the gray and filmy look of shucked oysters.

Lola Damon laugh nervously. "She's scared you're going to hurt her new boyfriend!"

Larry Prohaski nodded. "She should be scared."

"Please, don't hurt him," Franny said. "I didn't tell him about Bob. It's not his fault."

Lola Damon stepped closer to Larry Prohaski. "You see how it is, Larry? Franny's in *love* with this new guy."

Larry Prohaski rocked his head from side to side, as if he had a kink in his neck, a casual gesture that unnerved Franny. Didn't boxers do something like that before they went into the ring? "You," he said to Lola Damon, "I'm not talking to you," and he motioned for Franny to follow him between a pair of carnival trailers that sat in the parking lot of Pynch Lake Savings and Loan.

"Don't go with him, Franny!" Christy Strawberry and Joan Harvett cried, but Franny was sick of their silliness, and if for no other reason than to disassociate herself from it, she went after Larry Prohaski.

"I'm sorry if I made Bob feel bad," she said when the two of them had moved out of earshot of the others.

Larry Prohaski turned his head to one side. The streetlight caught on the thick lenses of glasses and turned them white. "It's girls like you make guys hate women," he said, though not in her direction. "You Wahls. You think your shit don't stink. Darren Rutiger's my buddy. I know how your sister Rosamund treated Darren once she went off to college."

Automatically, Franny protested that Darren was her friend. "Artie Stokes, too. You ask. And I did like your brother—"

"Hey." Without warning, Larry Prohaski pulled her into his

chest. "You're not going to cry, are you?" he murmured. He turned her chin up to his face with roughened fingers. He smiled, then. "My brother said you cried a lot."

Did he mean to kiss her? Should she let him kiss her? The question occurred at some unanswerable, appalling distance from her watery knees, where the kiss could occur before she even summoned the answer. In shame, she lowered her eyes.

"Franny Wahl." Larry Prohaski pressed his cheek to the top of her head. "You're lucky you ain't a guy, Franny Wahl. If you was a guy instead of a pretty, sweet-smelling girl, I'd have kicked your teeth in." Then he took a noisy breath through his nose and stepped back from the girl.

"Okay." He rapped his knuckles on the metal side of a trailer that read HAMILTON SHOWS. "We don't hurt your boyfriend, but you stay away from Bobby, right?"

She nodded. "Oh, thank you, Larry. Thank you so much."

"Don't thank me." He shook his head. "Just—go on back to your friends before I change my mind."

"Franny!" Christy Strawberry, looking as fay and dark-eyed as some fairy-tale changeling, jumped down from the law office planter. "Are you okay?"

"I'm okay."

Christy held out her hands to the deserted sidewalk. "I'm the only one who waited."

"Well, thanks."

"So *you* better not ditch *me*!"

"Of course not."

They found Ryan Marvell with Tim Gleason in a group that watched a man with a waist-length beard bring down the sledge at the "Test Your Strength" booth. Ryan Marvell smiled at Franny, then said something to Tim Gleason and, alone, started their way.

"That Tim probably doesn't want to come over because I'm here," Christy Strawberry whispered.

"No, he's mad because he wants Ryan to get back with his old girlfriend. And because Roz hasn't been hanging around with him lately."

Something in the roll of Ryan Marvell's gait suggested he had been drinking since she had seen him before, and when he drew near, his breath confirmed the fact. Peppermint schnapps. She knew the scent from car trips with her father. Her father always drank schnapps on car trips because he said it smelled like mouthwash if a cop pulled you over.

"Hey, Ryan," Christy Strawberry called, "Franny talked to that Larry! He's not going to beat you up!"

"Well, that's nice." Ryan Marvell laughed. "What'd you say to him, Franny?"

She shrugged. "I just told him it wasn't your fault."

"Every boy in trouble needs a girl like you, huh? But, wait! You're the one who got me in trouble in the first place!" He wrapped his arms around her when she began to object. "Just kidding. So, come on! I got a car over by the drugstore."

"But—" Franny gestured toward Christy.

"That's okay. You come, too, Franny's friend."

"Christy," Franny said.

"Christy. Either of you girls ever tried schnapps?"

"My dad—" Franny began, then broke off.

"Your dad?" Ryan Marvell gave a comical scratch to the top of his head—a Stan Laurel sort of scratch—and he clicked his heels together. "Your dad—uses colorful language when he's been drinking, doesn't he?" He winked at Christy Strawberry. "Her dad didn't think too much of my coming by the house."

The car to which Ryan Marvell led the girls was a black Cadillac, brand-new, shining. His father's car, he explained as he unlocked the door. It seemed that, the night before, Ryan had put his own Ford into a ditch. With a laugh, he explained how a farmer had pulled out the Ford with his tractor, then invited Ryan and his friends—Tim Gleason and some other boys—to come inside his farmhouse for a drink of what turned out to be wine that the farmer had made from Hi-C and rhubarb.

"Then we had to compare vintages." Ryan Marvell lay his forehead on the steering wheel and laughed weakly. "Grape Kool-Aid versus Tropical Punch. June versus May." Later, trying to leave the farmyard, Ryan had put the Ford in another ditch, and then the farmer put the tractor in the ditch while trying, again, to help with the Ford; and Ryan and his friends had ended up sleeping on the farmer's porch until morning, when a second farmer with a tractor came to help.

Franny thought of, but did not mention, the fact that her own parents had met under similar, if less colorful, circumstances.

"Here." He pulled a fifth of schnapps from under the seat and handed it to Franny.

"No, thanks," she said, but Christy not only wanted a sip, she was eager to pass the bottle back and forth over Franny's lap. Very soon, Christy was singing along with the radio, very loud, and Ryan Marvell said, "Listen—Christy, right?—do you mind if I kiss your friend in the backseat for a minute or two?"

"My friend in the backseat?" With much hilarity, Christy Strawberry twisted around and rose up on her knees to face the backseat—one of her bony elbows knocking Franny hard in the temple—"I don't have a friend in the *back*seat," she said, "but Franny's my friend, and I know she'd love to kiss you!"

"Are you getting drunk, Christy?" Franny whispered while Ryan Marvell opened the driver's-side door and climbed out of the Cadillac.

"I'm fine! Go on! I won't look!"

It was wonderful to be in those arms—she lightened, lightened—but then Ryan Marvell began pressing her down on the seat, trying to get her under him. He slipped his hand between her thighs, an area that she had not dreamed she would need to guard for years. Not that she did not want to give herself to him entirely. She did. But she did not want whatever that sly hand thought it wanted, and implied could be shared, and so she felt only grateful when—with a whoop—Christy Strawberry spilled right over the Cadillac's front seat and into their laps.

"I'm drunk, you guys! Look at me! I'm drunk!"

After they had untangled themselves from Christy Strawberry, in an effort to sober up the girl, Ryan Marvell and Franny began to walk her back toward the carnival. Which was nice. To be out of the car, working on a problem together.

"I suppose I can't hold your hand here?" he asked.

"Better not."

"He wants to hold your h-a-a-and," Christy sang, making others in the street turn and laugh. They had reached the chamber of commerce building by then, the spot where Franny's mother was to pick up the girls. Franny set her hands on Christy's shoulders, and said, "Christy, listen, do you think you can act okay in front of my mom?"

Christy Strawberry grinned. Reached into the bag of popcorn she had been carrying around with her all night and scrubbed her face with the popcorn.

"Great. That looks real normal, Chris."

Ryan Marvell was not much better. "Look, Franny." He slipped into an indentation in the face of the chamber of commerce building. "I'll stand right here, and we can talk until your mom comes, and she'll never see me!"

"You're nuts," she said, his enthusiasm for her both a thrill and a terror. She scanned the street for the Wildcat, the old worry washing over her: *Her mother would not come at all.* She moved closer to grinning Ryan and his peppermint breath. She wanted to tell him how crazy her parents had been after he came to visit, but suppose he took that story as a sign of sickness with which he would not wish to be associated.

"I love to breathe!" Christy Strawberry cried. She gulped at air and grabbed her fingers toward the sky. "Breathing is fun! Do you know that, you guys? I have pores—everywhere! I have pores in my eyes! I'm mentholated!"

Franny stroked the girl's back. "But you have to settle down, honey. And you"—she shook her head at Ryan Marvell—"you've got to go!"

"I can't!" Head cocked to one side, he pressed himself flat to the chamber of commerce wall. "Your charms have turned me to stone. I can't move!"

"Her mom's always late anyway," Christy Strawberry said.

"Christy!" Franny protested. "That's not true!"

"Almost always," Christy said, ducking as two boys with peashooters ran past, laughing, jostling people, forcing an old finned Dodge to stop with a terrible screech.

She could walk north, Franny thought, pretend she saw her mother's car farther up the street, waiting. She squinted in that direction to make the pretense real.

"Hey!" Christy tugged at her arm. "There she is! No—it's like your mom's car, but it's a guy."

Franny nodded and pretended she merely continued staring up the street, watching for Peg—while Darren Rutiger drove by in Peg's Wildcat, Martie's head on his shoulder.

She could not have said precisely why she felt she should pretend not to see. Because she suspected Martie would feel embarrassed at being with Darren after he had behaved so badly at that party? Or because Rosamund might expect Franny to tell her if Franny were to see the pair together?

"There's Brick!" Christy Strawberry pointed to the old Mercedes, now inching forward along that section of Main narrowed with rides and booths and people making their way on foot. "Better stay back, Ryan." Christy shook a finger at Ryan Marvell and he made a funny face of fear that kept the girls laughing even as Brick Wahl drove them toward home.

CHAPTER FIFTEEN

IT HAPPENED, EVERY NOW AND THEN, THAT BRICK WAHL TOLD an old air corps story of how, in the mess hall, certain men who were too full for their desserts, but wanted to save them for later, would stand up in plain sight of the other men and spit on the dessert, a piece of pie, a slice of cake.

"It was important you did this very publicly," Brick would say with a laugh, "because men were less concerned with eating food some other fellow spit on than being *known* as a person who would eat food another fellow spit on."

In her bedroom, the curtains bouncing in the late morning breeze, Franny wrote Brick's air corps story into her journal with the secret notion that she would use the story, years later, as a means of remembering that ugly night when Eduardo from Lake Okoboji—and that entire party crowd—had watched Martie stumble up the drive with Darren Rutiger. She could not imagine that she would *not* remember that night—or the more recent night at the carnival when she saw Martie with Darren and pretended not to—still, the people around her seemed to remember things incorrectly more and more often. Rosamund already needed prompting from Franny in order to recall the names of girls with whom she had been high school friends just two years before.

In memory of her own experience of the carnival—with the girls and Ryan Marvell and Larry Prohaski, too—Franny copied #320 in her journal:

We play at Paste—

Till qualified for Pearl—

Then, drop the Paste—

And deem ourself a fool—

The Shapes—though—were similar—

And our new Hands

Learned Gem-Tactics—

Practicing Sands—

She had entered a strange world, hadn't she? The carefree world that she once imagined awaited her—the big game, 45's spinning at the sock hop, you and your honey sipping one malted milk with two straws—maybe that world had never existed. Though something like it must have existed. There was evidence: the big girls' formals in plastic bags in the cedar closet, Martie's dried corsages and ticket stubs, Rosamund's photo albums.

At any rate, Franny's world had collapsed in upon itself like a sinkhole, and, like a sinkhole, it had its own climate. Really, she could scarcely see the world above from her sinkhole—though who cared when such rare flowers grew there?

Not that she believed that Ryan Marvell loved her as she loved him. Not that she could convince herself that he was actually with her in the sinkhole. Still, he was with her, somewhere. They met in an echo, maybe, and when he laughed, his laugh sounded like something out of a book—that is, he had the sort of laugh that, whether high or low or beautiful or not, the writer let you know, that laugh was a kind of natural wonder, not to be forgotten.

"Franny." Spray bottle of window cleaner in hand, Ginny Weston stood in the bedroom doorway. "Your dad wants you. Kitchen."

Franny called down from the top of the stairs, "Dad?" At noon, her mother was to take her to meet friends at Woolf Beach—though not really; really, Franny meant to go across the road to Mother Goose to see Ryan Marvell. "Did you need me?"

Brick Wahl stuck his head into the stairwell. He looked aggrieved. "Hurry it up. Your mother's stuck at the dentist and she says I've got to haul you to the beach."

"But, I don't need to go for another hour."

"Well, I'm here now, so you're going now. Chop, chop."

Chop, chop. She raced to her room. She was not ready at all. Luckily, she had laid out her yellow shorts and top; however, when she went to pull the top over her head, some string or tag caught in the three rollers in her hair—

WA-SAAAH! An inboard ripped past the house with a terrible blast of its air horn. *WAH-SAAH!*

She dashed to the window. Suppose Ryan Marvell had sounded that air horn. Suppose it contained a message for her. Stay home. Go away. Come now.

The inboard had disappeared when she pulled back the curtain, but upon the wake the boat left behind—no question about it—there floated Franny's rowboat, loose, a good fifty yards from shore.

Long, short, short, Brick honked in the drive.

"Franny?" Ginny Weston called. "He's getting mad!"

"I'm coming!"

The boat could not go far, she supposed. It had a license. Surely someone would call if it washed up on their beach.

Brick frowned when she climbed into the car. "I don't like people who keep me waiting," he said.

I don't like people who keep me waiting? Well, he was preposterous, she thought, and relished the silence that followed as they moved up the road. The sharp morning had lost its edges and it seemed to puff up, leaven, as the sun climbed to its midpoint in the sky. *No. Please, don't talk,* she thought when Brick made the peculiar bee buzz deep in his throat that signalled he meant to speak:

"You know, I'd be more than willing to haul your friends back to the house rather than have you at that crummy beach."

She tried to sit up straighter in her seat, and to remind herself that she could not be too angry with him for trying to change plans that were all lies, anyway.

"We *want* to be at the beach," she said, then added—the name sounding almost like an afterthought, or an accusation—"Dad."

Dad. She blushed and looked down into the depths of her beach bag. She hoped her interest in the beach bag suggested she had not the slightest interest in the miniature golf course, now coming up on their right.

"Say"—his voice was suddenly lively—"you ever notice that spot, there, Fran?" He pointed to a scrubby area that lay just between the miniature golf and the trailer court. "There used to be a road through there not—four or five years ago. Remember that? I used to take it all the time, when I was going south. It hooked up with a gravel stretch that met Highway 65, but some dumb bunny closed it off—who knows why—and now it's almost disappeared! A solid road! That's how quick nature takes things back!"

She nodded. She remembered driving on that road with him, or maybe the big girls, once or twice. She wanted to share the moment with him, but he made her feel too helpless. Loving her, pushing her around. Where did one end and one begin?

"Damned mutt!" Brick gave his horn a toot as the trailer-court setter—barking, tongue lolling—careened toward the Mercedes. To Franny's relief, the creature did not follow when Brick turned into Woolf Beach, and began to make his way past the fields of stubbly grass that served as parking lots for the overflow of summer visitors.

"Where you supposed to meet your gang?"

"Anywhere's fine." She put her hand on the doorknob, waiting for him to stop. "They're probably on the beach."

"Hm," Brick said, and turned onto a dusty, narrow road that wound back into the park campgrounds.

"This—isn't the right way," she said, but quietly, quietly, hoping he might almost imagine the words his own thoughts.

MEN read the grainy stencil on that small concrete block building alongside of which her father stopped the car. She could smell the sewage, but he leaned forward over the wheel and looked this way and that as if he did not notice a thing. "I hate to have you wander around in here all by yourself," he said. He glanced her way. He smiled. Tenderly, she thought, and, instantly, she was ready to give up, go home—

"But then I ask myself"—Brick lowered his forehead to the steering wheel and began to laugh—"what kind of nut would come to a dump like this when they've got a lovely beach of their own?"

The remark not only offended her—did he believe her too dumb to see through such easy manipulations?—worse, it made her feel unsafe in his company. Which released her from guilt. Before she could climb out, however, he began to drive again. They passed a section where tents and makeshift clotheslines could be seen through the trees. More campground.

"This isn't the right way," she said stiffly. "It's back the other way."

"Puh!" He drew his mouth into a purse of disgust, then braked hard enough that she had to put a hand on the dash to stop herself from falling forward, and a woman alongside the road grabbed up her small child with a shriek. "Settle down, babe," Brick muttered as he brought the car around and began to drive out from the trees and toward the beach area once more.

Franny's heart beat fast. Could he tell? Like a wild dog who turned wilder if it sensed your fear? Up ahead, by the concession stand, there stood a heavy girl in a red swimsuit and she was familiar, yes, a girl who had gone to Roosevelt the first semester of seventh and then transferred out. Anita Grant—she had sat near Franny in homeroom, and Franny said, "There's Anita!" not exactly to Brick, but for his benefit. "Hey, Anita!" she called from the car window.

The girl, chewing on a bite of hot dog, turned to peer sullenly at the old Mercedes.

"*That's* a friend of yours?" Brick said.

"That's Anita. The other girls are probably in the bathhouse, changing."

"She looks awful rough," Brick said.

"Well, thanks for the ride." Franny gave him a peck on the

cheek and climbed from the car. She could feel precisely how he bent over the steering wheel, watching her, waiting. Then the driver behind him laid on a horn and Brick moved down the road.

Anita Grant pointed her hot dog—the white of its bun daubed rose with lipstick—in Franny's direction. "I remember you."

"So are you going to Adams now?" Franny asked, eyes on the Mercedes, making certain Brick headed to town.

Anita Grant nodded. "I shoulda always gone there. It's a million times cooler than Roosevelt."

Franny stared at the back of the refreshment stand. People had gouged names and telephone numbers and obscenities, there, exposing the cheap fiberboard beneath the stand's coat of white paint. In one spot, the *F* in a certain "FUCK" had been worked at so hard and long you could actually see through the F-shaped hole to something moving inside the stand. The dark pants leg of some worker?

"Was that your dad that dropped you?" Anita Grant asked.

Franny said yes, then excused herself, *Guess I better change.*

The high odor of bathhouse mildew mingled with the smells of wet concrete and shampoo and hair spray. Immediately, she locked herself in one of the toilet stalls. Inspected her face in the compact she had recently purchased on a trip downtown. At the drugstore, the sales lady said, "You have lovely skin! Honey Kiss is your perfect color!" At the time, it had seemed the selection of the perfect color might make a world of difference, but Franny had not yet been able to bring herself actually to use the compact.

Only once did someone knock on the door during the forty-five minutes that Franny sat in the stall, waiting for it to be time for her to cross the road to Mother Goose. Still, it was dank and uncomfortable to sit there. She dabbed at her underarms with tissue from the toilet paper dispenser. Suppose Ryan Marvell had changed his mind. Suppose he did not want her to come. He had never seen her in the sunlight. Suppose he did not like her in the sunlight.

When she emerged from the bathhouse, Anita Grant was gone. Franny made her way through the rows of parked cars to Lakeside Drive. Looked right and left—a good pedestrian—then, heart trembling with fear and happiness, she hurried across the road.

Ryan Marvell stood in the Mother Goose parking lot, dumping a small trash can into the larger trash barrel. For a moment, from behind, she did not recognize him. His beautiful hair had been cropped into the familiar muffin of her male classmates; on top, some concession had been made to the desire for length, but the rest was chopped short.

Shyly, he ran a hand over his head, a display of vulnerability that made her love swell into new lands. "So, can you still like a guy who looks this goofy?" he asked.

She nodded.

"That's good," he said, smiling, drawing his finger down her nose, "since I'm in love with you."

She reached up for his hand and squeezed it and wished she knew how to let the love show on her face in just the right way. The way he did. What she felt—she wanted to offer it to him in its finest form, like some perfect song or poem from which she had removed all dross—

"Hey, I picked a name for you to use here," he whispered. "You're 'Michelle,' okay?"

Both of them glanced, then, toward the house where the golf course manager lived. Though it was a shabby little bungalow with a plastic OFFICE sign over the front door, when Ryan hurried off to help a customer at the snack shack, Franny imagined fixing up the house for the two of them. She would paint it, of course. Maybe just white. Plain white. And replace the torn screen door. Get rid of the dead Christmas tree and other trash by the garage . . .

The day had turned out hot but she was thrilled to sit on the split-rail fence encircling the little course and watch Ryan Marvell sweep the sidewalks and dispense golf clubs and balls and packets of potato chips, bottles of pop. The setter from the trailer court ambled through the course, and she called to it—funny and wonderful to see the animal up close, look into its big brown eyes. She smoothed her hands over its silky head, delighting in the fine bones. "What a sweetie you are," she crooned.

Ryan Marvell turned from his sweeping to laugh. "That mutt?"

"She's not a mutt, Ryan. Don't say that. I hate that word. 'Mutt.'"

He shrugged. "She lives over there," he said, and pointed to the trailer court. "I bet you're too young to even remember when the trailer court was the ice rink."

"No way! They didn't have enough records so they always played 'Sunday Kind of Love.'"

"That's right." He smiled. "And 'Rubber Ball.'"

"See? I've been around for a while. I remember when Mason's had nickel cones and"—she hesitated—"and the roller coaster was still running at Funland."

He raised an eyebrow at this last assertion, then asked, *by the way,* had her sister Martie mentioned talking to him at the Romero the night before? "She wanted to tell me I was a bum, and I better stay away from you if I know what's good for me."

"Don't pay any attention to her," Franny said in a rush.

"Franny." He opened his hands in a reassuringly helpless gesture. "I can't pay attention to her."

When he next hurried off to set up a group of golfers, she wondered if she could inject "purple mountain's majesty" into a poem about him, for both the comedy and the rightness of it, the way it expressed the glory and the dopiness of her love.

A pair of little kids in plaid sailor suits approached the knee-high barn that was the course's last hole, and she smiled at them. The barn was an easy hole-in-one if you knew—as Franny knew from years past—that the swinging doors on the front opened on the count of three. She was debating telling them—would it ruin their fun?—when here came Ryan, this time carrying a case of pop bottles from the manager's house to the snack shop. As he approached Franny, she leaned forward from her perch on the fence to drop a kiss on his arm.

"Whoa!" He smiled, but frowned, too, before he was past. Then he turned to whisper over his shoulder, "You don't want me getting fired, do you?"

"Of course not." She ran her hand along the rough blocks of

the exterior of the shack while, inside, he busied himself with packing bottles of soda into an old refrigerator. She could see how it was: Each time he tilted his head one way or the other, he shaped her, chipped away at her. Which meant it might very well be necessary for her to pretend to be someone else so that he would not actually be able to change her into whatever it was he had in mind.

"Here." He stepped from the shack, holding out a bottle of Coke. "And don't look so worried. My dad owns this place. I'm not likely to get canned. So, what'd you tell your folks today?"

"I'm at the park, swimming."

He grinned and toed her beach bag. "Your swimsuit in there?"

"Hey, lover boy." A woman in a cut-off sweatshirt and cut-off jeans stepped up to the shack. "Who's your friend?" she asked and gave Franny a grim up-and-down glance.

Hefty, Franny's dad would call her. *A hefty old broad,* although the woman was probably no more than twenty-five.

"Karen, this is Michelle," Ryan Marvell said. "Michelle, Karen Johanson. Karen"—he made a teasing bow of deference—"is the wife of the boss."

The woman whose husband Bob Prohaski had threatened. Karen Johanson. "How do you do?" Franny said.

The woman rolled her eyes. "Okay, Ryan," she said, "now that I've met Michelle, here, would you like me to tell her to get her butt off the fence, or do you want to do it?"

Immediately, Franny slid from the fence; immediately, wished she had not.

"Okay," said Karen Johanson. "Now maybe you can do the batting cage, Ryan? If you're not too busy entertaining?"

"Now, don't worry about Karen, Michelle," Ryan Marvell said. He winked at the woman as he began to back toward the batting cage. "Karen doesn't really mind if girls come by now and then."

"He shouldn't be so sure about that," Karen Johanson muttered; then she lifted the hinged piece of countertop that allowed employees into the snack shack and began to clip packages of potato chips to a display rack.

Stck, stck, went the baseballs as Ryan Marvell tossed them into the pitching bin.

Franny stared down at her sandalled feet and the bright crushed limestone that surrounded the snack shack. When she stared at her feet and the crushed rock—and not at the golf course or the cornfields at the back of the property or the swamp to the west—she could imagine herself in a Mediterranean country, some hot and dry and exalted land where people wrote poetry and honored their passions, someplace like the land in the poster on Rosamund's wall.

Other girls came by Mother Goose to see Ryan Marvell. The idea filled her with despair. She closed her eyes. She whispered to herself, *Nayr.* His name backward, a spell, a lover's incantation. *Nayr.* Martie had done that, once, during a bad period with the ROTC member. Not that it had done much good.

The hiss that sounded when Karen Johanson lit a match for her cigarette made Franny turn.

"You smoke, Michelle?"

"No, thanks."

"I wasn't offering you a cigarette, just asking if you smoked."

Franny nodded. "You have to understand," she said—very slowly, so the words would come out right—"I'm used to being around people with manners, so you confuse me."

"Uh-huh." The woman aimed a finger Franny's way and pretended to fire a shot. "Gotcha."

Her cheeks hot, Franny turned to lean on the fence and watch the pair in the sailor suits begin to work their way around the course a second time. They would have to be brother and sister, she supposed. And their mother was probably that pretty redhead who waited—windows rolled up, engine running—in the Mother Goose parking lot.

"Siren!" the pair of kids began to shout and, sure enough, an ambulance now headed down Lakeside Drive, a streak of white and red coming around the curve just beyond Woolf Beach.

Franny wished, as she always wished, that the ambulance would stop, soon, nearby, so that she would know that the driver had reached the proper destination, delivered help.

"Siren!" Gleefully, the little kids ran toward the parking lot, but the ambulance shot past before they reached the car of the red-headed woman. Even the trailer court setter seemed to know not to try to chase the thing.

"Hey, here comes a buddy of mine."

Franny turned as Ryan Marvell stepped up behind her and pointed to the dusty sedan now entering the Mother Goose lot.

Every inch of Ryan Marvell's friend carried the even anonymous coat of dust common to workers just off a shift at the cement plant. The moist flickering eyes and mouths of Pynch's local cement plant workers always struck Franny as eerie—that look of live men trapped inside dead. Still, Franny recognized Ryan's friend. He had helped Tim Gleason take Eduardo to the hospital. He had stood on the bank with Tim Gleason to argue with Ryan Marvell the night she and Ryan met. Warren something-or-other. Now this Warren crossed the lot, calling, "Marvell, you got scalped." He nodded Franny's way. "Miss Wahl. I guess your parents will think twice before they ever let you get near one of your big sisters' parties again, hm?"

Ryan pretended to protest, and Franny laughed, but after that, Warren addressed all of his comments to Ryan Marvell. It seemed Warren had spent the past weekend at the teachers college he would attend in the fall, and Ryan asked him questions about the trip, and then both boys joked about Ryan's attending Stanford Fanning Fellow in the fall.

"But, hey, man," Ryan said, "how could I leave Pynch when Franny's here?"

Without answering, Warren looked up the road toward the causeway. "I wonder if that's the ambulance that passed me on my way here," he said.

"Is it good or bad if the siren's off?" Franny asked, not just Ryan, but Warren, too, because it had been her experience that a boy would answer a girl's question whether he liked her or not, and whether he knew the answer or not, and it might help things if Ryan witnessed her in conversation with his friend.

Before either boy could answer, however, the trailer court's setter streaked out into the road, and the ambulance rode over the dog, a quick lift of the right-front tire, and the ambulance drove on as if the driver had not even noticed.

A cry rose from the group at Mother Goose. The car behind the ambulance braked for the dog in the road, which lifted its head, howled miserably, and careened off in the direction of the causeway and swamp.

"Where're you going?" Ryan Marvell shouted when Franny started after the animal. "Come on back!"

She held up one finger—just a moment—but did not turn around. Really, she felt gratified to have a purpose that was not him. She was useful now, running down the road in an effort to help the dog.

Somewhere in the swampy ground that lay west of the manager's house, a splashing sounded, and it grew louder as she drew near. "Here, puppy," she called. A stand of cattails buckled and parted but she could not see into them. "Let me help you, pup."

With a howl, the creature shot from the swamp, and up onto the shoulder of the causeway, then zigzagged across Lakeside between the passing automobiles, and ran toward the makeshift parking lot at Woolf Beach.

"Sorry!" Franny called to a driver forced to come to a dangerous stop on her behalf. "Sorry." She hurried across the road. Ryan Marvell and his friend still stood in the Mother Goose parking lot, but she did not give him any sign that she noticed him there. Because she did not want him to think that she would assume he continued to watch for her.

"Here, buddy." She crouched down, and called beneath the cars parked on the grass at Woolf Beach. "Here, pal." She whistled. Clapped her hands. "Here, buddy."

While she moved between the rows of cars, someone on Lakeside Drive began to honk very insistently. Someone parked on the shoulder of the road? She did not turn to look at the source of the honking until she recognized the voice calling, "Franny! Franny Wahl!"

Her mother. Standing up in the convertible to call to her.

Franny raced toward the car. Just across the road, at the edge of the Mother Goose lot, stood Ryan Marvell and his friend, and she called ahead of herself, "There was a dog, Mom. It got hit and I'm trying to find it. I think it went under one of these cars."

Peg Wahl lowered herself into the driver's seat. "You need to get in," she said.

She looked ashen. She knew everything. The golf course manager's wife had figured out everything and she had called Peg and told Peg everything—

"That Bob Prohaski—" Peg turned her face straight ahead as Franny climbed into the car. Her voice was strangled. "He—"

"What?"

Peg put the car in gear and pulled back on the road. She reached for Franny's hand. "I got a call as I was leaving the dentist's, Fran. That Bob came by the house today after you'd gone. Ginny was still there. She told him you weren't home. She thought he'd left, but then she heard him yelling for you, and, by the time she went outside, he was in the lake. Your boat was out on the water and apparently he was trying to reach it, and"—she glanced Franny's way—"he got in trouble."

"Oh, Mom!" In alarm, Franny lowered her head to her knees. "What happened?"

"I came as soon as Ginny called. There was an ambulance on the way. Somebody next door went in after him—"

"But the ambulance went by already! You have to follow it, Mom. What's it mean if they don't run the lights and siren?"

Peg shook her head. "Let's just stay calm and go to the house. We don't know that the ambulance you saw was the ambulance Ginny called. Let's just wait and see."

Franny wrapped her arms around herself, tight. If Bob Prohaski only were okay, she would like him again. She would. She would.

Please, God. "It's my fault! I didn't answer, once, when I was out in the boat and he was calling me! He probably thought I was hiding from him!"

"Now, sh, come on, honey. We don't know"—Peg broke off to look in her rearview mirror—then said an indignant "somebody in that car made an obscene gesture when we went by!"

Franny grasped her ankles with her hands. She could not bear to see Lakeside Drive, and how slowly they moved up it. *Please, God,* she prayed, *if only*—but her heart rebelled. *Please, let him be okay, but don't make me have to love him.*

When she felt the car turn, she knew they had reached the main drive, and she sat up. There was Ginny Weston, running toward the car. "He's gone!" she called as Peg brought the car to a stop.

Franny and Peg gasped, and reached for one another.

"Not like that! He *left*!" Ginny Weston began to cry. "I shouldn't have called the ambulance! I'll pay for it, Mrs. Wahl, don't worry."

"But—where's Bob?" Franny asked.

"He hightailed it out of here, as mad as a wet hen."

"Well, thank goodness." Peg smiled at Franny.

"But we have to find him, Mom. To make sure he's okay."

"Ginny said he was okay, Franny."

"He could be hurt!"

"Oh, I doubt it." Now that she knew she was not in trouble, Ginny Weston seemed to be irritated with the boy. "He stuck out his thumb and somebody picked him up—bang—wet clothes and all."

Even so, Franny persuaded Peg to drive her back toward town. "I'll watch the right side of the road, and you watch the left," she said, and when they reached the causeway once more, she asked Peg to keep an eye out for the setter, too.

Franny caught a glimpse of Ryan Marvell, on his way to the batting cages.

Oh, Peg said—trying to distract her, Franny could tell—*did Franny know that Roz had received another letter from Turner?* In

Peg's opinion, Turner seemed like just the one for Rosamund. Actually, Peg was thinking she might make one of her enamels for his father for Christmas. Of course, only if Turner and Rosamund were still serious at Christmas. Though maybe it would be more appropriate to send it to the mother. The problem was, Peg had a *feeling* she'd like the father better. Because the mother sounded like she might be too hoopty-doo.

When they reached Tanglefoot, Franny directed Peg to the Prohaski house.

Did Franny want Peg to walk up to the door with her?

No. But thanks.

The only time that Franny ever had been to the Prohaski house had been on a night in May when she slept over at Joan Harvett's. Franny did not know Bob Prohaski, then, except as a handsome boy from the school wrestling team, but Joan Harvett had kept saying he liked Franny, and that she and Franny ought to walk through his neighborhood because maybe he'd be outside. It had been pitch dark that night. In Tanglefoot, the streetlights were few and far between, and there were no sidewalks, but by the time Franny announced that she wanted to turn around, Joan Harvett said no, up ahead, the one with the window broken out in front was his, and then Joan began to rummage in a garbage pail that sat alongside the Prohaski garage.

"What're you doing?" Franny had whispered, and Joan whispered back, "I'm trying to find a piece of glass so I can cut myself, and then we can ask to use their phone." Franny had thought Joan was crazy, but at that point a light had come on at the Prohaski house, and Bob Prohaski stepped out into the garage. The tough look on his face softened once he saw the girls. "What's up?" he asked. While Franny invented a bumbling story of collecting pop bottles for Y-Teens, Mrs. Prohaski appeared in the door behind Bob, and invited the girls inside. All of it had stirred Franny: the yellow Formica dining table and metal chairs, the handsome boy who had apparently noticed her without her doing a thing, the brightly colored drink that sweet Mrs. Prohaski had poured from a can into plastic glasses.

Three months ago.

The sheet of plywood, now blackened and swollen, remained in the broken picture window. Shafts of summer sunshine made their way through the trees overhead and dappled the damp and dark yard below. Franny felt as if she moved inside a minnow bucket.

She paused at the door before she knocked. Wires dangled from the spot where, once upon a time, there had been a doorbell. Through the screen, she could see both Bob and Larry Prohaski on a long couch in the living room. They watched the TV—*P.M. Matinee*—but Larry Prohaski saw her, and he called, voice thick with warning, "What do you want?"

"I want to talk to Bob. Just for a second."

Bob Prohaski rotated his head her way, then back to the movie, which was one Franny herself knew: Mitzi Gaynor starring as Eva Tanguay in *The I Don't Care Girl*.

"Bob?" she said. "Could we talk a second?"

He pushed himself up from the sofa and came to the screen door. He had changed into dry clothes, but his hair remained damp. Instantly, Franny wanted to take him in her arms. Maybe she did love him after all—

"What do you want?"

She drew closer to the screen door. She supposed he would not have told his brother about the ambulance, the indignity, and so she whispered, "I wanted to see if you were okay. I heard—"

"Was you out in that boat?"

"*No*. I was—at the beach."

"Still, you can drop dead." He took a whistling in-breath. "I almost died 'cause of you."

"Oh, Bob." She pressed her hand to the door. She did not say that if he had died, it would have been an accident. She knew what he meant: His feelings for her had made him fail to treat his life with care.

"Okay." Larry Prohaski moved toward the door, arm extended, finger pointing. "You had your say. Now get a move on."

"I'm glad you're okay, Bob."

Larry Prohaski nodded. "He's fine. Now, go."

The Prohaskis had no sidewalk, just a few wobbly, concrete circles set into the patchy yard, and as she returned to the car, Franny made an effort to step on each circle, and hoped this conveyed a sense of respect for their property.

"Franny!" From down the pocked road, and across the shady yards, Lola Damon and Joan Harvett now ran her way. "Franny!" they called. Each carried an orange Popsicle in one hand, a cigarette in the other—though Joan Harvett paused to toss away her cigarette as soon as she saw Peg in the Wildcat.

"Hi, Mrs. Wahl," blushing Joan called to Peg, while Lola Damon said an icy, "What're you doing here, Franny? I thought you and Bob were all through."

Franny nodded. She could feel the boy, watching from the doorway. His gaze lay on her back and her neck like cold, wet rags. "I just had to talk to him for a second. No big deal. So—you live near here?"

Lola Damon did not answer but waved toward the Prohaski house. "Hi, Bob!" she called; then, with a shrug, "'Bye, Bob."

"Here comes Diane, Lola." Joan Harvett pointed to the sedan that now picked its way around the road's numerous potholes; according to Joan, the driver was Lola's big sister.

Who now proceeded to drive her sedan directly up against the front end of the Wildcat. *Bump.* Bumper tapped bumper. Looking both impressive and silly, Peg rose up out of the driver's seat to peer over the windshield at Diane Damon and the hoods of the two cars.

Diane Damon—bigger, and with bigger hair than Lola—gave a hoot of laughter at Peg's concern. "Come on, girls," she called in a voice that was almost a parody of those weary mothers who managed to retain a little spunk despite where they found themselves in life, and Franny noticed that Peg used this same voice when she said, "Yes, come on, let's go, Fran."

CHAPTER SIXTEEN

THOUGH SPEEDBOATS STILL SHOT ACROSS THE LAKE, AND mothers continued to lug home bags of briquets for picnics, and girls and boys in swimsuits lined up at the window of the Dairy Queen, there was no denying that the winding down of summer had begun.

According to Rosamund, this was a good thing since she no longer wanted to spend time with anyone in Pynch Lake—"Present company excluded, of course."

Franny smiled at this—she was elated, just then, walking with Rosamund toward City Park and a meeting with Ryan Marvell— still, the season's changes pressed on her heart as if they were not the result of the tilting of the earth in relation to the sun, but, instead, messages of consequence. Not that she could say precisely what the messages might be, but she did feel more alive in their presence. She sensed a swelling in the world, a sensitive skin. She sometimes found herself leaning against things in an oddly cozy way, stroking the bark of a tree, even pressing her lips to the refrigerator door as she took a call on the telephone.

"I appreciate you bringing me into town, Roz."

Rosamund wrinkled up her nose. "What else do I have to do on a Saturday night? Oh—there he is!" She gave Franny's elbow a squeeze. "I forgot how darling he is!"

Darling, darling, darling—

"I hope you girls won't hate me for this." Looking sheepish, Ryan Marvell gestured toward the band shell and the barbershop quartet now singing for a tiny audience.

The girls laughed and took seats on the grass. Rosamund said, "Actually, one of my friends"—she raised her eyebrows at Franny in a way that let Franny know that Roz referred to Turner Haskin— "he says it's interesting to look deeper at things that might just seem corny on the surface. Like, you could ask, what do some people like about a barbershop quartet?"

"Maybe it reminds them of music?" Ryan Marvell said.

The look that Rosamund gave him was one that Franny knew well: a pursing of the lips that suggested disapproval followed by an upturning of the corners of her mouth that showed amusement.

Franny herself was so pleased to be with both Ryan Marvell and Rosamund that she hardly felt jealous that the pair talked to each other as much as they talked to her. It was Franny's knee, after all, upon which Ryan Marvell rested his head—pure treasure—while he explained to Rosamund that he had taken a lot of ribbing about enrolling at SFF but his parents wanted him to stay near home so he could learn about the family business. In case he ever took it over.

He had never told Franny any of this, and she was impressed by how grownup he sounded. Rosamund seemed impressed, too. They were having a nice time, weren't they? When Ryan Marvell took out his package of cigarettes, he offered one to Rosamund, and Rosamund, who never smoked, said, okay, and they all laughed at the way she exhaled like a little kid blowing out birthday candles.

But then, in the middle of a sentence about a movie he had been to see—*What's New, Pussycat?*—Ryan Marvell looked up at Franny and smiled and said, "You know what, Roz? I can hardly eat since I fell in love with your little sister."

Which turned out to be a mistake.

Immediately, Rosamund stood. "I don't want to hear about that," she said. "I can't be party to that." She stared off at the barbershop group and their friends, all of them now standing at a foldout table and eating slices of neapolitan ice cream.

Ryan Marvell lifted his head from Franny's knee and sat up, then. "Listen, Roz," he began, but Rosamund cut him off.

"*Okay*," she said, quite loud. She looked only at Franny, as if

Ryan Marvell had disappeared altogether. "I'm supposed to get a few things at the Red Owl. I'll be at the car in ten minutes, Franny. You be there, too."

"What was that all about?" Ryan Marvell asked as Rosamund strode off across the park.

Franny shook her head. "I guess she wants to think we're just friends."

Rosamund was quiet in the car, but when she and Franny got home, she acted friendly. She showed Franny that, along with eggs and bread, she had picked up a bottle of fudge sauce and a can of whipping cream so they could make sundaes. "We do this at the dorm sometimes," she whispered, then opened her mouth wide, and squirted it full of whipping cream.

Martie was out with Deedee Pierce the evening Rosamund and Franny visited Ryan Marvell and made sundaes. She did not arrive home until four the next morning. At breakfast, Peg declared to Rosamund and Franny and Brick that she had no sympathy for a girl with a hangover; and, not long after, she posted herself outside the girls' upstairs bathroom and detailed what chores Martie needed to do as soon as she finished vomiting.

This was at about the same time that Ginny Weston arrived and began to vacuum the bedrooms. Brick had left for the day when Martie appeared in the kitchen. Martie made no effort to appear perky that morning. Her wet hair hung in limp noodles down either side of her face? So be it. She slumped at the table, smoking a cigarette and rolling her eyes at Peg's clanging of pots and pans. However, it was possible, just then, for Franny and Rosamund to exchange smiles, as if the household were—amusing. A fresh pot of flowers sat on the table. Birds could be heard in the yard. The air outside the house, and in, was sultry, as if some thread had been pulled free from whatever stitching bound each summer day to the fate of the days before, and now it was no longer the end of August, but June again, June once more.

Franny did not really mind her chore: rubbing the dining room furniture with sweet O-Cedar oil. Rosamund and Peg polished silver in the kitchen, and that was the best job as its results were visible so quickly; still, at least Franny had not been sent with Martie to sweep the garage and, now and then, Rosamund added a little festivity to the work by putting a song on a record player, something Peg would not mind too much: "Come Rain or Come Shine," "Scotch and Soda," "You Better Love Me While You May."

Franny was singing along with the latter—moving Peg's milk glass pieces out of her way on the breakfront—when Peg called from the kitchen, "Telephone, Franny. For you."

A girl. Someone with one of the fake, breathy voices that advertisers liked females to use on television and radio. The Julie London voice. A product all wrapped up in a feather boa and a wreath of cigarette smoke. A voice very much like that of the woman who sang "You Better Love Me While You May."

"Franny," that voice said after Franny said yes, this is Franny, "we're going to kick your face in, Franny. We're going to rip your tits off, slut."

Franny set the receiver back in its cradle. Brick's old emergency siren sat on the cookbook shelf above the telephone, and it held a reflection of Franny's white face, warped across the siren's curve. Nauseated, ashamed, she hurried back to her chores.

As soon as she was free, however, she walked down Lakeside to tell Susan Thomas about the call—she had to tell someone—but telling Susan did not help. That evening, when dinnertime came, she excused herself from joining the others. She lay in her darkened bedroom until Rosamund came upstairs again; then she crossed the hall to Rosamund's room.

"What do you think? Should I tell Mom and Dad?" she asked after explaining about the call.

Rosamund looked up from addressing a letter to Turner Haskin. "Well," she said, "given how angry Mom was at Martie this morning, you might want to wait awhile. Most likely, the calls were just pranks. I used to get prank calls in high school. Remember? Remember how people used to TP the house?" Rosamund smiled and opened her eyes wide, as if there were some pleasure to be found in all this. Then she asked if Franny would like to ride into town with her while she dropped a letter at the post office.

Ryan Marvell would not be working at Mother Goose that night, Franny knew; still, she could not help looking at the golf course as they passed, just in case. What Franny wanted, at all times, was more chances to see Ryan Marvell. Any road she walked down, let him be there. Any store she walked through, she walked through with the hope of seeing his face. Could he be around the next corner?

As she and Rosamund drove along Lakeside in the dusk, she studied the grilles of all approaching cars, hoping for the grille of the brown and white Ford. She studied the people on the sidewalk in front of the Romero. She glanced in at houses with their curtains open. For split seconds, she imagined she spotted him in men too old and boys too young to have possibly been him.

"I wonder if Martie and Deedee are there," Rosamund said as they passed the Top Hat Club. "Martie likes to think her going there, now, is just the same as when Mike took me as a guest. It's so pathetic."

Franny turned to look back at the Top Hat. A modest place, but its white and red neon script always appeared magical at night. She doubted Martie would meet Darren Rutiger at the Top Hat. If she did not want people to know she were seeing him. But, then, Franny had no idea if Martie had seen Darren Rutiger at all after the night at the carnival. He might be in the service now. Maybe he was off in Vietnam, living in the jungle.

When the Wildcat passed the China Castle, Franny wondered if she and Ryan Marvell had ever sat in the same booth at the restaurant. No doubt they had. She wished the China Castle were open now. That she and Rosamund could go sit inside the cafe, near the window, and that Ryan Marvell might drive by and see them there.

She did not want to go home. Just let her drive around the lake, around and around, make circles in the circles in which he moved.

"Damn," Rosamund said with a groan as she turned in beneath

the Poddigbattes Camp sign and started up the drive. "Mike Zanios is at the house."

The music on the stereo was quite loud—some old Louis Armstrong thing—and when the girls stepped into the kitchen from the garage, they found Brick there, smiling, singing, using his index fingers to conduct Martie and a pretty woman Franny did not recognize (French twist, pink spaghetti-strap dress).

Martie nodded at Franny and Rosamund, and opened her arms wide. "Join in, you guys!"

Rosamund pressed her two palms together, then raised the hands to one cheek and tipped her head: sleepy. She climbed the stairs while Franny went to look in the refrigerator for something to eat. Lately, she was hungry all the time. That morning, she and Susan Thomas had eaten an entire loaf of bread made up as cinnamon toast, and they could have eaten more if there had been more bread—

"Hey, Frances Jean!"

She turned as Mike Zanios entered from the den. "Where's Roz?"

"Oh, she was real tired. She went up to bed."

Mike Zanios consulted his wrist watch. "Tired—at nine-fifteen?" He glanced at the woman in the French twist and she smiled. His date? A new girlfriend? Franny remembered that the singer from the club was a brunette, but this woman's hair was the same champagne color as Rosamund's.

"So, tell me, Frances," Mike Zanios continued, "has your sister been hiding from me lately?"

Franny was too flustered by the question to answer, but Brick laughed and said, "What's all this, Zanios?"

Mike Zanios smiled in a way that showed both his upper and lower teeth—a wincing kind of smile, though surely he did not mean it to look that way. "I was just asking Frances, here, if your eldest had been hiding from me," he said.

For a moment, Brick's mouth went slack, but, with a little effort, he rooted up another expression: dubious amusement. A smile delivered with a creased forehead as he bent to rinse a shot glass beneath the tap. "Now, why would she hide from you, Zanios?" he asked.

Mike Zanios grinned and looked down into his drink. "I thought she might be—embarrassed."

"Aw, Mike." Brick shook his head. "Why don't you just come out and tell us what you mean?"

· "Well, I assume she figured out that her Prince Charming and our chanteuse went off together."

Her eyes wide, Martie asked, "Turner Haskin?" and a small "Huh" escaped Brick:

"But, how could that be?"

"Oh, hell." Mike Zanios put his arm around the woman with the French twist. "They went off to Minneapolis, and spent a week at the Radisson. She came back, alone—sadder, but no wiser, I'm afraid."

"I can't believe it," Martie cried, and looked beseechingly toward Franny, who realized that like Martie, she, too, had tears in her eyes.

The woman with the French twist coughed into her hand. "One of us should go keep Peg company," she said, and exited the kitchen.

"Now, tell me, Zanios," Brick said, "by what lowlife did you come by this nonsense?"

"It's not nonsense, Brick. I had a drink with them before they left town. Very sophisticated of me, right?"

Brick shook his head. "You may find your part in this amusing, but that's our little girl upstairs. We don't laugh about somebody hurting our little girl."

Mike Zanios shrugged, but his face was chalky. "I didn't know that you didn't know," he said. He set his half-full drink down on the kitchen's central island. "Hey, Dorothy," he called toward the den, "we ought to get going, babe."

"But, how do we know it's true?" Peg asked when Mike Zanios and his date had gone and Brick told her the news.

"It's true." Brick poured himself another scotch. "Mike had a drink with them the night before they left town. And to think of him telling us that in front of a stranger! Practically—gloating!"

"His pride's hurt," Franny said—like the others, keeping her voice low. "He probably wants Roz to feel bad, too. He was mad she liked Turner more than she liked him."

Brick reared back with a dramatic "What?"

"Mike," she said. "He *liked* Roz."

"Don't be ridiculous," Brick said, and Martie, as if scandalized, "Really, Franny!"

Peg pulled out a chair at the table and sat. "Maybe we shouldn't tell Roz. If that's all Mike's up to, why ruin things between her and Turner? Things are lovely between them. He's written her and—"

"For Christsake!" Brick cried. "The guy's a fraud!"

Peg stared at Brick, almost as if she dared him to go on, but that did not stop Brick. "He deceived us, too, for that matter! He took advantage of our hospitality, and now we all look like idiots, and you can bet Mike's new gal won't waste time telling people how the Wahl girl's boyfriend came to town and—"

"You guys?" The four of them turned to the landing where Rosamund stood, white-faced, waiting. "What's going on?"

"Oh, honey." Peg and Brick immediately made their way across the kitchen to the girl, oh, honey, honey, and Martie and Franny joined them, there, hugging Rosamund, who repeated, now with real anxiety, "What is it? What's going on?"

In the morning, when Franny went to Rosamund's bedroom to say, again, how sorry she was about things with Turner, Rosamund turned from her dressing table to hand Franny an envelope. "Look at the postmark," she said.

Minneapolis, Minnesota.

"He was clever, but not that clever, huh?" Rosamund raised the back of her hand to her mouth as she smiled. Rueful, Franny thought, but not heartbroken. Somehow, while showing all the signs of love, enjoying what appeared to be the best of it, she had managed to keep her essential self on dry land. Franny would have liked very much to know if this had been something Rosamund had decided to do, or if it all had just happened that way, the way that this difficult love had happened to Franny; but she doubted that Rosamund would know the answer, or even how to pass along such skills, if they existed.

"I promise I won't tell anyone what he did," Franny said.

"What do I care if people know?" Rosamund smiled. "I'm not the one who had sex with him. I'm the one he respected."

Franny felt glad for Rosamund that she was so good at making the world be what she wanted it to be, but the ease with which Rosamund could perform such adjustments did leave Franny feeling inept and lonesome. To make matters worse, this day was to be Susan Thomas's last in Pynch Lake until next summer.

Gloomily, she went outside. Descended the stairs to the dock and the rowboat. The boat had been pushed up on the shore since that business with Bob Prohaski and she felt a twinge—aversion, guilt—as she pushed the boat out into the water and climbed in and began to row toward the Thomas cottage.

They would go for a walk, the girls decided. Once they were around the bend that led farther out into the country, away from the lake and cottages, they began to sing. "Chances Are," "Young and Foolish," "I'll Never Smile Again." They turned off Lakeside and onto a gravel road that ran between two farms. On a rise above a battered pigpen, they stopped to watch as two immense sows trotted across the muddy pen. The soft tents of the sows' ears flapped up and down. In the quiet, you could hear the sows' breathing, and the flapping of the ears, but then, seemingly from nowhere, like a dumped bucket of balls, a cluster of squealing piglets spilled across the ground behind the sows, racing to catch up with the mothers.

Though Franny knew her mother would not have liked it, she told Susan Thomas, "My mother's dad raised pigs. That red one's a Duroc. And the others are Hampshires. I think I might like to raise pigs. I might like to be a farmer. Something simple like that. I think I might be happier that way."

Susan Thomas nodded, but said, "I figure I'm probably as happy now as I'll ever be."

"Susan! I couldn't go on living if I thought I'd never be happier than I am now!"

Susan Thomas scowled. "Franny, you're smart and pretty and this adorable guy likes you and—what more do you want, for Pete's sake?"

"Well"—she felt embarrassed—"to be sure of something, that's all."

"Oh, that's all." Susan Thomas shook her head, then continued on up the gravel road.

Flushed, worried that she had somehow diminished her love for Ryan Marvell by her confession, Franny wanted to shout after Susan Thomas that circumstances, not a failure of love, cramped her happiness. As she did not know how to say such things to another person, instead she made her way down into the steep ditch alongside the road and flicked at the transparent green pods of the touch-me-not growing there. Just as they had when she and her friends used them for play food in their games of "house," the ripest pods of the touch-me-nots snapped open, ejecting yellow seeds and curling their insides outside, like the petals of lilies.

After a time, she could hear Susan Thomas coming back, the rustle of the fine gravel growing louder beneath Susan's shoes.

"I didn't mean I wouldn't *like* to be happier," Susan said. "I just mean I don't think I will be. That's all."

Franny squinted up at the girl, who made a kind of sepia tower against the sun. "But maybe if you don't think you will be, you won't have a chance to be," she said.

"And if you keep thinking you will be—in the future—maybe you won't be happy with what you've got now!"

Franny clawed her way up out of the ditch, grabbing at weeds, laughing at her trouble with the unsteady footing. On the way back to the house, she showed a new poem—a short thing—to Susan Thomas.

On my way to you, I haul up

the One and Only

from the popular song

long gone over the bridge

and sunk in the lake.

I punch my face through

every blue-skied calendar page. Yes,

I'm ruffed as Shakespeare or a clown.

Do you like the meadowlark?

The cardinal singing "pretty, pretty, pretty"?

The worship that belongs to them

and Bethlehem will have to do—for You—

until I have a tune of my own.

Susan Thomas nodded and smiled. "Did you show it to Ryan?"

"Oh, no." Quickly, Franny stuffed the thing in her pocket, and she changed the subject to Bell Academy, and Susan's poetry class there—for how could she have explained to Susan that it would be utterly impossible to ask Ryan Marvell to think about what she thought about their love?

That afternoon, Franny and Susan Thomas made the most optimistic of plans for getting together at Thanksgiving and Christmas and Easter. They walked about the house with their arms over each other's shoulders, sad, but exhilarated, too: proud of their friendship.

When the Thomases finally drove off to Des Moines, Franny ran down Lakeside Drive after their car. She waved wildly and cried, "Adieu! Adieu!" as if she mocked those movie scenes in which a person ran alongside the train that carried away the beloved, but this was only to conceal the fact that she felt precisely the way she imagined the people in the movies felt—that is, the way the characters felt, not the actors.

CHAPTER SEVENTEEN

THE SATURDAY BEFORE LABOR DAY, A CREW CAME FROM Moore's Marina to take out the dock and pull the hoist for the inboard onto the bank. The rowboat could spend the winter on the bank, upside down, but not the inboard. While the crew worked, Franny and Rosamund drove the inboard over to Moore's ramp where Brick waited with a car and a boat trailer. The three of them then drove the inboard into Moore's big, echoey warehouse for the winter, and Brick and Rosamund acted as if this were a jolly end-of-summer ritual. Franny went along, but secretly wondered if her father ever had paid his bill at Pynch Marina, and if he now ran up a bill at Moore's.

The day after Labor Day, Roosevelt Junior High opened, and Franny found she felt some of the old excitement of school starting again. She carried a new three-ring binder and a vinyl pouch holding four as yet unsharpened pencils and one pen. She wore a clean, white oxford cloth shirt with a button-down collar. *I'm Rip Van Winkle,* she thought as she hurried down the familiar halls and into the familiar morning light of her homeroom, #112; *that is, I'm me, but a me who's been through an experience nobody else knows about.*

At lunchtime, across the crowded cafeteria, she caught a glimpse of Bob Prohaski. Fear made gooseflesh rise on her arms at the same time that her heart sank with remorse. Bob Prohaski now wore eyeglasses with stern black frames that did not seem quite wide enough for his broad face. It occurred to Franny that he must have needed glasses for a long time as his lenses had the same greasy-looking thickness as the lenses of his big brother's glasses. But, then, maybe they were his brother's glasses?

He was trying to use his brother's glasses to help himself see?

Or: He wore his big brother's glasses, which he did not need, in order to resemble his brother?

There sat Christy Strawberry and Joan Harvett—with Lola Damon—the three already finishing their lunches at a table near the wall of floor-to-ceiling windows. As she made her way to the girls, Franny held her face turned slightly to one side, in part because she felt shy in their company lately; in part because she did not know how to respond to Joan Harvett's imitation of Lola Damon: that black hair, the chalk-white lipstick, the twin ribbons of black liner that seemed to weight her eyelids.

"We were just talking about Greg," Lola Damon whispered as Franny took a seat. "Joan's having trouble with him."

It seemed Greg Hopper—now the boyfriend of Joan, and *not* Christy; Christy now preferred a Ralph True from Holy Family—it seemed Greg Hopper was now threatening to break up with Joan. And why? Because he had made out with another girl over Labor Day, and when he reported the incident to Joan, Joan had failed to cry. The picnic girl, however, *had* cried when Greg Hopper told her that he liked Joan best—all of which made the boy wonder if maybe he should like the picnic girl.

"Everyone knows I can't cry!" Joan wailed. "Right, Franny?"

Franny nodded. She tried to appear sympathetic. Really, it depressed her that she did not feel sympathetic toward Joan, or even especially friendly toward her. And look at Lola Damon. Lola seemed intensely interested in Joan's problem. Lola leaned forward in her chair to say, almost sternly, "Start carrying an open safety pin and stab yourself with it whenever he expects you to cry. Or bite your tongue! It's *not* that hard."

Christy turned from sneaking a look across the cafeteria at Greg Hopper. "I've got it, Joan," she whispered. "You run to the john and we follow. You put soap in your eyes, like they do for movies, you know? Then you and I go up to Greg's table and I say, like I'm real mad, 'You creep, Greg, you made Joan cry,' and you're all red-eyed and everything."

While Christy spoke to Joan, Franny sensed that Lola Damon had turned her gaze Franny's way. She pretended not to notice until Lola said, her voice clearly taunting, "So, Wahl, you think that's a good idea?"

"Worth a try," Franny said. The words sounded odd, crumpled, and she repeated them—"Worth a try"—as she stood up from the table. "But I've got to go get my lunch. Before the bell." She looked toward the cafeteria line, the ladies in their white uniforms and hairnets. "Is there anything worth eating today?"

It was a great comfort to arrive home after that first day of classes. Once she was off the bus, and inside the house, she wanted nothing more than to turn on *P.M. Matinee.* However, no sooner had she lain on the floor in front of the television than Martie thundered into the den.

"Some girls called for you earlier! They said they were going to beat you up!"

"Sh!" Franny looked toward the kitchen where her mother was folding laundry at the breakfast table. "Jeez, Martie."

"I already told her." Martie lowered her voice to add, "She was, like, 'Oh, well, just some pranksters,' but I think we should call the police if it happens again. Tap the phone."

Franny tried to concentrate on the TV movie—Jimmy Stewart as a young clerk. She tried not to think about someone punching her in the face, kicking her ribs, but Martie set a penny-loafered foot upon Franny's arm, and she leaned down to ask, "You're not still seeing that Ryan Marvell, are you?"

Franny hesitated, then whispered, "You're not still seeing that Darren Rutiger, are you?"

Such narrowed eyes! Such tight lips! "What are you talking about, Frances?"

"At the carnival, I saw you guys. In the Wildcat."

Martie glanced toward the kitchen. "Did you tell anyone?"

"No."

"Good." As if they were spies passing messages, Martie, too, stared at the television as she whispered, "He's off at basic training now. And he was just using me, trying to get at Roz. So, are you happy, Miss Busybody?"

Franny looked back at the television. "Some days more than others," she replied. "Now, may I watch this show in peace, please?"

Unfortunately, once Martie left the room, Franny found she could no longer concentrate on the story; and so she turned off the set and went into the kitchen to see if Peg would mention the telephone call.

"Here." Peg tossed the end of a warm bed sheet to the girl and they began the familiar dance of folding: drawing apart, together. Apart. Together. Peg took the sheet for its last fold, then placed it in a box marked MARTIE WAHL that already contained a set of pink towels for Martie's dormitory room. Her voice low, she said, "So Martie told you about that call? You girls. Honest to God."

"Mom, I don't even know who these people are!"

Peg gave a skeptical snap to a pillowcase, then nodded at the basket of socks and things that remained to be folded. "You got something in the mail, by the way. A brochure from the Bell Academy for Girls. Do you know anything about that?"

Franny nodded as she began to lay white socks out on the table for matching. "That's where Susan Thomas goes."

"Well, I know that, but don't you start thinking we can afford to send you to some snooty school, because we can't."

She nodded. She was not thinking about Bell Academy. She was thinking about Saturday. On Saturday, Peg and Brick would drive, first, Rosamund to the Des Moines airport, then, Martie to Iowa City. Which meant that Franny would have the entire day to spend with Ryan Marvell. The problem: She still had not figured out in what way she could phrase the question, "How much of the day would you like to spend with me?" so that Ryan Marvell's answer did not expose possible deficiencies in his feelings for her.

*   *   *

A waste of effort, she realized when he called her at Karlins' Grocery on Friday afternoon. There *was* no perfectly safe way to ask the question, and when they made their plans for Saturday, she said nothing at all about the fact that her parents would be out of town.

She did, however, mention the threatening phone calls. There had been another just the night before.

"You don't know who it could be, do you?" she asked, and Ryan Marvell said, "Franny, I don't know girls who go around beating up other girls."

Offended, it seemed, so she did not pursue the subject.

On Saturday, by the time Rosamund and Martie had all of their things packed inside the Wildcat—suitcases and hair dryers and boxes—the only place for Franny to sit for the drive to town was Martie's lap, in the backseat.

"Delightful," Martie said and asked Franny to lift herself up, now and then, so that Martie could pull her skirt straight.

Brick and Peg and Rosamund chatted away in the front seat. Peg and Brick were looking forward to seeing friends in Iowa City. One of the friends had a new house and Peg and Brick would go there after Martie was settled in her dorm.

The car passed Mother Goose Miniature Golf. Ryan Marvell had quit the job once school started. Still: she had sat on that very piece of split-rail fence and talked to him.

"Now, Fran." Peg smiled and craned around in her seat. "We may not get back before late. The Harvetts are bringing you home after dinner, right? If I call at nine or ten, you'll be home?"

Franny nodded, right, but her mother's smile made the lie more painful than usual, and when her father stopped the car in front of the children's entrance of the public library, she did not point out that she had not used the children's library for over two years. She kissed each family member goodbye and told her sisters to write, and then stood, waving, until the Wildcat pulled into the street.

The children's entrance to the library featured a clumsy

wooden foyer, a shanty that had been tacked onto the stately building to provide a place in which children might remove and put on
their snow clothes in winter, and Franny stopped and took a fond
sniff of the foyer's odor of battered wood and rubber matting. The
benches were wonderfully low, as was the water fountain just inside
the building proper.

Did Miss Ivy remember Franny? A big woman in a tube of
mauve lace and a French twist as dun and matte as a discarded
chrysalis, Miss Ivy looked up from the checkout desk and smiled as
Franny passed through Children's to the hall that led to Adults.

A maiden lady, Miss Ivy. Someone to pity.

Between Children's and Adults sat an alcove that held a wall of
coat hooks and the pay telephone upon which Ryan Marvell would
call Franny at noon.

Of course, he might not call. He might have stopped loving her
since they last saw each other. Such things happened with heartbreaking regularity, she knew.

In Adults, the clock in the reading room showed the same time
as the clock over the checkout desk and also the clock over the door
leading to the Francis Wahl Nature Walk: eleven-o-three.

She pushed open the door. A pretty day, the air thin and bright.
She stopped before the memorial plaque that stood at the entry to
the nature walk. "Beloved husband." Hard to imagine her grandmother speaking of gruff Francis in those terms. But, then, she supposed "beloved husband" was the language of public memorials,
useful where private sentiments would feel wrong.

The plants that grew around several of the big trees were
hostas—one of her grandmother's favorite plants—and her grandmother had installed markers that identified which variety was
which, and Franny stopped, now, to straighten a marker that had
fallen over.

The grounds were not extensive but there were many short
trails and as she continued on, she spotted, up ahead, a stooped figure in a green dress moving very slowly through what seemed to be

a group of gooseberry bushes. Someone elderly? Who had lost something?

In an effort not to startle the woman, Franny called hello as she drew near, and the figure straightened and turned and it was her grandmother, wearing—along with the green dress—canvas garden gloves that rose all the way up to her elbows, and bright red rubber boots.

By way of greeting, Charlotte Wahl raised into the air a filthy pop bottle, several scraps of paper, and what appeared to be a small child's sweater, gone stiff with rain and sun. "The maintenance men don't always keep things as nice here as they should, so I came by to do a little straightening."

"I'm taking a break from homework." Franny pointed a thumb back at the library. She never knew exactly how much to say to her grandmother. It might be that her grandmother knew every detail of the trip to Des Moines and Iowa City, and would be offended if Franny assumed she did not know; or it might be that she knew nothing at all, and would be offended at that; or she might be offended if you presumed she wanted to know something.

Charlotte dropped the trash in her hands into a paper grocery bag she had already filled almost to the top. She was meeting her friend, Gen, at the country club for lunch, she said. Would Franny like to join them? Then they could bring her back to finish her homework?

Oh, thanks, but she was going to Joan's later, and needed to keep working now.

She had promised herself that she would wait until eleven forty-five before she went to stand in the neighborhood of the pay telephone. She made it until eleven-forty. The hall, thank goodness, stood empty. Framed autographs and letters from famous people—Walt Whitman, Herbert Hoover, Helen Keller—lined the walls, and Franny, reading one, then another, hoped they seemed to give her a reason to be in the hall.

A very large young woman in white majorette boots and a

hairdo as big as a tumbleweed ambled past. Had she looked at Franny oddly? It seemed so. It also seemed to Franny that the young woman was not the library type, but the type who might make anonymous telephone calls and pull a girl into a rest room and pummel her bloody. She had hardly finished thinking this, however, when the young woman came back down the hall, pushing a library cart of books.

The framed letter closest to the telephone came from Samuel Clemens, who wanted to inform a draper that he and his wife were dissatisfied with the curtains they had ordered. Curtains! A complaint about curtains exhibited on the walls of a library for all to see and admire! Franny laughed aloud, but just as quickly understood: a letter from the hand of Samuel Clemens. If she had received a letter from Ryan Marvell, wouldn't she have kept it forever?

Cherished it? Framed it?

A pretty woman now advanced toward the alcove (petite, agitated, wearing very high heels with very tight pants, a combination Franny knew only from the record jackets of certain jazz albums belonging to her father). The woman smiled and took a seat on the bottom step of the set of chained-off stairs that rose out of the alcove. "You waiting for a call, too?"

Franny nodded.

"A secret sweetheart?"

While Franny hesitated, the telephone began to ring, and the woman popped up to answer it, *bang,* much faster than Franny would have answered it. Franny would have let it ring at least twice, three times if she could have stood it, so as not to appear overly eager.

"No," the woman said, "but just a minute." She turned with a wink. "Franny?"

All her life, Franny had been told that only cheap girls rode next to boys in cars. "That girl's going to cause an accident," her mother would say if they saw a girl sitting close to a boy, "crawling all over him like that." Her father usually laughed, but Franny knew that he could laugh at things that, later on, you realized he found utterly revolting.

She had felt awkward the first time that Ryan Marvell asked her to sit next to him but she did love to have him put his arm over her shoulder and hold her close. She loved his grownup stink of cigarettes and coffee, and look at him, now, better than a god because he was a man, a big man wearing a black and red hunting jacket, beard unshaven, he was a regal lumberjack, and see how the concrete pillars of the library flew away behind the Ford like streamers on the bride and groom's car. She had known those pillars all her life, but now she sat beside Ryan Marvell and the world became the setting for what happened in their story. She was giddy with it, and it seemed he was, too. Look at him smile her way.

"Whoops! Better keep my eye on the road."

They stopped at a red light, too fast, and several things slid forward from beneath the seat: an empty beer can, a shotgun shell, and a book. She did not recognize the book at first glance because it had a different cover than the edition of the book that she had read, but she picked it up.

1984.

"This is one of my favorite books in the whole world," she said. "Are you reading it?"

He sucked in his cheeks for an ironic effect. "That's just something I'm supposed to read for school. But, listen, I've got to tell you about Thursday night."

On Thursday night, he had almost been arrested for underage drinking at the Lagoon. He and a number of others had been taken to the police station to be booked, but he saw a chance to run, and took it. "Here." He reached in his glove compartment. "A souvenir for you from the booking desk."

A small card held upright by a metal coil soldered to a metal base. NO SMOKING read the card. Franny pulled the card from the coil, then slipped the coil over her ring finger before extending her hand to exclaim, "But, darling, you shouldn't have!"

He laughed. "I should get you a ring, though, shouldn't I? What kind of a ring would you like? Turquoise, or—amethyst? Opal?"

She colored with pleasure and confusion. "I'd like anything you gave me," she said, a little frightened he might say it had been a joke, but he went on. "That's a good idea. I'll have to think about that. Maybe for your birthday? Only forty-eight days to your birthday, right?"

Because they came upon The Craft practice house from a different direction than when she and Martie had come upon it in July, and the formerly scruffy lawn was now mowed trim, at first she did not recognize the place even after Ryan Marvell parked.

"What's here?" she said while he stretched his arms out over the steering wheel and yawned—a little theatrically, it seemed to Franny.

"This is where The Craft practices," he said through another yawn. "Richie said we could stop by and listen."

Franny leaned forward to peer at the house in a way that felt at least as theatrical as his stretch. She wondered if he would think it bad if he knew she had been there before. "It doesn't look like anybody's there," she said, but then a noisy guitar twang sounded and they both laughed.

The band began to play "Turn On Your Love Light" just as she and Ryan Marvell reached the front door. Maybe that was the time to tell him about her earlier visit to the house? Or maybe not?

Richie Craft smiled and nodded at both of them as they took seats on the carpet at the back of the room. The band practiced "We Got to Get Out of This Place," which was a current hit, and the Dovell's "You Can't Sit Down," which was not. Ryan Marvell smiled at her, and began to move his arms like some old cornball doing the twist, and she laughed, and wished she could join in with his antics, sing to him, bounce around. Maybe he would like her better if she were able to be her whole self in his company, but to be her whole self in front of him would—require acting. Acting the part of herself. Which sounded odd. And, of course, there was the danger that if he knew her whole self he might not like her at all.

In the lull after "You Can't Sit Down," Richie Craft looked at

Franny and Ryan Marvell, and began to warble "I Only Have Eyes for You"—a parody, Franny understood, but a pretty one, and then the bass player cut in with the theme song from the old TV show *Have Gun, Will Travel*, and the lead guitarist transformed that theme into "Muleskinner Blues."

Bring the buck-buck-bucket, boy!

When Franny laughed, Ryan Marvell squeezed her tight, and said, "You are so great," and everything felt perfect, then, but you could not stop at perfection, you could not stop anywhere, and there should have been some place to which they could go next: A football game. A movie with friends. Out to eat—

He smiled and stood up from the floor. So they were going. "Come on." He gave her his hand. "Let's take a tour."

He meant to lead her to a bedroom, she supposed, and she found herself closing her eyes as they moved down the hall. She let her fingers drag on the wall's sandy paint, and though her heart beat with fear, she laughed. In the company of boys and men—even in the company of her own father—she often seemed to be laughing when she did not want to laugh. She could not even say if it were wonderful or awful to let Ryan Marvell lead her down the hall by the hand. According to Tim Gleason, Ryan Marvell had planned to marry Noreen Frye, which maybe meant that he had sex with her. Franny could not ask him about that, though. You didn't ask a boy about things like that.

"Franny! Open your eyes!"

They stood in a room papered in light green horses drawing light green buggies. He took a seat on a bare mattress. "Ding dong," he said, and ran his hand down her pants leg to the hem of her bell-bottom trousers. Did they look faddish? Did the big black and white checks seem absurd? Rosamund had assured her they looked nice, but maybe Rosamund was just being kind.

"Whose room is this, Ryan?"

"I don't know, honey."

She crossed the room to the group of familiar donation bags that stood, filled, in the corner. "Charity Village," read the bags, and each one carried a life-size picture, from the waist up, of a trim, uniformed man. The man smiled, and tipped his hat as if he stood at your door, right this minute, waiting to take away those items you no longer needed. His face was meant to be a face that you could trust: firm and forthright, teeth even, smile open, a tiny wrinkle of kindness around each eye. She and Susan Thomas had laughed over that perfect face when Mrs. Thomas gathered donations for Charity Village at the end of the summer. Franny started to tell Ryan Marvell how they had decided the Charity Village man actually came from another planet, like in *Invasion of the Body Snatchers*, only his ploy was to trick the earthlings into believing they gave to charity when, in fact, they were contributing DNA samples to the legions of—

She did not watch when Ryan Marvell got up and closed the bedroom door. While she talked, she picked up a set of deer antlers from one of the bags, and let the prickly hair at the base of the antlers work under her nails, the way she had with her teddy bear's plush when she was small. It seemed necessary to behave as if she and Ryan Marvell were not here, doing what they did. But when he came up behind her and whispered, "Hey, hon, it's not nice to get into people's private stuff," she wanted to cry. It was just the sort of thing her father would have done: try to make her feel in the wrong by chastising her about something that did not matter a bit. She wished, then, that she did not love Ryan Marvell at all, and she set the antlers down and walked to the double-hung window that looked out on the neighbor's yard.

"So, what're you thinking about, Franny?"

While she shook her head, he put his arms around her from behind. She drew a mental line between a corner of the Crafts' bedroom window and the bedroom window of the house next door, and then she connected that line to the corner of an air-conditioning unit across the street. She did want to be in his arms. Just let them stand there, together, forever and ever. But he reached out and pulled down the window blind and guided her over to the bed.

"What are you doing?" she asked.

"I thought we'd just lie down for awhile. I thought it'd be nice."

Really, she had no desire for him to take off her clothes, except that she felt it would be ugly and wrong—coy—to fight over her clothes if she meant to let him take them off eventually. And why not? When what was precious was his love?

Of course, a thirteen-year-old girl could not have sexual intercourse—that is, so absolutely *should* not, it might as well be *could* not. But she found she could lie on a bed in a bedroom, wearing nothing but her underwear, while Ryan Marvell took off his own clothes, and there was the shape of what she knew must be his penis—it made her want to cover her eyes—swaddled in its clean white jockey underwear. His bare legs were there, of course, too, below the underpants. Arms, legs, torso. Ryan Marvell—all alone in a room with Franny Wahl.

Ryan Marvell lay down beside her. His arms and chest and legs were there—bare skin—and then the skin and all of him lay on top of her.

"You're my girl, right?" he whispered. "Forever and ever?"

Of course. Of course. She adored him, but it was not from desire that she allowed him to push his knee between her thighs. Did he like that? She thought: a gift. Even when she saw that he believed he robbed her of something—that part of him seemed to *wish* to believe himself a robber—she thought: a gift.

How long did they roll about and rub limbs? At some point, the house had gone quiet. Hours must have passed, surely, while she hovered high above that striped—and slightly stained—mattress and Ryan Marvell stroked her breasts and whispered his delight. She gathered material for the nest in which she meant to hold them forever, yet could not help feeling frightened at the way he moaned and tried to steer her somewhere with his swaddled erection.

"Look at that," she said finally—she needed to hear her own voice say something more than *no*—"it's so white out there, Ryan, it's silver." She pointed to a seam of the afternoon world that entered the room where one window blind did not quite touch the base of its window frame, and he lifted his head and looked and said a fuddled, "What? Oh, honey."

Abruptly, he rolled off of her. He rubbed his face with his hands and cleared his throat and made odd noises just the way her father did when trying to collect himself before a cop came up to the window of the car with ticket book in hand. "Okay," he said. "Okay."

He turned from her while he pulled on his pants. She touched his back, the muscular shoulders with their dusting of freckles. She wanted to be brave for him, for his love, but could not tell what brave might be.

When they stepped out of the hall and into the kitchen, they found Richie Craft, alone, gluing a chair rung back into a chair. He looked up at the two of them and smiled, then said, "Jesus, Marvell, do you think you could have scratched up the poor girl's face any worse?"

Though the remark embarrassed Franny, she appreciated Richie Craft's friendliness, and the way that he spoke to her and Ryan Marvell as if they were just any couple. *Where are you two off to now*, he asked, and *Had her big sisters had any more of their crazy parties lately*, and she felt reassured by the comfortable conversation—until he mumbled an apology about "that business with Patty when you and Martie came by."

A look that she had never seen passed over Ryan Marvell's face; something sour and knowing.

"So, Franny"—he jingled his keys as they started down the sidewalk—"you'd been here before, huh?"

"Just once. With Martie. To listen to them practice."

"Hm. I suppose Martie didn't just listen to the practice, though, right?"

"She certainly did," Franny said, though it did not escape her attention that he had just expressed disapproval of a girl doing what Franny herself had just done with him; and maybe this occurred to Ryan Marvell, too, because he ran ahead of her, then, and tossed his keys high into the canopy of a sugar maple, catching them as they fell. "The thing is," he said when she came abreast of him, "I know Louie Nicholson."

"Louie Nicholson?" Franny remembered Louie Nicholson. A

thick-limbed boy with blond hair as curly as a lamb's coat. Years ago, Louie had come by the house on Ash Street to play four-square with Rosamund and Martie. "What about Louie Nicholson?" She opened the passenger-side door. Took a seat.

Ryan Marvell slipped in behind the wheel. So—*jaunty*, he looked. It made her even angrier with him. "The thing is," he said, "your sister did it with him, Fran."

"*Did* it with him? Martie liked Louie when she was in sixth grade. She kissed him once under Rubners' pagoda when they went there with Deedee Pierce and Max Hawkins to smoke lake reeds." Franny paused, then added a fervent, "Also, Ryan, if she *had* done it with him, I wouldn't think she was some kind of awful person."

He raised his eyebrows and smiled, as if she had said something pleasantly damning. She didn't care. "I mean it," she said.

"Okay, honey! Okay!" He pulled her over to him. "Take it easy, now."

She let him hold her. She wanted him to hold her, but after a few minutes, she looked at the little clock on the dash, and she said, oh, four-thirty, if it were four-thirty, she had to get home.

He sat back in the seat after he had switched on the ignition. He let his head drop forward and looked at her out of the corner of one eye. "You know, sometimes I wonder, why couldn't we just have met in the future, when you were, like, eighteen?"

She smiled at him, then, though the idea made her heart constrict. He would rather not be with her now? When all she wanted in the world was to be with him? Still, such thoughts did not change her plans, and soon after, when they came in view of the Poddigbattes Camp sign, to make certain that he had the impression she needed to be careful—*someone at home could be watching*—she asked that he let her out at the rise before the Nearys' farm, and she made her way on foot to the empty house from there.

CHAPTER EIGHTEEN

IN THE MORNING, WHEN SHE AWOKE, THE HOUSE STOOD COMpletely silent, as if her parents had not returned at all. A squirrel or a chipmunk chattered in the trees—she could not tell which. Somewhere, a motor droned. Barefoot, frightened by the possibility that she had spent the night all alone, she stepped warily into the hall. Filled with morning sunshine, even Martie's room seemed more vacant than it had the night before.

She hesitated before she looked into her parents' bedroom. From the door, she knew, you could see the end of the mattress.

There were her father's big feet, pink, hanging over the end of the bed, but she found this less reassuring than she had imagined.

Impossible that her parents would not know where she had gone and what she had done the day before. Still, they slept on while she made coffee and read the Sunday paper and ate a bowl of cereal. On and on.

For company, she took Snoopy out of his cage. He seemed tired, irritated. She set him on her shoulder while she added food to his dish though he hardly seemed to have eaten anything from the day before.

"You okay, buddy?" she whispered. "You okay, little pal?"

It was almost eleven when her parents began to move back and forth between their bedroom and the bathroom. As she could not bear the suspense a minute longer, she started up the stairs, calling ahead of herself, "Hi, you guys. How was your trip?"

Through yawns, they said good, Roz got off fine, they'd had a nice visit with the Malcolms in Iowa City.

And that was that.

Back in her own room, she lay down on the bottom bunk. She pulled a chunk of covers over her feet and took out the notebook marked "Franny Wahl's Selected Poems of Emily Dickinson." She wished she could write something about her afternoon in the bedroom at Richie's Craft house, but she hardly knew how she felt about it. Because she loved Ryan Marvell, the afternoon had had great weight, emotional density, yet hadn't it lacked the erotic luster of those childhood games of slaves and king in which everything was imagination, untrammeled by the awkward reality of disrobing, touching actual body parts?

"So maybe the Dickinson poem was wrong? Paste is sometimes more than pearl?" she wrote. Then closed the notebook and her eyes.

When she woke up, she felt disoriented. It seemed to be late afternoon, and there were voices downstairs—in the living room, she guessed, which meant company.

She paused at the top of the stairs to listen:

Her father's partner, Walter Trelore. She could not remember Mr. Trelore's being a guest in their house for some time, but she recognized his pleasant, rumbling voice as he said, "We can't afford to get a reputation for this sort of thing when we have bills to collect ourselves. And, you know, Harold, if you make enemies where you owe money—especially if you're drinking too much—they're more likely to talk."

"Oh, Christ, Walter"—

Franny could tell her father barely contained his anger.

"—we're talking peanuts, here! These people know they'll get their money in the end, but, at the moment, I'm putting two girls through college. And, I might add, a number of the good citizens of our town owe me dough!"

Franny could hear her mother and another woman—presumably Mrs. Trelore—exchange quiet, regretful remarks. *It's a shame we don't see each other more often.* That sort of thing. Then the sighs and squeaks of people standing up from chairs and sofas sounded, and shoes scuffed on the floor.

"Well," said Walter Trelore, "your father was my best friend, Harold, and he's not here now, and I feel—" He paused. "Even if you'd take care of just that one bill at the country club—apparently you ruffled some feathers there—I think that'd do a lot of good."

If her father made a response to this bit of advice, Franny did not hear it. The next sounds were goodbyes. A car starting. And, then, there was arguing, in the kitchen.

Peg wanted to know why Brick had not paid off the bill at the country club with the check his mother had given him. Brick answered that he had used that money to pay off the bill for the enameling kiln he had given Peg.

"That kiln didn't cost anywhere near nine hundred dollars!" Peg protested. "And I wouldn't have wanted it at all if I'd known we had bills to pay!"

"We always have bills, dear." Brick's voice was dull and slightly sarcastic, as if he spoke to an ignorant child for whom he cared little. "I figured the kiln would save us money since you were running up such big gas bills going back and forth to the Hobby Shack."

"Ha!" said Peg. "If you hadn't insisted on moving out here, I could still *walk* to the Hobby Shack!"

Franny waited to see if Peg would also say something about the fact that Brick had given Mr. Trelore the impression that he was paying for the big girls to go to college; but, abruptly, the argument stopped. Footsteps sounded on the stairs to the landing, and Franny bolted down the hall to her room. Maybe they were coming to see her, now. Her heart beat hard both from her rabbitlike bolt, her fear. Maybe while she slept, the Trelores had told her parents something about yesterday. Someone had seen Franny with Ryan Marvell and told the Trelores.

But her parents did not come down the hall. They went into their own bedroom and closed the door, and she never heard anything about Mr. Trelore's visit again.

That fall, the weather remained unseasonably warm. On Wednesday afternoons, Franny usually skipped Y-Teens, and Ryan Marvell picked her up at the public library and they drove around Pynch Lake with the windows down. If WLS came in on the radio, there were bouncy advertisements for Imprevu Perfume and H.I.S. jeans and events in Chicago, and Franny felt their romance gained a certain sophistication from contact with that world without their needing to participate in it. They climbed out of the Ford at Woolf Beach and took walks through the now empty campsites. They drove down odd roads and sat in the deep grass by bits of creeks that neither one of them had ever seen before. Thursdays were always activity days for Franny, with cheerleading practice or football games after school, but Fridays she got off the bus at Karlins' and Ryan Marvell called her at the grocery's pay telephone and they established their weekend plans.

They had few choices, of course. Once, he talked about sneaking her into the dorm room of an SFF friend—just to watch TV, he said, wouldn't it be fun just to watch TV together?—but, to her relief, he abandoned that idea. They could never have gone to a football game together. Not a football game, a restaurant, not even to his father's own Lake Theater—

"And I could get us both in free!" he teased. "I can't even impress you by waltzing you through the door without a ticket!"

Usually, when they saw each other at night, they spent some time parked in the country or at Woolf Beach. Afterward, they stopped at a hamburger stand if he were hungry. She never felt hungry in his company. She could not imagine eating in front of him.

She was embarrassed the time they went to his father's *drive-in* movie theater. Everyone knew what people did at drive-in movies—and to make matters worse, she had to be back at Mr. Pizza by ten, and the movie he wanted to see had not even started by then.

He joked about it, later: "Now all I need is a girlfriend who can't go out *before* ten o'clock at night."

They were at Woolf Beach, at the time. The Ford sat under the trees where they could look out over the sand at the choppy water, the darkening sky. Other cars parked alongside them, most containing couples, a few empty while their owners huddled close to picnic fires along the shore. Ryan Marvell had beer in a cooler in the backseat, and while he fetched himself a can, and opened it, he told Franny how, the night before, he and a friend from SFF had made a trip to Des Moines to fetch several cases of liquor purchased by the friend's parents.

"These are cool people. They know we can make good money selling the stuff on campus, so they're glad to help."

Franny smiled and nodded, but she did not want to admire these strangers in Des Moines. She wanted to admire only Ryan Marvell, and for him to admire only her. That would keep things simpler, wouldn't it? She leaned back against the passenger side door and tucked her stockinged feet under his hip. He was so handsome. So happy. But where did he get that happiness? He never told her anything about himself, really. Nothing about what he felt except that he loved her.

Later that night, in view of everything else that happened, she supposed it was not so awful that while they had sat at Woolf State, one of his SFF friends came up to the brown and white Ford and threw open the door she leaned against.

"Whoa!" the friend said as she toppled backward. Franny had looked up with a gasp at a large young man who now helped her regain her seat in the car.

"Nice going, Monk," Ryan Marvell said. "You okay, Franny?"

"She's okay," said Ryan's friend, and lowered himself onto his big haunches outside the open car door. "Sorry, Franny. Hey, I'm Monk, one of Ryan's buddies."

Ryan Marvell tilted his head back on the seat and made a noise of dismay—a soft nickering—that caused his friend to laugh:

"I can tell you're overjoyed to see me, Marvell. So this is the jailbait, huh?" Monk gave Ryan Marvell the thumbs-up sign, then tapped Franny's shoulder. "You don't have any sisters at home, do you?"

"Listen, Monk"—Ryan started up the Ford—"we were just getting ready to take off. Catch you later, okay, buddy?"

"Jailbait?" Franny said as he backed the Ford from its spot under the trees.

"I didn't call you that." He tossed his now empty beer can over the seat, and it hit the floor with a soft *ping*. "Of course, I could go to jail because of you."

She kept her face straight forward, watching the way the headlights swing across the beach and the tree trunks and—as Ryan Marvell shifted into drive—that sere stretch of grass leading back toward the main road. "But who's going to press charges against you?" she asked.

"Your parents. The law. Actually, just about anybody could if we got caught together."

They drove toward town in silence. She felt as if she would like to bite him, hard, on the arm or leg, hit him with something, a stick, a bat, again and again. But when she looked his way, he appeared calm. Smoking a cigarette, fiddling with the radio.

When they finally reached the business district, he turned off Lakeside Drive and drove up Clay. Her father's office sat on the right. She supposed he must drive by her father's office often, as he went about his day. Did he think of her when he drove by and saw the name that was her name?

She suspected he did not, while—with no provocation at all—she was forever thinking of him.

He turned the Ford onto Main. Scooping the loop. He had never before scooped the loop with her in the car. She might have teased him about it if things had not been tense between them just then.

They passed Tony's Shoe Repair and Ralph's Bicycle Shop. The Card and Party Place. These were shops she went into in her regular life. The man in the shoe repair shop was not Tony, but a gnomish Negro named Elliot, and Elliot's shop fit like a tiny cave into the front of an old red sandstone apartment building. The Elgin. Supposedly, The Elgin had been impressive once upon a time. Supposedly . . .

She glanced over at Ryan Marvell. He was driving slower and

slower. When they came up to a red light, he stopped, and lay his cheek against the steering wheel. He looked across the space between them with eyes that seemed sad, worn. "I've been thinking," he said, "what if I put on a jacket and a tie and tried meeting your folks again? You know, played the gentleman? The whole bit?"

Oh. She found the offer breathtakingly dear. And terrifying. Once again, her father grabbed her by the hair and threw her into the wall, and once again, the pain did no good, the pain bought her nothing, and she did not know what to say to Ryan Marvell, she could only slide across the car seat and, knees folded beneath herself, lay her arm over his shoulder. "I think I like you best when you've been drinking." That was what she said. "You're sweetest when you've been drinking."

"I'm serious. And, when you're sixteen, we could get married. You ever think of that? You and me getting a little cottage?"

A cottage. She stared at the dashboard clock. Its glow-in-the-dark hands read eight-fourteen. The word "cottage" was as sweet and promising as Ryan Marvell's chewed-down nails. Ryan Marvell had said he wanted to marry her. At eight-fourteen. On October ninth. 1965. She wanted to box up the moment, save it—please, let him save it, too, because how could she possibly use it now when she was thirteen and still had to finish high school and, then, college?

Behind them, a car began to honk. Ryan Marvell pulled into the intersection. Sounding both downcast and confused, he said, "You know you're driving me nuts, right? You send me messages or something, right? Like, by thinking about me when we're not together?"

Though she let the corners of her mouth turn up in a smile, Franny felt uneasy. Suppose she had tricked Ryan Marvell into love by her persistent song? He would be like those lovers in *A Midsummer Night's Dream* whose love was only the result of a potion, and not based on something real that occurred between the two.

"Is your clock right?" Her voice came out nervous, wrong. She pointed to the chamber of commerce light board. "Your clock says eight-fifteen and theirs—"

"What's this about?" He turned toward her sharply, then looked away. "You want me to drop you at Mr. Pizza right now? I can take you there right now, if that's what you want."

"That's not what I want. I just wondered—" She lay her hand on his arm, and he lowered the arm, moving away from her touch.

"You're sure?" he said—so casually, so casually. "'Cause I can take you now, if that's what you want."

"I want to be with you. You know I want to be with you."

"I don't know what you want. Just—don't sound sad, okay?"

He drove the car out into the country then. By the light of the moon, he removed her clothes. She made her best effort to pour her love into him, to fill him up. He breathed furiously above her. Drove his penis against the crotch of her underwear and kissed her breasts in a way that she felt certain would leave a mark. Still, she did not cry out—No!—until he made a thrust that moved the penis beneath the edge of her underwear and flesh touched flesh.

No!

He sat up. His bare shoulder was as round and gray as marble in the moonlight and she kissed him there and whispered, "I'm sorry, but you know I can't do that."

"Yeah." He yanked on his pants, his T-shirt. Started up the car.

"I'm not dressed," she said, and quickly began to feel around on the floor for her things.

"Hey. Wait." His hand ran down her bare back. "Don't get dressed. Just—grab me one of those beers, and, then, sit in my lap. Like that, in your panties. Facing me. It'll be nice. It'll be fun. Come on."

It would not be nice or fun. She knew that even before she maneuvered herself between him and the steering wheel, but he laughed and he seemed to be happy with her again, so she did not mind so much. She focused on the night sky beyond the driver's-side window. Stars. White farmhouses gone blue. After a while, he began to drive a little faster, to pump the gas pedal in time to a song on the radio. This made the Ford lurch, which was meant to be funny, she supposed, and so she tried to laugh, but when the song ended, he drove even faster, and, now and again, the Ford skidded in those spots where the road graders had pushed the gravel into ridges.

"Maybe you shouldn't have any more beer," she said the next time they came to a stop.

"A little while ago you said you liked me better when I was drinking." He nuzzled her bare shoulder. "And remember the night we met? *You* were a little drunk that night."

She sat back against the steering wheel, crossing her forearms over her breasts. "I wasn't drunk. I had maybe two sips of your beer."

He sucked in his cheeks. "Well, you sure didn't fight me off."

So he wanted to believed that she had been drunk? That her being drunk would explain her lying down with him on the bank?

When he began to drive again, the sound of asphalt beneath the tires—the absence of the crisp snap of the gravel—let her know that the car now travelled a main road once more. They headed toward Lakeside, she realized, as a sign for Woolf Beach appeared. A car coming from the opposite direction drove past, its headlights on her skin a scald.

"You've got to stop, Ryan. Let me get dressed."

"But I like you like this."

The Ford whirled along the curve that straightened as they passed Woolf Beach and, then, the miniature golf course. "Eighty," he murmured, "eighty-five," just the way he murmured his love to her at other times. "Ninety." The car rattled. It slipped onto the shoulder, and rocked, and she cried out.

"That was close!" he said. He sounded cheerful.

"Do you want to get us killed? Just—stop!"

He downshifted, then. Braked. The car scraped up to the gas pumps in front of Karlins' Grocery.

"Ryan!" She scrambled off of him in a mad attempt to cover herself while he—in stockinged feet, pants, and T-shirt—jumped from the car.

"Here!" With a laugh, he turned and threw his hunting jacket her way, then called out a greeting to the sleepy-looking Karlin boy who emerged from the store, shrugging into a sweater. "Put in two dollars of regular, man. I'm going inside for smokes."

The Karlin boy laughed. "Hey, Marvell, you lost your shoes!"

He stuck his head into the open driver's-side door just as Franny covered her back with the hunting jacket and began to work her hands—as awkward as flippers—into the armholes.

"So how you doing tonight? Franny, right?"

"Good. Fine." Bent forward beneath the tent of the jacket, she pretended to scout for something on the floor.

"Getting cold," the clerk said, and stomped his feet while the gas ran into the tank and then, as Ryan Marvell came merrily hopping and shivering across the lot, "Ryan's a cool guy, isn't he? Hey, Ryan, how's SFF, man?"

"Oh, hell, I'm flunking out! Gotta go, man!"

While Ryan Marvell turned the car around in the lot and headed back toward town, Franny hurried into the rest of her clothes. He behaved as if he were alone in the car now. He sang along with a song on the radio—he had never done that before—and to remind him of her presence, she finally got up the nerve to ask, "So, are you really flunking out?"

"Oh, yeah." He steered the car with his elbows as he worked a cigarette from the fresh pack. "Going to have to start hitting the books or I'll get drafted. Hell, I might even enlist!" He grinned her way. "What would you think of that? Me as your soldier boy?"

Her breath collapsed in upon itself. Out of the corner of her eye, she watched his cigarette catch on the bright filaments of the Ford's automatic lighter. Her soldier boy? The prospect terrified and exhilarated her. It was not impossible that he would die if he became a soldier, and maybe death was the answer. If he died, she could love him forever, but not have to see him anymore.

CHAPTER NINETEEN

M ID-OCTOBER.

Across the road from the house, the swamp and the meadow sat empty and brown. A faint, scintillating reddish brown. *Sedge.* Franny climbed down from the school bus and stood beneath the old camp sign, looking out. As if at the sea. But it did not have to be the sea. Enough that it was what it was—with the school bus making a brilliant patch of yellow against the gray day and groaning around the next curve, hauling its load of farm kids farther out into the country.

"Sedge" was a word Franny wanted to use in a poem, but she did not have any other words quite like it. "Sedge" was not a verb, but it put most of her verbs to shame.

She smiled a little. She prized this day, and the word "sedge," and the lowering sky, the mist that hung over the meadow and swamp and made the bark on the Nearys' apple tree perfectly black.

"Tamp"? A soft, almost moist word, but firm, too. "Tamp." A brown sugar sort of word with twin connotations of compression and filling up one thing with another.

Head bowed against the wind, she started for the mailbox. Charlotte Brontë crossing the moors, that was who she wanted to be then. With a fringed wool shawl to pull up over her head. Some slip of a fay creature instead of Franny Wahl, with big breasts and big nose and bright green *R* on the front of her cheerleading sweater, green and white pompons in a dry cleaner's bag.

Gimme an *R! R!* Gimme an *O! O!*

At that time of year, the mailbox always contained a few uncollected letters for summer people who would not be back until May. The Wahls had been directed by the mailman to toss the summer people's letters toward the back of the box so that he might, periodically, reroute them to winter addresses. Today, however, all of the new mail in the box was for the Wahls.

Dear comrades—so began the fat letter from Martie that Franny read on her way to the house.

> *Just kidding, but, really, these are exciting days, aren't they? Sorry I haven't been in touch, but I've been sooooo busy! Amazingly enough (considering I dropped out of the political scene last spring) I had the good fortune to run into Milton, and he and his friends (all completely brilliant) have been opening my eyes to all kinds of things that are wrong with our culture.*
>
> *Remember how you used to say that thing about the country needing a good revolution every ten years, Dad? Looks like we're going to make up for lost time! You'd be so proud if you saw the stuff I've been reading. Whew! Marcuse and other philosophers. But, hey, it's worth it, right? We're all gearing up for the big teach-in. I'm sure you've heard news of it, even in good old Pynch Lake. Yours truly is going to help out at one of the major workshops . . .*

The letter ran on for several more pages. It was, Franny thought, as thick as the letter the ROTC boy had sent to Brick and Peg when he decided to break up with Martie.

Idiot stuff, that was what Brick would say in response to the letter. *If she doesn't change her tune fast, I'll pull her out of that zoo so fast her head will spin.*

When she opened the front door, Franny could hear the sounds of both the TV set and her mother's telephone voice (always crisper, more modulated). Peg covered the receiver when Franny entered the kitchen—"It's Roz"—and Franny waved Martie's letter at Peg and said, "Here. From Martie! Let me talk!"

Peg took the letter, but stayed on the line, and Franny sat down to wait. Drew her legs up under her skirt. Started to remove her jacket, then changed her mind. The weekend before, she and Peg had installed curtain rods over several doorways, and Franny could see that Peg had spent the afternoon in front of the TV, sewing curtain hooks to old blankets. Peg's plan: to hang the blankets on the curtain rods and trap in the kitchen and den whatever heat the poor old furnace could supply.

On the TV, a news program showed footage of trash-filled American rivers, and rivers with freakish, bubbling brine at their edges. Then there were soldiers. One of them, anonymous beneath his helmet, darted out from behind a tank with arm raised in a signal that made him look like something right out of a movie, and Franny wiggled her fingers at Peg, and said, again, "Let me talk." She wanted to let Rosamund know about the newspaper article on Darren Rutiger. Darren Rutiger had been injured in a truck accident at his training camp, and though the newspaper article had not provided details, Ginny Weston had heard that Darren lost a leg.

"Mom," Franny protested as Peg set the receiver into its cradle, "I wanted to talk to her, too!"

Immediately, the telephone began to ring and, as Peg answered, Franny said, "If that's Roz again, let me say hi."

Peg grinned. "It's that McCartney boy from John Adams," she mouthed, as if today she and Franny existed in some cozy world in which Mom and Daughter await Daughter's call from Mr. Right.

What was that all about?

While Franny spoke to the boy—a nice boy from the other junior high; too bad she could not like him—she watched Peg read Martie's letter, shake her head.

The boy wanted to know if Franny meant to go to the high school football game that Friday. Oh, she couldn't say just yet, she told him. A lie. Why lie to him? Already, she had lied to her mother about Friday night: *The Coles are coming to their cottage for the weekend, and they called to find out if I could baby-sit.* That had been a daring move. Suppose her parents drove by the Cole cottage on Friday night and saw the place all dark. Or suppose the Coles really did drive up from Des Moines for the weekend. Franny had picked the Coles because they kept their cottage open all year, but suppose the Coles ran into Brick and Peg at Karlins' Grocery or the gas station.

Or, suppose, she thought when Friday night arrived—suppose the Coles were to drive up just now, and their headlights swept over Franny as she sat on their front stoop, quaking with the cold, waiting for Ryan Marvell to arrive.

"The Coles will drive me home," she had told Peg, "and I said I'd just walk down."

Most of the cottages stood closed for the season. The dark walk down Lakeside had taken Franny by surprise. And she should have worn a heavier jacket, gloves. The noise of her footsteps on the road's shoulders sounded louder than in summer, almost as if it would drown out any warning she might need to hear.

The Cole property was a funny little pink and white place with a ragged picket fence, maybe just the sort of cottage Ryan Marvell had thought of sharing with her.

There was little traffic that night. Each time a car approached, she could not help smiling a wild smile that she covered with her hand. After a while, though, her cheeks hurt from the smiles, and the cold, too. A more sure sign, she decided, would be a slow-moving car, and then a car did go by slowly, and the sound of its engine pressed against her heart as the car continued up the road.

She rubbed at her legs, bare between knee socks and wool Bermudas. She should have worn a watch. She could not recall Ryan Marvell ever wearing a watch but the Ford had its dashboard clock with the turquoise glow-in-the-dark lines and the red second hand that moved with a click when you were very quiet.

Maybe something had happened. She felt sure, however, that she would know if something had happened. An accident. A flat tire. Somewhere—from Martie?—she had heard that human beings had an excellent sense of time. They were generally able to guess the correct time within fifteen minutes, either way.

If that were so, he was a good hour late.

Unless she had misunderstood. Unless he had meant tomorrow night, or maybe eight o'clock. No. He had said tonight. Seven.

A group of oak trees stood across the road from the Coles' cottage and now that her eyes were adjusted to the dark—she could see practically everything now, even the tiny rocks in the concrete stoop beneath her—now she could see the way a yard light down the road cast a yellow fog on one side of each oak tree's trunk.

The spring before, in late May, Susan Thomas and her mother had driven up to Pynch Lake one day to gather mushrooms, and they had invited Franny along. A rainy Saturday, and they all got soaked, and after finding nothing for hours in all kinds of obscure patches of woods around Pynch Lake, they had discovered a perfect patch of morels, right there, in among those oaks, and they took them to the Thomas cottage, and cooked them in butter, and ate them right from the pan.

The car that now approached was a dark sedan and, oh, it passed the picket fence, but then it turned in at the driveway of a cottage two doors down, and hadn't Ryan Marvell come for her in different cars on occasion? There had been the station wagon of his friend Warren. The Rambler belonging to Timmy Gleason's mother . . .

Breathless, she waited for a sign. The car came to a stop, the yard light down the road silhouetting the heads of numerous passengers. It seemed to Franny, however, that at least one of those heads belonged to a female with a bouffant hairdo; and, almost immediately, the sedan backed out of the drive and returned, moving much faster, in the direction from which it had come.

So. No Ryan Marvell.

Inside the Cole cottage, the telephone began to ring. She leapt at the sound. Suppose it were her mother, calling to check on Franny. Suppose her mother and father drove down to the Coles' cottage when Franny did not answer.

Would they do that?

Just in case, she went to stand on the lakefront side of the cottage and peer around the building toward the road. If Peg and Brick drove up, she would pretend she had just come out the lakefront door. She would say, *Hey, are you guys here to take me home?*

Say that, and see what happened next.

But they did not come. No one came. She waited on the lakefront side of the cottage for what was surely another hour, then went back to the stoop. She tried to clench her ice-cold hands together the way she had that first morning after she met Ryan Marvell. Diamonds from coal. Pearls from paste. It seemed her heart could hardly move her blood.

The moment she entered the house—quiet, but from the back hall she could see lights in the den and over the kitchen sink—she went straight into the downstairs bathroom. "STAFF ONLY," said the old stencil on the door, preserved as a joke by Peg and Brick, and there was her face in the medicine cabinet mirror. The face that Ryan Marvell no longer loved? Red from the hours outside. Its clown's nose ran and she shook with cold as she wiped away the ridiculous snot with tissue from the toilet paper roll. She let the hot water thunder into the sink until steam rose to the ceiling, and when she sank her red hands in the water, distorted, they looked like the hands of her father.

"Is that you, Franny?" Peg called from the den when Franny finally walked into the kitchen.

"Didn't you hear me come in earlier? I've been in the bathroom."

"How'd things go?"

"Fine." She could not stop herself from checking the kitchen clock—ten thirty-two—before she opened the refrigerator and moved jars and bowls around to generate some sort of commonplace noise. "Hey, did you try to telephone me at the Coles'?"

"No. Why?"

She pulled an apple from the refrigerator, some leathery thing that had been in there for months. For a disguise, she took a bite from it; now she was one of the Cleaver boys home from school, and she said around the mush, "Oh, somebody called, but Mrs. Cole had told me not to answer so I didn't. I thought it might have been you."

"No. Not me."

"Hi, Fran." Brick stepped into the kitchen from the den, sci-fi paperback in one hand, empty glass in the other.

"Hi, Dad."

"Getting chilly out there, huh?" he said as he drew his bottle of scotch from its nighttime position by the toaster. She did not look while he poured. Let him pour. Just then, she felt, what the hell? They were all in this mess together, and she kissed his cheek and said "'Night" before she walked out to the den to kiss her mother, too.

•   •   •

You sit still.

While others jostle my elbow,

I try to thread a needle. I mean

To pierce your heart and bind you,

Round and round,

Thick with thread as a bobbin.

I will be a spider.

No, a glorious seamstress!

I mean, a song.

But I stitch my mouth shut.

I prick and I prick

And fall into a sleep.

You sit still.

I wait for the rousing kiss.

Your head turns right,

Left,

Enough for you

Who live under the revolving sky.

In the early morning—it had to have been after four-thirty because she remembered looking at the clock at four-thirty—she finally fell asleep, sitting up in bed, surrounded by a blizzard of rough drafts and one fair copy of her poem.

When she awoke at eight, it was to the sounds of her father shouting in the upstairs hall. From what Franny could gather, Martie's photograph had appeared in that morning's *Des Moines Register*. Franny's grandmother had telephoned to let Brick know, and now Peg and Brick were trying without success to reach Martie at her dormitory.

Franny made her way down to the landing. In the kitchen, Peg—looking as blanched as Brick looked boiled—stood with newspaper in hand. Brick was on the telephone with the housemother at Martie's dormitory.

"We're ruined," Peg whispered to Franny. Her eyes drooped as if the eyeballs themselves had grown heavy with blood. "Martie was in some protest yesterday and they got her on film."

While Franny took the paper from Peg, Brick put his hand over the telephone and asked, "So what do you have to say for your sister now?"

Sure enough, there was Martie in a sea of anonymous faces.

Could Ryan Marvell have been in that crowd? Suppose Ryan Marvell had gone to Iowa City to see a university friend and been caught up in that crowd and unable to make it home for his date with Franny?

"Well?" Peg said.

Franny shook her head. "Is she in some kind of trouble because of this? Did she get arrested?"

"I'd say you're in trouble if your picture's plastered all over the front page of the state newspaper!" Brick barked. "And your poor grandmother's footing the bill for this nonsense!"

After that, Franny carried a cup of coffee to the window in the back hall. A black car passed by the house slowly. Suppose it were him. Suppose that was the car she had seen last night, and he had been in that car with a group of friends, and, because he was late, imagined that *she* had gone home?

"Mom?" Franny stepped into the kitchen. Peg sat at the table, one hand covering her mouth so firmly it appeared she stifled a scream.

"Mom."

Peg did not lower her hand, but she flicked her eyes toward Franny as Franny said that maybe she could have lunch with her grandmother that afternoon. Wouldn't that be a good thing for Franny to do? Before she went to the library to work on her history project?

(A history project sounded perfect, didn't it? And, no doubt, there was some history project that she should have been doing, and, if she could find Ryan Marvell and things turned out all right, from then on, she would do everything perfectly, all her school-work, everything, perfectly.)

"That'd be fine," Peg said, then she stood and crossed to the planter that hung on the kitchen wall. With a tug, she uprooted the planter's half-dead ivy plant and proceeded to carry the mess over her cupped hand to the trash basket.

Franny hardly knew how to make plans with her grand-mother—she had never done such a thing before—but she did it that day. For Ryan Marvell. For Ryan Marvell, she put on the bur-gundy plaid Bermudas and knee socks and tennis sweater she had bought with such care for the back-to-school life promoted in the fall's issues of *Glamour* and *Seventeen*. For Ryan Marvell, she brushed her teeth twice and flossed and used mouthwash and set her hair and sat underneath the hair dryer.

"Don't you look cute!" her grandmother said when she came to open the door to Franny and Brick.

"Well, Mother"—Brick rubbed his cold hands together as he stood on Charlotte Wahl's front steps—"I'm sure you'll be gratified to learn I'm on my way to the office."

"On Saturday?" Charlotte held the door open so that Franny might pass inside.

"That's right. Death and taxes await me!"

Charlotte nodded, then she and Franny told Brick goodbye and they made their way through the muted-green interiors of the house to the big old-fashioned kitchen at the back.

"I ran out earlier and filled the feeders," Charlotte said as they sat down to eat. She pointed out her bay window to the crowd of birds now taking off and landing. "I thought you'd enjoy them over lunch."

Franny smiled and nodded. She had already calculated that she ought to stay at her grandmother's for an hour and a half. If she stayed two hours, she would have only two and a half hours in which to try to find Ryan Marvell before Peg picked her up at the library—

"You don't like the sandwich, Franny?"

"It's delicious! It's just—rich."

Her grandmother laughed. "That was what your grandpa and I used to say when we didn't like something. 'Delicious, but very rich.'"

"Your sandwiches really are delicious, though." Franny was sorry she could not pay more attention to her grandmother—she had been saying something about a train trip she meant to take with a friend—but Franny felt she could somehow help herself reach Ryan Marvell more quickly if she mentally *polished* the route to him, and so she imagined, again and again, opening her grandmother's front door, making her way down the walk in the direction of the library—

"You know, Franny"—Charlotte Wahl shook a playful finger at the girl—"I never can tell whether you're being polite or what. With my own children, I knew. They were always charming to me, but rarely meant a word they said!" She laughed—almost as if she had taken herself by surprise—and then Franny laughed, too, though it felt strange to have her grandmother comment upon the character of her father and her aunt and Franny herself. Really, it had never occurred to her that her grandmother had an opinion of her, one way or the other.

"And what about this business with your sister being in the newspaper?" Charlotte asked. "What do you think of that?"

When Franny hesitated, Charlotte raised a finger in the air. "Hold that thought," she said, and took a pair of binoculars from the lazy susan in the middle of her table in order to look out the window. "No. Nothing." She lowered the binoculars. "I see a finch or sparrow in a different light sometimes and think it's a new bird. But, say, has your sister turned political, or is this a boy thing, or what?"

Franny murmured that she had read that the college years were a time for trying out different ideas, and she didn't think Martie was committed to any one way of looking at things.

Charlotte nodded grimly. "Your father was like that. Always taking up some new thing. He couldn't be a lawyer because he had to be a writer. No, he was going to be an architect. No, a pilot."

"And a piano player," Franny said.

"Oh, yes. He was going to play piano and Sally Vayless was going to sing. Look out, Manhattan!" Charlotte raised her hands to her doughnut of hair and—an old habit—without quite touching the doughnut, made her way around its circumference, checking for loose ends. "Poor Sally," she murmured.

"Why poor Sally?"

Charlotte raised the binoculars. "Don't you kick my bird seed around like that!" she said, and then, "Sally was a dear girl, Franny, and she died."

"Was she the one in the accident?"

Charlotte set the binoculars back on the lazy susan. Gave the lazy susan a little spin. "Yes. An awful thing. I prayed your dad would quit drinking after that—but to no avail."

"But I thought he started drinking—*hard*—because of the accident. Because people thought he'd been driving, when really he only said he was driving to—" She broke off, doing her best not to flinch as her grandmother reached forward to tuck her hair behind her ears.

"That's better," Charlotte murmured.

"But, was he the driver?"

"Oh." Charlotte stood and began to clear the dishes. "He always said he was the driver. It's just—he gave the impression he *wasn't*."

Franny stood then, too, automatically shaking the placemats in preparation for wiping the table. "So what do you think, Grandma?"

"I figured out a long time ago that what *I* think about it doesn't matter."

How irritating Franny found this response! How coy. The clock in the hall began to chime. *She should get going,* she said. *Of course, she'd help pick up first—*

"No, no, you run along, but I'm afraid I've upset you. Your cheeks are bright pink."

"I'm fine. I just—do you have any aspirin?"

"I'm sure we do. *I* do. I'm always saying that: *we*. Run up to my bathroom. Left side of the vanity."

Left. Right. Franny hesitated before her grandmother's vanity. That odd conversation and the climb up the stairs after so little sleep had left her feeling woozy. When she pulled open the left-hand drawer, it tipped forward, and dented tubes of Ben-Gay and Preparation H and tins of Doan's pills fell toward the front, along with a new bottle of aspirin.

The bottle was made of that same grass-green glass as the empty bottle of aspirin that the caramel-corn girl had handed Franny at the house of Richie Craft. Franny took two aspirin from the bottle and returned it to the drawer. Then—the artery in her neck pulsing—she took the bottle out of the drawer again, and stuck it in the pocket of her Bermudas. In the mirror, she adjusted the hem of her tennis sweater to cover the lump before returning downstairs.

Her hope: He would see her while she walked to the library. Which meant she took her time once she left her grandmother's house. Which was all that she really felt capable of, anyway. She—daw-dled. She stopped and picked up pretty leaves. All the same, she must have moved too quickly, for soon she stood in front of St. Mark's Episcopal, with the library only half a block away.

She stepped inside St. Mark's, which sat empty and dark except for the light that came from the small bulb above the altar and the crimson candle that burned in the corner. The Perpetual Candle.

Just last May, with the church full of people and light, she had been confirmed up at the altar rail. She had longed to feel something more than pleased at the chance to wear the white dress Martie had worn for the Sweetheart's Dance, but when the bishop lay his hands on her head: nothing. The longing with which she had approached the rail was the same longing with which she left.

The Perpetual Candle: Had she made up that name?

She removed the bottle of aspirin from the pocket of her Bermudas and stuck it inside her purse. The modest beauty of the church was a comfort: the dark wood, the stained-glass windows that looked the way stained-glass windows should—dark, mellow, full of depth, like something medieval, not daisy-bright and new.

In a pew close by the door, she knelt down. The kneeling provided some solace. *Please make Ryan love me*, she prayed, over and over. She stared at the Perpetual Candle and hoped it might focus and direct her prayers, keep them ascending even after she left. But, then, it occurred to her that there ought to be a back-up candle for the Perpetual Candle, and it, too, should be called the Perpetual Candle. Then, if the first candle went out, you could say that it did not matter.

Though two candles might not do the trick. Three. Four. No. There was no end to the number of candles you could worry over. So perhaps it was better not to call the candle the Perpetual Candle. Perhaps it was better not to have the candle at all.

Like a bolt, she rose from the kneeler. Suppose, right then, Ryan Marvell drove by the church.

Down the aisle, and out the door, she rushed into the sunshine. "Franny!"

A large hand rose from a station wagon in the alley between St. Mark's and the neighboring congregational church, and she walked toward it, slowly. The station wagon belonged to Mr. Estep, father of her old Sunday School pal Kimmy, but, might, by some mysterious process, Mr. Estep's car be found to contain Ryan Marvell?

"Saw your big sis in the paper this morning!" Mr. Estep called as Franny drew closer. Also in the car: Kimmy and Mrs. Estep, who worked as a secretary in the St. Mark's office. Kimmy wanted to know whether Franny would be coming back to Sunday school soon. Franny did not know how to explain that her parents were uninterested in going to church lately, and she found it hard to focus on what the Esteps said—they were talking back and forth with one another and she was unclear whether Mr. Estep meant what he said about Vietnam, that the soldiers should not be in Vietnam—still, she stayed beside the station wagon, nodding, as this allowed her to remain on the street, in view, and she half-regretted it when Mr. Estep finally said, "Well, we better get going."

She was still waving after the station wagon—its back bumper layered with faded stickers from the Corn Palace, Wall Drug, Dinosaur Monument—when the brown and white Ford came to a stop at the curb.

"Get in!" Ryan Marvell called, and leaned across the seat to throw open the passenger-side door. "I can explain! There was an emergency and I had to help out!"

She got in. He chafed her hands as if he knew how cold she had been the night before. He spoke as if he were a little out of breath; as if he were, in fact, still caught up in the emergency. "The crew guy for The Craft screwed up and left the amp cords in Pynch and I had to drive them down to the gig in Cedar Falls!"

"Oh," she said, thankful he cared enough to offer her an excuse, even if it were an excuse so stupid that it could be accepted by only the most hopeless of lovers. Really, it was such a bad excuse, it might even be true. Worse: Somehow he knew that if he behaved as if the excuse were reasonable, she would have to accept it.

That was who he was. Who she was. Who they were together.

Eyes soft, voice tender, he asked, "You're not mad at me, are you, Franny?"

Unfortunately, it had not occurred to her to be mad at him.

"I even called your house, but you didn't answer!"

"Ryan—"

"Oh, right, right! You couldn't answer! You weren't there!" He smoothed her hair back from her face. "I missed you," he said. "Do you know it's been almost seventy hours since I last saw you?"

He prattled on in this way as they drove along. Seventy hours since he had seen her. Seventy-one days since they had met. And only thirteen days until her birthday! *Gonna have to get you something nice for your birthday. If I'm not too broke. The big fourteen. Hey! Only seven years till you can vote and buy beer!*

Up ahead, in a vacant lot, a group of boys about Franny's age played touch football. Ryan drove up alongside the boys and parked. "That kid in the gray sweatshirt's my cousin," he said, and, just like that, he hopped out of the car and began to play with the boys, calling for the ball, running up and down the lot, laughing, his neck turning that perfect red that was a banner of his vitality.

She lifted her purse from its spot on the floor and gave it a shake. The aspirin made a soft rattle as they moved in their bottle. Seventy hours since he had seen her. She was charmed but not deceived by such calculations. That is, she appreciated each effort he made to show that he thought of her, but understood such efforts meant little. That is, she was not taken in by him, but loved him as helplessly as if she were. So what good did it do to not be taken in? Not much good at all. She did not even dare to let him know she was not taken in. If he knew, he might be embarrassed and go away and never come back.

In the evening, Martie finally returned Brick and Peg's calls. It was Franny who answered the telephone. Brick was in the den, reading. Peg worked at something new in the basement: Sumi inks on rice paper.

"So, did you see me in the *Register*?"

"Yeah." Franny glanced at the photo, which now sat propped against Brick's old emergency siren on the cookbook shelf. Martie's face had been circled in pencil. IS THIS HOW YOU WANT TO BE SEEN BY THE WORLD? read the note that Peg had written in the newspaper's margin.

"What'd you think?"

Franny lowered her voice to say, "Mom and Dad are pretty upset. They talked about making you leave school."

"I'm thinking about dropping out," Martie said gaily. "How would they like that? Their daughter, the dropout?"

While Martie chattered on about the revolution, and her SDS boyfriend—*Milton is so brilliant, Franny, and not just brilliant, but understanding, too*—Franny considered the newspaper photo. It had been evening when the photo was shot and most of the protestors looked as if they were underwater, but Martie was curiously identifiable in that anonymous bunch, as if the photographer saw something in her raised face that he wanted everyone else to see, and so he had arranged to make her the center of attention.

Dedication? Was that what the photographer saw in Martie besides her pretty face? Some sort of shining belief in the future? Franny blew a breath onto the old siren. A fine bloom of condensation rose on its silvery side, then disappeared, and Franny thought how, if she were to put the siren to her lips, its coolness would be a surprise—a predictable surprise, if you could say such a thing. That is, a thing you might have experience with but could never quite get used to.

"But, listen, Franny"—the little squeak on the other end of the line signalled to Franny that Martie was suddenly near tears—"you're sure Mom and Dad aren't on the phone, right?"

"Right."

"Because there's something they don't know." Martie paused. "Do you know?"

"Do I know what?"

"You can't tell Mom and Dad, promise?"

Franny shook her head, her features dissolving into bands of color that moved back and forth across the bell of the siren, but when she spoke she said, "I promise," because she suddenly understood: Martie was pregnant, and needed to tell someone the news.

CHAPTER TWENTY

FRUIT PIES IN THEIR CLOUDY WAX PAPER WRAPS. CUPCAKES. Wonder Bread that built strong bodies twelve ways. Twinkies. Snowballs covered in pink and white coconut. She kept her face turned toward the bakery rack while she sipped at her bottle of pop. Through the rack, it was possible to see the Pynch Lake telephone directory, which dangled like a hanged animal from the black pay telephone above.

All over Pynch—on bedside tables in apartments and motels, in the homes of farmers and on the reception desk of her own junior high school's front office—you could find a telephone listing for the home of Ryan Marvell. Turn to the proper page of the directory and there it was. "Marvell, Ben." Visible. Accessible. Would it make sense to anyone if she tried to explain that this appeared a miracle to her mind? Something like proof of God?

At four o'clock she put her empty pop bottle in the crate by the counter and went to the telephone, but she did not dial the Marvells' number. As if she had come to Karlins' to make a call rather than receive one, she dialed the number that gave the local temperature and time, and while the recorded voice reported its loop of message, Franny enacted a brief conversation about getting together to do homework with a person she called Donna.

I just wanted to make sure you were home, Donna. I'll see you in a few minutes, then.

It had been a week since she had last talked to Ryan Marvell. Nine days since she had seen him. And told him about Martie. A sacred thing, telling him that sacred secret that no one else knew. That had also been the afternoon when she first let him slip his hand inside her underpants. They were parked at Woolf Beach, back in the campgrounds, lying side by side. He turned his face away and wet his finger on his tongue and rubbed it down there, which she supposed was the prelude to what her friends called "finger-fucking," though she could not imagine how that was accomplished, and she felt frightened because he wanted so much to take off her underpants, please, and she could not let him do that, and he was so miserable.

"You don't trust me," he said. "I know you don't trust me. I don't see how you can love me if you don't trust me."

She had imagined that telling him about Martie might show him that she trusted him, and so when they were sitting up again, putting their clothes back on, she did tell him. While she talked, she stared at an enormous boulder that sat in the campsite where the Ford was parked. The boulder appeared magical in the late autumn sunlight, gilded, and so did Ryan Marvell, pulling his T-shirt on over his head.

But he had laughed about Martie. "See, I told you. So, who's the father? Or doesn't she know?"

Nine days ago.

Seven days ago, during the last telephone call, she had felt as if she were some lost soul who clung to a limb while the alligators circled below: safe only so long as her strength lasted. "I can't see you this weekend," she said, trying to keep the conversation as short as possible. "I'm really busy."

It seemed he waited for her to say more, and when she did not, he said, sounding almost amused, "Shall I call you Wednesday at the library, or will you be too busy then, too?"

She meant to say, *Yes, don't call me anymore at all, if all you can do is laugh when I tell you my sister's pregnant,* but her strength ebbed too fast. Her teeth began to chatter and she said, "No, call Wednesday."

By Wednesday, she had been unable to eat or sleep. She was

convinced everything was her fault. She should not have told him about Martie. Or she should have done it differently. But he had not called on Wednesday. She left the library in a sort of daze. Narrowly missed being hit by a car as she crossed the street.

Today was her birthday. Fourteen. She was getting a cold or maybe the flu. Her breath felt hot in her nose, her armpits were slippery. Even the wind that blew through her jacket as she began to make her way from Karlins' toward home—even that biting wind could not cool her. Still, she kept her cheeks sucked in, her jaw strong: to make her face feel more like she imagined his perfect face must feel.

After all, any car that came down Lakeside from either direction might be his Ford. Her brain retained a perfect template of the grillework of the Ford, and she inspected every grille. No car mattered but his. Unless some other car held him. Then only that car mattered.

Did Martie feel this way about Darren Rutiger? Franny supposed Darren Rutiger were the father of Martie's baby, but she had not asked Martie for a name, and Martie had not offered one. Martie had said, "I'm not ready to tell Mom and Dad, Fran. I'll tell them at Thanksgiving." Then she laughed nervously. "Maybe I'll bring Milton along."

"But Milton's not—"

"No, but he says it's cool. He says all babies will be raised communally pretty soon. Like, it won't matter whose kid is whose, everybody will love everybody's kids just the same. Won't that be great? He and some friends are going to find a farmhouse where we can all live together in the spring."

Franny had not known how to respond to Martie's enthusiasm, and while she hesitated, Martie said, a little bossy, "But don't tell Roz *any* of this. I want to be the one who tells."

That had been two weeks ago. Maybe Martie had telephoned Roz since then.

At the top of the rise for the Nearys' farm, Franny stopped. Now, she shivered. She could not imagine she had been hot before.

Yet she regretted that her walk home was almost over. When she reached the mailbox, she lingered, though there was little to see. A *Life* magazine. A birthday card from Rosamund containing a photo in which Rosamund and her roommate were busy "wall-papering" with aluminum foil and Scotch tape the kitchen of their little rental house.

Franny dawdled on her way up the drive. It would be terrible if he drove by just as she reached the door and turned the knob. She would not be able to go back to the road if her mother heard the turning of the knob.

From the hall, she called, "Mom, Roz sent me a picture."

In the basement, busy transferring wet clothes to the dryer, Peg peered at the photograph in Franny's hand. "That was foolish, her moving out of the dorm," Peg said. "Did you know she meant to move out of the dorm?"

"No." This was not a lie, but there were things that Rosamund had told Franny that she felt sure Peg did not know: A new boyfriend had entered Rosamund's life, and he was a poet from New York who smoked marijuana and owned a macaw and lived in a van.

Peg sighed. "I still can't get over that Turner Haskin's turning out to be such a skunk."

"I always knew he was a creep," Franny said.

"You?" Peg laughed. "You were as starry-eyed as the rest of us."

Franny did not feel like arguing the point. She walked up the basement stairs to the kitchen. To her relief, a box containing a birthday cake sat on the counter. She had been afraid her parents had forgotten her birthday altogether, which would have been just—too embarrassing.

Upstairs, in her bedroom, she lay down. She wished she had not agreed to meet Christy Strawberry and Joan Harvett at the high school football game that evening. She would have preferred to stay home. She stared up at the satellites and moons on the underside of the top bunk mattress. It was nice here, out in the country. Martie ought to come home—unless she and this Milton were truly in love and wanted to get married. The baby could have Franny's room and Franny could sleep in one of Rosamund's twins. Franny could take care of the baby after school and on weekends. She did not care about cheerleading and going downtown after school. The other day, Franny and Christy Strawberry had been in line at the Red Owl behind a lady with a fussy baby, and the baby had calmed right down when Franny talked to it. Even the baby's mother had commented upon this: "You have a way with little ones!"

Aunt Franny. Aunt Rosamund.

Franny wished that Martie would not tell Rosamund about the baby until after it was born. Would that be possible? She did not know how far along Martie's pregnancy was. Rosamund would think Martie a fool for getting pregnant and planning to keep the baby. Maybe Franny should call Martie and say, "Keep it a secret. Don't tell anyone but me."

Preposterous. Advice from Franny. Who had told Ryan Marvell—who was not even a friend to Martie, let alone a member of the family.

That night, as she and her father approached the high school in the old Mercedes and she saw the white glow in the sky above the stadium, she remembered the excitement she had felt the fall before, when she was first allowed to go to the games with friends: all that looking forward, that habit of expectation. She missed it now.

Of course—she should have known—Lola Damon leaned up against the whitewashed walls of the stadium with Joan Harvett and Christy Strawberry when Franny approached. "God, Wahl, you look terrible!" Lola Damon said, and put the back of her hand to Franny's forehead. "And you're hot!"

"Yeah"—Franny jerked away from Lola's hand—"it's a cold."

Christy Strawberry had a birthday present for Franny and she wanted Franny to open it right there.

A bottle of cologne. Franny's favorite. She gave Christy Strawberry a hug, and Joan Harvett said she had a present for Franny, too, only she had forgotten it at home, sorry. After that, all four girls

joined the crowds that walked back and forth on the section of cinder track in front of the home bleachers. Franny had not been to a
high school game that year, but she remembered walking back and
forth on the track with Joan and Christy last year, all of them peeking at the boys who passed, wondering if this one or that one might
be the one. Now, she looked only for Ryan Marvell.

Could he possibly be in the crowd? Looking for her?

When the girls finally took seats in the bleachers, Franny made
certain to position herself at the end of the group. "Sit by me," she
whispered to Christy Strawberry, but Christy was tugging at Lola
Damon's arm and murmuring, "Look."

Bob Prohaski and his big brothers now strode past on the track
below. If they were freezing in their tight T-shirts, they did not show
it. Muscles bulging, jaws set, walking almost in step with one
another—they looked more like enforcers of the law than law-
breakers.

"Hey, Prohaskis!" Lola Damon called, and—all in unison it
seemed, the three heads pivoting as one—the brothers looked up,
gave a nod, and kept on walking. Lola Damon sighed. "They won't
come up 'cause of Franny."

"You want me to leave?" Franny asked—not really meaning
it—and Christy Strawberry whispered, "Don't be silly."

The football field was almost neon green beneath the big lights.
Franny still failed to understand the game, despite the fact that
cheerleading had required her to recognize forward movement;
however, she found the high school boys impressive in their shoulder pads and helmets, their white pants so bright they left an after-
image on the eye. She could understand a girl falling in love with a
football player if she saw him only in uniform, she told Christy
Strawberry; then added in a whisper, "Maybe I shouldn't have broken up with Bob."

"Franny!" Christy drew back, wide-eyed. "Lola likes Bob now!
And he hates you."

She nodded. What she wanted was not Bob Prohaski, anyway.
She wanted to back up. Never to have seen Ryan Marvell. Because

she did not understand how she could go on if she did not have him anymore.

"Christy"—at that moment, some craven loneliness in her dreamed that if the girls knew she were truly depressed, they might draw her to them again, and she blurted—"sometimes, lately, I think I may kill myself."

"God." Christy set a hand on Franny's arm, then she closed the wax paper liner of her box of Milk Duds and turned to whisper in Joan Harvett's ear.

Joan Harvett leaned forward in her seat to look at Franny. "Don't be crazy," she said. "Anyway, I just read this thing that said girls hardly ever kill themselves. I mean, they aren't successful. Like, they cut themselves *across* the veins in their wrists, when people who really want to kill themselves go all the way *down* their arms."

Christy Strawberry protested Joan Harvett's demonstrating the proper movement on the sleeve of her jacket: "Great, Joan. Like, you're telling her how to do a better job killing herself?"

"It's not like she's going to do it," Joan said, then turned to whisper in the ear of Lola Damon.

"Don't go telling everyone," Franny murmured as Lola Damon turned from talking to a boy in the row behind them. Something familiar in that boy's chubby face, the blond hair that clutched his brow like a hand:

Bob Prohaski's friend, Roy Hobart.

"Franny"—Lola Damon shook a finger at the girl—"negative thinking never got a person anywhere."

Franny smiled at Lola Damon as if she had no idea to what the girl referred; then she smiled at Christy Strawberry and said, "Hey, let's drop it. That's a pretty bracelet. Did Ralph give you that?"

Christy nodded happily, then asked a demure "Want to see something?"

Franny suspected that her answer was no, but that she had to say yes or lose Christy entirely, and so she nodded, and Christy slipped her arm from her jacket and pushed up her sweater to exhibit three nasty sores on her forearm: two round, the size of thumbtacks; one a worm of sienna that made Franny shudder.

"Is that what I think it is?"

Christy grinned. "Three in one night."

Joan Harvett leaned forward to drawl, "And we're all so impressed!"

"Ralph beats me out every time," Christy told Franny.

"Ralph, darling!" Lola Damon clutched at her heart.

"Eat your heart out," Christy said. "He's meeting up with us at the Maid-Rite later."

Joan Harvett stood and wiggled her hips, then exposed her own arm, burned, and scarred, too. "I beat Greg twice yesterday, and Greg can beat Ralph."

"You guys are nuts." Franny meant to hide her revulsion beneath an air of amusement, but maybe the girls could see the hiding. Maybe it left a bump or a hole in all she said or did in their company.

The people who paid attention to the football game now stood and yelled. Something good must have happened for the Pynch Lake side as the band played some sort of celebratory tootling and drumming, *bum, bum, bum*.

Christy elbowed Franny, then pointed to Joan Harvett, who had begun to write in nail polish on the wool coat of a lady in front of her, "F-U—"

"Joan," Franny whispered, "stop it!"

Though Joan ignored her, Roy Hobart leaned forward to hiss, "Shut your trap, Wahl. Everybody knows you're such a whore, if you didn't keep your legs crossed, your guts'd fall out."

The words made the world in front of Franny go granular and jumpy, like a color TV screen looked at from too close. For a moment, her ears closed up, the way they did at high altitudes, and though she sensed Christy Strawberry now whispered something consoling in her direction, she also had seen the moment in which Christy and Joan Harvett glanced at each other, as if they wondered whether Roy Hobart's saying the words made them true.

Roy Hobart went back to talking to Lola Damon, making her laugh by analyzing the bodies of the women who passed on the cinder track below.

Joan Harvett completed her nail polish "FUCK" on the back of the woman's coat despite the fact that, at least twice, the woman had glanced over her shoulder and sniffed, apparently wondering at the smell.

Franny did not notice the boy from John Adams on the track below until Christy Strawberry shook her shoulder. "It's that guy," Christy whispered. "Tom McCartney. He's waiting for you to invite him up."

A handsome boy, with dark curly hair and olive skin. She smiled as he and his friends loped up the bleacher steps and took seats on the bench behind her and the other girls. She made an effort to talk, and the effort helped, but then he and his friends joined Roy Hobart in making spitballs and shooting them at people passing below, and she felt, no, this is impossible, and when they all got up at the end of the game to go to the Maid-Rite, she wanted only to go home.

Last year, she had found it exciting to walk with a noisy group of boys and girls to the Maid-Rite. Now it seemed childish. When they emerged from the darker neighborhood streets surrounding the stadium, and onto brightly lit Main, she whispered to Christy Strawberry, "Can't we walk on the other side of the street? I don't want anybody in the pool hall to see me, you know?"

"What's the big deal?" Christy said, her voice irritated, and so Franny stayed with the group, but turned her face toward the street as they passed the pool hall.

You could often see people through the pool hall windows, she knew: young men watching a game, or waiting to take a shot. A sinister and inviting world, dark and light, the fake river continuously running past the north woods in the Hamm's beer clock in the window.

"Franny!"

The entire group stopped and turned. Behind them, on the steps of the pool hall, stood Ryan Marvell.

He came toward her, smiling, at the same time casting glances at the other members of the group. "What're you doing here, honey?" he said.

"Just"—she pointed down the street—"going to the Maid-Rite."

"Well, don't go there now! Let me get my jacket. I need to talk to you." He watched her face. His eyes held her face. She knew he was proud of how he could hold her, and she did not want to look at Christy Strawberry or Tom McCartney or any of the rest of them to see if they saw it, too.

"You'll be here when I get back, right?" he said.

Roy Hobart mumbled, "Shit, are we going to stand here while she decides whether she's too good to come with us or not?"

Franny glanced at Tom McCartney as Ryan Marvell went back inside Viccio's. Tom McCartney looked away. "I'll catch up with you guys in a minute," she said.

"Yeah?" Roy Hobart laughed. "Give him a quickie for me, too, why don't you?"

She watched the group move up the street. With little kicks, she bounced her toe off a parking meter in front of Viccio's—some nonsense meant to dispel that agitation she felt, though it was so ineffective that she barely was able to stop herself from taking off at a run as the old Mercedes trundled up Main, and Brick gave a honk and pulled to a stop beside her.

"Fran"—he leaned across the seat of the car to speak to her through the open window—"what're you doing here?"

Though she did not look back at the pool hall entrance, she could hear the door open behind her, steps coming her way.

"Dad, thank goodness you're here," she said, very loud, and quickly climbed inside the car. She wanted to look back at Ryan Marvell, to send him a message, but did not dare. "I was going to call you and Mom. Some kids and I were walking to the Maid-Rite, but they were acting like such jerks, I couldn't stand to be with them anymore."

Brick nodded. "I know all about that," he said. "Say, are you coming down with something? You sound sick as a dog."

*   *   *

In the morning—hot, thick-headed—she lay in bed and tried to will her body to fight off whatever ailed her. A cough shook itself loose from her chest with surprising strength as she forced herself out of bed; but imagine the problems that would arise if she stayed in bed, and then Ryan Marvell called and wanted her to meet him.

After breakfast—her mother down in the basement, Brick sleeping—she wrote on the blackboard "Gone for a walk." She headed for Karlins' Grocery. Maybe it was crazy to think he might call her, there, on a Saturday morning, but she hung about the store for a bit and, then, since she was already halfway to Mother Goose, she continued on down the road—just in case he might have been called in for a little part-time work.

She was quite close to the miniature golf course when she realized that Karen Johanson and a stout man who was surely Mr. Johanson were at work on the course, preparing for the winter closure. Two small children toddled about while the adults dismantled The Old Woman Who Lived in the Shoe.

Franny had just turned to head back home when Karen Johanson called out, very friendly, "Hi, Franny!"

A trick, but Franny missed it, and turned to smile.

Karen Johanson did not smile. In her Screaming Purple People Eater sweatshirt, with her hair in disarray from the wind, she looked slightly maniacal. "That's Franny Wahl," she said to her husband, then turned back to Franny with a shake of her head. "I suspected you all along. *Michelle.* You could've gotten my husband killed."

Franny shook her head. "It was a mistake, and I fixed it as soon as I could."

"You're the girl?" Ted Johanson wiped his hands down the sides of his work pants as if he meant to come greet her, but his wife gave him a sharp look and he stayed put.

"Ryan's not around, is he?" Franny asked.

The man shook his head. "You're a troublemaker," his wife said. "I could smell you coming."

Franny turned again and started back the way she had come. "Bye-bye!" called the little Johansons, but their mother shushed them.

At home, Peg demanded, "Where have you been?"

"Walking."

Peg began to empty the dishwasher at a furious pace. "Some boy called for you. Are you sure you weren't meeting some boy?"

Some boy. It made her hopeful. "Was his name Tom McCartney?"

"He didn't give his name, but that cough of yours is awful. You should take some of my turpinhydrate."

In her mother and father's bathroom, upstairs, Franny found the bottle of turpinhydrate that her mother kept on hand for her bouts of bronchitis. She drank a swig of the stuff. Nasty. It reminded her of last summer and the bourbon she had sneaked to Artie and Darren.

Back in bed again, she continued to cough into her pillow for a time, but then she began to feel better, rosy rather than hot. She listened to music on her clock radio. The clock radio's face *did* look like a face. In the upper-right quadrant of the circle, an open square showed the date, and that was an open eye while the other side was an eye shut in a wink.

She slept most of the afternoon, then picked at a little dinner in front of the television while Peg worked in the basement. Brick was not at home, but Franny did not ask about that.

Later in the evening, Peg came out into the den, holding up a half-full bottle of cough syrup that she had just found in the downstairs bath. "So you didn't find this earlier?" she asked.

Franny hesitated, then answered, "No, I didn't."

"Well, here. It'll help that cough a lot." Peg gave the bottle to the girl. "Take two teaspoons. Keep it with you."

Like a good girl, Franny went out to the kitchen with the syrup and took the two teaspoons Then she went upstairs to hide the bottle of cough syrup she had found earlier. She placed it with the bottle of aspirin taken from her grandmother's house and a packet of razor blades from her father's side of the medicine cabinet. If need be—if Ryan Marvell did not come back to her—she could numb herself with the cough syrup, then take the aspirin and slit her wrists. No, her forearms.

It was difficult to measure what effect the syrup had on her cough, but it did put everything off a little to one side: Ryan Marvell, the fever. The next evening—Sunday evening—when Tom McCartney called her, she lay on her parents' bed and stared into the receiver, which made her feel a little like a dog listening to a call from its missing master. A weary RCA Victor dog.

"Excuse my cough," she said to Tom McCartney. She *would* like him. Probably lots of boys who were thirteen spit spitballs. Ryan Marvell probably had. Ryan had probably not been as mature as Tom McCartney when he was thirteen.

She had to get back to thirteen.

In and out she drifted from the conversation, but the boy had a number of friends around him, and, now and then, they would get on the line and say, "Hi, Franny!" and that would rouse her a bit.

On Monday, she sipped at the turpinhydrate in the bathroom stalls between classes. Her English teacher asked if Franny weren't too ill to be in school, and Franny made a little humming noise—the cough syrup made her feel like humming—and she said, "Oh, I think it's just allergies, Miss Rozen."

At lunch, the light wood of the stage at the end of the cafeteria flickered with static, tiny dots of green and pink. Joan Harvett and Christy Strawberry teased Franny about how jealous Tom McCartney had been when she did not go with them to the Maid-Rite, and Franny laughed as if she were elated by the news, and then she told them how crazy it had been when her father drove up and she had to leave with him while Ryan Marvell watched from the pool hall steps. She did not tell them that to lose the pain of losing Ryan Marvell would be to lose him even more completely, and she had no intention of doing that. She did not tell them that, before first period, she had gone to their cheerleading coach, Miss Bright, and quit the squad. Miss Bright—a muscular little woman with a skunk's streak of white in her black hair—had asked, "Now why would you want to do that?" The bones in Franny's face had vibrated as she said, "I'm not feeling well," and bent to leave the pompons in their dry-cleaner's bag by the door.

After school that day, she walked to St. Mark's. The chapel was dark but someone had cranked open one of the stained-glass windows and that jeweled wing against the autumn sky made the bright world beyond tilt and gasp, become a magical glimpse caught in a magical mirror. That was Ryan Marvell, too. Life was him. God is love. Or life is. She knelt and bowed her head. Ryan Marvell had filled her brain. She had not had a chance.

In the dark church, her cough brought stars and bits of glitter to her eyes. She stared at the saints in the stained-glass windows. She, too, was surrounded by a hot corona, her body light, almost transparent. Soon, now that the cold was coming, ice would begin to build up inside the base of the stained glass windows—old metal things, poorly sealed. When the sun shone on the windows in winter, the ice became a lens for the window's colors. Blue ice. Pink. The irregular gold of melted butter.

She closed her eyes. She prayed. The same prayer, over and over again, and the truth was, what she believed in was love. Love. Love. Only love could save her, make her whole, lave her wounds. What was the passion of Jesus to her? She prayed for the love of Ryan Marvell. She prayed for help. Who was God but someone to whom she could address the insufficiencies of her life? The comfort of God was only that he might answer her prayers.

Her ribs ached from coughing. The light from the Perpetual Candle flickered, and she squinted at it with one eye. Something told her that a person's taking medicine in church—particularly medicine that made you feel so much better—might be sacrilegious, and so she waited until she reached the alcove before she took another sip of the turpinhydrate.

It seemed too good to be true that Susan Thomas and her mother sat in their Corvair outside the entrance to St. Mark's, and so Franny did not immediately walk up to the car, but waited, grinning, on the St. Mark's steps, hoping the long-haired girl on the passenger side, who was surely Susan, would turn her face Franny's way, eliminate all uncertainty.

It was Mrs. Thomas, however, who showed herself first, her bowl of gray hair rising into view as she climbed from the Corvair.

"Mrs. Thomas!" Franny called.

"Franny! We just tried to call you!" Mrs. Thomas exclaimed, and then Susan Thomas was unfolding herself from the car and giving Franny a hug. It seemed Mrs. Thomas had taken Susan out of school early that day so she and Susan could see a litter just born to a Pynch Lake breeder's prize weimaraner; and, as a favor to their minister in Des Moines, Mrs. Thomas was now delivering literature to the sister church in Pynch Lake.

"You want a ride home?" Mrs. Thomas asked. "As soon as I run this box next door, we're going out to the cottage to pick up a few things."

Franny nodded. She did want to go home. To get in bed and rest her cheek on a cool pillow. Gratefully, she sat down in the back of the Corvair with Susan to wait for Mrs. Thomas's return. Susan told Franny all about the weimaraner pup she had selected—the owner had given her a sweet Polaroid of the litter and exhausted mother, and Susan had made a ballpoint X beneath her dog.

When Mrs. Thomas got back in the car and they started out of town, Susan asked if Franny had received the brochure from Bell Academy.

"What? Oh, yeah." Though happy to see Susan, Franny found it hard to concentrate on what her friend was saying: Would her parents let her go to Bell next fall? Susan's literature class was reading *The Canterbury Tales* and Susan just knew Franny would love them, too—

"You know, Franny"—Mrs. Thomas interrupted Susan as they approached the Poddigbattes Camp sign—"you should be in bed. You look like you feel miserable, and that cough—"

"I'm okay, really. Would you drop me here so I can get the mail?"

Franny squeezed Susan's hand before she got out. "I miss you," she said, then patted Mrs. Thomas's shoulder, and added, "You, too."

"We miss you, Franny," Mrs. Thomas said, and Susan said, "Yeah. Write me. You should be getting a letter from me, like, tomorrow. And keep bugging your parents about Bell."

There was not much in the mail, but at the back of the little orchard, the small red peppers that clung to Mrs. Neary's dead plants were as bright as Christmas lights. Everything was bright.The shaggy grass along the camp's old baseball diamond burned. One of the Wahl garage doors stood open, a velvety, black rectangle.

She looked up the road at the sound of a car pulling to a stop, its tires biting into the grit from the shoulders. A dark car. Not the brown and white Ford, but this car came on as if she were its goal, and when it rolled to a stop alongside her, she screwed up the courage to look at the car's passengers.

There was something wrong with their faces, something deformed. The car was filled with deformed people. Embarrassed at having seen, she looked away.

So stupid. As soon as they were out of the car and upon her, she knew they were just girls with nylon stockings pulled over their heads.

It was Ginny Weston who found her and drove her to Dr. Hanson's office.

"I made trips like this before with both my ex and Billy," Ginny said. "You don't have to tell me *what* you been up to, but don't try to tell me you ain't been up to nothing."

Franny did not try to tell Ginny Weston anything.

Dr. Hanson's pretty nurse, Jane Wiener, winced as she cleaned the sand and dirt from the cuts and scrapes on Franny's face and hands and legs. "I'm sorry, sweetie," she said, her voice lovely and low, "but we have to get you cleaned up so Doctor can evaluate what we've got here."

"Looks to me like her hand's broke," Ginny Weston said from a plastic chair in the corner of the examination room. "I'd like to find the monsters that did it, I can tell you."

Jane Wiener nodded as she made her way around the table. Polio had left her with a severe limp, and after practically every visit that Peg made to the doctor's office, she commented, *Poor Jane*, because the nurse's fiancé had broken their engagement when she contracted polio, and no one had ever asked for her hand again.

"You've got a fever, too, haven't you, Franny?" Jane Wiener pulled the thermometer from its holder and stuck it—ripe with alcohol—under the girl's tongue.

"One-o-three," she reported when Peg arrived at the office. "She's a sick puppy, Mrs. Wahl, as well as a mighty sore one."

Ginny Weston offered Peg her chair, but Peg waved the offer away. "She didn't tell me she was sick," she said. She squeezed Franny's hand, but her eyes were on the face of the nurse. "I just knew she had a little cough."

Dr. Hanson opened the door the way he always did, with a knock that allowed no time for a response. Peg and Jane Wiener stepped back from the examining table. "She's got pneumonia," the doctor said shortly into the examination, but he didn't think her hand was broken. *Where else are you sore, Fran?* She pointed to her head—someone had kicked her there. Her ribs. *Other than the cut, the mouth looks okay. Probably want to take a couple stitches on that cheek, though.* The doctor spun around on his examining chair to speak to Peg. "We'll have her x-rayed—she may need tape on her ribs—but she ought to do fine at home once we get her on some antibiotics."

"But, Dick—" Peg tilted her head toward the door.

Jane Wiener went back to work with her tweezers and gauze while the doctor and Peg left the room. From the corner, Ginny Weston said, "Somebody ought to call the police."

"Maybe that's what they're doing," Jane Wiener said.

The door opened. Peg, smiling now, stepped into the room alone. "The doctor decided it would be good for you to spend a few days in the hospital. Until your cough is better," Peg said. She turned her smile toward Jane Wiener and Ginny Weston. "And he agreed with me that nobody else needs to know about the other business."

Peg expanded upon "the other business" when she and Franny were alone in the car, driving to the hospital. "This isn't the sort of thing you tell your friends. Those girls—don't give them the satisfaction of spreading the news!"

Lying in the backseat, dopey, bandaged and bound with tape, Franny stared at the bars in the Wildcat ceiling where the canvas folded over upon itself as it lowered into the boot. She considered her various pains. The ones under her eye and by her mouth glowed like branding irons. Her ribs ached. At least no one hit or kicked her anymore. She remained grateful that the hitting and kicking had stopped.

"Oh, honey," her father said when he approached the bed in her hospital room. Though it was dark by then—Peg had not been able to locate him for a time—he shielded his eyes with a hand, like a person trying to observe a distant object on a bright day. "Oh, Christ."

Franny was glad of the pain pills they had given her; otherwise she knew she would begin to weep. With shame that she was in such a predicament, and pain at the pain in her father's eyes, and self-pity. There was no denying that.

He took her hand. He looked pale. But then a nurse sashayed into the room to check Franny's temperature, and he laughed and said, very merry, "How come you've got so many sick people around here?"

The nurse's smile was thin—maybe she smelled the alcohol on his breath—and, after that, Brick sat quietly until she left the room.

"So, what's this all about, Fran?"

"I don't even know who they were, Dad."

"I find that awfully hard to believe," her mother murmured, but continued in her normal voice, "Dick says he can keep her a week or so. She should look a little better by then." For a moment, Peg leaned over the bed and stared into Franny's eyes—implying she could see deep inside her? Put a spell on her?

Franny felt better after they left.

She liked life at the hospital: calm, quiet, accommodating. A Catholic order owned the hospital and certain of the nurses were nuns whose long, white habits swished as they moved up and down the hall. Also, the idea that Ryan Marvell could not possibly know she was there lessened her pain at not seeing him. If he did not know where to find her, she need not suffer over not hearing from him; and maybe, she thought, she could take instruction from this. Maybe the thing to do was to place yourself in unexpected locations. Then you would not need to feel bad if no one ever reached you.

Her mother brought a letter from Susan Thomas to the hospital when she came the next day. The envelope's puffed and stiffened look suggested it had been steamed open and glued shut, and Franny was thankful that she once had warned Susan that she must write only the tamest news in her letters.

"Aren't you going to read it?" Peg asked when Franny put the letter on the bedside table.

Franny was coughing. Little stars sparked in front of her eyes as she shook her head. "Later."

Peg took a seat between the window and the bed. "I called Mrs. Deever about your piano lesson. Christy and that boy—McCartney—they called. Christy wondered why you weren't in school. I told her you were sick. I don't think she knew anything. About the other, I mean."

The sunshine that streamed in the window hit Peg's face. She looked as pretty as always, but tired. The skin under her chin was starting to go a little soft, a little wrinkled, like a peach that had sat too long. As if she knew Franny noticed this, Peg raised the back of her hand to her jaw in the way that people beyond middle age so often did in studio photographs. Probably, she had not slept much the night before. Franny was sorry. It was too bad she was not the sort of a daughter who could please her sort of mother. But there you had it. She certainly did not intend to try to make herself over to please Peg.

Well! With a smack of her hands against her thighs, Peg stood. She was going to run down to the machines and bring back a cup of coffee! Did Franny want a cup of coffee?

No. No thanks.

No sooner had Peg left the room, than the telephone began to ring. Was it magic? Had Ryan Marvell, somehow, heard what had happened to Franny, and did he now want to come to the hospital to tell her he loved her?

She stared at the telephone as it rang a second time. You always had to let it ring twice, no matter how much you wanted to answer, and suppose it were those girls, calling to say they were not finished with Franny yet.

The receiver felt greasy in her hand, as if the last person to use it had been smeared with ointment, but Franny managed to say hello, not drop the thing.

"Franny." It was Martie. Crying as she explained that Peg had called that morning to tell her Franny was in the hospital.

Did Franny want Martie to come home? Just say the word. Milton could bring her—

Then, suddenly, Martie was not crying but laughing. "I can't believe you haven't even met Milton yet! Hey, maybe this would be as good a time as any for me to break the news to Mom and Dad, you know?"

Franny waved to Peg, now entering the room. "Mom's back with her coffee, Martie," she said by way of warning. "Anyway, I'll be home really soon. It wouldn't make sense for you to come, so— I'm going to let you say hi to Mom now."

"I just talked to her this morning," Peg said, but she came to the bed and took the receiver, and Franny turned onto her side so she could look out the window and try not to think about her various pains or the coughs that pushed against her lungs.

"Miss Wahl?"

One of the nuns—a smiling old lady—stepped into the room.

She carried a vase of pink flowers. "These seem to be for you," she said and set them on the bedside table.

Pink baby roses and carnations. Peg leaned close as Franny pulled the small green envelope from the flowers. "Who're they from?" she asked, one hand over the receiver.

The card's border of violets was visible even before Franny pulled the card from the envelope, and if the card bore the name Ryan Marvell—well, just then, Franny did not care if Peg saw. If the flowers came from Ryan Marvell, and he wanted her to, Franny would run off with him tomorrow.

The unfamiliar handwriting on the small card seemed to break up and form again, but surely that was an *R*—

Go away, she wanted to say to her mother, *go away*, but then Peg was telling Martie, "Roz sent Franny a lovely bouquet of carnations and roses," and she was right. The unfamiliar handwriting was the handwriting of the florist, that was all. GET WELL SOON, read the card. LOVE, ROZ.

The day before she was to leave the hospital, the newspaper carried an account of how a Baltimore man had poured kerosene over his body and set himself on fire outside the Pentagon. The man's wife told reporters that her husband had become increasingly despondent over the war in Vietnam, but the story was complicated by the fact that the man had brought his small child with him. A number of bystanders said they had been forced to plead with the man in order to make him release the child before he set himself aflame. Others said the man had shooed the child away on his own.

No photographs accompanied the article, but Franny remembered the photographs of a Vietnamese monk who had set fire to himself a few years before. Eyes closed, the monk had looked perfectly calm, as if the flames surrounding him could do no harm. Franny's father had called the monk's actions "show-off stuff." Franny had not known what to think, but for the man at the Pentagon to hurt himself like that in front of his child—he had to have been sick in the head, didn't he?

She tried to write a letter to Susan Thomas about the cigarette burns on the arms of her friends. *Do you honestly think a boy would like a girl better for burning herself that way?* she asked, but then tore up the letter and lay back against the hospital's stiff pillows and stared at the cross on the wall.

She had seen Catholic crosses before, with their bodies of Jesus, crucified and nailed to the cross. Some people considered Jesus's gesture the grandest gesture of all. There were people who seemed to love Jesus because he died—for them, supposedly. To save them.

It seemed to Franny that she would risk her life to save Ryan Marvell if he were in danger, but she knew that such a gesture would not win his love. Ryan Marvell either loved her or he didn't. And that was all there was to say about that.

CHAPTER TWENTY-ONE

Aᴼᵀᴱᴿ Fʀᴀɴɴʏ ʀᴇᴛᴜʀɴᴇᴅ ꜰʀᴏᴍ ᴛʜᴇ ʜᴏꜱᴘɪᴛᴀʟ, ʜᴇʀ ᴘᴀʀᴇɴᴛꜱ spoke much more softly when they were upstairs. The noise of their conversations distracted Franny little more than the chirps of the birds outside her window or the whistle of the wind. If she sensed one or both of her parents might come to her room, she often closed her eyes and lay back against the pillow and pretended to sleep until they went away.

Both of them were nicer to her than usual. Brick had brought her peach ice cream from the dairy her first night home and, the next night, he came up to her room and seated himself at the foot of her bunk bed. He gave her toes a pat through the blankets and said he'd been thinking about their getting another dog. *What kind of dog did she think she'd like?*

Peg came up to the bedroom to cheerfully deliver messages from Christy Strawberry and others who telephoned (*Roz says I should tell you she'll be bringing home your birthday present at Thanksgiving*). Franny thanked her, and said she would like it if Peg continued taking her calls—just until Franny was feeling better—and Peg seemed to consider this a good idea.

"You want to fully recuperate before you try going back to school," she said, widening her eyes in what Franny understood as her mother's way of trying to politely convey the message that Franny still looked like a girl who had received a beating.

"A smart girl like you—what do they teach you at school anyway?" Peg asked. In return, Franny smiled. If it were up to Franny, she would never go back to school. She found, in fact, that she did not even care to get up to brush her teeth.

When Peg came to Franny's room, she never stayed long. The bedroom was cold enough that, even during the day, you often could see your breath, but Franny preferred to spend her days there. Each morning, she built an immense collar of blankets around herself and, within it—writing, reading—she became an Antarctic explorer in her tent, a Buddha, an American Indian looking out from the edge of the continent, a Chinese scholar got up in elaborate robes and a black silk hat with a tassel on top.

Most of the time, in that chilly world, she did not think about the fact that Martie was pregnant. Sometimes, when she did think about it, she decided it might not be true. Maybe Martie had been mistaken. Or—made it up. Or maybe, by now, Martie had told Rosamund, and Rosamund had helped her get an abortion through some friend or other in Florida.

Most of the time, Franny thought about Ryan Marvell. One afternoon, after Peg drove into town to the Hobby Shack, Franny made a careful copy of one of her poems to send to him:

> I made myself still as the water in a bowl
>
> to hold your most perfect reflection
>
> So that whoever looked at me
>
> would see you.
>
> You were that beautiful.
>
> Loving you became a kind of vanity,
>
> I suppose.
>
>
> What I felt—my love—
>
> it was surely the whole mountain range,
>
> sunstruck, and the sun coming up, going down, a complete view
>
> Upon which you could feed forever.

But I was not water or mountain or mirror.

I was the cupboard

behind the mirror

Where the shelves hold the base rubber appliances

and a comb, a brush, a tiny cup—the child's

bowl of heaven—that a woman must bring

to her sickened eye

to wash it clean.

She put the poem in an envelope and addressed it and carried it downstairs, startling Ginny Weston as she brushed out her pin curls in the front hall.

"You about scared me to death!" Ginny said.

"Sorry." Franny patted Ginny's arm through her heavy coat. "But would you, please, put this in the mailbox for me?"

With one hand, Ginny Weston fluffed her old-fashioned curls across the collar of her coat; with the other, she stuck the envelope in her coat pocket. "I ain't even looking at the name on it. That way, I ain't involved."

Franny laughed as if she were her old self, and did not let on that she had to hold on to the hall bureau to keep from falling down.

That night, while her father drunkenly banged Cole Porter songs on the piano, she knelt beside her window, face and bandaged fingers pressed against the screen. *Nyar.* The waves conspired with her call. *Nyar. Nyar.* Her patience grew gorgeous: purple and green and blue iridescence, as eyed as peacock feathers.

It was true, she thought, though a miracle, that Ryan Marvell had said, "You're my girl, right? Forever and ever?"

Though maybe not a miracle. Maybe something like Double-speak. Maybe the kindred soul she had recognized in him was like the kindred soul Winston Smith had recognized in O'Brien. Maybe at some time Ryan Marvell would have been the perfect love, but they had gotten to him and ruined him long ago.

*   *   *

In her bed, she wrote. She recited poems. She memorized Keats' "Ode to Beauty" and "The Love Song of J. Alfred Prufrock." It seemed like a life that could go on and on. However, when Charlotte Wahl telephoned Peg about the upcoming Thanksgiving, and learned that Franny remained at home, she drove straight to the house.

"Frances," she called before she even reached the doorway to the girl's room, "I know about the beating and that you've been sick, but it's time to face the world again."

Peg had followed Charlotte up the stairs, and she and Franny exchanged a glance around Charlotte's grand fox fur collar: How did Charlotte know about the beating?

"I usually manage to find out most things in this town, whether people want me to or not," Charlotte said in answer to the unasked question.

Franny studied her grandmother's face as she pulled the chair from the dresser over to the bed. What if Ryan Marvell had told someone about Martie and her grandmother now knew about Martie, too?

But Charlotte Wahl said only, "At seventy, I don't have anything more important to do with my time than see that my granddaughter returns to the world," and with that she sat down and took a book from her bag—some fat history by William Manchester—and she raised her reading glasses from their chain around her neck and opened the book to chapter one.

After four days of such visits—which always included a period in which Charlotte washed Franny's face and combed her hair—Franny felt so besieged that she got out of bed and dressed and went downstairs to eat breakfast at the table before her grandmother could leave her own house in town.

The following Monday, she returned to school.

At first bell, when all of the students pushed toward their homerooms, she found she needed to step back to wait in the dead space under the stairs leading to second floor. Certain kids skittered past with heads down. Others used elbows and knees and hard parts to ram and gouge those in their path. Two boys in identical striped shirts grinned at one another, then picked up a smaller boy by his ears and started him down the hall.

"Stop that!" Franny shouted.

To her surprise, the three boys ran off together, as if she were the enemy.

In algebra, she had missed two quizzes, one exam, and the explanation of factoring. In the lunchroom, Christy Strawberry waved to Franny—*over here*—and as Franny took a seat beside the cafeteria's big windows, she noticed: no leaves in the small trees staked with tough wire and sections of green garden hose in front of the school. No leaves in the yards of the pink and yellow and blue tract houses that sat across from the junior high.

"God, you're skinny!" Joan Harvett said. "I wish I'd get pneumonia for a while."

"But, hey"—Lola Damon took a bite of her sandwich, then chewed while the others waited for her to finish her sentence—"Claudia and Janeen asked if you still liked Ryan Marvell 'cause they saw him at a party with some girl."

"God, Lola, she doesn't want to talk about that!" Christy Strawberry said, and Franny shrugged as if she had been too ill these last weeks to have given a thought to Ryan Marvell. She could do this because she was down deep, like a diver who hears the speedboats overhead and knows she must stay submerged for as long as possible if she does not want the top of her head ripped off.

"Claudia and Janeen," she said. "Who are Claudia and Janeen?"

"Our Y-Teen leaders," Christy said softly. "They go to SFF, Fran."

"Oh." Franny nodded. Big girls with blue eye shadow and hair dyed the color of corn silk.

"But, hey, Franny"—Christy smiled—"what do you think of Barry Monahan?"

Franny appreciated the change in conversation. She batted her eyelashes at Christy. Pretended to bite a lengthy cigarette holder, tap a little ash. "Rahly, dahlink"—Natasha the Russian spy from *Rocky and Bullwinkle*—"I don't know zis Barry. Vy don't you introduce me sometime?"

"Ho, ho," said Lola Damon. "Nobody gets to talk to Barry but Christy."

Christy dipped her head closer. "He's cool but he's kind of fast. He wants me to do some stuff, you know?"

Franny nodded. Smiled. The smile stunk. She stunk. She was a mildewed cadaver her old pal now inspected for bad news and clues? Was that it?

"I think I'd go all the way before I'd—you know, let him finger me," Christy whispered. "Wouldn't you?"

Terrible not to trust Christy. Last fall, Franny and Christy had sung all of the songs from *The Wizard of Oz* together. Last winter they had bought matching stadium coats with wooden toggles, and the night Christy learned her dad was moving out, Franny had rocked Christy in her arms. But she did not quite trust Christy now, and she said, maybe a little more Germanic, less Russian, "Ah, ah, ah! But ze finger does not contain ze spermatozoa." She lifted her index finger, made the top digit bow. "Ze finger iz your little friend."

Christy giggled behind her hand. "You're awful."

"Undt have you never heard ze visdom of sages who tell us ze penis is like ze loaded gun, safe till it shoots?"

Christy repeated this tidbit to Joan Harvett and Lola Damon who said, "Ick!" and "Ho, ho!" and, then, "But that's really true, isn't it?"

Billions of sperm swam in a single ejaculation. Six or seven "good ejaculations" contained enough sperm to repopulate the entire earth. That afternoon, she read all about it at the Pynch Lake Public Library. Why had it never occurred to her that the library owned books and magazines that contained such facts? And pictures? A Swedish photographer had shot beautiful opalescent photographs of sperm swimming in cervical mucus; pink fallopian tube folds as delicate and lovely as the petals of a peony.

At just six weeks, while still so small it could fit on a thumbnail, the human embryo showed minuscule rag doll hands, a fog of fingers. By eleven weeks, the embryo weighed no more than a letter sent with a single stamp—three quarters of an ounce—yet it now looked like a human baby. Little legs and toes and arms and even the beginnings of a nose in that spooky miniature head.

She glanced up from the book's slick pages and out the window at the library's front lawn. Resemblances everywhere. The trunks of the pale-barked sycamores reminded her of the long legs on the three Holsteins the Nearys kept for milking. The tears that rose in her eyes surprised her. If Ryan Marvell were to walk into the library, now, and see her, sitting here, looking out the window, and he could tell what she was thinking, would he fall in love with her again? No denying she had hoped she might see him here, today. Absurd. Yet she had imagined him in the reference room, yawning, loafers propped on one of the big tables. In the stacks: *Well, if it isn't Ryan Marvell!* Said oh, so lightly. The trick would be to make it possible for him to be not too embarrassed at seeing her. To make it possible for him to move toward her, if he liked.

Better: to make it impossible for him to move away from her. But that would be magic again. Miracles. Potions.

When she finally thought to check the clock that afternoon, she found it was already after five, and she hurried down to the alcove to call her father's office. A man in a yellow rain slicker was using the telephone, barking happily into the receiver, "Yes, yes, exactly! That's exactly the way I remember it, too."

She went to stand a few paces off, to wait.

"Hold it!" A young woman stepping out from under the alcove's stairs grabbed the collar of the parka of the toddler who moved one step ahead of her. The woman knelt. Wrenched the parka hood onto the child's head. Tugged the strings that pulled the hood into a pucker around the tiny face.

"You drive me crazy all day long, don't you?" the woman muttered.

Franny smiled at the tiny, squashed face that stared her way while the mother took miniature mittens from her own coat pockets and worked them onto the child's hands. A woman not much older than Martie. Her hair looked rough and her skin was grainy. *Ill-used,* Franny thought, not sure where she had seen the phrase.

A terrible mother? A tired mother?

"Come on, hurry up," the mother called to the child as she advanced down the hall. Then they were gone and the man in the rain slicker left, too, and Franny stepped up to the telephone, which looked full of promise.

Suppose—on a whim—Ryan Marvell decided to try to telephone her at the library. Right this minute.

Just in case—so no one else could use the telephone—she picked up the receiver and discreetly depressed the cradle. A woman in a Chanel-style suit descended to the base of the alcove's chained-off stairs and unhooked the chain and passed by Franny, who said into the telephone, "That would be nice. Sure. If your mom says it's okay." But when a second woman stopped in the alcove, Franny had to drop her dime into the coin box and dial her father's office.

Closed.

She tried home, next. Busy.

"May I use the phone if you're not getting through?" the waiting woman asked. "I'll only be a minute."

Franny wandered down the hall to Children's. Eyed the beat-up display rack of early readers that stood just inside the door: the story of the fellow who woke up to find his head turned into a parsnip. A Ricka, Dicka, and Flicka book. A story of Babar the Elephant. *Make Way for Ducklings.* All of them, books she had loved. So maybe the young mother in the hall had not been so terrible of a mother. She had brought her child to the library, after all.

"May we help you?" Miss Ivy called from the checkout desk—quite loud, apparently because no one else was in the unit at the time.

"I'm just waiting for the telephone," Franny said. She walked the length of Children's, to the Story Room—the prettiest room in all the library, a circle of windows and window seats. When you were small, you could sit on the window seats while Miss Ivy read stories, or you could work on the simple wood puzzles at the central table, fit the piece of blue sky to the scallops formed by Bo Peep's pink bonnet, lay the sheep-shaped pieces into their appropriate spots at the base of Peep's hoop skirt.

"Oh, Lord," Peg said as she drove Franny out of the library parking lot, "Martie called just before you did, all in a tizzy. It seems her latest, this Milton, left for Washington, D.C., and he didn't want Martie to come along."

"Oh, no."

"I tried to get her to calm down. She makes a fool of herself. That's why they leave." Peg scarcely stopped at the four-way half a block up the street. "I could see nobody was coming," she murmured. "'Don't throw yourself at them, Martie.' How many times have I told her that? A girl can't throw herself at a boy and hold his interest."

Franny sighed. "That's so sad."

"But you agree, don't you?" Peg said sternly.

Franny watched two nuns climb out of a beige sedan in front of the rectangular brick building that was their home. The yards and yards of their habits caught in the breeze and lifted and luffed, black sails against the gray sky.

"That it's sad?" Franny said. "Yeah, I agree."

CHAPTER TWENTY-TWO

THE TRAVEL PLANS ARRANGED FOR MARTIE AND ROSAMUND Wahl's trips home for Thanksgiving included Rosamund's flying into Des Moines on Wednesday afternoon, and Brick's picking her up at the airport. Peg had arranged for Martie to receive a ride from Iowa City with the nephew of her hairdresser, who was to drop Martie at the house at around eight on Wednesday evening.

"You would have thought I'd sold her to the Indians!" Peg said, then added with a whine, "'I suppose you guys are driving to Des Moines to get Roz!' As if she couldn't see the difference between an unnecessary eight-hour trip and a necessary three-hour trip."

"Sometimes, you just have to plug your ears when she talks," Brick said.

This was at breakfast, Wednesday morning. Her parents would know about Martie's pregnancy by the time they went to bed, and yet there was nothing for Franny to do but act as normal as possible. Eat her toast. Explain that Mrs. Harvett would bring her home from Y-Teens. Go wait for the bus.

In English class, however, Franny jiggled her foot so hard that her shoe flew off and hit the shoulder of a girl several rows up; and, at lunch, when one of the more popular of the ninth-grade boys entertained his friends by sending love notes to a girl from Special Education, Franny found herself yelling at the boy and his friends where they sat, smirking, on the cafeteria stage.

"Ooo, Franny." The boys raised their knuckles to their mouths and leaned back, pretending to be afraid of her. "Ooo, don't hurt us, Franny."

All day long, she watched the clock. "IBM" read the small black letters on the face. The father of a boy Rosamund had dated during her freshman year of college had been employed by IBM. Would she have to remember that forever and ever? Every time she looked at an IBM clock? The father of a boy she never even met?

At the ringing of the release bell, she wandered out into the hall to her locker. Lola Damon stood in the foyer, using the trophy case as a mirror while applying her lipstick. Joan Harvett joined Lola Damon there. She looked down the hall toward Franny and waved *come on.*

"Lola and Chris want to get some nylons before Y-Teens," she explained as Franny drew near, "so we got to hustle."

Moisture in the air, moisture in the gutters from a recent rain. She had never lived through a winter in love with Ryan Marvell, but the smell stirred a nostalgia in her that was linked to him. Because her whole life was now linked to him? Was that what it was?

At Drew's Department Store, several women already waited at the stocking counter, and when Christy Strawberry and Lola Damon joined the line, Joan Harvett asked if Franny would do her a favor and come with her to Spragues' Drugs to buy her a pack of cigarettes.

Franny was more than willing to leave the store and walk outside, to get away from Lola Damon. Sometimes, she wondered if Lola Damon might have had something to do with the beating.

"But, listen," she said as she and Joan Harvett entered the old drugstore—she gave a laugh and lowered her voice as if she were about to say something risqué—"I want *you* to do *me* a favor, too, Joan."

"Me?" Joan Harvett's smile was forced. "What?"

As she did not like to say, for a moment, Franny busied herself with rooting a dime from her purse. "Here!" She smiled and offered the coin to the girl. "I want you to make a call. All you have to do is say, 'Is Ryan there?' and if he's not, you just say, 'Would you, please, tell him Franny called?' and if he is, then you give the phone to me."

Joan Harvett looked toward the drugstore's front door.

Because she wanted the other girls as witnesses? Support? "But if I'm just doing that," she said, "why don't you call, Franny? If he's there, you'll talk to him, right? You don't want me to talk to him."

Franny grinned. As if this all were—fun. "Come on, Joanie. Humor me." She pulled playfully on Joan Harvett's arm. "It'll take you all of two seconds."

A very old telephone booth made of dark wood, with a wooden seat, the Spragues' telephone booth sat in one corner of the store, tucked behind carousels of postcards and sunglasses. "I'm handing the phone right to you," Joan whispered as she dialed the number. "Don't you dare move."

From where she stood, Franny could hear the faint ringing of the Marvell telephone. It filled her heart with joy and fear. She squeezed her hands into fists she raised to her face, and then Joan Harvett was saying, "Is Ryan there, please?" She smiled at Franny. "Okay, well, would you, please, tell him Franny called?"

Joan Harvett laughed as she hung up. "So?" Franny asked, now very stiff, as if her interest in Ryan Marvell instantly had cooled to vain curiosity.

"It was his dad! He was *so* sweet, Franny. 'I'll tell Ryan you called, honey!' Did you ever meet him?"

Franny shook her head, no, and stared at the telephone booth's molasses-dark finish, its white stars of reflection. Mr. Marvell probably had no idea that a person named Franny even existed. And Mr. Marvell had liked Joan, the girl who had called, not Franny. Furthermore, while the lady at the counter rang up the cigarettes—one pack of Winstons, one of Marlboros—it occurred to Franny that it might have been Ryan Marvell who took the call. Joan Harvett would not have known. Ryan Marvell could have pretended not to be himself just as easily as Joan Harvett pretended to be Franny.

The SFF girls who served as leaders for the Y-Teens group acted as if they were gratified to see Franny enter the Y-Teens room. "We've missed you!" they said. "Are you feeling better?"

From the way they studied her face, she suspected that they, too, knew about the beating.

"We're making Thanksgiving decorations for Good Shepherd," the taller and prettier of the two leaders said, and pointed toward the back of the meeting room where a number of girls sat at fold-out tables, adding pipe cleaner handles to nut cups. Two girls Franny knew from honors sprawled on the floor, drawing turkeys on sheets of oak tag.

"Brownnosers," murmured Joan Harvett.

"Thunder-thighs," said Lola Damon and pointed at an exposed section of leg belonging to the heavier of the two girls. Renee Bowen. Franny liked Renee Bowen. At the beginning of seventh grade, Renee had used to invite Franny to join her and her friends for lunch. Those girls had not, however, been the friends that Franny had wanted back then; and now they considered her wild.

Wild.

Even the hoody girls at her school—the ones with lilac eye shadow and hair teased into transparent mantillas, the girls with hickeys all over their necks—Franny could hardly believe anymore that they acted with the sort of reckless joy she once assumed went with true wildness. Maybe, like her, they were dragged about by terrible bonds they could not understand or even see.

She took a seat at one of the fold-out tables and began to work. Inane. And was this what life ended with? Being wheeled into some disinfected dining hall so you could get a nut cup made by the Y-Teens?

The last time she had been at the Y, she had not actually attended the meeting. She and Ryan Marvell had parked along Lime Creek and skipped stones while, supposedly, she walked with the other Y-teens, collecting money for UNICEF. That day, before Peg arrived to drive her home, as an act of contrition—Franny had seen the photos of babies whose heads balanced precariously above stick bodies—Franny stuck her entire October allowance in the collection box at the Y's front desk. That was just before Joan Harvett had returned with her UNICEF group, and said a haughty, "Are you really coming to the meeting next week, Franny, 'cause we're getting tired of lying for you," and Franny had snapped, "I never asked you to lie for me. Tell the truth: You *don't* know where I am."

Today, she hardly cared enough to be touchy with the girls. After the meeting closed, she volunteered to be the one who sat on the front steps and watched for Mrs. Harvett's arrival while Joan and Lola and Christy went to smoke between the Y and the neighboring boarding house.

Winter was coming. Cars now drove with their headlights on. The headlights glimmered on the moist streets, and behind them, the cars appeared sly as cats preparing to pounce.

One car—a dark sedan—pulled up to the curb and made Franny's heart lurch, but the female driver immediately hurried into the boardinghouse.

A radio tower's distant light plucked, red, at the teal sky. She stood to look in through the glass doors to the lobby. Five twenty-three said the clock over the reception desk. Two and a half hours until Martie would arrive home. Rosamund might already be at the house. Franny was excited to see her but also wished that the whole evening could somehow be put off, indefinitely delayed.

Yes.

A group of girls played table tennis at the back of the lobby, and, just then, the game's blond paddles and taut green net struck Franny as particularly therapeutic, a game to restore normalcy.

If Franny had gone inside, and asked to join the girls' game, they might have exchanged frowns at her intrusion, but they would not have turned her away. If she were patient, and flattering, and disapproved of the girl who had been in love with Ryan Marvell, in time they would probably let her be their friend.

She could be patient, and maybe even flattering, but she could not imagine that she would ever disapprove of herself for loving Ryan Marvell. As far as she was concerned, she never had a choice in the matter. Loving Ryan Marvell was very much like being born into the family she had been born into, a mixture of good luck and bad.

So she sat down again on the cold staircase. She played a little game she often played when alone and waiting for her parents to pick her up. She became, for a while, that old lady coming down the street with her little shopping cart rattling behind her. Her back had a terrible hump, oh, her old chest ached, her tongue flapped around in her toothless mouth like a fat seal.

She entered a spring-footed boy—maybe nine or ten years old—who ran a bike up to the front of the boarding house, and she felt his hands vibrate on the handlebars, and his scalp tingle as his sweat began to cool in the early evening air.

The dinner made in honor of Rosamund's return was ham and navy bean soup with garlic bread, salad, and date bars. Franny was hardly able to eat, she was so nervous about the impending arrival of Martie, but the kitchen looked cozy—Peg had lit a candle in the center of the breakfast table—and the other three went back for seconds, and Brick toasted everyone with the wine that he had opened.

It seemed clear to Franny that Rosamund remained as ignorant of Martie's condition as Peg and Brick.

"Daddy," Rosamund said after the table was cleared, "can we get you to play a few songs for us?"

Brick rubbed his arms and pretended to shiver. "I don't know. It's mighty cold in the living room since your mother decided we ought to live like pioneers."

Peg laughed. "I think we pioneers can brave the cold, but let me start the dishwasher first."

"We'll be right with you, then, girls," Brick said, and, with a bow, he held back the blanket that hung in the kitchen doorway so they might pass through the dining room and proceed to the living room.

Rosamund scampered to the shantung couch. Took a seat. Drew her legs beneath her. "How can you stand it in here?" she whispered when Franny drew near. "I have goose bumps!"

"My virtues produce an inner glow," Franny said, then pulled out a blanket she kept hidden behind the couch and tossed it Rosamund's way.

"You're sweet." Rosamund wrapped the thing about herself. "I could never live in Iowa again!"

"Never?"

"I'll visit, of course, but there's nobody here except family I want to see. Mike's called me a couple of times at school, but"— She shrugged to show lack of interest.

"Mike Zanios," Franny said. She was surprised, somehow, although she recently had realized that, despite last summer's fury, Brick himself had resumed going to the Top Hat Club for lunch.

"Oh, and Timmy, too. He's called and written."

Franny hoped Rosamund would say more, or ask about Ryan Marvell, but Rosamund stuck out a hand from the blanket's folds and picked up the *Vogue* lying on the coffee table and began to flip through its pages.

"So"—Franny glanced toward the kitchen door, watching for the arrival of her parents—"have you talked to Martie lately?"

Rosamund shivered beneath the blanket. "Should I have? She called me when you were in the hospital. She wanted us to form a vigilante group to hunt down whoever hurt you—and, incidentally, from the way Mom cried about you on the telephone, I half-expected you to have an eyeball hanging out of its socket, or something."

Franny raised a finger to an irregular groove on her cheek that still felt tender to the touch. "I'll have a couple scars."

Rosamund rapped the magazine against Franny's leg and smiled. "They'll make you look distinguished and give you a good story to tell your grandchildren!" she said, then raised a finger to her lips as Peg and Brick—him, with the tray of shot glasses and bottle of scotch—entered the room.

"This ought to improve the temperature in here," Brick said, and Peg laughed at the sight of Rosamund, bundled up on the couch:

"You can't go around in a sleeveless dress here, honey!"

"I'll probably be rusty." Brick slid back the bench and sat down at the piano. "With your mother's new economies in force, I hardly come in to play."

"Mood Indigo" was Rosamund's request, and Peg asked for "Bewitched, Bothered and Bewildered," and then the front door flew open and Martie called, "Halloooooo! I'm home!"

The four in the living room stood up for hugs. Franny felt moved at embracing this Martie who was more than Martie. She did her best not to look below Martie's neck as Martie picked up the bottle of scotch.

"I guess you need a drink to keep from freezing in here, don't you?" Martie smiled and screwed up one eye in a kind of wink at Brick. "So, how do you think good scotch will sit on top of cheap red wine?"

Peg drooped. "Oh, Martie, you weren't drinking in front of Leona's nephew, were you? I'll never hear the end of that."

Martie leaned into Peg's shoulder with a laugh. "Hate to break it to you, kid, but Leona's sweet nephew *gave* me the wine, and also assured me that if I, or any of my friends, ever wanted any drugs, he was the guy to call."

Peg shook her head. "How can it be that I go out in the same world as you, and no one ever offers me such things?"

"I don't know." Martie looked up mischievously from pouring her drink. "Maybe you need to change the way you dress."

You could not tell she was pregnant. She wore a big sweater and, if anything, her legs and face looked thinner than Franny remembered.

"Cheers!" She lifted the glass. Downed the shot.

"Say, toots!" Brick said. "That's sipping scotch!"

"Now, Brick," Martie said, and this was it: Martie's eyes began to brim with tears. Franny felt her heart constrict. Martie was going to tell them, any moment now—

"Brick"—Martie grinned and pressed her fingers to the inner corners of her eyes, stemming the tears—"didn't you ever just want to drink something really good straight down?" She sniffled and laughed. "Sure you did."

Brick turned toward Peg, then, to mutter, "What's all this?" which Peg took as her signal to stand with a clap of the hands and

declare that *she* needed to get cracking on peeling potatoes for
mañana, and didn't she have some volunteers lined up to help?

"No, no!" Martie set down her empty glass as Franny rose from
the couch, eager to move off to the kitchen before another word
was spoken.

"Everybody, listen up!" Martie said. "Rosamund, put down the
magazine, please. I want your full attention."

Rosamund looked askance at the request, but closed the magazine in her lap.

"I have an announcement to make." With a grin, Martie raised
a finger to the group. Closed her eyes. Took a deep breath and
released it. "Just wait!" she said tearfully, then raised her shoulders
up to her ears, dropped them. Up. Down.

"For goodness sakes, Martie, what is this?" Brick asked.

Martie's face crumpled. "What it is—" She looked at Franny.
Shook her head. Then mouthed, as the tears started down her
cheeks, *You tell*.

Franny's heart sank. "Are you sure?"

Martie loosed a shuddering laugh. "Please."

"Well." Franny's forehead and cheeks prickled like a foot gone
to sleep. Around the small lighted spot in which they stood, the
room was black and gold, and everyone looked her way, waiting.
"Well, Martie's going to have a baby."

"Hh!" Peg Wahl bent over, her arms clutched to her stomach. "I
knew it. I think—I'm going to be sick."

"Oh, Mom!" Franny said, just—*ashamed* of Peg's response, but
then Brick grabbed Martie by her upper arms and he lifted her right
into the air. "Is this true?" he shouted, and when Martie cringed
and sobbed, "Yes," he set her down with a shove that sent her toppling into the table that held the bottle of scotch and the tray of
glasses, all of which fell with a crash and splintered and spilled
across the floor.

"Dad," Franny cried, "what are you doing?" and there was
Brick's snarling face up against hers, yelling, "You keep out of this!
You knew and didn't tell us?" He looked over at Peg, his face

bloated with disbelief. "What kind of brothel are we running here, anyway?" he demanded.

"She's ruined our lives, Brick." Peg sat down on the floor where she stood. "We're ruined because she wanted to spread her legs for some boy."

Martie, stranded in the mess of glass and scotch, leaned into the curve of the baby grand like a boxer thrown against the ropes. "That is so *low*," she moaned. "I'm having this baby, and—you need to show respect. It's your grandchild—"

"No!" Head in her hands, Peg wailed, "Don't even talk! You are no longer my daughter! Don't you imagine for one minute that we'd ever, ever let you bring it here. Never. And you"—she pointed a finger at Franny as Franny began to pick her way through the broken glass and scotch to Martie's side—"you stay away from her! Get!"

Franny shook her head. At least there was some comfort in holding Martie.

"We're probably the laughingstocks of Pynch Lake," Brick said. "If you told that damned Deedee Pierce—did you tell that blabbermouth Deedee?—oh, Christ. You're a perfect idiot, aren't you?"

Rosamund did not say a word until the point at which Brick demanded, *And who the hell's the father?* Then Rosamund stood, dropping the blanket back on the couch. "Daddy," she said, "may I, please, speak to Martie alone for a few minutes?"

"Oh, hell." Brick turned from Martie as if he could not bear the sight of her. "I don't care what you do with her."

"Dad!" Martie and Franny wailed then, but Rosamund appeared calm, if shaken, and she extended one hand to Martie and pointed the other toward the stairs:

"Come on. Let's go to my room for a minute and talk."

Brick kept his back turned as Martie and Franny began to make their way out of the mess on the floor. The scotch was sticky. It was sticky on their shoes even when the girls had moved beyond the wet.

"You stay here, Fran," Peg said, but Rosamund said, "It's okay, Mom," and Franny kept moving.

Rosamund, Martie, Franny. Heading up the stairs. Entering

Rosamund's room. Franny and Martie took seats on the twin bed closest to the door.

"Here." Rosamund pulled the spread off the second bed and wrapped it around Martie from behind, meanwhile shooting Franny a stormy look: *Why didn't you tell me?*

"I figured they'd be bastards," Martie sobbed. "They've always treated me like there was something wrong with me—I was too noisy, I was too whatever. Still, I hoped that I'd get some support here—and Mom's saying I'm not even her daughter!"

"I wish you'd talked to me about this first, Martie," Rosamund said. She sounded calm, if slightly irritated. "Mother and Daddy wouldn't have needed to know, and you could have been spared some of this."

"But I wanted them to know, Roz! It's going to be their grand-child!"

For Franny's benefit, Rosamund raised her eyes toward the ceiling to show how forbearing she had to be. "But how could you possibly have thought they'd accept this, Martie? And how could you possibly have a baby now?"

Martie cast an imploring glance toward Franny. "I have ideas, don't I, Fran? Some people were talking about getting a farmhouse. I'm not sure that's going to happen, now, but—oh, and I was think-ing maybe I could come here and get a job in Dad's office. I must have been out of my mind to think he'd help."

"I'd help," Franny said. "After school, I could baby-sit. And on weekends. And the baby could have my room—"

Sh! Rosamund signalled Franny as she began to massage Mar-tie's shoulders. "Martie," she said, "you're smart and attractive and you've got your whole life ahead of you. I'm sure you'll make an excellent mom—"

"I will!" Martie said. She let her head fall forward with a moan. "That feels so good, Roz."

"I meant *someday,* Martie. Also, you haven't mentioned the father, which is fine, but it doesn't sound like you're getting mar-ried, right? And—you're still in school!"

From beneath her curtain of hair, Martie murmured, "Flunking out. I was taking care of Milton and his friends, cooking and cleaning. It was hard to get to classes—"

According to Rosamund, Martie looked at things incorrectly. Didn't Martie realize that Peg and Brick could figure out a way to get Martie a medical excuse? Then, if Martie got the pregnancy taken care of, Rosamund doubted Martie would have to deal with anything much worse than filing for a few "incompletes."

Martie leaned back against Rosamund now, and looked up, tears streaming down her face. "But I don't know, Roz."

"Sure you do." Rosamund lifted Martie's hair with one hand while she massaged her neck with the other. "Mother and Daddy are kind of in shock now. You have to think not just about how hard your having a baby would be on them, but on the baby, too, and it could make it hard for you ever to find a husband."

"I don't care!" Martie pulled away from Rosamund then. "The baby and I would have each other. Anyway"—she swiped her nose across the back of her hand—"it's too late to do anything now."

A roar sounded below. Brick. Just—roaring, making a big sound of pain without the shape of words. Rosamund acted as if she did not hear the roar. "Don't be silly," she said. "I know a girl who had it done in her sixth month. How far along can you be?"

Martie shrugged. Three and a half months, she guessed.

Three and a half months? According to Rosamund, that was not bad at all! "We can get this taken care of, Martie. I can make a few phone calls to the right people. What do you say?"

"I have to think." Martie pulled the bedspread up over her head and looked out like a monk from his cowl. "I tried all those dumb things Mom tried on me. The gin. The horseback ride. I even bought a pair of knitting needles."

"Martie!" Rosamund clapped her hands to her mouth.

"I didn't get very far." Martie shook her head. "I figured, if I bled to death or something, what good would it have done me? Except Mom and Dad might have felt too bad to be pissed."

Rosamund hugged Martie. Franny could not remember having

seen her hug Martie in that way before. A really *tight* hug. The sight made Franny want to hug both of them, and she did, albeit awkwardly, and then Rosamund—with a small, sniffling laugh into that circle made up of herself and her sisters—Rosamund said, "Listen, the worst is over now that you've told them. So—just stay here and think and I'll try to calm them down, okay?"

After Rosamund left the room, Martie curled up on the bed and stuck an edge of the corduroy spread into her mouth and began to chew on it. "I need a cigarette," she said.

Franny stroked Martie's hair. "At the library," she said, "I looked at some pictures of babies developing inside their mothers—"

"Sh." Martie lifted her head from the mattress. "It's quiet down there." She settled her head on the mattress once more. "Roz was great, wasn't she?"

Franny nodded. "But you ought to do what you want to do, you know, Martie?"

"I know. In the beginning, I prayed and prayed I wasn't pregnant. Then, when I knew I was, I told the guy. I won't tell you what he said, the bastard."

Franny nodded. "That's fine."

"Unless you really want to know."

"No," Franny said.

Martie waved a hand in the air. "You can guess, right? Like, he was the only one I'd ever done it with, but he was, like, 'If you did it with me, I bet you did it with other guys.'"

"Not very original," Franny said, and then Rosamund's footsteps sounded on the stairs, and she returned to report that she had told Brick and Peg that Martie was too young to be a mother, and that the pregnancy had only occurred because Martie got tipsy on spiked punch—

"I got tipsy on spiked punch?" Martie made a face.

"Since they don't like your drinking, I made it a spiked punch. Anyway, they agree it would be best if you ended the pregnancy. And they're willing to help out and, after, to act as if it never happened." Rosamund lifted a finger in the air: Wait. "And remember: Whoever the guy is, it's better they don't know. That way he doesn't need to exist for them."

Martie rolled off the bed and went to stand before the dressing table. "Look." She pulled up her big sweater to examine the minor bulge of her belly in her jeans. Head-on, then profile. "So"—she dropped the sweater—"I get to be a virgin again, huh?"

Rosamund turned toward the door. "They're coming."

Brick made his way through the suitcases that Rosamund had strewn on the floor and he laid a hand on Martie's shoulder. "Rozzie talked to us, and—we're willing to agree this never happened if you are." He began to cry, then, ripping sobs, terrible sounds, and Peg added in a small, bleating voice, "If anybody asks, we'll say we don't know what they're talking about. And we won't, right, Brick?"

While the three of them cried and embraced and kissed each other and Martie said that she was sorry, so sorry, Rosamund set her arm around Franny's waist and whispered in her ear, "You should have told me, though. You know that, right?"

CHAPTER TWENTY-THREE

OUTWARDLY, THAT THANKSGIVING DAY DID NOT APPEAR SO different from any other Thanksgiving. The usual din of the football game filled the house before the family drove to Charlotte Wahl's, and then it filled Charlotte's house once Brick entered her den and turned on her television.

In Charlotte's big, white kitchen, Rosamund and Martie got into a typical debate, this one about war resistance, and who could claim more authority, and Charlotte and Peg discussed the turkey. Should it stay in a while longer? Begin the half-hour sit?

Franny had taken up a post by the bay window where her grandmother now directed her attention to the cedar waxwings feeding in the crab apple tree.

"Wow," Franny said once she found the birds in the binoculars, and Charlotte gave her a pat on the shoulder before going back to Peg at the oven.

It seemed to Franny that, upon her family's entering Charlotte's house, Charlotte had given Martie's belly exactly the same sort of furtive look that Franny had given it the night before. So Charlotte knew? And also knew that something had been decided?

Would Franny's father have told Charlotte such a thing?

Franny had no idea.

Earlier that morning, when she had gone downstairs, she found Peg and Brick and Rosamund seated at the breakfast table in a whispered conversation that stopped entirely when Franny reached the landing.

"Martie?" Peg asked.

"Franny," Franny said, and pushed aside the blanket covering the entry. "Martie's still asleep."

Peg nodded, then continued, "Anyway, I've worried she was oversexed ever since that Roger Dale."

"Oh, Mom," Franny protested, but Brick wagged the piece of toast in his hand her way. "Like it or not, some women are."

"It's true," Rosamund said. "There's even a name for it, Franny: 'nymphomaniac.' Still"—she turned to Brick and Peg—"I never thought she'd put you two through something so awful."

"We didn't either, dear," Brick said. "Let's hope she can act more ladylike in the future."

Franny had wanted to run upstairs, then, and tell Martie not to do it, they were tricking her with their hugs and forgiveness, but what was the use? Martie probably *was* too young to be any sort of mother. Too young, too irresponsible. Still, when Franny finally heard Martie start to move around upstairs, she did go to talk to her.

"Martie," she said—this was in the bathroom, where Martie was slowly brushing her teeth, staring in the mirror at her punchy reflection—"you're sure you want to do this thing, Martie?"

"God, Franny!" Martie spit into the sink. "You're not going to *ruin* this for me, are you? Dad and I sat up talking till two this morning. It was great. When'd he ever do that before?" Martie massaged her temples. "Which is not to say I don't feel like shit from all the scotch we drank."

"But, Martie, you were looking forward to the baby, weren't you?"

"Water, water." Martie ducked her mouth under the tap and drank and drank. "I can have babies later," she said when she raised her mouth from the sink. "Oh, and Dad said he and I might end up going to Mexico to do the thing. Roz knows some people who've gone there. Wouldn't that be cool? Mexico?"

She seemed so hopeful, Franny had to nod yes. "Martie," she said, "did you tell Deedee?"

"Of course I told Deedee."

"Did you tell her who the father was?"

Martie set her hands on her hips and laughed. "It could only have been *one* person, Franny. Don't you know—"

"Don't tell me!" Franny closed her eyes and covered her ears and hummed. "I don't want to know. Please."

"God"—Martie flung open the bathroom door, which bounced against the hall wall with a great bang—"don't be thirteen, okay, Fran?"

"Fourteen," Franny muttered. "I turned fourteen over three weeks ago. You just forgot."

"Franny," Charlotte Wahl said, "if you see that darned squirrel, rap on the glass! It's eating me out of house and home!"

Franny knocked on the glass. The handsome squirrel, so delicately stashing rude amounts of sunflower seeds into its bulging cheeks, seemed not to notice Franny's knocking, but the birds nearby flew off and even some of the waxwings left the crabapple tree across the yard. It was while following the waxwings' flight that Franny saw the brown and white Ford pull up to her grandmother's curb.

Immediately, she left the kitchen. Maybe she was in a dream? No. Because when she stepped out into the front hall, there was her father, coming from the den, empty glass in hand.

"It seems we have visitors," he said as the doorbell began to ring, and then he made a neat left turn into the foyer.

The wooden door opened with its usual *whiff.* The storm door squeaked. Shoes scuffed the mat in the foyer.

"Hello, hello," her father said with no evidence of rancor. "You come by to watch a little football with me?"

At that low murmur of reply, Franny could wait no longer and she stepped toward the foyer—just as Tim Gleason stepped out from the foyer and into the front hall.

"Franny," he said. His hair was much longer than she had ever seen it. He had lost his summer tan and looked as pale as a blanched almond. "Just saw your car out front," he said, perhaps more to

Brick than to Franny. "Thought I'd say hi to Roz. If she's around."

"She is, indeed," Brick said, as if nothing in the world pleased him more than going to fetch Rosamund for Tim Gleason. "I'll tell her you're here!"

Franny waited until Brick had moved down the hall and out of sight before she asked, "So how's Ryan, Tim?"

Tim Gleason nodded. "He's okay."

"When I saw the car—"

"I just borrowed it. It's smart you guys aren't seeing each other. It's better for both of you."

She hoped he would say more—just more words, anything connected to Ryan would be something, but he looked away from her and touched a finger to the sleeve of a porcelain statue that Charlotte Wahl always kept on her hall bureau. The statue depicted a Chinese courtesan with flowing robes, plump lips, minuscule fingers. Years ago, Franny had accidentally broken one of the statue's delicate hands and all five tapering fingers. A disaster, she thought, but her grandmother had done such a fine job of putting the tiny bits back together that, for years, no one would have guessed that the hand had been broken at all, and now that the glue had darkened with time, the mends appeared a minute and charming glove of brown lace.

"Say, Timmy?" Brick stepped out into the hall. Gave his nose a back and forth rub—the way he often did when feeling flustered or awkward. "I didn't realize, but Roz went out on an errand. I'm sorry."

Franny did not care if Tim Gleason did not want her to walk him out to the Ford. "I just want to see the car," she said, "for old times' sake."

She let her hand trail along the front fender, which was dusty, as if the car recently had been out on country roads. She cupped her hand around the curve of the side mirror. He would have touched that, making adjustments, looking at himself. His face had been there. Think of that. Again and again. She sneaked a peek at herself in that mirror. A pretty girl? An ugly girl? She did not know.

Tim Gleason opened the driver's door and climbed inside. "Well," he said, "tell your big sister happy Thanksgiving."

"But, wait. Just—"

On the dusty driver's window, with her finger, she wrote:

Franny loves Ryan

Tim Gleason squinted at the words—backward for him—then shook his head. Maybe he was disgusted, maybe he was amused, or a little of both. "You don't give up, do you?" he said.

She shrugged. "Tell him I said hi."

He closed the car door, then, but she knocked on it, and held up a finger—wait—and she changed the *s* in her sentence to a *d*, which made it a fiction, but sometimes, she knew, by writing down a thing, you could make it true. Or alter its power. Or even change it into something else.

"'Bye, then," she said.

She watched the car start up the road. It seemed almost as if something could happen—something like the *d* replacing the *s*—so that Tim Gleason could become Ryan Marvell, and that change would mean another change in which the car might drive toward her instead of away from her. Stop, instead of moving on.

But she was thinking of miracles again, wasn't she?

She started back to the house. Just out of sight of the bay window, her grandmother kept bags of birdseed in a covered trash pail. Sunflower and black niger and millet. Franny took one handful of the sunflower seeds and one of the millet and she laid them out on the top bar of the pretty fence that ran around her grandmother's yard. A "rill" of seeds, she thought. The visit from Tim Gleason had left her vibrating. Like a violin string or a tuning fork or a piece of old glass. Hmm, she sang. *Hmm*—to see if her voice carried the vibration, and she thought that it did.

The rest of them stood in the kitchen when she went back inside. Brick opened a bottle of wine while Martie cut the turkey with the electric knife and Rosamund and Peg and Charlotte transferred pots of vegetables and things into serving bowls and carried them out to the dining room. They all seemed quite jolly.

"Tim said hello," Franny told Rosamund.

"Hello," Rosamund said as she rapped a spoonful of stuffing into its dish.

"Grandma," Franny said—blurted out, really—and, on impulse, she grabbed Charlotte Wahl's dry old hand. "I want to ask you—I'd like to ask if I can use my college money now. To go to Bell Academy for Girls in Des Moines."

Peg had just started for the dining room with her dish of potatoes, but she stopped and said, "What are you talking about?"

"It's what I'd like to do," Franny said. "I thought I'd ask Grandma. Since I don't think—I'm getting a good education. Here. In Pynch Lake."

"It was good enough for your sisters," Peg said.

"And your father," said Brick.

"Maybe it's changed, though." Franny did her best to look each of them in the eye. "Or I just want something different. And I think if I went to a good school, I could get a college scholarship."

"I know something about Bell," Charlotte said. "The Heberlings sent their daughter there, and the Nelson girl went there, too. There's no question that it's a good school."

"Did she talk about this with you?" Brick asked Peg.

"Not a word," Peg said.

"Is that why you spent so much time at the library this fall?" Charlotte asked Franny. "Trying to get a better education?"

Franny looked down without answering, uncertain if her grandmother were teasing or not.

"Well, I applaud her initiative," Charlotte said to Brick.

"Me, too." Rosamund hesitated, then gave a meaningful look to both of her parents before adding, "I think it'd be good for her to get out of Pynch Lake. And go to an all-girls school."

"But, when were you thinking of doing this, honey?" Brick asked.

"Now. As soon as possible."

"*Now?*" said Peg.

Brick smoothed his hand down Peg's back. "Obviously, it's something we'll have to give some thought to. We're not going to decide anything while we're putting the dinner on the table."

Peg nodded, then, and carried the casserole dish into the dining room, but Franny stayed behind long enough to whisper to her grandmother, "I brought the brochures. I can show them to you after we eat."

Later that afternoon, when Brick started to pull into Charlotte's drive in order to turn the car around for the trip home, Martie asked, oh, please, couldn't they take the long way home? Drive the rest of the way around the lake? So she and Rosamund could see the old house and the high school and all?

"Why not?" said Peg, and so Brick backed the car out the same way that it had come and the Wildcat continued on up Lakeside Drive toward the business district.

"Coming up on City Park," Martie announced.

Franny pitied the band shell, its ugly plaster so exposed now that the trees were bare.

"Scoop the loop, Dad!" Martie said. Brick groaned a little, but then he drove up Clay, past his offices, and turned down Main, which was perfectly empty except for themselves and a VW bug that waited at a red light. The Hamm's beer sign in the window of Viccio's had been turned off for the holiday and, for all the life that the pool hall showed, the place looked as if it might have gone out of business.

"There's the Maid-Rite!" Martie said. "There's Drew's and the hardware store and Spragues'!"

"Did you think they might have gotten up and run away?" Brick asked, and everyone laughed, but Franny knew what Martie meant by her surprise. She felt it herself every time she went down the street, or anywhere else for that matter: amazed. Amazed at being alive.

Lights shone in a few of the apartment windows of The Elgin but the only shop on Main with its sign burning was the one that hung in the cobbler's window: a work shoe with a red neon wing attached. "You don't suppose old Elliot's in there, cobbling, do you?" Brick asked, but the shop itself was dark and surely empty.

They drove past the high school and the Romero Ballroom—and the Top Hat Club, though nobody mentioned that. They drove past the old house on Ash Street and Peg gasped at the children playing in the tree house that her own children had built.

"It's lasted pretty well," Brick said.

"I can't bear to look," Peg said, her face turned aside. "I could never bear to look when you kids were up there."

"It's amazing we survived, when you think of all the crazy stuff we did," Martie said gaily.

"You were lucky," Peg said. "A person shouldn't count on her luck holding out."

Taking the long way home meant driving through a good deal of cropland on roads set far from sight of Pynch Lake. For several miles, the family passed fences and fields and the occasional gravel road that led to farmhouses and barns and outbuildings for animals and machinery.

Franny lay her head back against the seat while they drove. How many more times would she and her sisters ride together in the back, like this, the way they had always ridden, Brick at the wheel, Peg in the front passenger seat? Franny always ended up between Rosamund and Martie—unless, for a change, on long trips, she rode between Peg and Brick, up front.

"I think people who grow up in Iowa are lucky," Franny said, not to anyone in particular. "Some people drive through here, and they say it's flat and boring, but, really, it's subtle. It helps you to see things if you grow up someplace subtle."

"So, let's hear it for Iowa!" said Martie, and began to sing, very loud, the boisterous state song—

"Martha!" Brick said. "For Christsake, knock that off!"

Martie looked startled. "Hey, I'm doing what you guys want, aren't I? I thought you were happy with me."

Peg gave Brick a look of warning, then said, "We are, honey. Just—wait till all this is over. We seem tense now, but when all this is over, we'll be our old selves again."

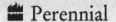 Perennial

Books by Elizabeth Evans:

CARTER CLAY
ISBN 0-06-092982-0 (paperback)

Carter Clay, Vietnam Veteran at loose ends, is involved in a hit-and-run accident with the Altiz family—killing Joe Altiz and seriously injuring his wife and their daughter. Horrified, Clay seeks redemption while concealing his culpability, by becoming the questionable caretaker of the two survivors' damaged lives.

"A writer working her way into the literary stratosphere."—*Newsday*

ROWING IN EDEN
ISBN 0-06-095470-1 (paperback)

An extraordinary novel about a family during one summer at a lakeside resort in the 1960s. Told through the eyes of the youngest daughter who, at thirteen, is just beginning to see her family, and the world, as they truly exist. *Rowing in Eden* is a masterful portrait of adolescence and a powerful, if unusual, love story.

"*Rowing in Eden* brings readers through a gamut of emotional experiences, and leaves them wiser at the close."—*Denver Post*